THE
LAST DISC!PLE

To Amber,
may all your
journeys
be blessed . . .

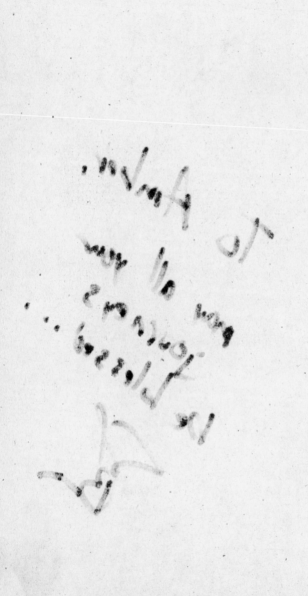

THE
LAST
DISCIPLE

HANK · HANEGRAAFF
SIGMUND · BROUWER

TYNDALE HOUSE PUBLISHERS, INC.
WHEATON, ILLINOIS

Visit Tyndale's exciting Web site at www.tyndale.com

TYNDALE is a registered trademark of Tyndale House Publishers, Inc.

Tyndale's quill logo is a trademark of Tyndale House Publishers, Inc.

Find out more about The Last Disciple series at www.decipherthecode.com

New Living and the New Living Translation logo are registered trademarks of Tyndale House Publishers, Inc.

Designed by Julie Chen

Edited by James H. Cain III

Scripture quotations are taken from the Holy Bible, New Living Translation, copyright © 1996. Used by permission of Tyndale House Publishers, Inc., Wheaton, Illinois 60189. All rights reserved.

Scripture quotations are taken from the Holy Bible, New International Version®. NIV®. Copyright © 1973, 1978, 1984 by International Bible Society. Used by permission of Zondervan Publishing House. All rights reserved.

Library of Congress Cataloging-in-Publication Data

Hanegraaff, Hank.
  The last disciple / Hank Hanegraaff and Sigmund Brouwer.
    p. cm.
  ISBN 0-8423-8437-5 (hc) — ISBN 0-8423-8438-3 (sc)
    1. Bible. N.T. Revelation XIII—History of Biblical events—Fiction.   2. Church history—Primitive and early church, ca. 30–600—Fiction.   3. Rome—History—Nero, 54–68—Fiction.   4. End of the world—Fiction.   I. Brouwer, Sigmund, date. II. Title.
PS3608.A714L37 2004
813'.6—dc22   2004010713

Printed in the United States of America

09 08 07 06 05
5   4   3   2   1

To Ron Beers
Your character, competence, and courage
are a gift to us and to the body of Christ.

Acknowledgments

First, we would like to express our deepest appreciation to Tyndale House Publishers for their relentless pursuit of truth. We are especially grateful to Ron Beers, Becky Nesbitt, Jan Stob, Carla Mayer, and Jamie Cain for their input and editorial expertise. They personify Tyndale's mission statement as "determined, driven, bold, risk-taking, frontier-driven distributors of God's truth."

Furthermore, we are deeply grateful for the staff and ministry of the Christian Research Institute—especially Stephen Ross, Adam Pelser, Brenda Marchak, Amy Leonhardt, and Kristen Ross. Thanks also to Dr. Paul L. Maier and Gretchen Passantino for their historical and literary expertise. Together they embody the maxim "In essentials unity, in nonessentials liberty, and in all things charity."

Finally, we want to acknowledge Kathy Hanegraaff and the brood—Michelle, Katie, David, John Mark, Hank Jr., Christina, Paul Stephen, Faith, Grace; and Cindy Brouwer and the kids—Olivia and Savannah. Most of all, we are grateful for the grace that our Lord has lavished upon us.

I TELL YOU THE TRUTH,

THIS GENERATION WILL CERTAINLY

Seventy "sevens"
are decreed
for your people
and your holy city
to finish transgression,
to put an end to sin,
to atone for wickedness,
to bring in everlasting righteousness,
to seal up vision and prophecy
and to anoint the most holy.

—Daniel 9:24

NOT PASS AWAY UNTIL ALL THESE THINGS HAVE HAPPENED.

—MATTHEW 24:34

The revelation of Jesus Christ, which God gave him to show his servants what must soon take place. He made it known by sending his angel to his servant John, who testifies to everything he saw—that is, the word of God and the testimony of Jesus Christ. Blessed is the one who reads the words of this prophecy, and blessed are those who hear it and take to heart what is written in it, because the time is near.

—Revelation 1:1-3

CALENDAR NOTES

The Romans divided the day into twelve hours. The first hour, *hora prima*, began at sunrise, approximately 6 AM. The twelfth hour, *hora duodecima*, ended at sunset, approximately 6 PM.

hora prima	first hour	6 – 7 AM
hora secunda	second hour	7 – 8 AM
hora tertiana	third hour	8 – 9 AM
hora quarta	fourth hour	9 – 10 AM
hora quinta	fifth hour	10 – 11 AM
hora sexta	sixth hour	11 AM – 12 PM
hora septina	seventh hour	12 – 1 PM
hora octava	eighth hour	1 – 2 PM
hora nonana	ninth hour	2 – 3 PM
hora decima	tenth hour	3 – 4 PM
hora undecima	eleventh hour	4 – 5 PM
hora duodecima	twelfth hour	5 – 6 PM

The New Testament refers to hours in a similar way. Thus, when we read in Luke 23:44 (NIV), "It was now about the sixth hour, and darkness came over the whole land until the ninth hour," we understand that this period of time was from the hour before noon to approximately 3 PM.

The Romans divided the night into eight watches.

Watches before midnight: *Vespera, Prima fax, Concubia, Intempesta*

Watches after midnight: *Inclinatio, Gallicinium, Conticinium, Diluculum*

The Roman days of the week were Sun, Moon, Mars, Mercury, Jupiter, Venus, and Saturn.

The months of the Hebrew calendar are Nisan, Iyar, Sivan, Tammuz, Av, Elul, Tishri, Heshvan, Kislev, Tevet, Shevat, Adar I, and Adar II. In AD 65, the date 13 Av was approximately August 1.

ROME

CAPITAL OF THE EMPIRE

Four great beasts, each different from
the others, came up out of the sea.
The first was like a lion, and it had the
wings of an eagle. . . . And there before me
was a second beast, which looked like a
bear. . . . After that, I looked, and there
before me was another beast, one that
looked like a leopard. . . . After that, in my
vision at night I looked, and there before
me was a fourth beast— terrifying and
frightening and very powerful.
It had large iron teeth; it crushed and
devoured its victims and trampled
underfoot whatever was left.

—Daniel 7:3-7

INTEMPESTA

In the royal gardens beneath a full moon, Vitas stealthily pursued the man he had once vowed to serve with loyalty or death. His emperor.

It was a night unnaturally still and hot, heavy with the unseen menace of a building storm, with the moon above Rome and the seven hills that guarded the city—a moon that bounced mercury light off the placid lake of the royal gardens into thinly spaced trees along its shore.

Nero was fifty paces ahead of Vitas, lurching beneath an elaborate costume that impeded his progress. The costume had been pieced together from animals imported to the arenas to kill convicted criminals. Head to foot, Nero was draped in a leopard's skin. Two pairs of eagles' wings were sewn onto the back of the costume. A lion's head from a massive male had been attached to the top, and Nero's head fit completely inside the skull, allowing him to see through the empty sockets. His arms and legs were covered by the skin from a bear's legs, which had also been sewn to the leopard skin that covered the bulk of Nero's body. In the quiet of the night, the bear claws rattled with each of Nero's steps.

Another man walked beside Nero. Helius. Nero's secretary and confidant. Helius—along with a man named Tigellinus—had been a companion since Nero was a teenage emperor, when the three of them roamed the streets of Rome at night to bully and rob strangers, like common thugs.

Helius held aloft a torch, which illuminated the dull iron chain in his right hand, and it dragged along the ground, rattling in odd unison with the bear claws of Nero's costume.

Because of the noise and the apparent focus on their destination, Vitas was not worried that his emperor would notice his pursuit. He was far more worried about Nero's intentions. There had been times when Nero dressed in wolf skins and attacked slaves chained to stakes, but that had been part of very public celebrations.

This was too different. Too eerie. Vitas needed to know why.

Vitas was the single man in Nero's inner circle whom the Senate trusted. There were times when Vitas felt he was a thin string holding the Senate and emperor together. If Vitas lost his awareness of Nero's actions, he would lose the Senate's trust that gave him such value to both sides. The string would snap. If that happened, the inevitable war would be disastrous for the empire.

Ahead of Vitas, the roar of a real lion thundered from the inside of a gardener's hut, roiling through the heat and stillness back toward Nero's palace.

Vitas wondered if the echoes of the roar clawed into the dreams and nightmares of the slaves in their various quarters. If those who woke to the roar pretended sleep or silently held their children and whispered prayers to their gods.

The slaves knew there was danger in the roar. But, like Vitas, it wasn't the lion they feared.

✟ ✟ ✟

Helius had been instructed by Nero to make no noise when they reached the hut. Just outside the closed door, Helius nodded when Nero stopped and pointed at the chain Helius carried.

Helius was a man of arrogance and certainty except in the presence of Nero; he hated himself for fumbling with the chain as he tentatively attached it to a collar around the neck of the animal costume. Bowed meekly when Nero slapped him once across the face for his clumsiness.

Nero pointed at the door of the hut.

Helius opened it, and by the chain, led Nero inside.

Two men and two women were shackled to the stone of an interior wall, each sagging against the irons, each stripped to sackcloth rags.

They faced three cages. One held the lion. Another held a bear. And the third a leopard.

Helius stepped inside, leading the disguised Nero. He jammed the torch into an iron band bolted to the wall for that purpose. He fastened one end of the chain that held the beast to a bar of the lion's cage.

Helius turned to the first man.

They were the same height but obviously different ages. The captive was nearing sixty; Helius was in his twenties. Daylight would have shown the smooth and almost bronzed skin of Helius' features. His hair was luxuriously curly, his eyes a strange yellow, giving him a feral look that was rumored to hold great attraction for Nero. Helius wore a toga, and his fingers and wrists and neck were layered with jewelry of gold and rubies. There was something catlike about his examination of the captive in front of him.

Helius had a knife hidden in his toga. With deliberate slowness, he pulled it up and placed the edge of it against the man's face with sinister gentleness.

"The emperor wishes for you to bow down and worship the beast," Helius said. His fumbling fear was gone in service of Nero. Temporary as it might be, with Nero in the costume, Helius was now the one in control.

"No," the man said quietly.

"No?"

Helius moved to the woman beside the man. He drew the knife downward from her ear to her chin. A narrow line of blood followed the path of the knife and streamed onto her neck.

"Leave the woman alone," the first captive said. "Turn your attention to me." His hair matched his beard—greasy with days of unwashed sweat from being in captivity, gray hairs far outnumbering the remainder of black ones. His torso and arms were corded with muscle, suggesting a long life of physical labor.

"Then worship the beast," Helius answered.

"I cannot."

"Cannot?" Helius asked softly, waving the knife in front of the woman. "Or will not?"

"I will not betray my Master."

"Nor will I," said the woman. "I am not afraid."

"Listen to me, you Jews," Helius said. "If you bow to the beast and worship him as divine, I have been given authority to spare you this."

With his knife, Helius cut a piece of the rags that covered the first captive. He turned to the woman and used the cloth to wipe blood from her face.

Helius tossed the bloody rag into the lion's cage, and it savaged the cloth, pinning it with its mighty front paws and tearing at it with its teeth. Beside it in their own cages, the bear roared its fury, and the agitated leopard paced back and forth.

Helius ignored the cages, letting his eyes caress the face of each captive, searching for fear. Because he knew fear so intimately in himself, he was an expert at finding it in others.

Helius smiled his hungry smile. "Let me repeat. Nero wishes for you to worship the beast. Will you accept it as god? Or shall I let the beast loose to destroy you?"

The first man remained silent. Helius had expected the resistance. But it did not matter. Either way, Nero would be satisfied by a personal triumph over these Christians. They would worship him, hidden as he was beneath the costume of the beast, or he would take satisfaction in killing them as the beast. This symbolic victory would assure Nero that he truly was in control, that the widespread resistance to him from the Christians of Rome was meaningless.

Helius turned to the others, asking one by one if they were willing to bow down and worship the beast. None answered.

"Let me kill them!" The beast that was Nero spoke in a guttural, strangulated voice. "Let me tear their livers from their living bodies! Let me—"

"Silence!" Helius barked at the beast. These had been Nero's instructions. Play the role of the master of the beast so none of the captives would guess Nero himself was hidden beneath the costume.

To the captives Helius said, "Look at the beast closely. Do you not see it is a bear? a lion? a leopard with wings? Does it mean anything to you?"

The beast began hissing, a frenzy that ended only when Helius grabbed the torch and waved the fire beneath its head. As if it truly were beast, not man. Nero, the amateur actor, was widely known for playing his roles seriously.

After Helius calmed the beast, he spoke to the captives again. Anger tinged his words. "I understand far more about you Jews than you realize. I know of your prophet named Daniel. Hundreds of years ago, he foretold that Rome would be the fourth beast, greater than the kingdoms of Babylon and Persia and Greece. And here is your fourth beast, ready to destroy you."

"Death cannot destroy us," the first captive said. "Through my Lord and Master, it is a fate that we greet with peace. If you would believe in His love and——"

Helius slashed at the captive with his knife, a slash of rage. The blade flashed across the man's right bicep, instantly cutting through to muscle. Blood dripped down the man's elbow and onto the dirt floor. This had not been part of Nero's instructions, but Helius was at heart a coward and could not resist the power he'd been given for this role.

"You refuse to worship the beast?" Helius jeered. "Then tonight he will be the beast to destroy you! And in the next years, he will continue to destroy all the followers until the very last disciple is wiped from this earth. The name of Christos will be forgotten, but Nero will be revered forever!"

Helius spun, taking hold of the chain that held the upright beast to the lion's cage. "Ravage these men and women and destroy them," he spoke to the beast. "Leave their remains for the bear and the leopard and the lion!"

The beast howled.

"Yes," Helius told the beast. "Tonight you will sleep in peace, knowing the power of the fourth beast is greater than the power of their God. You will triumph!"

Helius was forced to yell above the roars of the animals and the high-pitched screaming of Nero playing the beast.

Then Helius froze as a lone man walked into the hut.

Gallus Sergius Vitas.

✝ ✝ ✝

Vitas had heard enough from outside to decide to stop this madness. And he knew how he would do it.

He'd made his decision to enter the hut based on a well-known story about Nero. During those years as a teenage emperor Nero had dressed himself as a slave and would roam the streets at night to loot shops and terrorize strangers. He and his friends, including Helius and Tigellinus, had attacked a rich senator and his wife. The senator was unaware that Nero was among the hoodlums and fought well, landing several punches directly in Nero's face. Nero and his friends fled.

While Nero had recognized the man as a senator, he made no plans to take action against him, realizing the senator had been perfectly justified in protecting himself from a mere slave. Unfortunately, when someone told the senator whose eyes he had blackened, he sent Nero a letter of abject apology. Because Nero could no longer pretend he'd been an anonymous slave and it was now publicly known that the senator had committed a treasonous act against the emperor, the senator was forced to open his veins in a suicide that prevented the trial and conviction that would have ruined the senator's family.

Yes. Nero was, first and foremost, an actor. Vitas counted on that.

Without hesitation, Vitas marched forward and yanked the chain from Helius. "If the emperor knows you are involved in illegal torture, he will have you destroyed!"

For Vitas, it was an all-or-nothing bluff, pretending he did not know Nero was inside the costume. Trusting that Nero would be too ashamed to admit it. Now. Or later.

Vitas shoved Helius hard toward the doorway of the small hut. "Outside! Now!"

Without hesitation, Vitas grabbed the chain and jerked it hard, treating the man in the beast costume as lower than a slave. "Don't move. I'll be back to deal with you."

Vitas forced himself to pretend outrage. But this was the moment. If Nero decided he would no longer play the role, Vitas was dead.

The beast snarled at him, an echo from inside the lion's skull. But the beast did nothing else.

Vitas knew he was safe. Temporarily.

Vitas spun on his heels and marched outside to Helius.

✝ ✝ ✝

"You feed his delusions," Vitas said to Helius.

The two of them stood outside the hut in the shadows of an olive tree.

Helius shrugged, a smirk visible on his face in the moonlight.

Vitas had learned in battle in Britannia how to detach himself from the emotions of the moment. Yet it took immense willpower to restrain himself from withdrawing his short sword from his toga and charging at Helius. But it would not serve the empire for Helius to die, for Nero clung to the man with a neediness that barely kept Nero stable.

"Of course I feed his delusions." Helius continued smirking, unaware of how closely the ghost of his own murder had passed by. "That is the whole point. His power. And how I survive."

"How does this serve Nero?" Vitas demanded, pointing at the hut behind them.

Vitas was not particularly large, but he was tall and carried himself the way a man with solid compact muscles does. He was also cloaked in his family's well-documented patrician background of generations of Roman purity, and by the stories, almost legendary, about his bravery in battles against the Iceni in Britannia. In daylight, his flat, almost black eyes made his thoughts unreadable to his opponents, and without a smile, his face was implacable, like unweathered stone. Here, his face hidden in the shadow cast by the moonlight, Vitas was that much more intimidating. Much as Nero needed Helius, Nero revered Vitas. Only Vitas could speak to Helius in this way and not fear later punishment in the stealthy form of poison or an assassin.

"His nightmares," Helius said, finally sensing the deadly anger simmering beneath the calm demeanor of Vitas. "Nero wants to be rid of them."

"By this travesty of justice?"

Helius shrugged. "No worse than anything else Nero has desired in recent years."

Vitas could not argue with that. "He is Caesar, the representative of our great empire. To protect the empire, we must protect our emperor's dignity."

"The empire?" Helius sneered. "You truly believe in the empire?"

That was the question, Vitas thought. Could he continue to believe in the empire? It had once been his whole life. Until that final battle in Britannia. There, he had fought to defend the empire against barbarians. Now, as Nero became more of a megalomaniac every day, Vitas wondered who were the true barbarians and if he needed instead to fight the empire.

"I believe," Vitas answered without betraying his thoughts, "that you enjoy Nero's worst instincts."

Helius smiled. "Nero gets what Nero wants. I do for him as he directs me."

"To secretly torture and kill these Christians."

"His nightmares have worsened."

Vitas needed no explanation. Nero, who had once shared a bed with his mother, had later ordered her murdered. As he did with his first wife, whose head he demanded as proof of death. His second wife he'd kicked to death while she was pregnant. He'd poisoned his adoptive half brother. The list went on, until the most recent atrocities—the executions of myriad Christians. It was no wonder that demons haunted the man in the dark of each night.

Yet, monstrous as the man was, Vitas well knew that to end Nero's life would likely result in civil war, as Nero had no successor. Civil war would destroy the empire. So Vitas served Nero and did his best as a trusted adviser to lessen the monstrosities.

"He expects this to quiet those nightmares?" Vitas said, gesturing at the hut.

"It's that Greek graffiti," Helius said. "That one senseless word that the Christians have begun to inscribe all across the city in defiance of him."

Vitas was aware of it. Three Greek letters. With the snake in the middle.

Helius continued. "Until tonight, their resolution to worship their Christos despite Nero's persecution had begun to shake Nero's belief in his own divinity."

"A man posing as beast is hardly divine."

"I've convinced him that if he defeats them as the Beast that their own prophet Daniel foretold of, he will break this curse upon himself. He has taken some potions to delude himself further."

The constriction around Vitas' chest eased only a little. If Nero's mind had been influenced by potions tonight, he would be all the more determined to remain in the role of the beast instead of giving orders to execute Vitas.

"I know about the Jewish rabbi you consulted," Vitas said. "So I also know of these Scriptures."

"How?" Helius demanded. "Who told you that I sent for—?"

"Secrets are difficult to keep in the palace," Vitas said wearily. "How I know is of far less concern than what I know. The prophet Daniel also prophesied that the fourth beast would be destroyed. You've kept that from Nero?"

"I'm not suicidal," Helius said. "Of course I did. It's what he believes that matters, not the nonsense of a Jewish prophet from six hundred years ago. Nero will never be destroyed and certainly never by a God of the Jews. Nero is convinced if they worship the beast or if the beast kills them, he is the victor. It's superstition, of course, but you know full well how superstitious fear rules him."

Vitas did know full well Nero's dread of the gods and of omens. He also knew that Nero, with his absolute power, had performed far stranger acts than this with far less motivation. In a twisted way, this horrible parody made sense. But could Vitas allow himself to stand by yet one more time?

"You think this will remain a secret?" Vitas argued. "That Nero is so afraid of the Christians he must dress up as a beast and kill them himself?" Every day Vitas was more fully aware of how the Senate would view Nero's actions. "Think of how the tongues of the mobs will wag further when they hear this."

"What Nero wants, Nero gets."

"If he continues like this, there will come a point when he will no longer be tolerated. The empire will revolt against him. And you will lose your own power."

"We are here and it is too late to stop this," Helius snapped. "Do you expect some sort of divine intervention to save those inside? to save you from the act of defiance you have just committed against Caesar?"

Images of the final battle in Britannia flashed through the mind of Vitas. Of the power of the empire unleashed on the innocent. He spoke quietly. "The persecution must stop."

"That's the real reason you're here tonight, isn't it?" Teeth gleamed in the moonlight as Helius smiled. "Your constant and tedious arguments to save the Christians. Perhaps you are one yourself?"

"Hardly. You and I both know they are innocent of treason. The empire cannot survive if it does not serve justice equally to all."

Helius shrugged. "Give me power over principles any day. It's a pity you won't learn that lesson."

"Take Nero back to the palace. With any luck, he won't remember this."

"It's too late," Helius said. "What's begun must be finished."

"No."

"No?" Helius echoed. "I doubt you'll stop me. You've become too soft, Vitas. Nero might not know it. But I do. The great warrior Vitas is a toothless lion. But what should one expect of one who married a barbarian?"

His neck muscles tightened, but Vitas held himself back.

"Tell me," Helius said, still taunting Vitas. "Is it true? Was it your sword that —?"

"Enough!"

"Enough or you'll kill me?" Helius said.

Vitas froze.

"See?" Helius said. "The great warrior Vitas would never have meekly accepted such an insult."

Helius turned his back on Vitas and hurried back into the hut.

✝ ✝ ✝

"No!"

Helius had just taken the chain off the bars to the lion's cage. The beast with the wings and head of a lion was pulling at the chain, reaching with bear claws to tear at the first of the four captives in shackles.

Vitas had made his decision. Over the last six months, he had allowed too much to happen already; his conscience could be pushed no further. He stepped back into the hut. Ready to defy Nero, even if it cost him his life.

"No!" Vitas repeated. He spoke to the beast. "This is enough."

Nero, addled by lust and anger and the results of whatever potions he had consumed, continued to hiss and snarl beneath the costume of the beast. "Kill him!" he hissed from inside the lion's head. "Tear his heart out! Vitas must die. I tire of his defense of the Christians!"

In that moment, Vitas knew he'd lost his gamble. Nero had stopped acting, spoken his name. No longer could Vitas pretend that he was unaware of who wore the costume. No longer was Vitas protected by his value as the only man of Nero's inner court respected by the Senate.

"Kill him!" Nero's voice became higher and unnatural. It goaded the real beasts in the cages into a frenzy of roars, a rumble.

"This must stop!" Vitas answered, resolute. If this was his final stand, he would not flee.

"Kill him!"

The noise of the beasts changed. Subtly at first. Then the low rumble became a distinct noise in itself, which slowly began to build and build.

The ground beneath them shook.

Helius swayed. Nero in his beast costume staggered. Vitas shifted his feet wider to keep his balance.

The cages rattled and shook back and forth.

As Vitas realized that the earth itself was quaking, lightning struck the thatched roof of the hut, and the rumbling was broken by a tremendous peal of thunder.

The roof burst into flames and again lightning struck, deafening them with instant thunder that followed.

Helius fell to his knees as the ground continued to shake.

Vitas saw that the cage doors had sprung open. That the animals were lurching out, dazed by their sudden freedom.

The huge lion advanced on Nero. He scrambled backward into the body of the first captive, then fell at that captive's feet, moaning from inside his costume.

Vitas pulled his short sword from his toga and stepped between Nero and the lion. Nero was emperor. Even though the emperor had ordered him executed, Vitas had his duty.

The lion crouched. It weighed three times what a man did, with teeth longer and sharper than daggers, paws as large as a man's head, and the power to take down an ox.

Vitas waited and watched, ready to fight, hopeless as it was.

Another boom of deafening thunder. The lion sank back, bewildered.

Lightning flashed again.

And the lion fled. The leopard and the bear followed.

Helius remained on his knees, cowering, tears streaming down his face.

In the calm that followed the next burst of lightning, the earthquake renewed itself.

Nero screamed, "The gods speak against me!"

He threw off his costume, dashed past Vitas, and fled the hut, leaving behind the leopard fur with its eagles' wings. Helius, too, retreated, following Nero into the trees as lightning continued to flash upon the grounds of the palace.

Vitas kicked aside remnants of burning straw that fell from the roof of the hut.

All four captives shackled to the wall stared at him in silence.

Vitas advanced on the first one with his sword.

"Please spare the women," the gray-haired captive said, the older one who had faced Helius with so little fear. "They have children."

"What is your name?" Vitas asked him, pressing the flat of his sword up near the man's chest.

"John."

"John," Vitas said, "you do not deserve to die for what you believe."

Vitas leveraged his sword into John's shackles until they separated. One by one, he released each of the other captives.

They made no move to flee.

Vitas turned to the first woman. Her bleeding had lessened. Vitas tore a strip from his toga and pressed it against her face. He lifted her hand until she held the cloth, then stepped away.

"Go to your children," Vitas told her. "All of you. Go. Now is the time to make your escape. Before Nero again convinces himself he is god."

ROME
CAPITAL OF THE EMPIRE

SMYRNA
PROVINCE OF ASIA

Do not be afraid
of what you are about to suffer.
I tell you, the devil will put some of you
in prison to test you, and you will suffer
persecution for ten days.
Be faithful, even to the point of death,
and I will give you the crown of life.

—Revelation 2:10

MERCURY

HORA DUODECIMA

At the end of the first day of the new games, the roars of animals and the howling of dying men and women inside the amphitheater were easily drowned out by the applause and cheering of tens of thousands of spectators.

Outside the amphitheater, these were the noises a young Jewish woman named Leah tried to block as she neared the main gates. Her brother was inside, but not one of the spectators.

She'd chosen nondescript clothing for this journey and tried not to look furtive. That was difficult for her. She'd lied to her beloved father to escape their apartment. It was the first time in her memory that she had deceived him. During every step toward the amphitheater, she'd felt as if every person along the way was aware of her vile crime against her father, as if the stain on her soul spread across her face like a disease.

Added to this discomfort was her fear that Gallus Sergius Vitas, a tall and quiet member of Nero's inner circle, might be here. To sustain the courage to make this day's journey, Leah had told herself again and again that even if Vitas was in the amphitheater, with the screaming thousands around him, it was unlikely he would notice her as she slipped past the main gates. Still, as much as she could convince herself of this on an intellectual level, she could not squelch her fear.

She remembered all too clearly the day Vitas had appeared at their home with soldiers to arrest her brother Nathan. Although weeks had passed since that horrible event, the vividness of Vitas' alertness and the piercing quality of his total attention to the sights and sounds around him were still impressed in her memories. It had seemed when he looked at her, standing so relaxed and dignified as he reprimanded the soldiers for prodding Nathan with spears, that he was able to read her very thoughts.

Worse—as she allowed her mind to worry about the presence of Vitas—she realized that here, near the main gates, the street had long since emptied of spectators rushing for seats inside, and now Leah walked alone on the cobblestone street.

Yet hers was not a walk of solitude. Leah was acutely aware of the stares of nearby soldiers who guarded the men and women hanging above her, lining each side of the broad street that led to the entrance of the amphitheater. Alongside charred stumps of posts were new wooden lampposts spaced every ten paces. Men and women dangled from each post, their bound wrists hanging from spikes in the post above their heads, their entire body weight wrenching at their shoulder sockets. As Leah hurried past them, she realized they could only listen to the nearby thunderous cheering and contemplate their own fate.

The soldiers sweated profusely, even while sitting motionless in whatever shade they could find. When a soldier rose occasionally to splash water against his face from a nearby public fountain and groan at the relief, it was a sight and sound that most surely added to the agony of those hanging from the lampposts.

This heat was a form of torture, adding to the excruciating pain of arm sockets slowly pulling loose. But the prisoners could not cry out for water from those passing the fountain. Their lips had been sewn shut to prevent them from disturbing Roman citizens with pleas for help or with shrieks of agony.

Like Leah, who hated her inability to help these tortured men and women, the prisoners knew the purpose they would serve when darkness fell.

Each wore the *tunica molesta*—a tunic black and gleaming in the sunlight and saturated in tar. Leah could scarcely imagine the suffocating sensation of the thick, heavy garments, soaking up the heat of the sun and clinging to their bodies as the tar oozed against their skin.

Yet beyond the imagination of that agony was one worse.

The waiting.

At sundown, by the orders of Nero, the guards would ignite their tunics so these men and women—the Christians—would become human torches to light the street for the half-drunk Roman revelers returning home at the end of the games.

This was the Great Tribulation. Hell did exist on earth.

Leah's worries about Gallus Vitas were groundless.

He was days and days of travel from Rome, roughly eight hundred miles away, across the mountains, across the Adriatic Sea, across Macedonia, and across the Aegean Sea in the center of an Asian port city called Smyrna. The afternoon had that late brightness that comes with the long rays of sun stretching across the aquamarine of the sea and bouncing up into the hills.

The tavern Vitas entered with Titus Flavius Vespasianus was so well shuttered that oil lamps were necessary for light, as if darkness, still an hour away, had already cloaked the city.

It took less than a minute for silence to settle upon the crowded tavern as, one by one, the patrons noticed the newcomers. The dice and knucklebones at the gaming counter stopped rattling, the prostitutes ended their chatter with the most promising drunks, and the lone singer near an oil lamp in the corner abruptly quit halfway through a verse.

"This is the trouble with visiting the slums," Titus said out of the side of his mouth to Vitas. "One must dress down to fit in. But to do so risks fleas of the worst sort."

Titus wore a spotless silk toga. Dim as the light was, it clearly showed his elegant handsome features. He'd been a best friend to Brittanicus, the son of Claudius, who had reigned as emperor before Nero. Titus' time in the royal courts showed in the confident way he held himself, in the style of his haircut, and in his articulate manner of speaking.

"Perhaps you could say that louder," Vitas answered. He wore a simple tunic and was slightly taller than Titus. Leaner. Vitas was nearing thirty, six years older than Titus. Each was obviously well muscled and healthy and showed a full set of teeth—ample evidence of their wealth and rank to the members of the underclass who filled this tavern. "Or perhaps you could repeat it for the few at the back who were unable to hear it the first time."

Already, a few large men—stooped from years of hard labor—had begun to rise from their tables, knocking over cups of beer in their haste.

"Speciem illorum uberum suis non amo," Titus said in clear reference to the two approaching men, using formal grammar to emphasize the common insult.

Vitas shook his head sadly as two more men rose from their seats. *I don't like the look of those sows' udders*, Titus had just called out.

"Please," Vitas said to the men, "no need to get up in greeting. We were told we might find Gallus Damian here."

As the prostitutes eased out of the way, none of the four men slowed his approach.

"Notice how they come in pairs," Titus declared loudly, calmly adjusting his toga so he could move freely in a fight. "It simply proves what I said. Sows' udders."

✛ ✛ ✛

At that moment, deep in the emperor's palace in Rome, the second most powerful man in the empire was about to discover a different kind of terror, hidden within a scroll with a broken seal.

"Leave me alone," Helius said to the slave who had entered his chamber with the scroll. "I'm extremely busy."

His sarcasm dripped with the authority of a man who'd once been a slave, now speaking to a subordinate. Because of his relationship to Nero, that meant nearly anyone else in the empire. The irritation Helius endured because of the summer heat was increased by the fact that he had always found this particular slave ugly.

"Tigellinus said—"

"I am occupied." Helius interrupted the slave, spitting out each word.

Indeed, Helius was busy allowing two other slaves to tend to him. A woman was trimming his hair in the latest style, and a teenage boy was applying makeup to his face.

The slave with the scroll—a man in his forties with sparse gray hair—seemed miserable. "Tigellinus wants you to look at the graffiti," he persisted. The slave only persisted because Tigellinus knew Helius was preparing for a night of debauchery with Nero and had foreseen that Helius would not be interested. Accordingly, Tigellinus had promised to have the slave severely whipped unless Helius read the scroll. And, since Tigellinus was the prefect of the Praetorian Guards, the emperor's soldiers who policed the city, Tigellinus was one of the few men in Rome with power nearly equal to Helius'.

"Graffiti?" Helius echoed. The first sensation of dread rumbled within his bowels. If this came from Tigellinus, it could only refer to certain graffiti that infuriated Nero. Nero's nightmares had not lessened; to-night's fun was intended to distract Nero from his demons.

"This . . . ," the slave said as he began to unroll the scroll. The back of it—the side facing Helius—revealed a single three-letter Greek word, large enough to be visible at several paces.

Helius sucked in his breath as his guess about the graffiti was con-firmed. He recovered quickly, hoping neither the woman behind him nor the boy applying his makeup had detected that quick intake of breath.

"This scroll comes from Tigellinus?" Helius said as casually as he could. "And where did he get it?"

"A young Jew stopped him in the streets and showed it to him. Tigellinus had him immediately arrested."

"You were with Tigellinus and witnessed this?"

"I was there," the old slave answered.

"Tigellinus read it?"

"Yes."

"And the Jew that he arrested?"

"Tigellinus instructed me to tell you that the young Jew has been detained and is under guard."

"By Tigellinus?" Helius asked, hoping the answer would be other-wise.

"By Tigellinus."

If Tigellinus had handled it personally instead of ordering soldiers to watch the young Jew, this was as important as Helius feared. For, if Nero got wind of it, he would be unbearable. Everything that mattered to Helius depended on the whims of Nero, whose patience was already nearing an end because of the apparent powerlessness that Helius and Tigellinus had against the symbol on the back of the scroll.

Helius forced his mind away from consequences. He was too familiar with the horrible ways that men and women who displeased Nero met their deaths.

Helius sighed, as if the issue of the scroll was a mere irritation. "As I said, I am busy. Have Tigellinus deal with this matter."

Obviously conscious of the whipping that Tigellinus had promised, the slave persisted. "He instructed me that you must read the scroll."

"I am very occupied." Helius needed to pretend that nothing about the scroll interested him. He paused, as if coming to a sudden thought. "You read it to me."

"Of course," the slave said.

"Wait. Are the contents of the scroll written in Greek? or Latin?"

"Greek," the slave answered as he unwound it. "Like the back of the scroll."

"Are you calling me stupid?" Helius said. His bad mood had worsened the instant he'd seen the single Greek word. Yes, the next weeks would be hellish if Nero discovered this.

"No, I—"

"I saw the back of the scroll. Telling me it is in Greek too is like telling me you think I'm too stupid to read Greek."

"I apologize," the slave said, dropping to his knees and bowing.

This humiliation pleased Helius. He hated ugliness.

The teenage boy giggled at the slave's apology. Since the boy was attractive, Helius decided not to reprimand him. "Go on, then," Helius told the old slave. "Read me this letter as Tigellinus has insisted."

✠ ✠ ✠

In Smyrna, less than a half mile from the tavern where Vitas and Titus were about to brawl, a man named Aristarchus heard screams on the other side of the blanket hung over the arch leading to the inner courtyard. With a fist already clenched, he punched the blanket, shook it off as it wrapped around his arm, and let it fall behind him onto the mosaic floor.

Marching through the arch, he ignored the views afforded by the courtyard's windows. To the west lay Smyrna's port and the sea beyond, while the hilltops stretched to the azure sky in the east. He had long taken his wealth and the palatial estate for granted, and this day was no exception.

He stalked toward the center of the courtyard, stepping into the long shadow that his body cast in the late afternoon. Directly ahead, a midwife and three other women were focused on his wife, Paulina, and did not notice Aristarchus until he was a few paces away. Their momentary shock at his breach of tradition nearly allowed him to reach Paulina, crouched on the birthing chair behind them. Paulina seemed unaware of his presence as she shut her eyes and screamed again, fighting the intense pain of a prolonged contraction.

"Move aside," he barked. But for the depth of his anger, his manner of expression would have been comical, for he was a small man with a high-pitched voice.

"How dare you!" the midwife said, breaking out of her brief frozen shock. "Out!" She grabbed his arm and spun him back toward the archway.

Normally, she would have prevailed. She was a large, wide woman and by nature, bad-tempered.

Aristarchus, on the other hand, had become *tamias*, "treasurer," of the town council of Smyrna, through cultivated deviousness, and rarely engaged in open confrontations. Today, however, his anger overpowered his instinctive political nature. He stiff-armed the midwife's belly with the hand he had not yet unclenched. As she staggered back, he twisted loose and turned on the three other women, Paulina's sisters, who had formed a protective half circle in front of Paulina.

Paulina gasped in relief when the contraction passed. The exertion had flushed her face and drenched it with sweat.

"Stand aside," he ordered. "I will speak with my wife."

The three women, dark-haired and dusky-skinned like their sister, all wore identical frowns.

"Leave," the eldest said. She'd never respected Aristarchus and had no compunction about showing her scorn now. "Men have no part in this. Ever."

Aristarchus opened his fist and dangled from his fingers a thin silver chain. A small silver cross hung at the end. "She will answer me this. I demand to know if what I've just heard is true."

"My sister," the eldest said, teeth clenched, "has been in difficult labor since last night. Wait until tomorrow. Better yet, wait until she has fully recovered. This is her time for a child not for an argument."

Paulina moaned as a new contraction gained strength.

The midwife rushed to her and mopped the sweat from her brow. With surprising gentleness, the midwife murmured, "One more contraction is one closer to bringing you a beautiful baby. Don't be afraid to push, my child."

Aristarchus opened his mouth to argue, but as Paulina began to scream again, he realized his efforts would be wasted.

When the contraction finally passed, he did not hesitate to continue. "Is she part of this cult?" he demanded, shaking the chain and the cross. "Is she one who shares the blood?"

The sisters closed ranks, and Aristarchus shoved them aside to shout into Paulina's face. "Are you? Is what I've discovered today about your secret faith true?"

Paulina was panting, exhausted, yet the light in her eyes was strong. "I am," she said simply.

"That Jew slave servant of yours, Sophia—she has corrupted you, hasn't she?"

"By leading me to the living Christos she has led me to a great peace. She—"

"She will no longer be part of this household. Now renounce Christos. Here and now in front of witnesses. It is not too late to save my reputation and the position that supports your family. Renounce your faith!"

Paulina's face tightened. "I cannot," she whispered. "The Christos is my Savior."

"No! I preside at a temple where Nero is worshiped as almighty savior. Do you want to destroy my livelihood?"

Paulina could not answer as the contraction overwhelmed her. While he continued to screech at her, she began to moan.

✛ ✛ ✛

"You're one of them, are you?" At the main gates of the amphitheater, a short guard with a powerful build leered at Leah. "You don't look it, but I've learned never to judge by appearances."

"One of them?" Leah asked. She could not guess at what the guard meant by "appearances." Leah was young, just at the age of marriage. She'd dressed plainly, covering most of her long dark hair. She knew men looked at her with desire but never felt that she was attractive enough to deserve their attention.

"Don't play stupid with me. You love to see their fear, don't you?" The guard took from her the bribe he had demanded earlier and jabbed a thumb in the direction of the chaos behind him.

On the ground level of the amphitheater, twenty or thirty people jostled toward the opening where prisoners were forced out onto the sand. The sunlight pierced the opening and clearly showed the lustful joy on the men and women jeering at a new group of men passing by on their way to death.

One of them.

Leah could not comprehend why the Romans enjoyed the death cries rising from the arena let alone understand the pleasure Nero himself took in all his public perversion and his imaginative manners of torture. A Jew born in Rome—the Jewish community was strong and large and vibrant—Leah had managed to avoid even being near any of the games that took place when politicians needed to placate the mobs with entertainment.

One of them.

Those in the small crowd ahead taunted the prisoners. Some—both men and women—reached out to grab them indecently.

"Take care you don't end up in the arena," the guard laughed, a sound more like a bark than anything. "At the last games, half a dozen spectators found themselves out on the sand. They died as quick as the condemned. What a spectacle that was!"

Leah hurried away and tried to shut out the sounds and sights of the guards using spears to prod the condemned forward. She left behind the opening of sunlight and the rumble of cheering, and she followed the tunnels deeper beneath the stands, down into a damp darkness lit by torches.

✠ ✠ ✠

The tension facing Vitas in the tavern grew as the four thugs approached.

"I say pretty boy cries for his mama first," one man called out, pointing at Titus. "And I'll put money on it."

"A simple yes or no is all I need," Vitas said, his voice loud but calm. "Have any of you seen Damian tonight? Help me and I'll gladly buy drinks for all."

That drew cheers but didn't stop the forward movement of the four thugs, though the spacing of the rough wooden tables made their approach difficult. As the first one neared, Titus smiled politely, then stepped forward and kicked him in the groin.

The large man fell to his knees, his body temporarily blocking the path of the other three. Seconds later, the man on his knees retched.

"Isn't it wonderful to go out on the town and get drunk?" Titus said pleasantly to the fallen man.

Two of the other men roared and leaped over the fallen man in an attempt to tackle Titus. He stepped behind Vitas, then onto one table and onto the next.

"Excuse me," Titus said to the patrons at each table, who were too stunned to react. "Excuse me again. And again."

Hopping from tabletop to tabletop, Titus was on the opposite side of the tavern in moments, leaving Vitas to deal with the large drunks.

Despite the beer they had consumed, the men were sober enough to appreciate the short sword that Vitas held in front of him, a sword he had drawn from beneath his tunic with such amazing quickness that it seemed he'd been standing on guard with it the entire time.

"Gallus Damian," Vitas said. "Surely you know him. I was told this is where many of the gladiators entertain themselves the night before the games."

"And who is asking?" This voice came from a man seated alone. All the other tables were crowded beyond capacity, but this man had his entire table to himself.

A low murmur went through the crowd in reaction to his question.

The man rose slowly. Moved toward Vitas.

The drunks fell backward trying to get away, dragging their stunned companion with them. Other spectators parted with reverent fear and made room for the new man.

The man repeated his question to Vitas. "Tell me, who is asking about Damian?"

✢ ✢ ✢

Standing directly in front of Helius, the sparsely-haired slave scrolled to the top portion. He held it at arm's length, betraying his farsightedness. The back of it showed the top of the single Greek word that had disturbed Helius.

"Wait," Helius said. "Unscroll it so these two can see the back of it again."

At his instructions, the woman and the teenage boy looked closely at the three-letter word.

"Do either of you read Greek?" Helius asked.

Both shook their heads.

Helius sighed his disgust at their ignorance.

"But I've seen it before," the boy said, eager to please. "Like graffiti . . . on the walls of the emperor's palace. And once at the games. A Christian was dying. A lion had swiped open his belly, then moved on to another one. The first Christian was near the wall. He rubbed his hand on his bleeding belly and with his blood smeared that same word across the wall for everyone on the other side of the arena to see."

This was what Helius had not wanted to hear. If this boy had seen it and recognized it, so had far too many of the people who wandered the city.

"You're sure?" Helius said.

"Most sure. Look at it. It's easy to remember, especially with the snake in the middle."

Yes, Helius thought, *easy to remember. Far too easy.* And Nero, too, had seen it on the palace walls. So far, Helius had managed to laugh it off with Nero, but the word had shown up far too often in the last weeks. If only, Helius wished, every Christian in the city were already dead so none remained to scrawl that mark in public places.

"What does it mean?" the boy asked.

"Nothing of importance," Helius said. "Make sure you don't powder my face so thickly that it is obvious."

In one way, Helius was telling the truth. It was nothing but three Greek letters.

$$\chi\xi\varsigma$$

But in another way, the center symbol gave the appearance of the writhing serpent and represented its hissing sound, and that made it truly ominous. The first letter was the initial letter of the name of Christ. The last letter was a double letter, which began the Greek word for "cross," *stauros*. And the symbol of the snake was trapped in between the two.

It was ominous in appearance.

And because its constant use in defiance of the persecution made so little sense to Helius, its mystery made it all the more ominous.

"Read the letter," Helius barked at the old slave. He spoke to the woman and the boy. "You two, both of you, keep busy."

✠ ✠ ✠

One of Paulina's sisters tried to push Aristarchus away from his exhausted wife as her birthing moans grew again in intensity.

He stood his ground, yelling at Paulina. "Don't you understand? I am treasurer! I am a priest in the temple of Nero! You can serve any god but the Christos!"

Her moans continued to grow louder as the next wave of pain crested.

Aristarchus spoke to the eldest sister, his anger slipping into pleading. "The Christos demands service to no other gods. Our city depends on the largess of the divine Nero. Will the people allow me to remain treasurer if word spreads that my own wife refuses to worship Caesar?"

Agony ripped another scream from Paulina.

"Push," the midwife urged. "Push!"

"Any other religion!" Aristarchus pleaded hoarsely. He struggled to make himself heard above the noise of his wife's screaming. "Any other religion would make room for emperor worship! There are dozens to choose from. I won't stand in the way of them! In every other matter of our marriage I give you what you want! But here, I put my foot down. No Christos, or I am ruined!"

"Push! Push!"

"Listen to me!" he shouted. "Even the Jews in this city reject the Christos! You must do the same. Listen!"

No one did.

The midwife lifted the sheet to check Paulina's progress. "Push! Push! Your child is nearly here."

Paulina shrieked, a mixture of torment and relief and joy.

"Push! Push!" The midwife caught the baby's head as it entered the world. Its shoulders twisted sideways and the rest of the tiny body followed.

Paulina wept with relief.

The midwife gently placed the baby in Paulina's arms, allowing the new mother to cradle it as she cut and tied the umbilical cord.

Aristarchus had stopped his ranting, mesmerized by the miracle that few Roman men witnessed. And briefly, one other item took priority over his fear for his employment and social standing. "Is it a boy?"

He didn't wait for the answer but peered for himself. A sneer crossed his face. "She serves the Christos and gives me a daughter."

Paulina ignored him and held her daughter close. "She's beautiful," she crooned, her pain and agony obviously forgotten. Serene joy lit her features. "Beautiful. And look at all her hair."

"What's her name?" one sister asked, sponging Paulina's face with a damp cloth.

"Priscilla," Paulina answered. "In honor of a woman in Ephesus who—"

"The baby will be given no name," Aristarchus snapped. "It will not live the nine days to the *lustratio*."

This was the official ceremony to name a Roman child and present it to the community.

"No!" cried the eldest sister. "This is Paulina's first child. She is young. She has many years to give you a son."

"Exposure," Aristarchus said firmly, sensing triumph. "I will not sell the child or kill it. Exposure is my decree and my command. Exposure to the elements until it dies."

✠ ✠ ✠

A cacophony of sounds assailed Leah in the darkness beneath the amphitheater, sounds of quiet desperation. Groaning. Fear. Beyond those sounds coming from the prison cells on each side of the tunnel, she heard the occasional distant roar of animals trained to do the executing later.

Since Nathan's arrest, Leah had slept only a few hours each night, spending the rest of the darkness tossing and turning as she tried to avoid thoughts of how her brother might actually die.

Yes, she'd spent far too much time in the horrors of the future; now it was upon her.

She wanted to be brave. Needed to be brave. For Nathan.

For her teenage brother. Nathan, the one of impetuous good humor who brightened their home and lives every day. Nathan! The baby of the family. Adored by all. About to die!

She lifted the hem of her dress, blocked out her fear, and moved deeper into the darkness. As she left the last shafts of light behind, the air seemed to close in on her, and her throat tightened as smells of suffering added to the sensation of smothering—body wastes accumulated in each cell, vomit, and the cloying, nauseating sweetness of alcohol from those fortunate few with enough money to bribe the guards and acquire the numbing forgetfulness from wine.

In this terrible labyrinth of doom and death, as darkness fell on Rome, Leah began to search for her brother.

✠ ✠ ✠

In the Smyrna tavern, tension increased as the hulking man approached Vitas.

"Who are you to be asking 'who is asking'?" Titus called from the corner. He began to move back toward Vitas. It was obvious that Vitas would not be able to easily defeat this new opponent.

The man didn't dignify Titus or his question with even a glance. He continued to lumber toward Vitas, his eyes focused on the short sword that Vitas held out in a defensive position.

"Who are you to ask about Damian?" he repeated to Vitas.

Someone shouted drunkenly, "Rip him apart, Maglorius! Your hands are enough!"

Maglorius. This name Vitas recognized.

A living legend.

Although Maglorius was in his fifth decade and bore the healed slashes of gladiator blades and lions' claws, he still radiated strength and power. His hair was not dark like most Romans', but a sandy gray, reflecting his Iceni heritage. Common lore among the mobs said that the army had captured Maglorius during his tribe's first revolt against the Romans in Britannia, then shipped him to Rome to be humiliated in the public display of Vespasian's triumph. Afterward they sent him to the arenas to die as a gladiator. Except, as his presence in the tavern proved, he'd survived for over a decade already, had found a way to live by killing others.

"Who am I to ask?" Vitas said, unafraid. Every nerve tingled as he watched Maglorius the way one lion watches another. "That is my business. Not yours."

"I have saved Damian's life during training half a dozen times over the last year in gladiator school," Maglorius said. "He is one of the most wretched citizens to take the oath. The only way he'll survive his first fight in the arena tomorrow is if I save his life again. I think I have the right to ask who is looking for him."

Vitas grinned and could see by Maglorius' reaction that it was unexpected. "Because anyone who wants Damian is either collecting an unpaid debt or wants to punish him for seducing a wife or daughter."

Maglorius grunted agreement.

That should have been the first warning for Vitas: that Maglorius, an obvious loner, had protected Damian over the last year. Damian, who'd been forced to make vows as a gladiator because of his gambling habits, was much more likely to inspire enemies than friends.

By then, Titus had reached Vitas' side. He, too, watched Maglorius with a wary eye.

"I don't understand you," Titus said to Vitas. "When we were younger, you would happily have begun a brawl. Now you exhibit nothing but patience and maturity. Let's have some fun. We'll fight this man, then talk."

"Forgive my friend, Maglorius," Vitas said. "After our time together in the legions he believes he is invincible."

"You bear a striking resemblance to Damian," Maglorius said quietly. "Are you the brother he has mentioned? Vitas? All the way from Rome?"

"I am. And this is Titus Flavius Vespasianus."

"Son of Vespasian? Who commanded a legion in Gaul?"

That should have been the second warning for Vitas. Maglorius asked about Vespasian's time in Gaul and avoided the much more obvious connection: Britannia, where nearly twenty years earlier, Vespasian had famously fought thirty battles, subjugated two tribes, and captured twenty towns.

"Yes, Vespasian is my father," Titus said proudly.

Maglorius reexamined Titus. And smiled slightly. Dangerously.

That should have been another warning for Vitas. He was too anxious to find Damian. Too anxious to prevent his younger brother from dying in his first fight as a gladiator. Vitas knew Maglorius was right in his judgment about Damian's poor fighting skills.

"I will lead you to Damian," Maglorius said. "You two appear able to take care of yourselves, but the streets of a harbor town like this are no place for strangers at night." He gave them a slight smile. "Trust me. It's too dangerous."

Vitas shrugged.

"But first," Maglorius said, "let us have a few drinks. I have no intention of going anywhere with a parched throat."

✠ ✠ ✠

As the woman continued to trim his hair and the boy continued to apply makeup, Helius listened to the slave with his eyes closed, as if the old slave were a harpist performing a beautiful melody. Yes, that was the picture Helius wanted to present to these three. Total serenity.

"'Here is a copy of something from the archives,'" the slave began, reading slowly from the scroll. "'If the emperor Tiberius found this important enough to bring it to Senate vote, then you should be aware of it and end the tribulation you have brought upon the innocent.'"

"That was the portion addressed to Nero?" Helius asked, eyes still closed, speaking as if the scroll were devoid of any significance, as if the cursed Greek graffiti on the back of it was a mere curiousity.

"Yes," the slave said, almost absently. It was obvious by his concentration on the scroll that he was reading ahead with considerable interest.

"And what comes next is from the archives?" Helius asked. "A matter brought before the Senate by Tiberius."

"It would appear so," the slave answered.

"Continue," Helius said with a wave. "All of you."

The slave read the rest of it to the audience of Helius and the boy slave and the woman slave. Helius was focused on the contents of the letter and unaware that both the boy and the woman had stopped their attentions to him, so absorbed were they by what they heard. It wasn't until the slave began to roll up the scroll that Helius opened his eyes and noticed they had listened so intently.

"Fine, then," Helius said. He was proud of his ability to remain calm. On the inside, he was shaking. If Nero heard of this—

No, he commanded himself sharply. *Do not think of consequences. Think of what must be done next.*

"No one else knows of this scroll except Tigellinus?" Helius asked.

"I was with him the entire time," the slave answered. "From the moment the young Jew was arrested to our arrival at the palace. Until I read this to you, Tigellinus was the only one to open the scroll."

Helius stood and addressed all three slaves. "Wait here until I return." He noticed the puzzled looks on their faces. His hair had not been completely trimmed, nor had all the makeup been applied. "Something I ate disagrees with me," he said as he left the room and closed the door.

That should have alarmed them. Men like Helius rarely explained themselves to people like them.

Helius found a couple of soldiers down the hallway. "In my chamber," he told them, "you will find a man, a woman, and a boy. I overheard them discussing a way to murder me."

Both soldiers straightened. When slaves spoke of murdering their masters . . .

"Yes," Helius said. "Go in there and cut off their tongues. Immediately. Then drag them to the Tiber and behead them and dispose of their bodies. Say nothing of this to anyone. Especially not to Nero. If he believes there is another plot brewing within the palace, no one will be safe."

The soldiers saluted.

The last plot against Nero had resulted in a six-month indiscriminate bloodbath.

"It will be done," the first one said.

"Good," Helius answered. "Very good. Remember, if I hear any rumors about this, I'll know who is responsible. And then Tigellinus will see to it that you are punished in the same manner."

"It will be done immediately," the second soldier stressed. "And we will say nothing."

They turned and half walked, half sprinted toward Helius' chamber and the slave and the woman and the boy who were unaware of how soon and how cruelly their lives were about to end.

Helius let out a sigh.

This, at least, would ensure no one else knew about the scroll. He'd find Tigellinus in the garden, and they would plan a course of action.

Helius touched his face. He did not anticipate this matter would delay whatever fun Nero had planned for them. Helius hoped that enough of his makeup had been applied so he would look decent for the evening's festivities.

But first he needed to speak to Tigellinus.

✛ ✛ ✛

In the courtyard, Aristarchus reached for his daughter. His firstborn. The baby he had decided to kill by exposure.

"No," Paulina wailed.

"It is my right as father," he said. "You cannot stop me."

Her sisters could not go to her defense. They knew the father's place in his household. He could deny the right of the newborn child to be reared. He could choose to sell, kill, or expose the child. And if he chose exposure, he could leave the baby outside the house or in a public place.

"Please," Paulina said. Exhausted as she was, desperation gave her strength. "Let me keep my child!"

Aristarchus smiled his satisfaction, thinking that perhaps the gods had favored him by bringing to his attention his wife's secret faith this very afternoon.

"Perhaps I will let you rear it." He paused.

The baby's suckling broke the brief moment of silence.

"Renounce this Christos," he said. "And the baby will live."

"I cannot." Paulina began to weep. "He gave His life to spare mine."

"Then the baby is exposed. Tonight. In the public square outside the temple of Caesar. Beneath divine Nero's statue. That will let all of Smyrna know that I honor Caesar despite my wife's foolishness."

Paulina tried to speak but could not through her broken sobs. She clutched the baby with one arm and stroked her head with her other hand.

"You are all witnesses," Aristarchus said, arms crossed. "Tell all who will listen. I give this baby as a sign of my allegiance to the divine Caesar."

"No! No!" Paulina managed to cry out again through her sobs.

"One last chance," Aristarchus said. "Will you renounce Christos?"

Paulina clutched the baby tighter.

"Trouble!" the midwife said. "She is . . ."

The midwife pointed. Beneath the birthing chair, blood was pooling in a dark, obscene circle.

The sisters hurried to find sheets to stem the hemorrhaging.

"What do you answer?" Aristarchus demanded of Paulina.

She was incapable of answering. She was slumped over the baby, unconscious, her arms still holding her tightly.

"There," Aristarchus said, "I have spoken. Let it be done as I have commanded."

VESPERA

When she finally found Nathan, Leah expected to see the same despair that she'd seen in the other cells crowded with prisoners as she had peered inside, straining her eyes in the dimness to find her brother.

The prisoners gathered in her brother's cell, however, were not catatonic or drunk or wailing like those condemned to the arena for murder or robbery or arson. Instead, they were quietly singing hymns as they held hands. They were men and women and children, a dozen of them, making a joyous sound that seemed to brighten the cell as surely as if each had been holding a candle.

Nathan noticed her immediately and rushed away from the group. It was only a couple of steps, and he tried to embrace Leah through the bars.

"Nathan!" Leah began to weep.

"My sister, my sister," Nathan said, stroking her hair.

It took several moments for Leah to realize that her brother was giving her comfort, when she'd fully expected in this situation that she would have to provide it for him.

He had matured somehow and was different.

"Why are you here?" he said. "You shouldn't have risked this."

"The message came that you needed to see Caleb. And he's . . ."

"Yes?" he said with a trace of his former impatience for life to move quickly. "Where is he? Is everything all right at home?"

She nodded, lying to a loved family member for the second time that day.

It was not all right at home. Their father was furious that Nathan had abandoned the Jewish faith, heartbroken that it would cost his son his life. Caleb, the eldest brother, shared the fury and heartbreak and had valiantly tried to reconcile Nathan with their father in the days after he announced his faith in Jesus of Nazareth as the promised Messiah of the Jews. The few months until Nathan's arrest had been almost as unbearable as the days that followed it.

"Where is Caleb?" Nathan asked. "I didn't want or expect you to come here. It's too dangerous."

"Caleb has been called by the emperor," Leah said. She knew it was the opposite, that Caleb had sought the emperor's ear; he'd taken her into his confidence so they both could lie to their father. And now she passed the lie on to Nathan.

"Called to the emperor? Called? Or arrested?"

Leah frowned, briefly clutching her throat. "No. Not arrested. Caleb has not turned away from our father's faith."

Nathan closed his eyes briefly. "I wish so badly that you would understand. It is not turning away from the faith of our fathers. Jesus is the fulfillment of the Law and the Prophets and the promises of God." He opened his eyes. "I'm sorry. You've heard me say that many times. I will continue to pray that you and Caleb find this faith."

Leah did not understand. Here was Nathan. In a horrible cell. Facing a horrible death. And he prayed for others to share his faith? Still, this was not the time or place to engage in the familiar arguments that had torn apart their family before Nathan's arrest.

She clung to the bars, wanting to hold her younger brother. He was so handsome. So young. He did not deserve to die.

"Nathan," she said softly, "you sent a message that you needed Caleb. He is now with the emperor. How can I help in his stead?"

"No," Nathan said. "I want you to go home as quickly as possible."

"I'm here now." Leah clenched the bars of the cell. "I refuse to leave unless you let me help."

Nathan tightened his lips. "Only because it's so important."

"Is it something I can bring to you?"

He shook his head. "There are letters in our household. If they are found by the authorities, all of you will be at risk. You need to make sure they are hidden so safely that a hundred searches would not reveal them. If you don't have the faith, you should not be punished for it."

"Why not destroy the letters?"

"There are precious few copies. And they are badly needed to comfort the believers in Rome. It is faith in the resurrected Christ that gives us hope through all tribulations."

She gestured at the prison cell. Helpless. Hopeless. "Even through this?"

He was emphatic and looked her directly in the eye. "We willingly face brandished steel, the lion's gore, the tunica molesta because we follow the Christ and we are utterly convinced that we, like our Master, will one day rise from the grave in resurrected, glorified bodies."

Leah bowed her head. Rubbed her face. What was it about her brother's faith that made him so resolute yet so joyful?

She lifted her eyes to his again. "The letters?"

"Someone will come soon for the letters. He will identify himself by showing you a Greek word, and he will tell you this as a password: 'The lamb that was slain before the foundation of the world shall destroy the beast.' Understand? Unless he gives you the password and shows you the Greek word, he cannot be trusted." He continued to speak, more to himself than to her. "We must be wise as serpents and innocent as doves."

The floor of the cell was dirt. Nathan knelt and used his forefinger to scratch a three-letter Greek word that Leah could dimly see. "Here is the word," he said. "Remember the symbols, because it is Greek and I know you only read Hebrew."

$$\chi\xi\varsigma$$

Leah was about to ask what it meant when a rough hand grabbed her shoulder, and a sudden tug spun her around. She found herself facing a man of almost unnatural thinness, a man dressed in ragged clothing that smelled so strongly like cat urine that even in this dank passageway filled with so many terrible smells, the power of the stench overwhelmed Leah.

"Leave her alone," Nathan cried from behind the bars, trying to reach for the man.

"You must talk to me," the man hissed, pulling her back from Nathan's grasp.

"No," Leah said. "I'm here with—"

"Listen to me," the man ordered. He pointed at the prisoners inside the cell. "And I will give them hope."

✠ ✠ ✠

The tavern's beer was almost rancid and dotted with flecks of gristle that Vitas could not and did not want to identify. Vitas had surreptitiously dumped each of several mugs beneath the table, confident that no one would notice the extra liquid on the filthy floor.

It wasn't a delicate stomach that compelled Vitas to do so. He had lived through months and months of field conditions, where a soldier learned not to inspect any food or drink too closely. He was afraid of alcohol, for he'd learned it no longer brought him pleasure. And he'd learned that too much alcohol no longer brought him temporary pleasure. Instead, losing his inhibitions unshackled pain he worked so hard to keep secure in a prison deep within his stoic facade.

Ever since the second and final revolt of the Iceni a few years earlier when the Roman soldiers had massed on a hillside under the leadership of Suetonius . . . Vitas did not allow his thoughts to stray much further. Because with those thoughts would come the searing images that— even after four years back in Rome from Britannia—sometimes brought him bolt upright in the middle of the night.

Images would bring questions, magnified now by the challenges that a teenage boy named Nathan had thrown at Vitas during what was supposed to be a routine arrest.

Vitas did not want the images or the questions.

Much better to think of duty. Duty to the empire, the only thing in this world that had permanence, a cause much more noble than the feeble graspings of any individual. Better, especially here in Smyrna, to think of duty to his father, of the deathbed promise Vitas had so recently made, unsure even if his father had been able to hear it in the final moments of life.

So Vitas had watched Titus drink with enthusiasm and watched Maglorius watch Titus drink.

Maglorius was one of Rome's most famous gladiators. Vitas had wondered why someone of his stature would be here. In the midst of the lower class. Yet determinedly alone. Did the man have demons, too? memories he couldn't escape? even self-loathing? It gave Vitas an immediate sympathy for the gladiator, for there were too many nights when Vitas could not bear his own company but could not find escape from himself in crowds.

Maglorius had waved off all attempts at conversation until he finally announced that they could find Damian in a villa he rented from a local estate owner.

Their exit from the tavern had been far less dramatic than their entrance. Because Maglorius stood at their side, a path was cleared immediately among the tables and they left untouched and unheckled.

The three men now traveled the main road that led past the houses and up toward the hills, where, at the crest—had they gone that far—the road split and they could turn north toward Pergamum or south to Ephesus.

Their journey, Maglorius had promised, would be a short one, for the villa was only halfway up the hills. They walked in the silence that the windless night draped over the city.

The harbor lay behind them, and had Vitas glanced backward, he could have seen the cliff that guarded the harbor from the Aegean Sea, jagged walls of rock outlined against the moonlight and the silver sheen of the waters.

His attention was ahead, however, on a pitiful wailing that sporadically ceased, then renewed itself. It came from near the temple of Nero ahead of them. The moon had risen above and behind it, throwing its light toward the sea to the west, casting the face of the immense statue of Caesar in ominous shadow.

Maglorius continued to lead them in the direction of the temple.

"I thought you said Damian was in a villa," Titus said, pointing at a cluster of dimly lit houses upward and to their left. "He would never be at a temple, unless he felt the prostitutes there had been neglected."

"Before we meet Damian," Maglorius said, "we have business at the temple."

"I don't," Titus answered, impatient. "Not unless it involves those same prost—"

Vitas put a hand on the arm of his friend. "Whatever his business is, I have my own business there."

The wailing rose and fell, drawing Vitas for reasons he did not want to examine too closely.

"You?" Titus said. "What business? You've never been a religious man."

Perhaps the little beer Vitas had forced down was having an effect already. The terrible thin noise from the darkness reminded Vitas of other wails that echoed through his mind, wails that haunted him in the restless hours before he found sleep each night. Despite the closeness of their friendship, this was not something Vitas was prepared to share with Titus.

Instead, Vitas answered Titus simply. "I am tired of death."

And, he thought, *tired of life.* There were times he found the irony amusing. He'd returned to Rome from Britannia as a military hero, returned to family wealth and power that any man would covet, returned to a choice of beautiful women drawn to that wealth and power. But it all seemed empty. Even exhausting.

"Tired of death?" Titus echoed. "By the gods, you are a Roman. One of Nero's favorite men. You deal in death. What is happening to you?"

"I wish I knew," Vitas said. He didn't wait for Titus to respond but marched purposely toward the pitiful wailing sound.

Titus caught him and grabbed his shoulder. "That's only a baby left out for exposure."

"If there is something I can do to help, I will."

"And breach Roman law? You, the self-appointed guardian of all glorious Roman traditions? Are you insane?"

"I hear a baby crying for help."

"What are you going to do? Rescue every child in the world?"

Had Titus simply let him go instead of challenging him with those final two questions, Vitas might not have taken more than a few steps. Vitas would have asked himself the same questions and turned around as acknowledgment of the uselessness of his self-imposed task.

But Vitas had already moved away and was too stubborn to admit to Titus that he was wrong.

So Vitas left Maglorius and Titus behind and continued to march across the vast empty square, toward the temple and the statue of Nero, unaware, of course, how his next actions would irrevocably and drastically change the direction of his life.

✢ ✢ ✢

"I trust you've already begun torturing the Jew who gave you the scroll," Helius told Tigellinus.

Helius was almost a head shorter than the broad, bearded man beside him. They stood in the palace hallway.

Torchlight flickered across the face of Tigellinus. His eyes were lost in the shadows beneath his heavy brows. "No," Tigellinus answered.

Another person might have waited for further explanation. Years of conversation with Tigellinus had taught Helius to expect short answers.

"Why not?" Helius asked. "If the contents truly came from the archives, we'll have to remove the scroll. Public sentiment is shifting. Nero will have our heads if he discovers we could have stopped this information from reaching the Senate. If the Jew knows where to find it, he must tell us."

Helius rubbed his temple. He pictured the extensive archives. How difficult it would be to sift through them for the specific records mentioned in the scroll. And he'd have to do it himself, because to ask one of the scribes would be like announcing it to the world. But if word got out that Helius was prowling through the archives, rumors would start.

Helius was getting a headache. "Worse," he told Tigellinus. "The mobs would pounce on this knowledge. We'll be lucky if our heads are removed. Nero will throw us into the arena."

"The Jew has no intention of making that obscure Senate record public. Not after I warned him that his father and sister would die if that happened."

"Then why go to the effort and danger of presenting the scroll to you?"

"He wants to negotiate," Tigellinus said.

"Negotiate?"

"Talk to him yourself."

Helius paced. "We don't negotiate."

"No," Tigellinus said. "I promise he won't leave the palace alive. But it will be valuable if he believes we negotiate."

Helius flashed a brief smile. "Of course. Another headless body in the Tiber." He frowned immediately. "And Vitas?"

Tigellinus understood. "Vitas is in Asia looking for his brother. I'll ensure he doesn't hear any of this."

"Good," Helius muttered. "Very good. If only the problem with Vitas could be solved as easily as with this Jew."

"I tell you again and again," Tigellinus said. "All we need to do is wait. Soon enough Nero will forget his fear and remember the insult."

Helius and Tigellinus had had this discussion many times in the weeks since the night Vitas had defied Nero in the garden hut and released the captive Christians. Because earthquakes had shaken Rome and surrounding areas with unusual frequency over the last few years, Nero would eventually decide it had been a coincidence that protected Vitas that night, not an action from the gods. And as the humiliation of Nero's cowardice ate at him, it would eventually overpower his gratitude for Vitas protecting him from the lion. When that happened, Vitas would lose his untouchable position in the inner court, and Helius and Tigellinus would find a way to destroy him. The man's principles were very inconvenient.

Tigellinus tapped Helius on the shoulder, interrupting his thoughts. He pointed at the entrance to the room nearby. "The Jew's in there. You'll find his proposition interesting and perhaps of value."

Helius nodded.

Tigellinus gripped Helius' shoulder and growled a final warning. "Don't let your temper get in the way of what's good for us."

✢ ✢ ✢

"Insane," Titus mumbled to Maglorius as Vitas disappeared into the darkness. "He's gone insane. In Britannia, we stood side by side, killing men, women, and children. He was a heartless cold soldier, one of the best. Yet since we've returned, he's a different man. I just don't understand."

"You were in Britannia?" Maglorius asked, barely audible. "You and Vitas?"

"Of course, of course. When the Iceni revolted for a final time. Queen Boudicca had the south of Britannia in an uproar. If Suetonius had not been so capable, the empire would have lost the entire province. I'm sure you've heard all of this, however."

"I have." Maglorius spoke with icy calm. "You were part of the triumph in Rome?"

"At the forefront."

"Leading the prisoners? The empire's future slaves and fodder for the arenas?"

"What else is a triumph?" Titus was not listening closely enough to the tone of the gladiator's voice.

"In Britannia, you fought Iceni warriors and destroyed their families?"

"They revolted." As if that were enough explanation.

"I was part of the Iceni revolt, too," Maglorius said. "The first one. I was part of a triumph that entered Rome as well. But not as a Roman soldier."

Titus shrugged. "Any battle has winners and losers. The empire never loses. Besides, I'm sure you live well as a famous gladiator. You would have never enjoyed life in this way otherwise."

"My wife died at the hand of a Roman general. As did my son, who was barely older than a baby. He would have been a man of your age today, had he lived."

Titus did not shrug this time. It would have been impossible. For Maglorius had spun his shoulder and placed a brawny forearm against Titus' neck, squeezing him in a deadly embrace.

"What should matter most to you," Maglorius said, almost in a whisper, holding a knife to Titus' ribs with his other hand, "is that my young wife was holding our son when that general executed them both with the same blow of a sword. As an example to my people. I was captive and could only watch and hate the man who did it. Vespasian. Your father."

Maglorius jammed the knife hard enough for the tip to pierce Titus' toga and draw blood. "It should not surprise you then," Maglorius continued. "I've been waiting a long time for this moment."

✝ ✝ ✝

"I am the *bestiarius*," the thin man said to Leah. His mouth was a blackened hole, his front teeth long since crumbled by decay. He stared at

Leah's lack of comprehension, as if he expected her to be pleased he had
bothered to speak to her.

"The beast master," he explained, obviously irritated. "In charge of
all the animals here. And I have a problem that you can help me solve."

He had pulled Leah away from the prison cell to speak with her pri-
vately. The only thing that kept her from fleeing was that he had promised hope.

"This is the first day of the games," he said. "The mobs are insane for
excitement, and I had no choice but to send out my best man-eaters this
afternoon. Now they are engorged and will have no desire to attack for
days."

"Man-eaters?"

"Lions," he said impatiently. "Have you lived your life in a cave?"

Leah shuddered. At the sight and smell of this man in front of her.
At the image of the man-eaters pouncing on helpless victims in the
arena.

Her brother . . .

Again, she forced the thoughts away.

"All I have for tomorrow afternoon's spectacle are untamed lions,"
the beast master continued. "Do you have any idea how difficult it is to
get them interested in attacking?" He thumbed in the direction of the
prisoners behind him. "Wild lions don't recognize them as food."

Leah couldn't help the tears that sprang to her eyes. *Them*. This man
was talking about Nathan, separated from freedom by only a few iron
bars. How could it be possible that tomorrow . . .

"These new lions have been in cages for weeks, so upset they've
barely eaten," the beast master continued. "Some of the lions are almost
too weak to attack. Then to set them loose suddenly in bright sunshine
with the screaming of the mobs . . . well, it frightens them so badly
some just lay down."

He grimaced. It formed an ugly mask across his face. "And if the lions
are afraid of the Christians, that will be catastrophic. I have senators to
entertain, you know." He lowered his voice. "Who is that man in there,
the one talking with you?"

"My brother," Leah whispered.

"Well then, this is where you can help. Talk to those people. They won't listen to me. All they do is speak of a resurrection and sing hymns, like tomorrow's carnage is going to be a great celebration for them. Tell them what I have to propose, and I'll make sure that your brother is spared along with the children."

"Spared!"

"He'll have to be sold as a slave, of course. But isn't that much better than facing the lions?"

She nodded.

"Then listen to this," he began. And he told her what he wanted.

✠ ✠ ✠

Nearby in Rome, Helius faced Leah's older brother Caleb in an opulent room in the center of the imperial palace, with an array of torches and expensive lamps giving ample light.

"My brother Nathan faces the lions tomorrow," Caleb said.

"I'm sure he deserves it," Helius said. "The empire dispenses justice without prejudice."

Helius sat in a large chair. No guards. No slaves. This needed to be a private conversation. But it would have been nice to have slaves fanning the air nearby; although it was evening, the air had not yet cooled enough to be comfortable.

As Helius regarded the handsome, black-haired, young Jew in front of him, he thought with regretful tenderness that it was a pity such a fine specimen would have to die.

"Nathan was arrested because someone reported to the authorities that he is a Christian," Caleb said. "A man named Vitas spent a great deal of time interrogating him."

Helius made a waving motion as if impatient. In the last months, Vitas had interrogated more than a few Christians, trying to learn if they were the threat to the empire that Nero decreed. Helius had been part of the interrogation of Nathan, as Vitas tried to prove the Christian beliefs were not treasonous.

"As I said," Helius answered, pretending not to be familiar with Nathan, "your brother deserves his fate. Nero has made it very clear that the Christians are a treasonous group. What does that have to do with this letter?"

Helius held up the scroll marked with the three-letter Greek word that Christians had been placing across the city in public places.

"It was the only way I could think of to get an audience with Nero."

"I serve in Nero's stead," Helius said. "Why did you want this audience?"

"I love my brother," Caleb said simply.

"How touching."

"My father is a famed Jew named Hezron," Caleb continued. "A man considered to be the greatest rabbi among the Jews in Rome. An excellent scholar and a wise old man with years of experience in debate. I have followed closely in his footsteps, and many feel I am already close to an equal in learnedness."

"Delightful."

"I do not say this to boast but to let you know that I can deliver on my promise. And that my reputation will have credibility in circles that matter."

"I haven't heard your promise."

"First," Caleb said, "I want your word that if I am successful, you will release my brother from the arena."

"Of course," Helius lied smoothly. "But that's assuming what you have to give in exchange is worthwhile."

"You have the material from the archives," Caleb answered, "and you know how damaging it could be to Nero."

Helius shrugged.

Caleb smiled with confidence. "A wealthy merchant knows a simple fact. If there is no apparent need for a good, create that need. Then the sales of it will be easy. I found what I did in the archives to create that need. That in itself should show you I am an excellent scholar."

"I fear nothing from the archives."

"Then why am I still alive?" Caleb asked. "You must think I possess something of value."

"You must love your brother a great deal to risk this."

"If I give you proof that makes the archive matter meaningless," Caleb said, "let him live."

Helius stared at Caleb.

"Yes," Caleb said, "I can prove for you that Jesus of Nazareth—whom the Christians call Christos—was not divine."

✠ ✠ ✠

The naked baby had been placed on the cold stone pavement directly beneath the statue of Nero at the temple in Smyrna. Vitas knelt in front of it and in the moonlight saw that it was a baby girl.

Vitas was filled with confusion.

What was he doing here? The father who had decided to leave the baby exposed was doing nothing wrong in the eyes of Roman law. Vitas had seen the bodies of dozens of exposed babies left in public places and had well been able to ignore their fading cries.

What was he doing here? It was against centuries of tradition to do anything but ignore the dying baby. And how could he save the tiny girl, even if he picked her up this very moment?

The baby's cries ripped at his heart.

What was he doing here? In Rome, he'd managed to spend four years in a cocoon, wrapped in the luxuries of wealth, determined not to step outside into a world filled with these tragedies. As a member of Nero's inner court, he'd taken great effort to remain a decision maker, to avoid involvement in implementing any of the plans that sent men or women to their deaths.

What was he doing here in front of this baby? Why did he care?

An image sprang to his mind: a young Jew named Nathan. Taken by arresting soldiers from a small Jewish household and hauled in front of the defacto triumvirate of Helius and Tigellinus and Vitas, the three men who formed the power base that served Nero. This young Jew had been utterly unafraid of the prodding spears of the soldiers and the harsh questions from Helius and Tigellinus. But the intended interrogation of the boy had become almost like a conversation between peers, almost to the point where Vitas had felt like a student at a master's feet, trying to understand where the young man could draw such strength and peace in front of the terrifying power of Rome. Strength and peace. Two things Vitas wanted to possess.

What was he doing here on the pavement, kneeling in front of the weakening baby?

Since the day of the arrest of that boy named Nathan, Vitas had been unable to escape the questions Nathan had posed. Questions about soul and purpose of life. Questions about a man named Jesus, crucified by Pontius Pilate during his clumsy attempts to govern Judea.

Vitas wanted his life in compartments, for compartments sealed away pain. Yet since arresting Nathan, Vitas had become too aware of the suffering of others. He was irritated at that growing weakness and irritated that the dreams he'd almost escaped since returning to Rome had recently begun to haunt him again.

What was he doing here?

If he took the baby, he breached law. And most certainly betrayed a long-standing tradition of the empire.

If he didn't take the baby, she would surely die within the hour.

If he took the baby, what of all the other children in this world who suffered? Titus had been right. The task was overwhelming.

Yet if he stood and left the baby where she was still wailing, would her cries join the other wails of his dreams?

Vitas sighed. He had enough money. Perhaps . . .

Vitas took the baby into his arms, trying to warm the trembling little girl. He would wrestle with what to do as he held her. That was his decision for now. The baby quieted briefly.

Footsteps alerted him to the presence of someone approaching from behind. "What do you think you are doing?" The demand came from a woman's voice.

Vitas rose awkwardly, still holding the baby. She began to wail again. He turned.

"I . . . I . . ." Vitas could not answer, for that, of course, had been the same question he'd been struggling with since reaching the baby.

The moonlight shadows from the statue that fell across the woman prevented him from seeing her face clearly. She was tall, seemed young. And she was clearly indignant, for her arms were crossed.

This attitude startled Vitas. It was night. The woman was alone. She should have been frightened. Her courage, however, intrigued him.

"Did Aristarchus send you?" She strode forward and pulled the baby from his arms. Moonlight flashed across her face. He'd been right. She was young. Perhaps a couple of years younger than his brother Damian.

A girl recently turned woman, with an air of something he could not define, but something that plucked at his heart.

"Are you not content that the baby has been condemned to exposure?" she demanded. "Or are you here to ensure her death arrives sooner?"

"No, I . . ."

The woman wrapped the baby in a blanket she carried, bent her head, and began to croon. The soothing sound worked and the baby's wails became whimpers of hunger.

"Are you the mother?" Vitas asked. He was bewildered at the turn of events.

"Go away," she said. "Don't follow." With that, she began to retrace her steps across the square.

Suddenly three men broke out of the darkness beneath the columns at the front of the temple. They ran toward the woman.

Vitas heard them first, then saw their fast approach . . . and the silhouettes of the swords in their hands.

"No!" the woman cried.

Without pausing to consider the rashness of his action, Vitas leaped forward.

✠ ✠ ✠

"Your brother." In front of Caleb, Helius made a great show of sighing. "Explain to me these Christians. Are they not merely a fringe of your religion?"

"No." Caleb lost his cool watchfulness. "They are blasphemous. They believe that Messiah already arrived. More than that, they claim that Jesus was the one and only Son of God, claim He is actually equal with God."

"Your brother, then, has chosen to die for the very same Jesus that you say is a fraud?"

"Yes," Caleb answered quietly.

"You still love him, even though it must be dividing your family?"

"Yes."

"It strikes me as odd how much people are willing to give for this man Jesus and what He teaches," Helius said. "Nothing in my experience has shown that kind of devotion to any other philosophy. Tell me, what would cause your brother to give up the Jewish faith and do this to your family? From everything I know about Jews, you would rather die than have your God insulted. Yet your brother and hundreds of others like him are turning their backs on their families, causing great rifts and hardships. And, yes, facing executions for their faith. What is it that gives them such determination?"

Helius realized he had spoken his thoughts in a way that revealed too much. He waved away any answer that Caleb might have given. "My job is to protect Nero," Helius went on quickly, as if explaining his slip. "My job is to ensure he doesn't face troubling questions. He has millions of subjects and the entire world to administrate. He should not have to worry about things like this."

Helius lowered his voice. He was excellent at faking sincerity, and he knew it. "I will continue to be frank with you. The Christians were a convenient scapegoat for the Great Fire of Rome. Yet now rumblings of sympathy have begun for them because of how cruelly they are killed."

Helius shook the scroll. "So, yes, your proof would be of value to Nero. What exactly do you propose?"

"I have gathered different letters circulating among the followers of Jesus," Caleb said. "I have the knowledge and skill as a Jewish scholar and rabbi to prove from them that Christ Himself was a liar and a false prophet."

"You don't need to prove it to me," Helius said. "I'm not a believer."

"I propose that you find a Jewish rabbi who is a believer," Caleb answered. "Let me debate him as if this were a Roman court and you were the judge presiding over the case. Record it as any other case brought before a judge. And when I have proved my point, release the records to the public. Once the claims of the Christians have been shown as ridiculous, they will no longer be a threat to Caesar."

Caleb was very earnest and naive, and Helius found that attractive.

"Then," Caleb continued with that naivety, "you will have no reason for my brother to die in the arena."

"Your proposal has merit," Helius allowed. "Let me think it over."

"Please," Caleb said. "My brother faces the lions tomorrow."

"It will take some time to find an opponent for you."

Caleb shook his head. "There is a respected rabbi already in your prisons; he is a Christian. His name is Zabad. Let him take the opposing side. Tomorrow."

"You've given this a great deal of thought."

"I love my brother."

"Enough, I suppose, to arrange with Zabad to lose this so-called trial case." Helius was a good enough negotiator to pretend resistance to the idea.

"I expected you would guess that."

"And?"

"There is a way to ensure that each side debates in fairness," Caleb said. "Offer freedom to the winning side. And death to the other."

✟ ✟ ✟

The suddenness of the treachery of Maglorius had caught Titus totally unaware. To save his life, Titus tried to stomp the heel of his sandal onto Maglorius' toes.

Maglorius kicked Titus' supporting leg as Titus lifted the other. Titus staggered to keep his balance, unable to deliver the blow he intended. Nor did it succeed in loosening the grip of the massive forearm around Titus' neck.

"You don't think I've seen and learned every trick a dying man tries to avoid his death?" Maglorius asked. "Meet your gods with dignity."

Titus fell slack against the forearm at his neck. As if he'd been choked unconscious.

Maglorius removed the knife from Titus' ribs and jabbed it into his buttocks, drawing a yelp. Titus straightened.

"Any words you want me to deliver to your father?" Maglorius asked.

"I can't believe fate transpired against me like this," Titus wheezed. "What are the chances of meeting the one man in the entire empire who—?"

"You Romans have a saying," Maglorius growled. "De inimico non loquaris sed cogites."

Don't wish ill for your enemy; plan it.

"It . . . wasn't . . . chance?" Titus could barely speak, so great was the pressure against his neck.

"It wasn't chance. When Damian joined the gladiator school and spoke of his brother and his brother's friend Titus, son of Vespasian, I knew I would have to keep Damian alive against the hope that someday you would visit him. So tell me, what shall I write to your father in the letter that will be delivered to him after your death?"

"He will have you crucified for this," Titus managed to say.

"Tonight you die, and tomorrow I will welcome death in the arena to free myself of the memories of watching my wife and child die. So speak your last words before I leave your body beneath the statue of Caesar to let the world know that I finally had my revenge against the empire."

Titus tried to twist free but knew the man holding a knife against him was utterly serious. And utterly capable of killing him in an instant. So he became serious himself. "Tell my father that I loved him dearly, although I didn't speak it in his presence."

"As you wish."

Titus closed his eyes in preparation for the knife to be slipped between his ribs.

A shout reached them.

"Help! Titus! I need you!"

"It's Vitas!" Titus cried. "My friend is in danger!"

Maglorius withheld the death stab.

"I owe him my life," Titus said. "If you understand honor at all, release me. Please. Kill me later, but let me first repay my debt to him."

The sound of running footsteps neared them.

It was a woman, impeded by a burden in her arms. She stumbled on uneven pavement and fell, shielding the baby from the fall with her own body. She shrieked with pain as she landed on her shoulder.

"Behind me," she gasped, lying on the ground beside Maglorius and Titus. "Three against one."

"I beg you," Titus said to Maglorius. "You did not hear me beg for my life, but I beg you to allow me to help my friend."

Before Maglorius could answer, the fight was upon them.

✛ ✛ ✛

"I don't understand why you won't agree to the terms given you by the bestiarius." Leah was in tears again. She'd delivered to Nathan the offer, and he in turn had spoken to the others. Now he was in front of her again.

"The children will be saved," Nathan said. "But I will not become a slave."

"As a slave, at least you'll still be alive. Our family can find a way to purchase your freedom."

"Could I live in peace," he answered, "knowing that I, of all the men and women in this cell, am the only one to flee from the chance to stand strong against tribulation?"

"This is your life!"

"'The people who are destined for prison will be arrested and taken away,'" Nathan whispered. He'd reached through the bars with both hands and gently cradled her face. "'Those who are destined for death will be killed. But do not be dismayed, for here is your opportunity to have endurance and faith.' These are the words of John, the last disciple of our Savior. We are living through the Great Tribulation, and he has given us comfort."

"I don't understand," Leah pleaded, grasping her brother's wrists and keeping his hands pressed against her cheeks. "I've explained how you can arrange it so you don't need to face the lions tomorrow. You can change your destiny."

"What is our destiny?" Nathan asked. "For all of us, is it not death?" He answered his own question. "I'm not afraid of dying, Leah. I am afraid that my family will never understand what faith in Jesus means. The real tragedy is not to die young. The real tragedy is to live a long life and never use it in service of the Master. If my death leads you to eternal life—"

"Live! Live among us! Teach us this faith."

Nathan shook his head. "I've done everything I can to show you and our father and Caleb already. If you understand that I'm not afraid of death, I pray you'll finally understand as well."

"Walk away from the arena! We need you."

"You are grown. Caleb is a fine young rabbi. Our father . . ."

". . . is heartbroken," Leah finished for him. *And feels utterly betrayed*, she thought. *So betrayed I was too afraid to let him know I've come here today.*

Nathan took a deep breath. He, too, was fighting tears. "I am heart-broken too. But if I have been called to be a witness in the arena with the others who believe, I cannot deny my Savior. And if Father will believe too, he is only a single heartbeat from joining me."

"A single heartbeat?"

"His final heartbeat. I wish I could get you to understand the urgency. All that stands between each of us and the end of time is our last gasp of breath on this earth. Then we will be joined in triumph." Nathan closed his eyes. "Or separated by the final battle as God destroys all those souls who have rejected Him. John gave us the vision of those times."

Nathan opened his eyes again. "You must believe, Leah. We must be on the same side when God judges the living and the dead. I am so cer-tain of it that I do not fear tomorrow."

"Please. As your sister, I beg you. Take advantage of what the bestiarius offers. It is your life! Nothing can be more important than that."

"Faith is more important." Nathan began to stroke Leah's hair through the bars. "The others have agreed to what the bestiarius asked. The children will be spared. That is a far greater blessing than we could have expected. They will be spared and always remember the faith of their parents. Rejoice in that."

"I cannot."

"Then I ask this of you. Ensure that the bestiarius keeps his word."

"How can I do that?" Leah asked.

Nathan explained what the others had requested.

"I can't," she cried.

"You must," he said. "Think of the children. Not of me."

Leah wept, and he simply held her hands until finally, he had to beg her to leave and return to their home.

✠ ✠ ✠

In Britannia Vitas had weathered the final stand against Queen Boudicca, when she and thirty thousand tribal warriors had attacked the legion.

He'd stood shoulder to shoulder with other soldiers, hacking and stabbing with his sword against waves and waves of attackers.

He was no coward.

But he knew the odds were against him now if he remained in the square.

Below were two others to help him fight. So after the initial charge that had deflected the three pursuers from the woman and the baby, he saw no shame in running away as well, following her down the hill, hoping to draw them to Titus and Maglorius, where the odds would suddenly change.

The moonlight was bright, and it seemed as he grew closer that Maglorius was standing behind Titus, actually holding a knife to his friend's side.

The woman was on the ground, cradling the baby.

Then, as if making a decision, Maglorius abruptly moved away from Titus and faced uphill, knife poised.

And Titus found his short sword.

The pursuers were nearly upon him as he approached. Vitas was in full stride, and his forward foot hit the same uneven stones that had tripped the woman. He too stumbled, and his shoulder rammed into Maglorius.

Maglorius fell to his knees.

In that moment, the nearest pursuer swung his sword at Maglorius.

Maglorius grunted in pain and tried to rise.

Titus had already begun to counterattack, and the next moments were a blur of frenzied action, of steel against steel.

Vitas gave no thought to each thrust and parry. For to think would be to hesitate, and to hesitate would result in death. He relied on instinct and years of hard training as a Roman soldier.

Almost immediately, it became apparent to the pursuers that these men were no fighting civilians who could be expected to quail under the barrage of an attack.

"Enough!" one shouted. And ran.

The other two instantly spun away.

Vitas leaned, hands on his knees, heaving as his lungs burned for air.

Titus leaned beside him, speaking as he gasped. "They'll be back. Did you see that they were city guards?"

"I see no cowardice in an organized and prudent retreat," Vitas managed to say. He turned to Maglorius to check for agreement.

Maglorius was on both knees, clutching his side. Blood soaked his tunic. He stared wordlessly at Titus and Vitas.

Titus picked up the knife that Maglorius had dropped. He advanced on the fallen man. Maglorius mutely clutched his wound as blood streamed through his fingers. He swayed as he watched Titus and the knife.

"This is yours," Titus said gravely, handing Maglorius his knife. "Thank you for allowing me to help my friend."

"We must go!" the woman said. "Those men were sent by Aristarchus."

Neither Titus nor Vitas responded.

"He's the treasurer of Smyrna," she said. "This is his baby. He must have known I would try to save it."

"Local government." Titus cursed.

"They don't know who we are," Vitas said. "We'll be safe." He stared at the woman. "But you won't be. Not if he had men waiting for you at the temple." Vitas made his decision. To the woman, he said, "What is your name?"

She bowed her head. "Sophia."

"You can find a wet nurse for the baby?"

She nodded.

"Then stay with us until we reach my brother's villa," Vitas said. "I'll keep the baby safely there while you get the nurse. And a doctor."

She hesitated.

"Listen," he said. "My brother is the last person any authority would suspect of hiding a baby."

More hesitation, then a slow nod.

"Vitas," Titus protested. "A baby. This is not our concern!"

"Maglorius," Vitas said, ignoring his friend, "you will direct us to Damian's villa."

Maglorius grunted, and it was obvious even that was an effort.

"But, Vitas, Maglorius—"

Vitas interrupted him. "Help me lift." He leaned down and draped Maglorius' arm over his shoulder. He stood and let the bleeding man lean against him.

"Ah, well," Titus said, the good humor back in his voice as he supported Maglorius from the other side. "With luck, we'll find a doctor skilled enough to keep you alive. And with more luck, I'll be out of this city before you are healed enough to fulfill your vow of vengeance against my father."

JUPITER

HORA QUINTA

Leah had lied to her father again and found another excuse to leave the apartment. But he was so distracted with worry about Caleb that he had only muttered and waved good-bye. A messenger had brought a note from Helius saying that Caleb had been invited to remain in the palace during the night, but no Jew trusted Nero.

She found a place to sit halfway up in the amphitheater. The smell of beer and wine was overpowering; most of those around her were drunk, and as they jostled to see the action better, spilled on themselves and those around them.

Leah was miserable—she was here to witness her brother's death, indeed to ensure it would be spectacular. This had been her promise to her brother, and it consoled her little knowing that her action—and the actions of the men and women who had agreed to help the beast master—guaranteed that twenty children would be released from the same death.

She wished she knew exactly when Nathan would be brought forth, for then she wouldn't have to endure the savagery below her.

A bull and a bear had been released onto the sand. Each wore a collar of leather, and both collars were attached by a long iron chain. Almost instantly, the bull spun and charged the bear.

The bear reared, roaring, and swatted a massive forearm in retaliation. The rush of the bull took it well past the bear, and when it reached the end of its chain, the weight of the bull snapped it backward, while the same force bowled the bear onto its back.

The bear bawled in more rage and found its feet.

The bull snorted and shook its head. Blood poured from a gash on its neck.

But this fight wasn't the real entertainment.

In the corner of the arena, three guards armed with spears and whips forced a man closer to the center of the sand. This man wore only a loincloth, and he was armed with a long pole that had a hook at the end of it. His task was to uncouple the chain between the bull and the bear.

His fear was obvious, and he repeatedly tried to get past the guards to the safety of the walls behind them.

The mob shouted out catcalls. Despite herself, Leah could not tear her eyes away from the sight as the guards snapped their whips and slashed their swords at the man.

Finally, he turned to his task.

In their anger, the bull and the bear were oblivious to his puny efforts to separate them.

✠ ✠ ✠

Distant cries of the gulls from Smyrna's harbor reached Vitas as he rested on cushions in Damian's rented villa. Soon after Vitas had arrived the night before, Damian and Titus had departed, promising to send back a doctor. The doctor had arrived, but they had not returned, and Vitas could only assume they were in pursuit of the pleasures that they expected would not be denied to Roman men with fat purses full of gold.

Bright as the morning was, little sunshine filtered through the windows, which Damian had draped to allow Vitas to sleep late.

This villa was much smaller than the one Vitas had secured. Still, given that Damian had had to pledge himself to a gladiator school to escape debtors, it was still substantially more than Vitas expected his brother could afford. Most of the other gladiators had stayed together at a squalid inn during the week of festivities before today's event.

Maglorius was on a blanket against the far wall, all but his face covered with a sheet stained with blood around his midsection. He was unconscious; his face was flushed and his breathing labored. Vitas had watched the doctor work on him through the night, cutting and sewing that had been hampered by the dim light provided from oil lamps.

In another corner of the room stood a wicker cage filled with swallows. The small birds fluttered from side to side within the cage, squeaking alarm as Vitas paced inside the room. He thought it strange that Damian found interest in them, but had not had a chance to ask before his brother had left with Titus.

There was a knock on the outer door, and Vitas hoped it was Sophia. She'd followed them to the villa to learn its location, then left the baby as she went for a wet nurse. Upon her return, the doctor was already there, and she'd left quickly again without stating her next destination, trusting Vitas with the wet nurse and the baby.

During the all-too-brief time together in the villa, Sophia had quickly explained the circumstances of the previous day. How Aristarchus had forced her friend Paulina into an impossible choice, how Paulina had awakened and begged her elder sister to find their servant Sophia and ask her to steal the baby before once again lapsing into unconsciousness.

The knock on the door was repeated. Vitas moved toward it, his hand on the hilt of the sword. He called out, and the answering voice was not Sophia's nor a city guard's.

Instead, it was Damian's.

Vitas opened the door, and the sunshine made him squint.

"My brother!" Damian said, not quite drunk but definitely not sober. "Maglorius still lives?"

Vitas nodded, deciding not to point out that if Damian truly had been concerned, he would not have left in the night to seek women and wine. "The doctor you suggested is excellent."

"The best your money could buy," Damian said. "And I assure you not a bit of it was spent on the wine that we enjoyed without you. As for the women . . ."

Damian was several years younger than Vitas. His body, despite the abuses he heaped upon it with great regularity, was still trim and muscular, his belly flat. His hair was a mixture of blond and red, and below a nose that had been broken several times and not once set properly lay the grin women seemed to consider irresistible. The lower portion of his left ear was gone, and the baby finger of his right hand crooked from a break that had not healed well.

Vitas smiled tolerantly at his brother, accustomed to seeing him in the high spirits brought on by spirits. Then Vitas frowned, suddenly understanding Damian's reference to women.

Behind Damian, Titus staggered through the doorway into view, clutching a wineskin in each hand. Three painted women in blonde wigs and diaphanous gowns, obviously prostitutes, followed Titus inside.

"Edepol nunc nos tempus est malas peiroris fieri," Titus announced with great gravity.

Now's the time for bad girls to become worse still.

"The sooner the better," one of the women said in a teasing voice. The three fanned out to examine the villa, cooing at the expensive art and furniture.

"What's this?" one of the women said, peering through an arch into an adjoining room.

"No," Vitas said quickly. "Give them peace."

"Them?" Damian asked, trying to focus. "You already have other women? Brother, how did——?"

"The wet nurse and a baby," Vitas said. "Didn't Titus explain that I would hide them here?"

"He was in no mood to listen," Titus said. "He had other things on his mind and I was very happy to follow." He swayed slightly as he pointed at the prostitutes. "See? I made the right choice, did I not?"

Damian leaned against a wall for support. "Titus, more wine! Eat, drink, and be merry, for tomorrow I may die." Damian burped and waved his hands with exaggerated eloquence. "*May* die? I am certain to die. And that will be today. With Maglorius half dead, there will be no one to protect my back in the arena. That baby you saved has cost me my chance at survival."

Another burp and a lurch toward Vitas. "What were you thinking, anyway? A baby girl? Why not save your energy for one much older?"

Vitas was trying to move the women away from the doorway to give the wet nurse peace. He turned and said over his shoulder, "No, Damian. This afternoon will not see the end of your life."

"Titus," Damian said, "more wine!"

Damian took the wineskin that Titus offered, tilted it, and drank deeply. "Yes, it will see the end of my life. Let me assure you, brother, I am a pitiful gladiator. Bet against me so that at least you will profit from my lack of skill. But save some money for the funeral, for my recent fortune has been spent on my own villa and these women."

"Didn't you tell him that either, Titus?" Vitas asked.

Titus gulped from the other wineskin, then gave Vitas a crooked smile as some wine dribbled down his chin. "Not a chance. I don't know where he got the money that he spent on wine and women to celebrate his last hours alive, but I have no intention of ending the fun too early."

Titus pointed at the women. "I mean, look. Would you want to send them away? They've promised to remain as long as we want."

They leered. One moved to Vitas and pushed him onto some cushions.

"As a matter of fact," Vitas began, trying to stand up. "I'm going to insist that—"

She pushed Vitas down again and forced herself onto his lap. She wrapped her arms around his neck and tried to kiss his ear.

"Hey, hey, stop that. Let him speak." Damian squinted. "What do you know about the arena that I don't?"

"Drink more wine," Titus encouraged Damian. "There is plenty of time to tell you later."

"Later I die in the arena," Damian said. He shrugged. "Perhaps getting more drunk isn't a bad idea. With luck, I won't even see the sword that kills me."

Titus winked at Vitas. "Come on, my friend. Listen to your brother and set aside your stoic front. Eat, drink, and be merry."

The woman in Vitas' lap began kissing his ear again as one of her friends wrapped an arm around Titus' waist.

Vitas looked up to see Sophia in the open doorway. Wordlessly, she marched past him to the room with the wet nurse.

"Sophia!" Vitas struggled to get to his feet, but the cushion was deep and soft and the woman on top of him too heavy, so he couldn't get the necessary leverage.

Moments later, Sophia emerged with the wet nurse, a heavy woman holding the baby.

"Wait!" Vitas pleaded.

Sophia gave him a look of burning scorn and ignored him as she stepped into the courtyard.

Vitas finally pushed the blonde-wigged woman onto the floor. He hurried past Titus and Damian, who stared at him with openmouthed amazement.

He dashed through the doorway and chased Sophia and the wet nurse and baby down the steps that led to the street. "Wait!" he called out again. "It's not as it appears."

✜ ✜ ✜

This morning in a room of the imperial palace, Helius surveyed the three other men with a measure of satisfaction.

One was a slave, ready with stylus to record the debate as if it were a legal trial. The man was gap-toothed and short and squat. Helius found the man's thick eyebrows disgusting. He'd chosen the slave for two reasons. The man was definitely excellent at transcribing conversations. He was also a man whom Helius found offensively ugly. Since Helius and Tigellinus had agreed that they did not want any person alive to pass on what happened in the room this morning, Helius had decided it would be efficient—if a slave must be executed—to ensure that the world has one less ugly person. Not even Vitas would learn what happened.

The second man was Caleb, who'd requested the help of slaves to groom him before this event. This was something that Helius found commendable, of course, and the man's obvious intelligence and good manners gave Helius some regret, given what he intended for the man's fate.

The third man was named Zabad. He was also a Jew, one with surprisingly red hair and beard. He was in his midthirties. Like Caleb, Zabad was a respected rabbi. With one difference.

Zabad had become a follower of the Christos. He and his family—a wife and two daughters under the age of six—had been arrested. His family was in prison this very moment. Helius had promised Zabad that if he successfully argued the divinity of the Christos Helius would end the persecution on the grounds that it was not seditious to proclaim another person divine, like Caesar, if that other person was truly divine.

Helius, of course, had lied.

He hoped that Caleb would be persuasive. If so, Helius would proudly bring Nero the transcript and set the emperor's mind at ease, ridding Nero of his insecurity because of the Christians' determination to die rather than give up their faith in the Christos.

On the other hand, if Caleb did a poor job, Helius had no intention of letting Nero even know this debate had occurred.

Yes, it was a politically astute move, and as the two Jews in front of him sat opposite each other on cushions, Helius congratulated himself on his brilliance.

Was it any surprise, he asked himself, that he was the second-most powerful person in the empire?

✜ ✜ ✜

In the amphitheater, the doomed slave darted into the melee between the bear and the bull. He bounced off the side of the bull as it spun to attack the bear. This met the lusty approval of the drunken spectators around Leah.

She bowed her head and closed her eyes. But curiosity overcame her when the shouts of approval reached a new level.

The bear had fallen, and the bull was too exhausted to do much more than push it along the sand.

The condemned man took this opportunity to reach in with his pole and snap loose the shackle at the collar of the bull's neck. The chain fell loose.

The man backed away, glancing in all directions for the guards who had forced him forward.

They were gone.

The arena was empty.

Except for the bull and the bear and the man who had freed them.

Seconds later, the bull realized it was free. Its monstrous head swung in the direction of the man stepping backward.

The bear had recovered too and was rising to its feet.

Both animals had found a new focus for their rage.

The man fled but, like a mouse in a bowl, had no place to go. He reached the walls at the edge of the sand and tried to scrabble upward, but he could not get any grip. At the last second, he dodged sideways, and the charging bull hit the wall with a tremendous thud.

A spectator had been leaning over the wall to taunt the condemned man, and the force of the bull's blow shook him off the wall and down onto the sand. At this, the crowd's shouting grew even more enthusiastic.

A new victim! What an unexpected delight!

Now the bear was approaching.

Both men ran in different directions.

Leah could not watch any longer. Again, she bowed her head. Beer sloshed onto her back, but she ignored it.

The minutes seemed endless, but finally the crowd noise died again.

She looked up briefly and saw slaves dragging the bodies of both men away. Archers stepped onto the sand to kill the animals. Spectators around her began to open baskets of food.

Leah had told herself that she would be strong and brave, but the apathy of those around her to the life-and-death struggles before them broke past the barrier she'd tried to erect against her emotions.

She wept silently, very conscious of the red scarf that she had folded and hidden beneath her dress. Too soon, she would have to wave it at her brother down below on the same sand.

And too soon, it would cause a horror far worse than what she had just witnessed.

✠ ✠ ✠

On the steps at the street below the villa, Sophia felt a tap on her shoulder. She turned to see Vitas.

"Let me explain," he said.

She felt instant anger at the handsomeness of his face. What a façade. He was like all other Roman men, only interested in physical pleasures. She'd been a fool to convince herself otherwise during the night, a fool to believe he was a noble man with pure intentions, a fool to think that a man of his wealth would be interested in a slave like her for any other reason than he might want a prostitute.

"I have no wish to talk to you," she said. Whatever problems waited in the future she would deal with herself. She would no longer hope for rescue from a man such as this. All women probably swooned over him, and it was obvious he used them as playthings.

"Please," Vitas said. He reached across and touched her shoulder.

She knew he was no hero, and her anger at deceiving herself earlier about him boiled over to an unthinking reaction. She'd spent the night dreaming about him, and he'd spent the night in the company of a prostitute. She slapped him hard across the face. "Good-bye."

She marched forward toward the street, where four large slaves were holding the poles of a litter that was draped closed. She heard laughter behind her, and that startled her into turning around.

Vitas rubbed his smarting cheek. "Thank you," he said, still laughing.

"Thank you?"

"I can see no other reason for your anger than jealousy."

"Hardly." She kept her voice icy.

"Wouldn't you expect a Roman to be entertained as it appeared I was?"

"What you do is none of my business." More ice.

"Then why your anger?"

"Because . . ." She paused. He was right. What business was it of hers that a Roman spent the night with a prostitute? Unless, as he was trying to imply, she did care about him. Which was nothing she would admit. She spoke more strongly. "Because of my concern for my friend's baby. Who knows what activities were about to take place in there?"

"My friend and brother had just arrived. With those women. I was trying to get them to leave when you appeared. Please believe me."

She shrugged. She refused to give this man the satisfaction of knowing she'd had any romantic intentions. What did it matter anyway? She was going to serve Paulina and help with the baby girl; he was going back to Rome.

"I thought you were a slave," he blurted.

"If it makes you feel better to diminish me, go ahead. But that says more about you than it does about me."

He pointed at the litter, almost stuttering as he tried to justify the statement. "You told me you were a servant slave in the household of Aristarchus. Is this how you normally travel?"

Sophia kept her voice cool. "Paulina is in there. She is not well. Aristarchus has already proclaimed a divorce and sent her away from the household, and she could only turn to me to find a place to stay. Until I saw you with your women, I had hoped that—"

"Not my women," Vitas said. "And I'll have them sent away."

This man was trouble. She wanted to be away from him, yet wanted him to stay near. She challenged him, finding herself enjoying it. "Why would they listen if they aren't your women?"

"Because . . . because . . ."

Yes, it was enjoyable watching this strong and confident man become uncertain. As if perhaps he, too, shared her feelings. Sophia reminded herself not to begin dreaming again.

"Please," he said, "let me help you."

"You have your life," she said. "I have mine."

"Have the servants bring your friend inside," he said. "We'll send for a doctor."

Before she could find a good reason to disagree, a half dozen armed men came into sight from the crest of the hill.

City guards!

Before she could react, Vitas boldly stepped in front of the litter, waiting for the approach of the guards. He braced his legs and crossed his arms.

Sophia moved beside him. She was not a helpless woman.

Still, when the guards arrived, she was glad that Vitas addressed the lead man, a middle-aged soldier with a prominent mole below his left eye. "Good morning."

"Stand aside," the leader said without emotion. "We are here to take this litter back to the treasurer."

"You make assumptions about the passenger in this litter," Vitas said.

Sophia remained silent, knowing her status as a slave dictated this.

"Hardly," the soldier answered. "Aristarchus had it followed. And the woman and baby behind you are ample proof of what he seeks. Stand aside."

"If I don't?"

The older man sighed. "You are outnumbered. And Aristarchus would send two dozen more if needed."

All of it was true. With the spears pointed at the belly of Vitas, any action he attempted would be useless.

Sophia could not help herself. She clutched Vitas by the elbow.

Vitas gritted his teeth and stepped aside, trying to move Sophia behind him.

She wrenched free and stood directly in front of the lead guard. "Please," she said to the guard, "leave us in peace."

He shook his head, implacable. "You may remain behind. But Aristarchus wants his divorced wife. And the baby."

One of the younger guards, hardly more than a boy, could not resist the opportunity for added drama. "He's going to kill the baby himself! There's nothing you can do."

"Shut your mouth," the lead guard said in a weary voice. "Making a woman cry is not a sign of manhood." He motioned at the others. "Take the woman with the baby." Pointing at the slaves standing with the litter, he said, "Follow us if you value your lives."

"You may remain behind," the soldier had said. Aristarchus, then, did not care to keep Sophia as a slave. She could finally return to Jerusalem. She could search for her family. Her mother and sister. When her father had died three years earlier, he'd left debts that could only be paid if one of them had been sold into slavery. Sophia had accepted it, had been taken to Asia. And now she was free to return?

For a moment, she considered this freedom. If she stayed, perhaps Vitas might help her return to Jerusalem. She banished the thought. Paulina, the woman she'd led to faith, needed her. The newborn baby needed her. Without saying good-bye, Sophia resolutely began to follow the litter and the guards.

She could not, however, resist one final look backward, just before the entire retinue disappeared over the crest of the hill.

Her heart soared.

Vitas had begun to sprint after them.

✠ ✠ ✠

In front of Helius, Zabad began speaking directly to Caleb in a soft, compassionate voice. "Please, my friend, treat this as something more than a debate. What you choose to believe about Jesus has eternal consequences."

Helius interrupted sharply. "This has far more immediate consequences. The one who pleases Nero will live."

Zabad showed no fear. "There is much more to our existence than our lives on this earth. If you even considered it for a moment, you would—"

"Enough!" Helius pointed at Caleb. "Begin. Let us understand why this Jesus of Nazareth is a false god."

Caleb nodded and addressed Zabad. "I would like to deal with the matter of the supposed resurrection of Jesus. After all, as your famous proselytizer Paul rightly says, if there is no Resurrection, everything you believe is false."

"That is everything. To ignore the Resurrection or deny it is to deny Jesus Himself. I, too, would like us to deal with that matter. So tell me please. Why was Jesus killed?" Zabad asked.

"What does that matter?" Caleb asked. "It is not His death that concerns us but the claims that He came back to life and walked among His followers."

"Are you afraid to answer the question?"

"Of course not."

"Why was Jesus killed?" Zabad repeated.

Helius was impatient. "We are aware of the trial. Romans are scrupulous when it comes to the law, and Pilate knew this might have political ramifications. He was careful to have the trial recorded. In short, Christos was crucified because of sedition. Let us move past this issue."

"Sedition," Zabad responded. "It is true those were the charges put forth by the religious leaders. If you are aware of the trial, you will know that the charges were not proven, that Pilate was forced to do the will of the religious leaders or face riots."

Zabad turned back to Caleb. "Why was the religious establishment so eager to have Jesus killed?"

Caleb shrugged. "He falsely claimed to be the Messiah. I stress *falsely*."

"Was it a false claim?" Zabad countered. "After all, every couple of years a madman comes out of the desert heat to make that claim. Dozens did before Jesus. Dozens have since. Few take notice, except to enjoy the entertainment."

Caleb held up a hand. "I can name a half dozen crucified for the claim."

"By Rome. And only because they actually gathered armed followers with the intent to revolt against Rome. The Jewish religious establishment refused—and refuses—to dignify the claims of most of them by paying any heed to their rantings. Yet the full force of the temple authorities was used to arrange the death of Jesus. So you'll agree that

Jesus—unlike the others who claimed to be Messiah—was actually a threat to the Jewish leaders?"

Caleb's face was expressionless. "I suppose."

"We agree Jesus was a threat," Zabad said. "Because He was a good teacher?"

"Certainly."

"You know that is wrong. Good teachers are welcomed and applauded among our people. Did Jesus contradict any of the teachings?"

"He . . ."

"You know as well as I do that He did not contradict a single teaching. He knew our laws completely. He stated again and again that He was here to fulfill the laws, not destroy them. So why was He a threat?"

Caleb shifted position slightly but did not reply.

"I will answer it for you then," Zabad said. "He was a threat because He performed miracles in validation of His claim. It is that simple. He healed the lame and the leprous. Raised a man from the dead. Asked if it was easier to forgive a man's sins or tell him to get up and walk, a man who had been lame all his life."

Zabad waited several moments before continuing. "You may try to deny the miracles, but you know the man did take up his mat and walk. You know there are ample witnesses still alive who will attest to that and to the rest of the miracles. Jesus had a power from beyond this world. It made Him so dangerous, the temple authorities had to kill Him. Will you agree with that assessment? Or should we make this a very legal trial and send for the witnesses?"

"We don't have time for that!" Helius snapped. "Move on."

Zabad smiled calmly. "You'll concede the point then?"

"For the sake of argument, yes." Caleb appeared calm and confident, waving away a protest that Helius was clearly about to make.

"Then let me emphasize this," Zabad answered. "I will proceed as if we are in agreement that Jesus performed miracles as attested to by hundreds of witnesses, and because of it, His following grew to the point where He—unlike any other to make the messiah claim—was such a threat to the temple authorities that they were forced to find a way to kill Him. For the record, do you agree with me on this?"

The slave with the stylus looked up. The conversation had obviously become interesting to him.

"Yes," Caleb said. Still calm, still confident.

"Now that we have established this point together," Zabad said, "I am prepared to deal with the matter of His resurrection. Can you assure me He was truly dead before He was taken down from the cross?"

"That is my question to you. The Resurrection cannot be debated unless we are both certain He was dead. And I have my doubts."

"Excellent," Zabad said. "Let me address those doubts then. Roman soldiers are trained to ensure that no one survives a crucifixion. Ever. Would you expect that they make an exception in His case?"

"Perhaps they were bribed."

"By a traveling teacher who depended on the generosity of those who listened to His teachings? Where would He and His immediate followers get enough money? And why would the soldiers risk their lives for a bribe of any amount? Crucifixions are public events—and this one more so. If you were one of the attending soldiers, would you risk anyone reporting that He hadn't died on the cross?"

Zabad continued after sipping water from a clay cup. "That's why if there is any doubt, the soldiers break the legs of the victim on the cross. Once the body weight cannot be supported, suffocation comes within minutes. Read the eyewitness accounts. The soldiers saw that Jesus was dead and didn't bother to break His legs. They pierced His side with a spear. Water and blood gushed out. Would a man still alive survive this? Would a man alive—?"

Caleb waved a hand. "I am prepared to agree that He was dead when taken from the cross."

"This is an important point. I want to make certain that you won't argue that He revived in the tomb."

Helius interrupted. "I will. Despite what you say, soldiers are not beyond taking bribes. A man with His following most certainly would have had supporters willing to pull together money to save His life. A man on the cross could easily pretend to be dead and act in complicity with the soldiers. While the witnesses say that blood and water poured from His side, a man can survive a substantial blood loss, and, as you pointed out, the legs were not broken to make certain suffocation had taken place. If the wound in His side was bound quickly enough . . ."

"Let's consider for a moment that—unlikely as this might be—Jesus did survive His time on the cross and that His followers somehow managed to solicit enough money in the few hours they had on that Friday morning, and out of the dozens of people they would have had to approach, not a single person has revealed the secret of the bribe."

Helius stared at Zabad. "Yes, let's consider it."

Zabad nodded. "This man's body was beaten and whipped and shredded after an illegal trial that kept Him awake all through the night, then hung from a cross on spikes and violated by a spear. You are suggesting that if He had somehow survived, that a man this broken and torn, single-handedly rolled away the massive stone that sealed His tomb?"

"Friends, perhaps," Helius said. He had not meant to get involved but could not help himself.

"Again, read the accounts. All His friends had fled, and would be committed to His deity only after His resurrection. Why would unarmed peasants face the well-trained soldiers guarding the tomb? And if they did, how would they manage to defeat them? And even if that had happened, how could they have kept this secret? Those same arguments can be used against those who claim Jesus was dead but His body was stolen from the tomb. No, all evidence and logic point out that He went in there a dead man and that some force beyond our understanding gave Him the life and power to leave that tomb without help."

Caleb smiled. "As you have emphasized, we should read the accounts. I've studied them closely. The first witnesses to the supposed empty tomb were women. Surely you realize the significance of that?"

"Because a woman's testimony is regarded to have such little value in our Jewish courts of law that if a man is seen committing a crime and there are only women to witness it, he cannot be convicted?"

"Exactly."

"That only speaks more fully of the truth of the accounts. Any person with intelligence determined to fabricate a story would not choose to include women as witnesses."

Caleb had no reply.

Helius was beginning to think the debate was going to turn out too disasterously to be of any use to Nero.

"Tell me," Zabad said to Caleb, "as a Jew and a rabbi, you have most certainly heard of James, the brother of Jesus, who lived in Jerusalem and was stoned to death a few years ago?"

"I have."

"This is the same James who, as the brother of Jesus, denied that Jesus was the Messiah, was embarrassed by Him. Then, later, this same James gave his life because of that belief, willingly died for the notion that one of his family members is God. You have to ask yourself what it would take for a man to change his mind like that. I'll answer that for you. James saw his brother resurrected. What gave Jesus' disciples the power to withstand jail and death threats and even death, when they acted like frightened rabbits the night of His trial? The same answer. They met Jesus after His resurrection," Zabad concluded.

Helius spoke to Caleb. "I suggest you find a different matter to argue than the Resurrection. I also suggest you do a better job of it than you have so far."

If the rebuke stung Caleb, he didn't show it. "Of course. I had all of the previous evening to read the eyewitness accounts of the man and His teachings. I will show that by His very words, this Jesus of Nazareth proved Himself to be a false prophet."

HORA SEXTA

A hush of expectation fell on the crowd in the amphitheater. They knew the lions were next.

To Leah, the hush seemed almost supernatural. There were fifty thousand spectators, and the silence was so complete it was as if all had decided to hold their breath.

Into this clear silence came the echoing clang of iron gates flung open.

Leah's soul groaned with agony. She'd never been at the games before, but she knew what that sound meant. Her tremulous fear was proven correct when suddenly the first men and women were pushed out onto the sand. Then more. And more. Nearly two dozen in all.

No cheers.

No roars.

Only the predatory joy that came from watching the Christians stumble across the sand, dressed in the hides of zebras and antelopes.

After their long imprisonment, the sunlight was too much for them. Each, without fail, flung hands across their eyes and moved blindly. Some stood tall and sucked in clean air, as if determined to enjoy, for the last minutes of their lives, the simple luxury of sunshine against skin.

Leah saw her brother, of course. He stood the tallest, and several of the women had gathered behind him as if he could provide protection against the inevitable.

As they regained their bearings, the people began to cluster, forming a compact mass.

It was still silent, and the roars of anger that came from the bestiarius reached clearly into the stands. He was standing at one of the dark openings into the tunnels beneath the stands, yelling at the Christians.

Spectators began to murmur.

But Leah knew the reason for the rage of the bestiarius. Her brother and the men and women with him were doing the one thing that would delay a lion's attack.

Despite the murmurs, there was still an atmosphere of expectation, the tension of it like a physical presence exerting a force on the crowd. Then came more clanking of iron bars.

The lions had been released.

✟ ✟ ✟

The city guards reached Aristarchus, with Vitas ten paces behind, the same distance he'd kept as he followed them through Smyrna.

"Who is this?" Aristarchus demanded, pointing at Vitas.

Vitas ignored him. The slaves had stopped in front of the gates that led to the villa, and Vitas did not want them to move into the courtyard, where he would no longer be able to follow.

"Take the litter to the house," Vitas commanded the slaves. He spoke harshly to Sophia. "And, you, ensure that the woman inside the litter is comfortable; then send for a doctor."

Aristarchus was apparently so astounded, it took him several moments to find his voice. And when he finally did speak, he squeaked with outrage. "Those are my slaves! How dare you give them orders."

"How rude of me," Vitas said, smiling broadly. He'd had the entire journey here to think through his next actions. "Did I actually forget to purchase them from you first?"

"Of course you did not purchase them. Nor will I actually sell them to—"

"Fifty thousand sesterces for each slave," Vitas said, knowing that it was triple the price Aristarchus would expect. "Except, of course, for the Jewish slave. She has already proven too stubborn and independent-minded to be of much value. Consider yourself lucky that I will take her off your hands as part of the bargain."

Sophia sucked in a breath, but obviously decided this was not a moment to protest.

"I see clearly what you expect to accomplish," Aristarchus said. "You want to buy your way out of trouble."

Vitas shrugged. "Nihil tam munitum quod non expugnari pecunia possit."

Nothing is so well fortified that money cannot capture it.

"You are mistaken. These slaves are not for sale at any price. I intend to have you arrested and the Jewish slave beaten. By morning, the entire city will know that their treasurer is a man of decision and power."

"Tread lightly," Vitas warned. He pulled Aristarchus to the side and spoke softly. Already he had decided that he did not want Sophia to find him interesting because of his wealth or background. "Have you inquired into my family background? Have you any idea of my closeness to Caesar?"

Aristarchus seemed to shrink.

"Let me enlighten you," Vitas said. "I am one of three men in Rome who report directly to Nero. My name is Gallus Sergius Vitas."

"The name means nothing to me. You are bluffing."

"If it's not a bluff, you have far more to lose than I have to gain by bluffing. You decide how much of a gambler you are."

"Regardless," Aristarchus said, less stridently than before, "it is my right to have that baby exposed. My right to divorce my wife. My right to choose what I do with my slaves."

"Do I understand," Vitas began, knowing that he'd succeeded in throwing the pugnacious little man off balance, "that all of this began because your wife refused to worship Caesar?"

"Former wife," Aristarchus stressed. "I am treasurer. As a connected man, surely you understand that my position depends on my reputation. Smyrna itself depends on the goodwill of the divine Caesar. There is no room in my household for one who belongs to the cult of Christos."

"Ah yes," Vitas said. "Let me ask you this: Now that you have decreed divorce, would Caesar not see it equally fitting if your wife and her baby simply departed from Smyrna?"

"My wife must be punished," Aristarchus said. He moved away from Vitas so that he was making a public declaration. "The city and Caesar must know that I will not tolerate someone who refuses to worship the emperor. I will ask you to let Nero know of my choice, if you truly are who you say you are."

"To punish your wife, you will kill the baby?"

"A girl. I have no desire to split the estate of my future sons with a daughter."

"And if the girl is adopted by a patrician family of Rome?"

"Why is it that you show so much concern?" Aristarchus suddenly looked at him differently.

Vitas realized his mistake in revealing what he really wanted. "I am a man of compassion," he said. It was time to use more leverage. "For example, because of that compassion I am trying to save you a great deal of trouble."

"Bah!"

"This afternoon the games begin for which Smyrna is so famous. Why else am I here along with thousands of visitors?"

"I tire of your talk," Aristarchus said.

"One of your patrons went to considerable expense to bring in a team of gladiators from Rome." Immediately upon their arrival in Smyrna the day before, Vitas had made arrangements with the owner of the gladiators regarding Damian, so he was very familiar with the financial arrangements for this local arena.

"If my memory is correct," Vitas said, "the *munerarius* agreed to pay fifteen thousand sesterces for each gladiator who survives tomorrow and sixty thousand for any who die."

"What of it?" Aristarchus snapped.

"The fact that I'm in a position to know this should warn you to tread lightly in my presence."

Silence. Vitas had hit the mark again. He continued. "Yet, as treasurer, I'm sure you are fully aware that one gladiator commanded a far higher price for his presence in Smyrna. A famous gladiator, who has not lost once in thirteen years. All through this city, his name has been included prominently on the advertisements painted on the walls."

"Maglorius," Aristarchus said with a touch of awe.

"The people of your city are going to be highly disappointed when he does not appear in the arena as promised."

"What!"

"You poor man," Vitas said. "If lucky, you may be able to prevent riots. On the other hand, when word reaches all that you were responsible for his injuries, I doubt you will remain treasurer much longer. You'll be lucky if the mobs spare your life."

"What!"

"They may well decide to amuse themselves by throwing you into the arena. I understand that often people live much longer than you'd expect after a lion has pulled their entrails out onto the sand."

"What!"

"I see," Vitas said, "that your guards neglected to inform you fully of last night's events. The Jewish slave girl and the baby fled to Maglorius from the square at Nero's temple. He was on his knees, unprotected, as your guards struck him with their swords."

Aristarchus turned on the guards. "Is this true?"

"W-we fought," one stuttered. "It was dark. How could we be expected to identify the man——?"

"So a man was on his knees when you attacked?"

"Yes, but——"

"The doctor to the gladiators spent hours in the middle of the night sewing Maglorius back together," Vitas interrupted. "You'll be able to confirm that easily enough. Maglorius himself and my friend and I are witnesses to the guards who attacked."

"I am lost," Aristarchus moaned.

"Not if all of us agree to silence," Vitas said. "Your guards will realize the prudence in protecting you and themselves from the wrath of the mob. As for your divorced wife and these slaves here, if they are on a ship headed back to Rome by afternoon, how could they whisper a word of it to any of the good citizens of Smyrna?"

It took little time for Aristarchus to come to his decision. "Fifty thousand sesterces for each slave is a generous offer. I accept."

"Good," Vitas said. "Have the money here at the villa in the next hour. Any later than that and I will have difficulty departing by sunset as promised."

"Are you mad?" Aristarchus screeched. "That was the price you offered me!"

"I *had* offered it," Vitas said, "but I've changed my mind. I've decided that's the price you are going to offer me."

Vitas did not like this man. It was childish, Vitas knew, but he wanted to punish him. And if the man loved money, that's what Vitas would take from him.

"You expect *me* to pay *you* for *my* slaves?"

"If I knew you well enough to trust you, I would consider banker's papers for payment," Vitas said. "But what I already know about your character tells me to insist on silver or gold."

"You expect me to pay you for my slaves? Not a chance!"

"Ah, you wish for the negotiations to continue further." Again, Vitas knew he was being childish to enjoy the man's discomfort. "I have no problem with that. Sixty thousand sesterces per slave. The Jewish slave, of course, is still not worth enough to barter for."

"Sixty thousand! Never!"

"What a shame," Vitas said, enjoying himself and the indignant reaction of Sophia at his insult of her. "I suppose the pleasure of watching the lions rip you apart in the arena will make up for our unsuccessful negotiations. Unless you want the negotiations to continue."

"I . . . I . . ."

"Sixty-five thousand per slave," Vitas said. "Let's draw this out as long as we can."

"All right! All right! Sixty-five."

"Well done," Vitas said. "Send Paulina and the slaves and the litter to my ship in the harbor. You'll have no problem identifying it, as it flies the emperor's flag. I expect the gold and silver there within the hour."

"Just be out of Smyrna," Aristarchus snapped.

"Of course." Vitas kept his face grave, hiding his sense of triumph. Mainly because he knew there was still trouble ahead.

Aristarchus was nothing compared to the outburst he fully expected to get from Sophia as soon as they were alone.

But he'd already decided he had a plan for her too.

✠ ✠ ✠

"Jesus was not a false prophet," Zabad said. "I have staked my life on it."

Caleb snorted. "Your poor judgment proves nothing except your poor judgment." Caleb rose from his cushion and paced tight circles in front of Helius as he continued to speak to Zabad. "You have placed great emphasis on the witnesses of the miracles of Jesus and the wit-

nesses of the Resurrection. Are we agreed then on the importance and
veracity of those witnesses?"

"Without doubt," Zabad answered. "We are still within the generation of those who witnessed Him. Only a fool would make claims that
could be contradicted by other living witnesses."

"Last night, I studied different letters about Jesus that have been circulating. I have one of the scrolls with me. A letter written by a fellow
Jew named Matthew. One of Jesus' disciples. You'll agree that few can
be a closer witness than that?"

"I agree," Zabad said.

"So we agree that what Matthew records as statements by Jesus can
be trusted."

"We agree. Witnesses have corroborated many of the events. Witnesses still alive today."

"I will assume then that you are familiar with the letter," Caleb
continued. "If not, you are welcome to refer to a copy of it. . . ."

"I am familiar with it." Zabad smiled faintly. "This letter was so con-
vincing that because of it, I began to consider Jesus as the Son of God. And
after much prayer, the Spirit of God opened my eyes, and I believed. My
family and I face death now because of our unshakable beliefs. So I will not
dispute you on the veracity of it, and yes, I am familiar with it."

"Excellent," Caleb said. "You'll recall what Matthew testifies about
the teachings of Jesus on the Mount of Olives just before His crucifixion."

"Just before His crucifixion *and* resurrection."

"Are you avoiding my question?"

"The discourse of Jesus on the Mount of Olives. It took place just
after Jesus left the temple grounds. He turned to His disciples and
promised them that not one stone would be left on top of another. They
were so astonished that they asked Him about it shortly after, as they
rested on the Mount of Olives and beheld the glory of the temple."

"Then you know His answer to their questions about when it would
take place, when they asked for signs of His return and the end of the
age?" Caleb asked.

"I do," Zabad answered. "And I am profoundly grateful for it. The
end of the age is upon us as Daniel predicted and as Jesus confirmed."

Helius snorted. "You are suggesting that time will end?"

"Someday, of course, it will," Zabad said calmly. "But that is plainly not what I mean. *The end of the age* is a common phrase used in our Scriptures in different ways. History easily shows that old epochs end and new epochs begin. Nations come and go. Even the Romans understand that the end of an age does not necessarily mean the end of time. And I am telling you that an evil era is about to end with the destruction of the temple and the ruling establishment in Jerusalem that rejected Jesus as the Son of God."

"Very well," Helius said, showing a flare of irritation. "Perhaps we can move on from debating terms."

"Something this important is not merely a debate of terms," Zabad told Helius. "With the death and resurrection of Jesus, a new age is upon us. One that does not require sacrifices at the Temple Mount. The covenant between God and Israel was broken with the rejection of His Son."

"Only if Jesus," Caleb countered, "as you claim, is the Messiah."

"He is," Zabad said. "Jesus has renewed and fulfilled the covenant between God and Israel, and now God calls all people everywhere to repent and believe the Good News that Jesus is Lord of all." Zabad turned to Helius again. "He calls you, too, to enter into His covenant."

"As I made clear, I am not interested in debated terms." Helius' irritation verged on rage. "And I am certainly willing to call only Nero divine." Helius pointed at Caleb, who had stopped pacing. "You have stretched my patience. I want proof that Jesus was a false prophet. Give me a good reason not to call in a soldier to behead you."

✣ ✣ ✣

One lion burst onto the sand, forced out from the chambers below the stands by a slave armed with a torch. Then another lion. A third. And fourth. More and more. In mannerisms, they were like mice scattering from lifted straw, but in appearance, they were monstrous beasts that caused women in the crowd to faint from anticipation of bloodlust.

The lions ran in confused circles. Several tried to jump up the walls, scattering the spectators who were leaning over for a better look. Several of the young males bumped into each other, which resulted in snarling fights as they rolled over each other in a savage display of pure rage.

The lions had yet to notice the cluster of men and women in the center, for the Christians remained motionless. Leah knew——only because she'd heard the bestiarius explain it to the prisoners—that the prisoners should silently separate and move slightly to let the lions know they were living prey. The bestiarius had also been careful to explain that if they remained clustered, it would intimidate the lions. Just as if any of the women in the cluster began to scream, it would actually frighten these wild lions, who were already amply confused by the sights and smells of the arena.

One lion began to dig in the sand, perhaps smelling the blood of a previous victim. Another lion began to stalk a nearby lioness.

Because there was no action, a few boos began from the crowd.

Leah faced the most difficult decision of her young life. She had to choose between prolonging her beloved brother's life or sending children into slavery.

Intellectually, she knew what choice she had to make. Because there was no choice. Her brother was going to die, whether it was in five minutes or thirty. If the children didn't go into slavery, they too would face the lions.

Yet her heart could barely take the strain, and her intellectual decision seemed meaningless against the emotions that overwhelmed her.

How could she do what she needed to do?

✛ ✛ ✛

"Homer returns." Damian spoke wryly as he looked up from reading a diptych.

"You're alone?" Vitas asked. Four slaves accompanied him. "What of your women—?"

Damian gave a wave. "You certainly know how to spoil a party. Titus heard enough of what happened out there to stagger after you. And all the moaning from our fallen gladiator hero spoiled the mood even more. I sent everyone away."

"Too bad," Vitas said, grinning. He gave instructions to the slaves to move Maglorius outside to the litter they had carried to the villa.

"Where's Titus?" Damian said, frowning at the activity. "Where are you taking Maglorius?"

"Titus caught up with me just after I'd completed negotiations with the treasurer," Vitas answered. "He's waiting down at the ship for you and me to arrive with Maglorius."

At the movement of the four slaves, the swallows in their wicker cage fluttered with panic.

"Easy now," Damian said to the birds in a soothing voice. "Easy. This will be over soon enough." He shot a frown at Vitas. "It will be over soon enough, correct?"

"Certainly," Vitas replied. "I doubt you have much to pack."

"I cannot leave Smyrna," Damian said. "The gladiator's vow . . ."

"Such a sense of honor," Vitas observed with an ironic smile. "I can tell you, brother, that I love you for it. You are nearly a perfect man, except for your weakness for gambling."

"Honor?" Damian rubbed his forehead and sighed. "Have you any idea how relentlessly a man is pursued if he forsakes the vow? And his fate is far, far worse than anything that might happen in the arena." He tossed the diptych at Vitas. "Here, this belongs to Maglorius. He'll want it if he lives."

Vitas weighed the diptych in his hand, curious about it for natural reasons.

Ink on leaf tablets—thin sheets of wood with tie holes that allowed a cord to keep several sheets together—were used for most correspondence. But a diptych contained thicker pieces of wood filled with beeswax on which the writer used a stylus to scratch out the words. Much more expensive than leaf tablets, diptychs were normally used for important documents, legal documents. Why would a gladiator receive such a document?

Vitas gave it a closer look. "The seal is broken."

"Of course."

"You broke it?" Vitas asked.

"As soon as the messenger departed."

"Some might decide it was illegal and immoral and—"

The slaves had taken Maglorius away. It was just Vitas and Damian and the cage filled with swallows.

"Relax, my brother," Damian said. "Maglorius gets me to read everything for him. He's a savage tribal warrior, remember? And that—" Damian pointed at the diptych—"that is a heated love letter. Very amusing. Not only is the woman in love with him, but she's married."

"Not interested," Vitas said. "Spare me the details."

Damian flashed his rogue's grin. "The woman begins by expressing her undying love for Maglorius that she's had even before I took the gladiator's vow."

"Enough," Vitas said. "This is no business of mine."

"Given her husband, I think you'd want to know more." Damian paused.

"All right!" Vitas grinned back, knowing his brother had been toying with him. "Who?"

"Lucius Bellator. His wife, Alypia, is in love with Maglorius. And has been for the last five years."

"Bellator! His family has been around since the founding of Rome! He's just been given a plum political office. He's to be transferred to Judea to oversee the collection of taxes there. As if he weren't rich enough already."

"Am I right?" Damian asked. "Would you have not eavesdropped? and read this letter?"

"I would have been tempted," Vitas said. But not tempted enough. He had the diptych now and would ensure that no one else looked at it but Maglorius.

"Let me tell you more then," Damian said. "She tells of her love and begs him to return safely, for she declares that enough time has passed that she could move him into the household as a bodyguard without arousing the suspicion of her elderly husband. Furthermore, she is finally able to reveal to him something of great importance. . . ."

"No," Vitas said firmly. He felt some guilt already at indulging in the gossip thus far. "I have little time and important news of my own for you."

"But really, it's too much! The fact that Maglorius has been unaware of—"

"No!"

Damian shrugged. "Have it your way."

"I'll see he gets it," Vitas said. "I expect someone as hardy as Maglorius to recover fully."

"Where's some wine?" Damian asked. "I've done my best to forget that I've lost my protector in the arena today. All this talk about Maglorius reminds me what's going to happen when I face the lions."

"Aren't you curious why I would come to Smyrna?"

"As the kind and decent older brother, I'm certain you are here to ensure the return of my mangled body to Rome, as unaware as the rest of the world that I had purchased the protection of Maglorius. Of course, with him nearly dead, the purpose of your visit will, ironically enough, be fulfilled. And once again, the world will see that you've acted wisely."

Damian grinned. "Won't complain though. No one else but me was responsible for the gambling debts that forced me to take the gladiator vows."

Vitas knew his brother well enough to understand that this forced cavalier attitude was an outer protection. Yet Vitas was not ready to give his brother the news that had brought him to Smyrna.

Vitas stepped past him. "Tell me about these birds."

Damian coughed and ignored the question. "Vitas, I'm sure it is for Father's benefit that you are undertaking this chore. Be sure to tell him that I do not blame my bad choices on him or the way he raised me. After all, look at you. A son to be proud of under any circumstances."

"Damian." Vitas spoke very, very softly. "Our father is dead."

✝ ✝ ✝

"Proof that Jesus was a false messiah," Caleb echoed Helius. "I will give you proof. In the words of Matthew, Jesus said this: 'I assure you, this generation will not pass from the scene before all these things take place.'" Caleb pierced Zabad with a stare. "Is this not in the scroll?"

"That, and more." Zabad nodded and quoted from memory. "'Don't let anyone mislead you. For many will come in my name, saying, "I am the Messiah." They will lead many astray.'"

Zabad drew breath to continue quoting Jesus, but Caleb interrupted and spoke to Helius. "Before he makes his point, I will admit there is truth in these prophecies of Jesus. I'm sure you are aware of Theudas, who persuaded a great number to follow him to the Jordan and promised he would divide it for their passage. And of Dositheus, the Samaritan, who pretended he was the lawgiver promised by Moses. And of the many false messiahs under the procuratorship of Felix."

"Yes," Helius snapped at Caleb. "I am keenly aware of the Jewish revolutionaries. Why is Zabad's argument so strong and yours so weak?"

"Patience," Caleb said. "Jesus also foretold this on the Mount: 'Wars will break out near and far, but don't panic. Yes, these things must come, but the end won't follow immediately. The nations and kingdoms will proclaim war against each other, and there will be famines and earthquakes in many parts of the world. But all this will be only the beginning of the horrors to come.'"

Helius glared at Caleb. "Patience? I thought you were supposed to offer proof that Jesus was false. It seems the opposite. If Jesus did predict these things, it strengthens the case against you. During the long reign of Tiberius, we had peace. Now, suddenly, in the years after the death of Jesus, unrest again."

Caleb shrugged. "The world as we know it has been in constant battle as the Roman Empire expands and holds its frontiers. Wars against the warriors in Britannia. Against the Gauls. The Parthians. Rome has dealt with a great famine in the last decade. Earthquakes seem to occur daily across the world. On the surface, Jesus seems to have made remarkable predictions."

Helius could hardly stand it. "*On the surface?* Have you no idea how to debate this matter? Wars and earthquakes and famines. When won't the world be faced with those? I would wager thousands of years from now it won't be any different."

Caleb put up a hand as if to silence Helius. This motion angered Helius more and he began to sputter.

Caleb ignored Helius. "Zabad, are you willing to say then, that Jesus applied all these predictions specifically to this generation?"

"Of course," Zabad said. "It could not be any more clear. Jesus said it would apply to this generation, and, even now, with the world at its most wealthy and civilized, famines and wars are still taking place."

"Debate this man!" Helius said. "Don't agree with him. By the gods, I'm half prepared to follow the Christos myself by the inept way you've handled this."

Caleb's eyes gleamed with triumph, and he grinned at Helius. "I want it remembered that we have all agreed that the truth of the prophecies of Jesus on the Mount of Olives is meaningless unless *all* the events He predicted occur, not just some."

"You are a stupid man," Helius told Caleb. "I think I shall order your immediate execution."

"I want Zabad to address this prophecy of Jesus on the Mount of Olives," Caleb demanded, his voice rising as he addressed Zabad. "Remember this one? 'I assure you, not one stone will be left on top of another.'"

"Jesus did say that," Zabad said.

"In other words, the temple will be destroyed?" Caleb said.

"Yes," Zabad answered.

Caleb turned to Helius and bowed. "There it is. Proof that Jesus was a false messiah."

"You call that proof?" Helius could hardly speak he was so angry.

"If but one prophecy is wrong, He is not divine," Caleb said. "And His most outrageous prophecy of all is clearly false."

Caleb turned back to Zabad. "Will you agree that the entire Jewish population in Jerusalem would fight to their deaths to prevent Gentiles from desecrating the Holy of Holies?"

"Of course."

Caleb grinned widely, not bothering to hide his triumph. "And that is where your Jesus is plainly a false prophet. The generation that was alive when he spoke is nearly ended. Yet the temple is standing strong."

"This generation is not over yet," Zabad countered. "Unlikely as it might be, I believe the prophecies of Jesus will be proven true before witnesses alive when He spoke them are all gone from this earth."

"How large are the stones of the temple?" Caleb asked.

"Each stone is twice the height of a man. Ten paces long. Two paces wide."

"So large it would take dozens of men to move one."

"So large," Zabad said, "that it has taken decades to build and finish the temple. That's what makes the prophecy of Jesus all the more bold."

"Bold?" Caleb said. "I would say plainly ridiculous. The Mount of Zion has a water flow that would withstand any siege. Those walls with massive stones are perched on cliffs. There is food to last ten years in the city. And those within would fight so zealously that not even the mighty Roman Empire would find a way to defeat them. Agreed?"

"Agreed," Zabad said.

"And you still believe that the prophecies of Jesus will be fulfilled within this generation?"

"I believe it."

Caleb spoke directly to Helius. "You are a man of great political shrewdness. You know as well as anyone that the authorities who control Jerusalem and the rest of the nation work closely with the Romans. Can you foresee any reason for the Jews with political power to allow a rebellion by their own people?"

"None," Helius said. He relaxed somewhat, as if he could finally understand where Caleb was taking the argument.

"You know Nero as well as any man alive," Caleb said. "Do you think he intends to waste time and energy sending in legions to destroy a temple when the Jews have given him no reason to?"

"Hardly."

"What I am saying," Caleb pronounced, "is that the temple is one of the wonders of the world. Massive. Unassailable. So unassailable that even if the mightiest empire the world has known tried to destroy it, that empire would be defeated. I am saying that there is no foreseeable reason for the empire to even try this. And the generation that Jesus addressed has nearly passed."

"Excellent," Helius said. "If the temple does not fall within this generation, then Jesus was plainly a false prophet. And a false prophet cannot claim to be inspired by God, far less have his followers believe he is the Son of God."

"This generation is not yet over," Zabad said.

Caleb ignored him and spoke to Helius. "Don't you see? Nero has the power. Not this Jesus. If Nero decides not to destroy the temple, Nero proves Jesus to be a false prophet."

Helius shared Caleb's sense of triumph. Yes! These were the words that would delight Nero.

"Well done," Helius told Caleb. "It is settled then. Zabad and his family will die in the arena."

"And my brother," Caleb said, "he will be released?"

"Of course," Helius lied. No sense in causing a scene here. He would leave the room and send in the soldiers to take away Caleb and the other rabbi for immediate execution. The scribe, too, for Helius wanted no witnesses alive.

Helius, happy now that he had something to set Nero at ease, began
to plan his evening. Wine first, as always, then—

He realized that Zabad had risen too and was speaking directly to him.

"Nero's death is imminent. It has been decided by God," Zabad said.
"And prophesied by man. Prepare to face the Judge of heaven and
earth—the King of kings and the Lord of lords."

✛ ✛ ✛

Leah somehow found the strength to stand from her seat in the arena.
And then somehow found the strength to lift her arm and wave a bright
red scarf.

Her brother, hundreds of feet away, lifted his hands skyward, as if
imploring God for mercy.

This movement told Leah that he had seen the scarf and understood
the signal.

The children had been taken away and sold as promised. This is what
her brother had needed to know. That the bestiarius had honored the
agreement.

And now the men and women gathered on the sand would honor
their part of it.

Leah's vision blurred with tears. She wished she could be spared the
sight. But her brother had made her promise she would watch with the
same bravery that he would show as the lions approached.

She watched, then, as the men and women separated slowly so they
would not startle the lions. Each began to sway slightly, lifting and dropping their hands to alert the wild lions to their presence.

Instantly, the beasts stopped the frenzied circling and responded by
crouching.

The crowd became silent as the moment of horror approached. In
this silence, a sound rose from the sand. It took several moments for
Leah to realize that her brother had begun to sing a beautiful hymn.
Others on the sand joined with him, and their voices rose like a choir.

This serenity and peace were not the reaction that the mob had expected, and the silence of the audience continued, more from surprise
than anything. The words of the hymn became more clear as the men
and women poured joy into their singing.

A few angry catcalls began. Then jeering and boos, and the momentary spell was broken.

A few lions crept closer.

Leah lost her breath as her brother stepped forward and dropped the zebra hide that covered him. He fell to his knees and clasped his hands in prayer.

The boldest lion suddenly leaped forward.

And Leah broke her promise.

She turned her head and closed her eyes in that last moment as the lion closed in on her brother with outstretched claws.

✛ ✛ ✛

"No," Damian said to his brother. Comprehension seemed to replace his denial. "Father? Dead?"

"Yes. Only days after your departure for Smyrna. He died alone. In his sleep. I'm told it was painless."

They shared wordless grief for several moments, the silence broken only by the restless fluttering of the birds in the cage.

"Well then," Damian said. He let out a breath. "That probably simplifies my burial arrangements. I wouldn't spend much, if I were you. Drink some wine in my honor and consider it done."

"I'll drink some wine *with* you, my brother. On the ship that returns to Rome this afternoon."

"I told you, gladiator vows are taken very seriously. If I fled Smyrna, there would be a bounty on my head for the rest of my life."

"No. Yesterday afternoon, I purchased you. It was a provision in father's will."

"By the gods!" Damian's face lit up. "Angry as he was with me, he still did that?"

"He loved you. Greatly. You and I share the estate."

"I don't believe you!"

Vitas nodded.

"You're the fool," Damian said, grinning. "You should have arrived in Smyrna a couple of days late, expecting that I would have been dead and the estate then entirely yours."

"Would you have done the same to rescue me?"

Damian nodded. "Without hesitation. Just don't make me admit that kind of love for you again."

"You are free, my brother. Return to Rome. You have been trained as a lawyer. You can start life fresh there as a respected man."

Damian snorted. He gestured at the birds in the cage. "So I can live like them? Well fed, safe, but in prison?"

"Your gladiator vows are shackles."

"You don't have any idea what it means to live on the edge, do you?"

"I fought in Britannia."

"But you didn't serve because you wanted to test life to its fullest. You served because of loyalty to the empire."

"What else is there?" Vitas asked.

Damian gave a crooked grin. He touched his nose. Showed his bent finger. Touched his nicked ear. "How about adventure?"

"Look for adventure in Rome; the ship is waiting."

Damian paced back and forth. "I'll go."

"Excellent," Vitas said.

"But not yet," Damian said. "I'm having too much fun with a certain game I've been playing." He pointed at the cage filled with swallows.

"Please," Vitas said. "Your games always end in trouble. Leave now."

"Leave Smyrna?" Damian asked. "The city of games? As a suddenly former gladiator? Think of the women ready to swoon at the mere sight of me. Especially now that I'm rich and I won't actually have to fight to earn my reputation."

"The ship is ready to sail," Vitas said. "Please. You know that gambling gets you in trouble."

"No," Damian said. "It's my craving for excitement that gets me in trouble. Gambling just happens to be one of the most convenient methods to find that excitement."

"I have something else for you instead," Vitas said quietly.

"Listen! This scheme is foolproof. These swallows are from Ephesus. I've made arrangements with certain gamblers down there who enjoy betting huge amounts of sesterces on the colors of the chariot races. Many of them bet on races here in Smyrna too, relying on couriers to bring them the results."

Damian didn't have to explain the colors, a longtime tradition in Rome.

There were four racing factions: the blues, greens, whites, and reds—the colors worn by the charioteers. These factions led to great rivalries, and great rivalries led to large-scale gambling. Damian had been forced to take the gladiator vows because of the debts he had accumulated.

"Titus is on the ship too," Vitas said. "Return to Rome. He and his father will vouch for you. Think of the political career ahead of you."

"Respectability is boring," Damian said. "Let me tell you about the swallows. My acquaintances in Ephesus also have a cage with swallows native to Smyrna. And we help each other."

"Help?"

"As soon as I know which faction has won the day's races," Damian said, "I paint a swallow that color and release it. Long before the courier gets to Ephesus, the swallow has arrived at its nest there and alerted my acquaintances on the team to wager. They, of course, do the same for me. The only horses I've bet upon in the last week have been winners." Damian grinned. "How else could I afford this villa?"

"Your scheme will eventually be discovered. No one bets correctly all the time."

"I agree," Damian said. "But by this time tomorrow I was either going to be dead or returned to Rome with the rest of the gladiators. In the meantime, I had Maglorius to protect me. So I spent everything as quickly as I could. Very enjoyably, I might add."

"How long before you return to Rome?"

"Look how many swallows remain in the cage," Damian answered.

Vitas sighed. He thought of the ship. Of Paulina and the baby whom he had made a vow to support. Of the Jewish slave who had beguiled him, whom he intended to court in the manner he would have courted a Roman woman of high social standing.

Vitas knew his brother would not be budged. And the others waited. "I've given your situation a lot of thought," he said. "I know you almost as well as you know yourself."

"You have my sympathy." Damian grinned.

"A month ago," Vitas said, "two slaves escaped Nero's palace. It hasn't been reported publicly, because they managed to leave with a substantial amount of jewelry. Apparently, Nero had been careless around those slaves."

"Handsome young boys, I presume, if Nero had dangled baubles in front of them."

"Hunt them down for me," Vitas said. "I think you'll find it as exciting as gambling, and it will give you an excuse to roam the slums that seem to draw you like a Siren on a rock."

"Not a bad idea," Damian said. "Not bad at all. Ex-gladiator turned slave hunter." Another crooked grin. "I can see how it would appeal to the sort of woman I find interesting."

"You'll do it then?"

Damian nodded. "I'll join you in Rome in about a month."

Vitas sighed. He walked to the birdcage. Lifted it. Moved it to a window. Ripped apart the bars of the cage. Held it at the window until all the birds had found their freedom.

He turned to see Damian calmly regarding him with arms crossed.

"I'll find more swallows," Damian said. "More for principle's sake than anything. You know I hate to be told what to do."

"You have two hours," Vitas said. "The ship leaves then."

As Vitas left the villa, he met three men walking toward him. Although they were not large, they were armed with pieces of wood and angry faces. They glanced at him but did nothing else as they passed.

Vitas turned and observed, without surprise, that they were entering the outer courtyard of the villa. What other business would they have at this hour of the morning?

Vitas shook his head and kept walking. Now that Damian owned half the family estate, he had enough money to pay them back. And a few bruises wouldn't be a bad way to encourage him to follow the road to respectability.

Two minutes later, Vitas heard shouting from behind him.

"Vitas! Vitas!" It was Damian, at a full run. His toga flailed around him and his sandals were not laced. "Vitas! Wait! Tell me where I can find this ship of yours!"

✣ ✣ ✣

"What?" Helius ordered the scribe to stop with the stylus.

"This is what has been declared by Jesus," Zabad said. "'Immediately after the distress of those days, the sun will be darkened, and the moon will not give its light; the stars will fall from the sky, and the heavenly bodies will be shaken. At that time the sign of the Son of Man will appear in the sky, and all the nations of the earth will mourn. They will see the Son of Man coming on clouds of the sky with power and great glory.'"

Helius cast questioning eyes at Caleb. "Coming on the clouds? You think this Jesus is about to return?"

"Zabad quotes from the scrolls of Matthew." Caleb gave a weary sigh. "If you were a Jew, you would be familiar with the imagery. *Coming on the clouds* is a familiar Jewish expression used by our prophets to communicate the majesty and sovereign power of God. His coming on clouds translates to judgment for those who resist Him and blessing for those who bow the knee."

"You are certain of this?" Helius said.

"This is common knowledge. Isaiah, for example, used this very expression to describe God's retribution on Egypt. When he prophesied that God would come in wrath and fierce anger to make the land of Babylon desolate, he said that 'the rising sun will be darkened and the moon will not give its light.' All these images are used frequently by our ancient prophets to describe God's judgment and retribution."

"Wrath and fierce anger?" Helius said to Zabad.

"From our prophet Daniel." Zabad quoted: "'In my vision at night I looked, and there before me was one like a son of man, coming with the clouds of heaven. He approached the Ancient of Days and was led into his presence. He was given authority, glory and sovereign power; all peoples, nations and men of every language worshiped him. His dominion is an everlasting dominion that will not pass away, and his kingdom is one that will never be destroyed.'"

"Enough!" Helius shouted.

If Nero heard that any god was about to deliver judgment on him, even as a rumor, the palace would be unbearable. Nero slept the uneasy sleep of a guilty man. He saw plots everywhere. "You're saying this Jesus will return to judge this generation?"

Helius turned to Caleb. "I want an explanation."

Caleb shook his head. "It does not mean a literal bodily return. It means God's punishment would vindicate Jesus and His death."

"Punishment?" Helius said. Nero was too paranoid as it was. This could not get out. "What kind of——?"

"If the temple does not fall—and it won't for all the reasons I described—all the other prophecies have no credibility," Caleb answered. "I've just established that."

"Yes," Zabad said, "if the temple doesn't fall, Jesus is a failed prophet. But this generation is not yet over. The temple will fall as judgment at a day and an hour that only God knows. And someday Jesus Himself will truly return to judge the living and the dead."

"I cannot bear this religious nonsense," Helius said.

"You also have your warning," Zabad told him. "A divine revelation as given by the last disciple."

"The last disciple?" Helius turned to Caleb. "Who is this last disciple?"

Caleb shrugged.

"Nero began the Tribulation after the Great Fire, but his time will be cut short," Zabad said. "He will be defeated by the Lamb. The Christ against the Antichrist."

"The lamb?" Helius repeated. Any prediction of Nero's defeat must not reach the emperor's ears. His voice rose as his question to Caleb became more insistent. "Tell me who is this last disciple!"

"Nero is doomed," Zabad said, as if Helius had not spoken. "And in his doom, so too will you find doom. Yet it is not too late to save your soul."

There was a torch on the wall, unlit because it was daylight. Zabad took it. Using its sooty end like a brush, he wrote a single word in Greek in large letters on the wall.

Helius knew what the symbols would be before Zabad finished.

$$\chi\xi\varsigma$$

In Greek, it was the word that the Christians had been placing as graffiti all across the city. Unreasoning rage drove Helius to an act he would later regret again and again. Had he let Caleb live, he would have been able to find the Senate records that were such a threat. Had he let Zabad live, he would have been able to torture him to learn more about the revelation of the last disciple.

Instead, he yelled for the guards.

"Kill them!" Helius screamed as they rushed into the room. "Kill them all!"

As Caleb and the innocent scribe backed away in horrified incomprehension, Zabad smiled a strange smile of peace and waited for the swords.

He died moments later, beneath the very letters that he had inscribed on the palace wall. Letters that also served as numbers. Letters that added up to a single sum.

Six hundred and sixty-six.

EIGHTEEN MONTHS
AFTER THE BEGINNING
OF THE TRIBULATION

{AD 66}

JUDEA

Do not seal up the words of the prophecy
of this book, because the time is near.
Let him who does wrong
continue to do wrong;
let him who is vile
continue to be vile;
let him who does right
continue to do right;
and let him who is holy
continue to be holy.

—Revelation 22:10-11

13 AV

THE THIRD HOUR

Silence or death," a voice whispered in her ear.

Queen Bernice woke in the Jerusalem palace to the voice and to the pressure of something sharp against her neck.

The flames of the lamps in her chamber had been snuffed. She was a restless sleeper and, because of her childlike fear of the night, made it a habit to burn several lamps filled with enough oil to last until dawn. Now, with the covering over the window as she always requested from her servants, it was nearly dark even though dawn had arrived hours earlier.

She could not see the intruder.

"As this knife proves," the ragged whisper continued, "I am a desperate man. I care nothing for my own life. If you call for your guards, you die along with me."

His breath tickled her ear, and the warmth of it washed over her face. The shock of this intimacy was as frightening as the knife. How had he made it through the labyrinth of corridors to one of the innermost chambers of the palace?

"On your side," the voice commanded.

"Who are you?" she whispered.

"I've never even struck a woman before," he said. "But this morning I am prepared to kill. Do as I say."

Slowly she rolled over. She slept in a silk gown, and it tangled against her legs.

Was this man an assassin? A *Sicarii* of the Zealots determined to punish one of the Herods for the family's collaboration with Rome? Then why not kill her as she slept?

From where he knelt at the side of her bed, the intruder took her left arm and pulled it in front of her. His gentleness was alarming.

Queen Bernice felt something tighten against her wrist. The noose of a leather cord?

"Although my knife is no longer against your throat," he whispered, "if you cry out I will kill you long before your guards arrive."

He fumbled for her other arm, using just one hand. That told her his threat was not idle, that his knife was in his other hand.

Again, the tightness of a narrow band around her other wrist. He'd had the nooses prepared, planned this carefully, she realized. It was a realization that raised her fear, and a tremor shook her body.

He tightened that noose, then cinched it farther so her hands were only inches apart. "Now on your stomach," he ordered.

She rolled over a quarter turn, her full weight on her bound hands, her knuckles pushing into the softness of her belly.

Silently, he bound her feet in the same way, with prepared nooses of leather cord.

"What do you want?" She felt her voice trembling as she whispered the question.

Without answering, he picked her up and threw her over his shoulder.

Did he expect he could leave the palace with her? Guards swarmed the corridors. Yet, she reminded herself, somehow he had found his way this far into the palace. Perhaps he truly did intend to escape with her . . .

No.

He took several steps away from the bed, away from the entrance to her chamber. It seemed effortless for him, and his strength frightened her even more.

He moved her to the far wall of the chamber. He set her down, propping her in a sitting position, her back against the wall, her feet in front of her, arms in her lap. Small protrusions of the wall dug into her back.

"Are you comfortable?" he whispered. From the sound, she guessed he was squatting beside her.

"My back," she said. "The wall hurts . . ."

"I will step across the room to get a pillow. But I say it again. If you call for help, I will kill you before the guards arrive. Understand?"

In the darkness, she nodded.

"I want to hear you say it," he whispered. "Do you understand?"

"I understand."

He rose. She felt the air move, a part of her mind amazed at her heightened senses. She heard the light clicking of the soles of his sandals. To the bed . . . and back.

"Lean forward," he said.

She did.

One of his hands grasped her shoulder. The other slid the pillow behind her.

Who was this man, ready to kill her yet concerned about her comfort? Fear and morbid curiosity sent flushes of adrenaline through her body.

"I'm thirsty," she pleaded. After years of facing the baser desires of men, she had the instinct of a seductress, an instinct that told her the more he aided her, the more sympathetic he would be toward her. "There is a small jug on a stand at my bed."

"Your life depends on your silence," he warned.

"You will have my silence."

Again, the movement that was invisible but sensed. Again, the slapping of sandals. Again, his return.

In the darkness, he found her arm and slowly moved the jug down until it reached her hands.

Bernice drank. Her thirst had been very real, a thirst of fear.

She was tempted to hurl the jug forward instead of setting it down, hoping the sound of it smashing against the far wall would bring a guard. The temptation passed quickly. Hands bound, feet bound, she was helpless. It would take only a heartbeat for him to find her throat in the darkness and slash it open.

"Who are you?" she asked as he took the jug from her. "What do you want?"

"We will have ample time to discuss what we need to discuss."

Ample time.

This meant he was acquainted with her habits well enough to know that she daily remained in bed for hours after dawn, shrouded from day-light by the covers over her window, demanding total privacy until she first opened the door of her chamber and called for a servant.

Frightening as this was, because he had made no attempt to harm her some of her royal composure returned.

"And what shall we discuss?" she asked.

"Judgment. Upon you."

✛ ✛ ✛

When Simeon Ben-Aryeh finally saw the man who walked with a staff marked by a red rag tied to its crook, the man's slow, confident manner of movement added to the instinctive dislike of Romans that had been simmering inside Ben-Aryeh since Queen Bernice had first directed Ben-Aryeh to wait for this man.

Gallus Sergius Vitas.

Ben-Aryeh sat on a blanket within a stone's throw of the arched outer entrance that guarded Herod's fortress. He'd arrived in Sebaste halfway through the morning before, wondering how many days it would take for the Roman to arrive; there was no sure prediction of when his ship would dock in Caesarea, no way of knowing in Sebaste when Vitas would receive the message directing him to look for Ben-Aryeh.

During his long wait for Vitas the day before, Ben-Aryeh had been utterly silent, for he did not want his accent to give him away as a Jew, not here in the stronghold of Samaria. Ben-Aryeh had watched for the man hour after hour—as the sun heated the day, as it brought the dry air to the point where it parched a man's lungs with every breath, as it fell again, leaving behind a chill that demanded another blanket for his old bones.

It had been enough, with the movement of the sun marking Ben-Aryeh's solitude among the crowds, for Ben-Aryeh to frequently set aside the simmering dislike and resentment for the joy of recalling the majestic poetry of God's questions to Job: *"Where were you when I laid the foundations of the earth? Tell me, if you know so much. Do you know how its di-mensions were determined and who did the surveying? What supports its founda-tions, and who laid its cornerstone as the morning stars sang together and all the angels shouted for joy? Have you ever commanded the morning to appear and*

*caused the dawn to rise in the east? Have you ever told the daylight to spread to
the ends of the earth, to bring an end to the night's wickedness?"*

It had been time enough to let those contemplations of the sun on its
path direct Ben-Aryeh to the other glories of the one and true God. To
glance past the walls of the city at the hills rising around it in all directions, patches of green dotted by the white fleece of distant sheep. To
watch the activities at the nearby communal well and ponder that something so simple and common as water sustained all life. To follow the in-
tricacies and vagaries of a sparrow in flight, and marvel as it moved
without concern above the troubles and greed of the men who cheated
and quarreled as they bartered without cease, dawn to dusk, at the
markets beyond the well.

Each moment of contemplation of another aspect of creation was a
moment of joy for Ben-Aryeh. The God of the Jews was a mighty God,
and Ben-Aryeh had gladly given a lifetime of service to that God.

Thus, even now, by contemplating God's glory to endure the waiting and to fulfill the task set upon him, he was serving his magnificent
God, and that eased—only somewhat—the resentment and dislike for a
man he did not know.

As for this man he finally spotted, the Roman who carried a walking staff with a red rag tied upon it to identify himself? Could such a
heathen—bound by the pleasures of eating and drinking and the pursuit of the flesh that Romans put before matters of the soul—even
dimly understand that every breath a man took was a breath granted
by God?

Ben-Aryeh knew the man would be looking for him but saw no reason to get up from his blanket. He had the advantage and would use it to
learn what he could about the man.

Where was the man's retinue? Ben-Aryeh wondered. Surely a man
of his importance would not travel without one of substantial size. Another man, much shorter and obviously Jewish, followed closely behind, holding the reins of two donkeys. Was this all? And had the
Roman actually chosen to travel from Caesarea on something as humble
as a donkey?

Yet there appeared to be no one else. No bodyguards. No bearers of
chests of luggage. No slaves or sycophants dogging his footsteps.

He was a man in a simple tunic, wearing no obvious jewelry. He seemed relaxed as he moved through strangers in a strange city in a strange land. A good observer would notice, however, that he held the walking staff not as an aid to plod forward but in such a manner that he could swing it suddenly with ease, either as a protective block or an aggressive thrust. Although his manner of dress was not what Ben-Aryeh had expected from a Roman with political power, the manner of readiness was indeed what Ben-Aryeh would expect of a man who'd once been a military hero.

The man moved past the well that was the focal point of the city, modestly averting his eyes when the women glanced up at him. When he passed, several of the women exchanged glances and comments.

Yes, Ben-Aryeh grudgingly agreed, he is a handsome man too, with close-cropped dark hair that spoke of one who didn't give much attention to appearance or the fact of his attractiveness, a man with a calm, dignified presence that would draw the attention of the fairer sex. Ben-Aryeh had no doubt the man took advantage of this at every opportunity.

A small boy dressed in rags chased another, each laughing loudly. The boy in front turned to shout and ran squarely into the man's thighs; he fell backward and began to sob. While the second boy backed away nervously, the man knelt, set his staff on the ground, helped the boy up with both hands, and dusted him off. Then the man picked up his staff and walked away without looking back. The boy opened his small hand and shouted with delight, then ran to find his friend to show him. A gift from the Roman? A coin?

The man was much closer now. He scanned the middle-aged men who stood and gossiped in small groups near the walls around Herod's fortress.

Ben-Aryeh knew what the man searched for, of course. Another man with a red rag tied to a walking staff. His own staff was on the ground, the crook of it deliberately hidden by the edge of the blanket he sat upon.

Ben-Aryeh sighed and pulled the walking staff out from the blanket. He used it to get to his feet.

The man saw the red rag tied to Ben-Aryeh's staff and paused.

Didn't smile.

Didn't frown.

Just paused and waited. And watched with dark eyes as Ben-Aryeh approached.

✝ ✝ ✝

Ben-Aryeh had his share of enemies, but only one who hated him so much that he was now contemplating the satisfaction of hearing stones thud into Ben-Aryeh's body at a formal execution.

This was Annas the Younger—former high priest, named as such because he was as famous and feared in Jerusalem as his father, Annas.

At the moment Ben-Aryeh rose to greet Vitas in Sebaste, Annas, the enemy who wanted Ben-Aryeh dead, was in humble clothing, riding a donkey in open countryside, gradually descending on the road from Jerusalem to Caesarea.

Annas had put Jerusalem's gates behind him a few miles before, and in that short amount of travel, the foliage had turned from faded reds and browns to vibrant greens. The soil had become less rocky, the cliffs along the road less steep and abrupt, until Annas neared the town of Givat Shaul, where the road to Caesarea split to the road going north to Sebaste.

Ben-Aryeh had been looking for a red cloth on a man's walking staff; Annas scanned his surroundings intently for three piles of rocks, side by side by side in a discreet triangle.

Annas was extremely conscious of his clothing, made from a poor man's rough hemp. It itched him in the heat, but what bothered him more was that he'd forsaken the prestigious outer garments of priesthood that would at least mark him as a man of consequence to passing strangers.

Pride was an integral part of his psyche, and Annas had no problem admitting it. For example, Annas was a handsome man and knew it. He had a face that shone warmth when he smiled and intimidated when he scowled. This, too, he knew and enjoyed. Yet, among all that he loved about himself, Annas was also proud that he could set aside pride for the sake of expediency. Today, it was more important that he appear as merely another traveler of many on this road.

When he saw the triangle of piled stones, Annas jerked the donkey's halter to force it to stop. All along, he'd been trying to decide what he should do when he saw the piles that marked this section of the road, and he still had his hesitations.

He looked at the crooked gully with high walls that led down to the road here. Noted that within fifty yards the gully twisted out of sight. Noted that this part of the road was lost in a dip, so it was invisible to travelers a half mile ahead or a half mile behind.

It *was* a good place for an ambush. He felt watching eyes on him and wondered if it was his imagination. He twisted on the donkey's back, looking in all directions for a sentry who might alert highway thieves waiting to kill a traveler here.

Except for the wind whistling through dried bushes, it was quiet. Vultures soared overhead, and Annas shivered at the sight.

So close to Jerusalem. Yet so isolated.

Would he have this opportunity again? The chance to destroy Ben-Aryeh in this manner?

No, he told himself. The old Jew hated to travel. It might be years before he left Jerusalem again. This, then, was so important that Annas knew he could not chance the slightest mistake. It was worth the risks to ensure the matter would be handled as promised.

So he turned his donkey off the road and moved along the gully, letting the donkey pick its way among the boulders and stones of the dried streambed.

And, as soon as he was out of sight of the road, Annas found himself surrounded by bandits armed with leers and curved swords.

✠ ✠ ✠

At thirteen, she'd been forced into marriage with her uncle, and at twenty became a childless widow, moving back into the isolation of the palace of the Herods. Unkind and unverified rumors said that her brother wanted—or treated, depending on which rumor one believed—her as a wife.

She was Queen Bernice, great-granddaughter of Herod the Great, almost certainly one of the most beautiful women of the Jews, and even more certain than that, the most hated and least respected.

And, perhaps, the loneliest.

Without children. Without husband. Without a true friend who might listen to her thoughts or troubles. Along with any luxury that she might choose at a whim, her wealth and ranking had become a metaphorical and literal barrier to the common ground that humans beyond it shared in their joys, triumphs, and agonies.

There were nights—because during the days and evenings she could distract herself with social events and spending of wealth —that Bernice toyed with the idea of running away, pretending that she was an escaped slave, throwing herself into the maelstrom of life. But she knew those were simply fantasies, because she believed herself too weak to take such a leap over the barrier.

Yet the loneliness had gnawed upon her soul for so long that she'd made a religious vow, one of fasting and prayers until the Passover. She'd taken the vow because she hoped for a sense of spirituality, hoped for anything to ease the unease.

What she did not expect, halfway through the thirty days of religious vows, was a visitor at dawn in the Jerusalem palace, one that had awakened her with the point of a knife pricking into the skin of her throat.

He stood in front of her now, and when he pushed aside the cover over her window, she discovered a partial reason why he'd been able to move through the corridors of the palace undetected. He wore the uniform of a guard.

But he was no guard she'd seen before.

He was a young man, she guessed in his twenties. Bearded. A gaunt face, eyes lost in the sockets of his skull. Yet his body radiated fanatical power, as if an inner force gave him the energy of ten men.

In his right hand he held the knife he'd used to threaten her in the darkness. In his open left hand, he held a round stone hardly big enough to cover his palm.

He averted his eyes and coughed.

Bernice looked down. While her open gown had not exposed too much of her body, there was still enough bare skin to make the young man blush.

She took this as an encouraging sign. Along with the respectful salutation, he was worried about her modesty. Perhaps captivity and the judgment he had promised did not mean her death.

Bernice adjusted her gown as well as she could with hands hampered by bound wrists. "Why are you here? Whatever you expect to gain, the guards will eventually know about this. And then . . ."

"Then my execution?" His question came with a smile of sorrow. "My life matters less than what brought me here."

"What is your name?" Bernice needed to make a bond with this young man. Needed to charm him. Whatever it took to save her own life.

He answered by putting the round stone in her palm and closing her fingers over it.

"What is your name?" she repeated.

"You will find out soon enough," he said. "Hold the stone in front of you."

Off balance, which was an unfamiliar sensation for her, Bernice lifted her hands and held them out in front of her.

"Heavy?" he asked.

"No." Lifting and holding the stone took little effort. It was a small ball, with her fingers nearly covering it completely.

"Good." He shifted his knife from one hand to the other. "You see, I have a simple task for you. If you fail, I punish you by taking your life."

Again, an unnerving calmness. The light had grown, and the intruder's eyes were no longer lost in the shadows of his sockets. She saw unwavering determination.

"And what is my task?" Bernice asked.

"You listen to my story."

"That is all?"

"Continue to hold the stone out in front of you as I speak."

"That is all?" Bernice asked again.

"That is all. But you must hold the stone aloft until I finish my story. If you drop it or fail to hold it in the air before I finish, I will become your executioner."

✠ ✠ ✠

Ben-Aryeh approached Vitas slowly. Ben-Aryeh was not yet an elderly man, but twinges in his legs from sitting motionless for so long reminded him that too soon would come the days when the light of the moon and stars would be dim to his eyes. It was good, Ben-Aryeh reminded himself as he began the task he had reluctantly accepted in

Jerusalem, to serve God in a man's youth, for when the silver cord was snapped, when the golden bowl was broken and the dust returned to the earth, a man's spirit returned to God who gave it.

"You are the one," the man said. Not as a question.

Ben-Aryeh stared back. Silent. Resentful. "'I saw a fourth beast, terrifying, dreadful, and very strong,'" Ben-Aryeh said after a pause. "'It devoured and crushed its victims with huge iron teeth and trampled what was left beneath its feet.'"

Ben-Aryeh had chosen this passage for the irony of it. Certainly this Roman could not realize he was quoting from a prophecy of Daniel, describing his own people and how they continuously devoured the Jews in fulfillment of the ancient words.

Ben-Aryeh added, "'It was different from any of the other beasts, and it had ten horns.'"

"Greetings," the man said. Without introducing himself. As if he, like Ben-Aryeh, was irritated by men who spoke to hear themselves speak. They each had the walking staffs with a red cloth. They'd each exchanged the passwords. There was no need for introduction, then, because each already knew of the other from the instructions they had received from different messengers.

Ben-Aryeh, of course, knew the Roman's name was Gallus Sergius Vitas.

Who would know Ben-Aryeh's name as well.

Ben-Aryeh's instinctive dislike of the Roman lessened at the man's quietness. Only slightly.

"You have something for me," Vitas said.

Ben-Aryeh carried a leather pouch, held by a strap over his shoulders. Wordlessly, he reached inside and found the narrow and tightly bound scrolls. Both he'd been instructed to deliver to Vitas. He passed them to Vitas and again watched him.

Vitas glanced at both seals. Ben-Aryeh did not take it as an insult. A man who did not examine the seal of a message was a fool.

Ben-Aryeh expected Vitas to set the scrolls aside, perhaps step back to the man who tended the donkeys, and place it in one of the travel bags to read later.

Instead, Vitas broke the seal of the first, the scroll from Queen Bernice. He glanced through it and nodded.

Before breaking the seal of the second, he moved away from Ben-Aryeh for privacy and read the other scroll quickly. Then started again and read it more slowly. Finally, he rewound it and tucked it inside his tunic. "Thank you."

Ben-Aryeh nodded his head slightly in acknowledgment, curious as to what Vitas had expected in the letter. Ben-Aryeh had his own guess about the second scroll.

While Queen Bernice had been the one to hand it to Ben-Aryeh, the seal bore the mark of the household of a Roman who lived in one of the most luxurious mansions in the upper city. An elderly man named Bellator. Rome's auditor of the tax collections of the city, who had arrived in Jerusalem less than six months earlier. The same Bellator who, it appeared, willfully ignored rumors about his wife and an ex-gladiator who served as bodyguard in their household.

"I hope we can spend as little time as possible here," Vitas told Ben-Aryeh. "I must leave for Jerusalem immediately."

Now Ben-Aryeh truly was curious. If the scroll did not contain bureaucratic necessities from one Roman official to another—as Ben-Aryeh had originally decided—what kind of personal matter had become such an urgency that the man didn't even bother to hide it?

✝ ✝ ✝

In the gully, with the bandits surrounding his donkey and silently eyeing him like wolves surrounding a lamb, Annas forced himself to be disdainful of them. It was a way to keep his fear at bay. He noted the gaps in the teeth of many of them. He was downwind, and the smells of their bodies washed over him.

He could not entirely quell his fear and was very glad not to be in his priestly garments. Annas ran his fingers through his long thick hair, a subconscious gesture that, as always in stress, reminded him of his handsome appearance and calmed him.

"I am not the one you want," Annas said.

"Don't tell us what we want," the biggest of the bandits growled. He was the largest man Annas had ever seen, and he tapped the side of his sword against his leg impatiently. "Perhaps we'll tear you apart then search for gold and silver."

The leader nodded, and three bandits moved forward. Before Annas could open his mouth to protest, they punched him across the legs and chest with a violent swiftness that toppled him from the donkey. He fell on his back, splayed across the ground.

Another put his foot on Annas' neck and began to apply pressure. Sharp stones on the ground dug into his back.

Annas gagged and flailed, then realized his fight only ensured more pressure on his neck.

The leader ambled over to Annas and placed the tip of his sword on Annas' belly. If he leaned into the sword, it would pierce Annas and pin him to the ground.

"Any gold?" the leader asked. "Tell me now and save us the effort of looking for it."

Annas tried to speak, but the foot on his throat choked him.

The leader gave that bandit a look of irritation, and the pressure eased. "Any gold?" the leader repeated. "Speak now or die."

✛ ✛ ✛

The man with the knife looked at Queen Bernice and smiled a sad smile. He gestured at the stone in her hand. "Seems effortless to hold, does it not?"

"What is your name?" Bernice asked again. She returned the man's smile. Anything to pierce his shell of detached calm.

"Matthias. But that doesn't matter. Nor does the name of my village. What does matter is that at one time I believed a man's actions could make a difference in this world."

The stone in Bernice's hand had begun to warm from contact with her skin. It was smooth and felt comfortable.

"Brigands raided the roads near our village regularly," Matthias continued. "Soon, few of our people dared to travel. We received no visitors either. Word reached us that many of the other small villages nearby faced the same danger. A few weeks ago, I took it upon myself to visit Caesarea, to appeal to Gessius Florus for help. I went through my village, telling others of what I intended, and collected a purse for the expenses. Most in the village were happy to contribute. All wished me well. I traveled to Caesarea. I sought an audience with Procurator Florus."

"He was not sympathetic," Bernice said. She was fully aware of the corruption of Florus.

"I did not get a hearing. His servants took my silver and promised I would see him. But the promises were hollow, and later I learned he wasn't even there. During my time in Caesarea, I learned more about the man that Rome had sent to rule us."

Matthias stared at his knife blade as he spoke. "Albinus, the former procurator, was a thief. I was told when he learned that Florus would replace him, Albinus cleared the prisons by taking bribes from all except those who deserved the death penalty. He infested our land with the brigands who plagued our village. And Florus—"

The man in front of Bernice sighed. He stood and stripped off the uniform of a palace guard. Beneath it he wore simple peasant's clothing, freshly washed. He threw the guard's clothing into a heap at the far corner of the chamber.

"Do your arms tire?" he asked as he paced in front of Bernice, the knife held loosely in his left hand.

With the stone out in front, her arms did feel the strain. Only slightly. She felt a quivering of the muscles on the underside of her upper arms.

"Florus," Matthias said as if he had not interrupted his own narration, "made Albinus seem benevolent in comparison. I was told that he joined in partnership with the brigands that Albinus had released, taking a share of their spoils. In short, even had I been granted an audience with him, my request for soldiers to patrol the roads near our village would have been ridiculed. So I decided . . ."

Matthias stopped at the window and stared down on the city of Jerusalem. He did not speak for minutes.

Bernice took advantage of his inattention and lowered her arms to her lap. She was surprised at the relief her muscles felt. Who would have guessed that a stone that small could take so much effort?

"A city of great beauty . . . ," Matthias mused, speaking to himself.

"And this view of the temple. So magnificent. I would have wished for my children someday—" His voice broke. He remained motionless, as if trying to regain his composure.

Bernice watched for his slightest movement, ready to lift the stone before he turned to her.

"I decided that if Rome could not help," he said, still facing away from her, "perhaps the king and queen of our own people would intercede. After all, if the people of Judea are happy with their rulers, it will remain at peace. And a peaceful Judea is a Judea that will send yearly tribute to Rome. And if Caesar is happy with the taxes received, Caesar is happy to continue to grant authority to the royalty. I am only a peasant, but have I judged the political situation correctly?"

He turned, knife still in his hand.

She was able to lift her arms in time.

He looked at her hands to assure himself that she still held the stone in front of her.

"What you say is true," Bernice answered. She stared at the stone in her hands. It was her life. And perhaps her death. "But if it was an audience with me or my brother that you sought, this is not the way to do it."

Although she'd rested her arms, they immediately began to quiver again. She hoped the trembling wasn't visible to Matthias.

"I'm afraid it is too late for that audience," he answered. His voice was dead. "Far, far too late."

Sitting against the wall, Bernice shifted her weight.

He noticed. "Your arms. How much longer can you hold it out like that? Until I am finished saying what I need to say?"

"Your story," she said. She was at the point where she desperately realized he needed to finish it. Soon. "Why are you here if it is not an audience you seek?"

"This audience is not the one I intended as I returned to my village to report what had happened in Caesarea. I wanted to see my family, to rest with my wife and two children. Then come here to Jerusalem. But a day after my return, a gang of brigands openly attacked our village. They were led by a certain man named John, of the village of Gischala. I pray to God that someday you will have him punished."

"That is why you are here? Because this John of Gischala raided your village?"

"It was not a raid. It was a warning to other villages. You see, the people of my village had united. Our attempt to appeal to Florus had failed. But that failure did not matter. It was our resistance to the brigands that drew John of Gischala into our village."

Matthias stopped. He moved to the window again and stared at the temple as he spoke. "And since it was I leading our villagers to unite, John of Gischala stormed my household. There were ten with him. He wanted to not only punish me but for my fate to be a warning to others."

Because he was staring down on the city again, Bernice dropped her hands in her lap. Her arms felt as limp as strands of dead grass soaked in rain. She could not believe how much the weight of such a small stone strained her muscles.

"Ten men," Matthias said. "Armed with short swords. You realize the significance of that, don't you? Short swords. Roman military weapons. Jewish brigands, armed by Rome. Ten plus their leader. Against me and my wife and two children. They bound me, just as you are bound."

He turned away from the window. Quickly. Too quickly.

Bernice tried raising her hands before he noticed, but the movement caught his eye.

He knelt beside her and placed the point of the knife beneath her chin. "You have failed. My story wasn't finished. Yet you could not bear the weight of the stone. You have brought your death upon yourself."

✠ ✠ ✠

Market sounds of Sebaste carried into the courtyard where Vitas and Ben-Aryeh stood in the shadow of Herod's fortress. While Vitas had watched silently, Ben-Aryeh argued with the guard to find a captain with the authority to allow them to visit prisoners.

Vitas did not want this distraction to keep him from immediately leaving for Jerusalem, but the message he'd received from Queen Bernice upon stepping off the ship in Caesarea had directed him to go to Sebaste, to the prison with Ben-Aryeh and learn what he could from the men they needed to see.

Until he'd received the message from Maglorius, the one bearing the seal of the Bellator household delivered by Ben-Aryeh, Vitas had believed there was little urgency to reach Jerusalem. But that had changed after reading the warning from Maglorius.

As Ben-Aryeh argued, Vitas observed, trying to get a sense of the man. As a fighting man himself, Vitas could see that although Ben-Aryeh appeared diminutive and vaguely comical as he walked, he was a man with a deceptively strong build. He had short, bowed legs, mismatched to a muscular upper body that should have belonged on a much taller man. Nor was his face particularly handsome. This was a kind way of describing the peculiar angles of his cheekbones and nose. Yet there seemed to be the power of a lion caged inside him. Vitas decided this was a man who deserved respect.

The guard departed to find his captain, and Ben-Aryeh leaned on his staff, the red rag now removed. "It would have been easier if you'd made it plain to the soldier that you have been sent to Judea by Nero. We would not be forced to wait like this."

"Fama malum quo non aliud velocius ullum," said Vitas.

"Ah, Latin," Ben-Aryeh said. "We're to stop speaking Greek between us as a common language? Good then. Let me reply in Hebrew. It will reduce what we can say to each other, and I might actually be able to endure any time I spend with you."

"I apologize," Vitas said. "The saying slipped out. What I said was that nothing moves faster than gossip."

But Vitas had established something. This cagey old Jew didn't understand Latin or preferred for Vitas to believe it. He'd keep watching and learn which it was.

"You," Ben-Aryeh said, "Nero's right-hand man, afraid of gossip?"

"I would prefer that Florus did not know I was here."

"So," Ben-Aryeh said, "you are not an official delegate sent by Nero?"

The man pretended surprise, Vitas thought. Through earlier correspondence, Vitas had arranged from Queen Bernice to assist him in all matters in Judea. Ben-Aryeh was obviously here because she had sent him to meet Vitas. The first scroll from the Jew, from Queen Bernice, had simply explained that if Vitas was here to learn more about the Roman rule of Judea, he should hear directly from the Jews of Caesarea the reason for their imprisonment in Sebaste. Did Ben-Aryeh know this already? Did Ben-Aryeh know the reasons Vitas had given the queen for his trip to this province?

Regardless of what Bernice told Ben-Aryeh about the circumstances, Vitas thought, *he would have seen in the market square that I traveled alone and certainly come to the conclusion that there was no official delegation.* Which meant the old fox was asking the question merely to see how much Vitas was prepared to divulge.

"This fortress," Vitas said, knowing that by evading the question he was also giving Ben-Aryeh a certain type of answer, "Herod built it. Impressive. Who did he need protection from?"

Ben-Aryeh did not follow Vitas' gaze to the high walls of thick stone blocks. "He imprisoned his own sons here. Alexander and Aristobulus. This was well after he'd murdered their mother, Mariamne. One of the enemies of Herod forged a letter implicating his sons in a revolutionary attempt. So he had them strangled. Herod also wanted the firstborn in every household killed on the day of his own death, so that the entire nation would be in mourning."

Ben-Aryeh finally looked up at the walls. "Who did he need protection from? His own people. Do you still find it impressive?"

"Only the hatred in your voice."

"You Romans have set up the politics well in our land. You give our royalty its power. Our royalty, in turn, has the authority to capriciously give or revoke the position of high priest. Our religious leaders, then, cannot cross the royalty without crossing Rome, and so Judea remains helpless against you because our royalty and our religious leaders always remain at odds. Do you have any idea how many priests Herod slaughtered, backed by Caesar's sword?"

"At least two hundred in three separate bloodbaths."

Ben-Aryeh glared at Vitas. "So now you let me lecture you on Jewish history when you think you have the answers?"

"Rome keeps extensive archives," Vitas said. "The Jews have a fascinating history." Vitas gave Ben-Aryeh a wry smile. "Very little seems to get solved by discussion."

"Our bloodshed is a result of Rome meddling in our affairs." Ben-Aryeh glared again. He turned his gaze from Vitas, making it clear that the conversation was over.

Vitas enjoyed the old man's prickliness. It was refreshing after years of sycophants in the imperial palace.

"I intend to begin my journey to Jerusalem immediately after we leave the prison," Vitas told Ben-Aryeh.

"You told me that earlier. I am not a stupid or forgetful man."

Vitas remained polite. "I repeat it to let you know that you are welcome to travel with me, if your affairs here are finished as well."

Ben-Aryeh snapped, "My affairs were to visit the men in prison. I have delayed that because I was forced to wait for you."

"Forced?"

"What Rome wants, Rome gets," Ben-Aryeh said, still looking beyond Vitas. "Your pressure on Bernice became pressure she in turn placed on me. If I please her, there are fewer difficulties at the temple. And that makes it easier to serve God."

"You have my apologies for Bernice's request. This detour to Sebaste was not my idea. I, too, am here at her suggestion."

Ben-Aryeh swung his head to examine Vitas, as if trying to decide whether Vitas was speaking truthfully.

"You could have visited the prisoners while you waited for me," Vitas continued.

"Nothing travels faster than gossip. Like you, I have no desire for Florus to know I was here until I am well on my way home. But unlike you, I don't have the protection of Nero, so my fear is well justified. What is your reason for fear?"

"Perhaps it isn't fear," Vitas said. Then, even knowing that Ben-Aryeh's resentment would probably make all of their conversations into a clash, Vitas went ahead and repeated his earlier invitation for the old Jew to travel with him to Jerusalem. "After all, if there is nothing else to hold you here and if you want to be gone before Florus discovers what—"

"I will make my own arrangements to travel. I prefer solitude to your company."

Vitas smiled. "I detect an insult there."

"Roman, don't get me started. Furthermore, we would have nothing to talk about. And lastly, I wouldn't want anyone seeing me with a Roman."

"Of course," Vitas said, amused.

"Listen to me, Roman." Ben-Aryeh pointed the tip of his staff at the sun. "You cannot make it to Jerusalem by nightfall. And I have no intention of staying at an inn with you."

"There's a full moon. I understand the road is clearly marked. I'll travel through the night."

"A full moon gives just as much light for brigands as it does for travelers," Ben-Aryeh countered.

"Why such concern if you'll be traveling without me?"

"A dead Roman will only cause more trouble for the Jews, especially one of your political stature."

"What did Bernice tell you about me?" Vitas asked.

"It's of no consequence."

Because now Ben-Aryeh was engaged enough to be looking at Vitas, Vitas raised a quizzical eyebrow.

"Whatever she tells me," Ben-Aryeh replied to his unspoken question, "I refuse to believe."

"Because she has a history of lying," Vitas asked, "or simply a history of lying to you?"

"Roman, you're a fool if you traveled all this way alone, without knowing whether you can trust her."

"I don't need to trust her. As you said, it's in her interest to keep Rome happy. She'll help me as needed."

"As needed. Am I to understand you want more than what you have represented to her?"

The old man was playing him, and Vitas enjoyed it. "What has she told you about that?"

Back full circle.

"It's of no consequence," Ben-Aryeh answered.

"Of course," Vitas said, "because you don't believe her. Nor, apparently, do you believe me."

"You are a Roman. Of wealth and political power. Why should you care what Florus does to the Jews?"

"She told you that, then. That I am here to investigate his methods of governing."

Ben-Aryeh grunted an unintelligible reply.

"If you don't believe her *or* me, then why are you here to help me?" Vitas enjoyed, too, the chance to be direct in return. In Rome, a wise man spoke obliquely. The commitment of directness could prove to be fatal if Nero chose to dislike what was said, whereas subtlety always left room for negotiation later about what had actually been said.

Ben-Aryeh shrugged. "What did Bernice tell you about me?"

"It's of no consequence."

"Roman, you may find yourself amusing, but I don't."

"Well, then," Vitas said with a smile, "at least I've provided you another reason to travel alone."

✝ ✝ ✝

"If you kill me," Annas gasped from his helpless position in the gully, "Florus will crucify you."

The mention of Florus was like a slap across the bandit leader's face. He squinted. Sounded less certain when he spoke. He gestured frantically at the man who held Annas on the ground to step aside. The leader helped Annas to his feet.

Annas tried to hide his relief.

"What do you know of Florus?" the bandit asked.

"That he gave you orders to wait here in ambush for an old Jew," Annas said.

"And if he did?"

"I am here to confirm for Florus that you have obeyed his orders and are waiting."

"We are here, aren't we?" the leader said. The others drifted away in boredom. Annas obviously was not prey. Or danger. "Tell him that."

"I will," Annas said, very glad that the mention of Florus had brought such immediate deference. "Repeat for me the instructions."

The leader shrugged. "Today or tomorrow or the day after, a young man coming from Jerusalem will pass by this spot on the road. We will know him because he will be leading a donkey and a foal, each without saddlebags. He will carry a walking staff and set it by the three piles of stones to let us know he is the one we expect. We are to let him pass by. On his way back to Jerusalem, he will be accompanied by an old man, and will ensure for us that no other travelers are near them. And then . . ."

The leader tilted his head and stared at Annas. "Has Florus changed his mind about what we are to do then?"

"No." Annas smiled. "Do what you do best."

✛ ✛ ✛

Matthias pulled Queen Bernice's hair, tilting her head backward. Her throat was exposed, the way a lamb's throat is bared at the altar.

"I . . . I . . ." Bernice was accustomed to sending servants running in terror. Now she could not even find her voice.

"Try it again," Matthias said, knife still beneath her chin. "Hold the stone in front of you. As long as it remains in the air, I will let you live. When it drops, I slit your throat."

"Please . . . ," she croaked.

He pushed the point of the knife harder. "Do as I say!"

Bernice lifted the stone again. It now felt like one of the massive rocks of the temple wall.

Immediately her hands wavered.

But her life depended on holding the stone high!

She found new strength. A low groan escaped her as she strained to hold her arms up. Yet against her will, they began to sag downward.

"This is a cruel torture, is it not?" Matthias whispered, pulling her hair even tighter and caressing her throat with the knife's blade. "You know that eventually you won't be able to hold the stone. Yet you are so desperate for life that you strain to keep it aloft for just one more breath."

He was right. Her every thought was consumed with the stone, with finding the energy to stave off death. Tears rolled down her cheeks. Her groan grew louder.

How much longer could she hold the small stone in front of her?

Then she decided. If she was going to die at the hands of this calm madman, she would ensure his death with hers. Her last strength would be to yell for her guards.

The stone fell downward as her arms collapsed.

She opened her mouth to scream.

Yet he was faster. He clamped a calloused palm across her mouth and cut her short. "Yes," he said. "Now you are dead."

With his hand over her mouth, he pulled her head into his chest. He touched the full length of the blade against the cartilage of her throat.

She was totally helpless.

In the moments before dying, her head against his ribs, she heard the beat of his heart. She smelled his odor and clothing, not entirely unpleasant. She saw the blue of the sky through the window. Tasted the copper of fear. And wondered why death and oblivion suddenly seemed simple.

Yet the blade was not drawn against the softness of her skin.

"I do not want you dead," Matthias told her. Without warning, he pushed her away. Unharmed. "Say nothing to draw the guards or truly I will kill you before they arrive."

Her own heart thumped so loudly that she expected the noise alone would draw the palace guards. "What is this brutal game you play?" She was angry. Confused. Relieved.

"For you, it is only a game. Because you still live." He closed his eyes. "I want you to imagine my small household. Unadorned and simple. Yet filled with love. My wife. A four-year-old daughter. A two-year-old son."

Matthias looked at her. Through her. As if he were peering into her soul. "Have you ever picked up a sleeping child to move him?"

Bernice shook her head.

"It is a wonderful thing. The child is so full of trust that he remains asleep. You rise with the child in your arms, and the child's arms wrap around your neck. Trust and love. Worth far more than this palace. That is what I had."

Matthias sat down beside her, as if he could no longer bear the weight of his own burden. He slumped, arms around his knees. His voice was muffled. "That day, John of Gischala and his ten men captured me and my family. He gave me the stone you held. Gave me instructions to hold it in front of me. Promised that as long as I could keep it aloft, my daughter would remain alive."

Matthias lifted his head. Tears streamed into his beard. "I held that stone out in front of me and begged for the life of my child. She had never seen me afraid, and my fear brought her to a panic. I only had eyes for her, my little girl. She tried to rush forward so I could hold her and comfort her as I had always done. The brigands held her back. I stood there, knowing she would live for only as long as I could keep the stone aloft. When one arm grew weak, I clutched it with the other. When both arms lost strength and the stone fell . . ."

In his grief, he could not speak. He fought for composure.

"Remember, Queen of the Jews," he finally said, "how badly you wanted to keep your own life when you believed I would kill you if you set the stone down. Know this. A parent would gladly give his life a hundred times over to save his child. Badly as you wanted to live, infinitely more was I desperate to keep them from killing my girl. Yet, when my arms collapsed, in front of my eyes they drew the knife across my little daughter's throat. Her blood spilled at my feet, even as she gasped to me for help until she could no longer gasp."

Matthias lifted his eyes to Bernice. "Can you comprehend my pain? Then? Now?"

She nodded. Horror and grief filled her for what the man had endured.

"My son," Matthias said. "First they allowed my arms to rest. Then they placed the stone in my hand again. Told me he would remain alive for as long as I could hold the stone in front of me. You will never understand the agony in my muscles as I fought and fought to keep my arms from betraying me and my son's life."

His voice became ice. "You know the inevitable. His blood joined the blood of my daughter. Then my wife's blood added to theirs. On the ground where we had played and sang songs. Then, most cruelly, they set me free to live with the memory of how I failed my family. Of how their eyes met mine as the brigands reached to open their throats. They wanted me alive so others would learn of what happens to those who oppose them."

Bernice took in a breath. Realized she had not taken one in far too long.

"That, my queen, is why I am here. Because of what you have allowed to happen to your people."

"I . . . I . . ."

"Make whatever excuses you want. If you are blind to what Florus is doing, you are blind by choice. While you live in luxury in the palaces across the land, all the sons and daughters of Abraham cry out for help. I accuse you of ignoring the plight of your people. That is why I am here."

"Did Ben-Aryeh send you?" she asked, her voice barely above a whisper. If any person in Jerusalem could have found a way to get this man into her private chamber, it would have been Ben-Aryeh. "If it was him, tell him I am sorry. That I will now honor the agreement we made two years ago. Tell him I will send a man out against the Christians to prove their claims about the Nazarene false. Tell him I will—"

"No one sent me," he said savagely. "I am here because of the memory of how I watched my family die. I am here because Florus is on his way to Jerusalem and I want you to meet him. Find a way to force the Romans to free us Jews from the injustice. You are queen. You have that power."

Just as quickly, Matthias lost his anger. Broke to his sorrow and bowed his head. Without wiping the tears from his face, he struggled to his feet. Overlooked the city. Spoke facing away from her.

"I am a Jew. God hears my cries. But He cannot take away my grief. If He allowed suicide within His laws, I would have ended my life that day. I have nothing to live for. Worse, living is what hurts me most. Who am I without my wife and children? Who am I with the knowledge of how and why they died? I don't want life but cannot end it myself. Yet I long for death."

"Whatever you want," Bernice said, "I will get for you. You will face no punishment for bringing me this story as you did. I will seek vengeance, justice. Your home will be returned. Your village compensated. This John of Gischala will die."

"What I want from you is a promise," Matthias said. "A promise that you finally accept your queen's duty to help your people. We have all suffered too long. Abused by the Romans. Ignored by our leaders. Help us. Ensure that Florus punishes the brigands instead of encourages them."

"You have that promise." Yes, Florus was on his way to Jerusalem. With an army. But she guessed he was appearing in force as part of the politics of ruling Judea. She would extend a dinner invitation to him. Cajole him. Threaten him. Do what it took to help her people.

Bernice thought of years earlier when she'd made similar promises to Ben-Aryeh for a different reason. Promises she now intended to fulfill. "You will have that," she repeated. "And more."

"More? Then I ask you for one last thing."

"Anything."

"Cry out to the guards."

"What?"

"Call them into your chamber."

"You will not be punished," Bernice repeated.

"Call."

She did.

"Louder!" he commanded.

"Guards! Guards!"

Footsteps clattered in the corridor.

Before the door opened, Matthias pulled a rag from his waistband. He wrapped it quickly around her mouth, tying it behind her head, gagging her.

Then the door crashed open. Four guards filled the doorway.

Matthias raised his knife, as if to kill Bernice. Then hesitated. And held his position as he waited for the guards to draw the obvious conclusion.

The guards rushed forward, raising their swords.

"No!" Bernice screamed into the rag. But her efforts to stop the guards were useless. They saw her life in danger and had only one response.

The swords came down.

THE FOURTH HOUR

Annas saw the full extent of the armies that Florus had assembled, and despite his satisfaction that Florus had made the arrangements with the bandits as agreed, Annas the Younger now raged.

At the temple, around subordinates, he had no hesitation at openly venting his frequent rages.

But here, out in the open countryside, with the hills rising on all sides instead of temple walls, he was forced to keep his rage hidden. Against the assembled discipline and equipment of two cohorts of Roman soldiers, he knew his personal strengths, reputation, and power as a former high priest of the exalted temple were inconsequential.

The soldiers passed and the horsemen came in waves on their way to Jerusalem. They towered above Annas on their fully armored beasts, and it irked him further that he sat on a donkey instead of on one of the magnificent stallions belonging to the temple stables.

He'd traveled five or more miles out of Jerusalem on the main road from Caesarea. Here, down from the mountains, the road was wide and safe. At any given time, one could look back or ahead and be reassured by the sight of at least a dozen other travelers moving along the road. Some walked; some rode horses or donkeys or camels. Some were on wagons or chariots. When it had stopped to encamp the afternoon before, a day's march from Jerusalem, there had been ample time for those continuing to the city to bring the word the army's presence.

An army!

Now, pushed off the road by the mass of soldiers and forced to plod on uneven ground on a stubbornly slow donkey, Annas felt his rage build. He maintained his outer air of calm until the end of the lines neared, with Florus, the Roman procurator of Judea, at the rear, seated in a chariot and holding the reins of a horse, while slaves on each side walked along and held umbrellas to shield him from the sun.

Annas dismounted and immediately caught the attention of Florus.

Florus barked an order to a nearby centurion. The order was repeated down the line, and both cohorts of soldiers stopped, remaining solidly in formation.

This was a light coat of balm on the rage inside Annas that at least his presence stopped a Roman army.

As Annas stepped closer to the chariot, Florus dismissed the slaves, another indication to Annas of his status with the procurator. Whatever would be said in their conversation was important enough to remain between the two of them.

Florus was a large man, a former soldier. His political astuteness and his rise to power as procurator of Judea were based on a simple system. Bully those who could be bullied, bribe those who couldn't, and learn quickly which category best suited his opponent. But whatever athletic poise and grace he'd once had as an active soldier had been lost to years of living far too well. There was redness in his face, broken veins in his nose. Wide as his shoulders were, the melon belly that strained at his toga dominated his upper body. His hair was thick for an older man—he was in his fifties—but he'd had it dyed black, and because of the deep wrinkles on his face and his sagging jowls, the vanity made him look like a parody of himself.

"Unusual," Florus remarked with a smirk when they had their privacy. "The prophet has left his mountain."

It was useless to try to explain to Florus that a temple priest was not a prophet, for he made the same inane comment every time he met Annas, something that fueled his anger. As a result, some of the rage inside Annas slipped past his efforts at composure. "An army—especially one of this size—was not part of our agreement."

"Where are your usual fawning niceties?"

Annas bit back the sharp obscenity that first leaped into his mind. He knew that in the eyes of Florus, he was not much more than the donkey on which he'd ridden from Jerusalem to meet the army.

Furthermore, Annas was acutely aware that Florus wielded a heavy stick. Despite Annas' high ranking among the Jews, Florus would have no hesitation at snapping an immediate command to have him slain on the side of the road. Especially here, where not a single witness would contradict any story that Florus wished to concoct.

On the other hand, the unchecked power in Judea that Florus was capable of sharing also meant he dangled a considerable carrot. Annas continued to play the role of donkey in pursuit of that carrot of power.

"The fawning niceties?" Florus repeated, raising his eyebrows.

"It is a hot day," Annas said. "I'm sure you would rather not have any of your time wasted."

"Don't presume to guess what I want or don't want."

Annas itched in the peasant's rough clothing. He felt a drop of sweat on the end of his nose. He resisted the impulse to wipe it away.

Florus waved for one of the attendants to approach. "Give this man the umbrella," he barked. "Then leave again."

Annas accepted it from the slave, surprised that Florus would be so considerate. The shield from the sun felt wonderful.

"Shade me as we speak," Florus said with another smirk, casually resting the reins between his fingers. "Then I won't have any concerns about the length of our conversation, will I?"

Annas felt his stomach clench with involuntary protest. He was a former high priest and would have the position again one day!

"Shade me," Florus repeated.

Still, Annas hesitated.

"Think of all you have risked and all you can lose if I speak a single word in Jerusalem about our arrangements." Florus was calm. "Shade me."

Annas finally shuffled forward and held the umbrella above the chariot, squinting as the heat of the sun baked him again.

Florus smiled in mock appreciation. He drew water from a leather pouch and drank deeply. "Now," he said expansively when he finished, "remind me of our arrangement. Not the one that involves the old Jew you want ambushed. But the arrangement that matters to me."

"It did not involve an army like this approaching Jerusalem."

"The public demonstrations you arranged against me were substantial, almost too much. If I let it go without some sort of token punishment, I risk a true rebellion as your people lose their fear of me. Or worse, word of it would get back to Nero, and he would remove me for being too weak."

"Seventeen talents of silver!" Annas said. "From the temple treasury. Gifts given by our people to God. We only agreed to five talents; your soldiers took seventeen! Worse, they spent an entire afternoon loading it in the temple square in view of all the people. If we hadn't protested as we did, the people would have thought we were in collusion."

"Your family and the temple officials have been in collusion with Rome for decades," Florus remarked. "Are the Jews truly so stupid that something like your demonstrations against me will actually distract them?"

Annas did not answer.

"Listen to me," Florus said. "I will appear with this army in Jerusalem. You and the puppet you control as a high priest will posture and bluff. I will posture and bluff. You don't have enough military power to send me away. And I don't have enough military power to actually take control of the city. Thus, after enough posturing and bluffing so that each side appears the winner, I will take the army back to Caesarea, and your people will believe that once again you have protected them. That I decided to bring an army to add to the show is meaningless. In principle, I am fulfilling our arrangement, am I not?"

"Along with the two talents of that silver set aside for me."

"Are you implying I have forgotten?" Florus' smile disappeared and he stared hard at Annas. "Or that I am going to steal it from you?"

"Only saying it aloud to satisfy myself."

Florus drank more water and pointedly did not offer any to Annas. Not that he would have accepted. Pigs—and Florus was definitely a cousin to the four-legged ones—were repulsive to a decent Jew. It would be like sharing a livestock trough.

"Something bothers me," Florus said. "You went to great trouble to meet me here in the countryside. We could have easily discussed all of this in the privacy of the palace where it would be expected for you to visit me."

"I come to warn you, and not even for this would I make any exception and send a messenger." Annas would never put any of his communications with Florus on a scroll where it could fall into the wrong hands and destroy his career and his life.

"Warn me?"

"Word of your arrival has already reached Jerusalem, of course. There will be a delegation waiting for your army outside the city walls. They intend to shame you with applause. I only say this because if your soldiers break rank and respond with any force, a true riot might break out. Any escalation would make it difficult for both you and I to simply, as you said, bluff and posture."

"I see," Florus said. He shifted his eyes to the horizon and then back to Annas. "I see indeed."

"There is something else," Annas said. "A matter of interest to you that we have discussed on other occasions."

"Yes?"

"Gallus Sergius Vitas finally arrived on ship."

"Vitas!" Florus lurched forward so quickly that the chariot shifted position, and Florus had to jerk the reins to keep the horse in place.

"According to my spies, he is now in Sebaste," Annas said. "With Ben-Aryeh. Your enemy has now joined with mine."

✚ ✚ ✚

"Do you think today you will die?" Quintus Valerius asked his sister. "I would very much like to watch. I've never seen anyone die before. All I know is what you and Maglorius have told me about the arenas."

Quintus was small for a seven-year-old. His hair was oddly dark and had been since birth. He wore a light blue tunic and laced boots of supple leather. In each hand he held a short wooden sword. He stood in sunlight, at the edge of the shadow cast by the courtyard wall, and squinted as he looked at Valeria and waited for her answer.

"Let me assure you that my death will not be a spectacle," Valeria answered her brother. "The only women to die in the arena are thieves or murderers or slaves." Valeria paused and sighed dramatically. "No, my death shall be dignified." Another pause. "And very, very tragic."

When only fifteen, Valeria had already begun to chalk her face and redden her lips and cheeks with the sediment from red wine. She'd looked fully woman then. Now at twenty, her beauty was amazing. She dressed accordingly. Her silk overdress was cream, with lace adorning the hem. She reclined on a couch in the shade, her bare feet tucked beneath her, her elegant sandals on the mosaic of the courtyard floor beside the couch.

"Will it be today?" One of the characteristics that marked Quintus was persistence. He had a beguiling mixture of naivety and self-assurance, and Valeria adored him. She also found it amusing that, intelligent as he was for one only seven, he did not quite comprehend death. To him, she knew, death was simply a different form of going on a journey. No different than if she actually left Jerusalem for Rome to marry an old man she'd never met, which her parents were forcing her to do. Quintus didn't understand death's finality, for he adored her as much as she adored him. If he really understood that once she was dead she would be gone from him forever . . .

With that, Valeria frowned. Her father and stepmother understood full well the consequences of death, yet they were prepared to watch her wither away in their very household as she starved herself to death.

Valeria replaced her frown with a set jaw. She'd show them. Especially her stepmother, a woman hardly a decade older than she, a woman who had obviously married her father for his wealth.

"Will your death be today?" Quintus repeated. "I would hate to miss it."

"Perhaps," Valeria answered, hiding the amusement that replaced her anger at her parents. If only Roman women weren't legislated to be under total control of their father. Quintus and his earnest innocence always did this for her. Took her mind from her troubles.

"Perhaps?" Quintus seemed vaguely disappointed. "You can be no more certain than that?"

Valeria pretended to give it thought. "I am feeling very weak. But as this is the first time for me, I have no experience in judging the symptoms. Perhaps one can feel on the verge of death for days before it actually arrives."

"Days?" Quintus echoed. "I can't wait that long."

"Days," she said firmly. "Perhaps even weeks."

"I believe that I would slit my wrists and open my veins," Quintus said gravely. "I can't bear the thought of missing one meal, let alone going without food for days and days and days."

"What would you know about bloodletting?"

Quintus snorted, indignant. "I am no longer an infant, in case you have forgotten. I am capable of listening as Father and Mother speak. Last month, all they discussed was how Nero had sent the invitation for suicide to our uncle in Rome and then confiscated his estate."

"You were visible to them as they had that discussion?"

"Of course not. How would I have learned anything?" He shook his head at Valeria's stupid question. "I know enough to choose a bloodletting in a steam bath. Wine first to the point of drowsiness. Then vertical slits up the inside of the wrist. Painless. Without inflicting upon the family all this suspense of wondering when you'll starve to death. It is difficult to make plans when no one knows when you will die."

"Well, forgive me," Valeria said, amused. "I shall search for a way to make my suicide convenient for you."

"Thank you," Quintus said. "I don't like listening to you and Mother argue."

"If you were older, you would realize those arguments were the point. Although I choose death over Rome, I would prefer to begin eating once again. Think of how little good it would do for me if Father changed his mind only after my life's blood began pooling at my feet. Once a knife cuts through the flesh of a wrist, it is difficult to repair the damage."

Quintus seemed to consider the politics of it as he rubbed his forehead with the back of his right hand, still gripping his *ludis*, the wooden practice sword. "Oh," he finally said. "Now I understand."

Another characteristic that Valeria adored about her younger brother was his short span of attention to any given subject.

Like now.

It was obvious that he felt he'd given enough thought to the issue of the arranged marriage she was determined to avoid, for without warning, he turned and charged a wooden dowel fixed in the center of the courtyard—a gladiator's training device called a *palus*—and screamed as he approached. He was shorter than the dowel and attacked it with the joyful fierceness of a ferret darting at a mouse.

His wooden swords were similar to the ones that gladiators used in practice. His had been fashioned in miniature so his small fingers could grasp the handles. The firstborn sons of rich Romans were accustomed to having every whim indulged, and Quintus had demanded that the swords even include his name carved on each blade.

"Death to the *retiarius!*" Quintus shouted, slashing at his mute opponent, rattling the dowel in quick succession, one hand after the other, then jumping back as if eluding a counterattack.

He raised his arms in triumph, pointing his tiny wooden swords at the blue sky above. "I am the greatest of *dimachaeri* to stride across any arena!"

In the silence, Valeria spoke again, calling across the courtyard. "And now the most dead. Must I remind you that a retiarius is far more fleet than the wooden dowel you cannot even scar with the greatest of your blows? The retiarius has a net, Quintus, and will snare you first, then spear you to death with his trident."

Quintus returned to the wooden dowel to inspect for marks to prove she was wrong about the scars he had tried to inflict. Not finding any recent ones for which he could claim credit, he faced her and glared.

"The dimachaeri, as you can plainly see, have two swords." He shook them at her as he approached on his short legs. "Each easily capable of blocking the thrust of a trident. Furthermore, you failed to note that the retiarius had already cast his net and missed me completely. I had run him to the point of exhaustion and knocked his trident to the ground before stepping in to administer the deathblows."

He cocked his head. "Listen."

"I hear nothing," Valeria said.

"The cheers of the crowd. In my time, I have defeated them all. Thracians, Samnites, Gauls. Today is the day that the emperor grants my freedom. I step from the arena famous and rich."

"Dreamer. When you are a man, you will sit in the arena as a spectator, like Father, blinking in the sunlight because of all your hours inside counting money. A collector of taxes for the emperor. You will be rich but not famous. Another respected administrator following the tradition of the Bellator branch of the Valerius clan. Father would never allow you to sell yourself into the bondage of the arena. Gladiators die, Quintus. Like kindling that disappears after a burst of flame."

Quintus raised his swords again and strutted a victory walk, taking him to the far end of the courtyard. He turned and called to his sister, "What of Maglorius? He was no kindling."

Valeria opened her mouth to retort but realized she had no reply. Thinking of Maglorius, she smiled. He'd filled many of her daydreams. "Finally," she said, "your first triumph of the morning. I must concede your point. Maglorius did the impossible."

She waggled a finger at Quintus, calling as loudly as he had called across to her, "Remember, however, even the great Maglorius has aged and now serves our family. What would you rather be? Master or employed freedman?"

Quintus was given no opportunity to answer, and Valeria instantly regretted her words and the volume at which they had carried.

A slave entered the courtyard, carrying a tray with bread and diced fruits and a small pot of honey. Valeria's stepmother, Alypia, followed the slave. Behind them both was Maglorius, ex-gladiator.

Immediately, because of how all three stared at her, Valeria knew her question to Quintus had carried loudly enough for Maglorius to overhear.

✠ ✠ ✠

The soldiers escorted Ben-Aryeh and Vitas to the prison in the depths of the walls; guarded on all sides by swords and clanking breastplates, it seemed to Ben-Aryeh that he too had been imprisoned. He consoled himself with the reminder that because the visit was early in the day, he could begin travel back to Jerusalem immediately after hearing from the prisoners, and be home with his beloved Amaris the afternoon of the next day.

Ben-Aryeh moved up to the bars of the prison cell. Five old men were crowded into a small cell that smelled like aged vinegar from their sweat.

Two moved forward as they saw Ben-Aryeh, recognizing him immediately. The other three remained in dejected heaps at the back of the cell.

"Did Florus grant our freedom?" Abel asked. The hope in his question spoke highly of Ben-Aryeh's political reputation.

Abel's look of hope was all the more pitiful because of the exhaustion that sagged the already deep wrinkles on his face. He was shorter than Ben-Aryeh, bald, and had a thin crooked nose. Ben-Aryeh knew the man, as he knew the others. All were leading Jewish citizens of Caesarea.

"I haven't had a chance to speak with him," Ben-Aryeh said. He wasn't here to try to get their freedom, but it didn't seem like the time to tell them that.

He pointedly referred only to himself, making it clear that Vitas was not a partner of any kind. The men in the cell remained focused on Ben-Aryeh, probably assuming that Vitas was merely a servant.

"Florus left Sebaste two days ago," snorted Tadmor, a man with thick gray hair who had obviously been a strong man in his youth. "When we were in Caesarea, Florus came here to Sebaste. When we came here from Caesarea to see Florus, he put us in prison and returned to Caesarea. He is playing games. Removing the leaders from the city to make it safe for him to return to his palace there."

It wasn't safety that Florus wanted. Ben-Aryeh knew this. Yet it wasn't the moment to tell them this.

Tadmor shook his head and made a sour face. "Florus. I pray his death will occur soon but be slow and full of agony."

"Ah yes," Ben-Aryeh replied. "That is a sure way for clemency. Insult Rome's procurator in front of soldiers who have been most certainly instructed to bring back every word of our conversation to him."

One of the soldiers shifted from one foot to the other; Ben-Aryeh took that as an inadvertent acknowledgment and smothered a smile of satisfaction at the accuracy of his guess.

"The way Florus has treated us is unjust," Tadmor said. "I don't care who knows what we say."

Ben-Aryeh cared. He knew Florus would not be the only person to hear reports of this conversation. No, even against such an enemy, the Jews of the temple were divided.

Vitas remained silent, watchful.

Tadmor shook his fist at the soldiers behind Ben-Aryeh. "Florus has already chosen what to do with us. Nothing we say—or even any argument put forth by the great Ben-Aryeh—will make any difference."

Ben-Aryeh ignored the sarcasm in Tadmor's voice. Had he been in Tadmor's place, he too would be in a foul temper, ready to lash out at anyone.

"Reports of the events in Caesarea reached us in Jerusalem," Ben-Aryeh said. "I understand you believe the riots were orchestrated by Florus."

"Believe?" Tadmor exploded. "It is not a matter of belief. But fact."

"Confirm for me those reports. That is why I am here."

"You are aware of our synagogue," Tadmor said. It seemed he was the only one with the energy to still be outraged. Abel had moved to the back of the cell to sit with the other three, defeat in his bowed head and shoulders. "And aware that the adjoining land is owned by a Greek."

"Also aware that you have repeatedly offered him a much higher price for that lot than it is worth," Ben-Aryeh said.

"One would think the Greek was in the employ of Florus," Tadmor said. "Not only has he continuously refused our offer, but when he began to erect workshops on our site, he laughed when we accused him of trying to insult us. Then he agreed it was exactly his intent. Worse, he deliberately left us a very narrow approach to our place of worship. Some of our youths—"

"I am proud of them!" Abel had found the strength to interrupt. "At their age, we would have done the same."

"Hotheads," Tadmor said. "Violence is no solution to violence. They tried to stop the workers. Unsuccessfully. It touched off a riot, but Florus sent in soldiers to protect the Greek."

"As he should have," Ben-Aryeh said. "We must work within the law." This was advice Ben-Aryeh wanted to reach Florus through the listening soldiers.

"Abel believed in another solution," Tadmor said. "An expensive one and totally useless."

"We all voted on it!" Abel rose, then collapsed again. "I should not be held responsible alone."

"Eight talents of silver," Ben-Aryeh confirmed. "That was the solution."

"So you've heard," Tadmor said to Ben-Aryeh. "Eight talents! Protection money that Florus agreed to take to stop the builders."

"Some would call it a bribe," Ben-Aryeh observed. "And a considerable one at that."

Eight talents!

"Either way, Florus was happy to accept it." Tadmor sounded bitter as he spoke. "And equally happy to retire here to Sebaste, leaving the riot to grow out of control on the following Sabbath."

Tadmor described it in detail. When the Jews arrived at the synagogue to worship, the entrance was nearly blocked by a sturdy young Greek who had placed a pot, bottom side up, in front of him. On this pot, he was sacrificing birds with an obvious smirk on his face, knowing this defilement would be unacceptable to the Jews. That this young Greek had foreseen their reaction was obvious when other Greeks sprang forward from where they had been hiding to defend the first Greek from attack. Within seconds, the riot had grown out of control, and the elder Jews, fearing the worst, had seized their precious copy of the Law and fled to Narbata, some seven miles away. From there, they had sent a delegation to Sebaste.

"As you can see," Tadmor finished, "we are that delegation. When we arrived to remind Florus of the eight talents of silver that he had accepted to protect us, he threw us in jail for taking a copy of the Law out of our synagogue! That man is provoking us beyond compare. How does he expect to keep the peace?"

Ben-Aryeh felt great sympathy for these tired old men. Sympathy for their physical state. And a greater sympathy for what they didn't understand about Florus.

"Think about what happened during the previous Passover," Ben-Aryeh said. Softly. "Don't you see? Florus doesn't expect to keep the peace. It's quite the opposite. What I fear is that he wants war."

"War?" Tadmor repeated in his prison cell.

Ben-Aryeh nodded.

A war in Judea would conceal all of the atrocities that Florus had committed since the departure of Albinus. If Rome were distracted by trouble that seemed to come from the Jews, Florus would be safe from criminal prosecution.

"My advice then," Ben-Aryeh said, "is to use all your influence to keep the people in your city from rising up against him again. You cannot allow any more riots. The entire nation depends on you ensuring that Florus has no excuse to let his soldiers loose."

This was not only Ben-Aryeh's advice but the collective advice of all the city leaders of Jerusalem. While Bernice had requested that he meet Vitas in Sebaste, that collective advice was the main reason that Ben-Aryeh had been sent. To counsel the Caesarea leaders for peace at all costs. If war began, Jerusalem would suffer most.

"You haven't heard." Tadmor seemed to be strangely amused and watched Ben-Aryeh closely.

"There is more to the events?"

"Ah yes." Tadmor stroked his beard. "You've spent all that time in travel. You haven't heard. When I tell you, just remember your own advice to us. And when you return to Jerusalem, see if you can get the people there to show the restraint you seem to so easily preach to us. See if you can prevent a riot in your own city."

"We will abide by the law." Again, Ben-Aryeh was speaking less to Tadmor than he was to Florus through the soldiers who would eventually report to him.

"We shall see whether you abide by the law," Tadmor said. "If, as you say, it is war that Florus wants, it explains the message that reached us today from Caesarea. Yesterday Florus assembled two cohorts of soldiers and began to march to Jerusalem. The soldiers should arrive there today."

☩ ☩ ☩

Gallus Sergius Vitas! Here in Judea?

Florus stared across the wheel of the chariot at the smug look that Annas didn't bother to hide, as if he'd enjoyed delivering the information. Florus kept the reins looped between his fingers and pressed his hands against his thighs to prevent them from shaking.

Gallus Sergius Vitas.

Florus knew of the family, of course, proud as it was of a lineage claimed to stretch back to the founding of Rome. Florus had met Vitas at various functions in Rome and hated him with the distrust that a corrupt man has for an honest man.

"Insperata accidunt magis saipe quam quae speres," Florus thought. *What you didn't hope for happens more often than what you hoped for.*

If there was a single man of influence in Rome who Florus hoped would never step into this land, it was Gallus Sergius Vitas. War hero. Patrician of unquestionable lineage. Favored by Caesar on one side and by the Senate on the other. A threat to neither. And a man known for integrity and uncompromising loyalty to the empire. Whatever reports he brought back would be seen as absolute, unbiased truth.

Nor could there have been a worse time for Vitas to enter Judea, not given what Florus needed to keep hidden from Rome.

Judea was a backwater, yet it had its riches to be plundered, as previous procurators had discovered. But it was far from the imperial courts, and for a century Rome had been accustomed to loud incessant complaints from the Jews, which meant that any complaints a new procurator generated did not seem unusual. In short, as long as a decent amount of taxes continued to flow from Judea to Rome, a corrupt procurator here could make a vast fortune, virtually untouched by the restraints of Roman law.

But Florus had been too greedy, worse still than his predecessor Albinus, and his recent abuses had gone too far. So far, in fact, that Florus desperately needed to find a way to cover up all his activities over the last eighteen months. He'd long anticipated an inquiry and had set aside considerable funds to bribe any representative sent by Caesar.

Any representative except for Vitas.

And from reports that Annas had gleaned from his extensive spiderweb of spies and passed on to Florus, Florus knew that Vitas had not intended to make this a public visit but a surreptitious one. Did it mean that Nero already had doubts about what had been happening in Judea?

Insperata accidunt magis saipe quam quae speres. Any other man but Vitas and any other time, and Florus would be totally safe from punishment by Nero. It wasn't the atrocities against the Jews that Nero would find offensive, but the fact that Florus had been siphoning far more tax money than he sent to Rome.

Even so, Florus might narrowly be able to escape the punishment of Rome. The army in front of him was his solution.

Annas did not know it, of course, but he was a fool. He actually believed that he would receive the silver that Florus had promised.

Just as Annas was stupid enough to trust that Florus had come with an army for the sake of appearance. His warning about making sure the soldiers didn't break rank and cause a riot outside the city walls? Florus appreciated it, simply because now he could tell a centurion to ride ahead with fifty horsemen and do everything possible to antagonize the Jews so that any report would make it look like they were the ones responsible for the riot he hoped would ensue.

Tomorrow Florus would have two cohorts in the city. And he had a plan to get another two cohorts inside. Then the balance of power within Jerusalem would tip in Florus' favor, and he could assure himself of such turmoil in the land that he would be absolved of any blame for treating the Jews as harshly as he had.

Yet if Vitas gathered enough information in a short period of time . . . and if Vitas lived long enough to get back to Rome with that information . . .

At these thoughts, Florus felt a rumbling within the depths of his bulk and a spasm of his guts. He told himself it was not fear but something he had eaten the evening before. He never liked or fully trusted food cooked in encampments, and this was the price he paid for leaving the luxurious accommodation in Caesarea.

"Sebaste? Vitas is in Sebaste?" Florus said to Annas. "You assured me that . . ." He paused to lick his lips. His mouth was dry—too dry. And it wasn't the heat of day up here in the mountains. "You assured me that he intended to go to Jerusalem and that he would see nothing of the countryside."

Florus left the rest unspoken. That Vitas would see nothing of the havoc Florus wreaked on the people of the countryside. That he would hear no reports to indicate how much wealth Florus had been stealing from the Jews.

"You know that Ben-Aryeh's assistant spies on him for me," Annas said.

Florus nodded impatiently. Annas always found a way to brag about his arrangements.

"I've learned from him, since you and I last spoke, that Ben-Aryeh is in debt of some kind to Bernice, a debt that forced him to meet Vitas in Sebaste at her request."

"Bernice and Vitas? That is new to me."

"And to me," Annas said. "I've just learned it from Ben-Aryeh's assistant, who listened in on his conversation with Bernice. There's an ex-gladiator in Jerusalem, a friend of Vitas. This ex-gladiator has served as a go-between for Vitas and Bernice, so no government officials would realize that she is helping him."

"What could she gain from Vitas?"

"The right-hand man of Nero?" Annas countered.

Florus grunted acknowledgment of the obvious benefits for Queen Bernice.

"The real question," Annas said, "is what does Vitas want from Bernice that he is prepared to owe her political favors?"

Florus grunted again. "And you will find that out for me?"

"That is why you need me, remember?"

Annas had become too confident. Which meant he had sensed that Florus was rattled by the name of Vitas.

"Perhaps you should remember that I've had occasion to order a soldier to split a man open," Florus said. "At which point I step on one end of his entrails and force him to walk away with the rest unwinding behind like a rope."

"I'm aware of those stories," Annas said, probably not as calmly as he wanted to appear.

Florus enjoyed his petty revenge. "You'd be surprised at how far a man can walk like that. And how long it takes for him to die. It can be amusing actually, watching some try to pile everything back inside. One man—"

"Yes, yes," Annas said. "I'm aware of those stories."

Annas ran his fingers through his hair several times. To Florus, it was an annoying habit.

"I want to know what Vitas wants here in Judea," Florus commanded. "Or better yet, I want him dead. Find someone to kill him in Jerusalem."

"A murder in Jerusalem would seem suspicious, would it not?" Annas said. "On the other hand, you already have bandits watching and waiting for Ben-Aryeh. It is more than likely Ben-Aryeh will travel back

from Sebaste with Vitas. Simply send them orders to kill Vitas also. To
Rome, I'm sure, he'll appear to be a tragic victim of random thieves."

"Vitas . . . dead," Florus agreed after a moment's thought. "It does
have a pleasant ring to it."

✜ ✜ ✜

"Remember, however, even the great Maglorius has aged and now serves our fam-
ily. What would you rather be? Master or employed freedman?"

Valeria's stepmother, Alypia, stood with Maglorius. Maglorius held
Valeria's stepbrother, Sabinus, who had been born about a year earlier
to Alypia. Both Alypia and Maglorius gazed directly at Valeria.

It was an indication of Maglorius' status in the household that Valeria
felt regret that he had overheard the insult. She would have had no such
concern about the feelings of any other of the servants, slave or not.

In the past, Maglorius might have erupted in sudden fury, something
he'd been famous for, even when he'd been their slave, not a freedman.
This, too, spoke of his status in the household. Any other would have
been flogged for such an action, yet it was something he had done regularly since joining the household.

But Maglorius had changed in the last weeks. He seemed more at
peace, and the simmering fury had disappeared. He smiled first at
Sabinus, then turned to Valeria and spoke calmly. "Stultus est qui stratum, non equum inspicit . . . ," he said.

After years among the Romans, he spoke almost without an accent.
His prowess had taken him to arenas across the world, including the one
in Smyrna where he'd survived a sword attack before retiring and ac-
cepting a contract with the Bellator family as a bodyguard.

His statement in the courtyard now pierced Valeria. "Stultus est qui
stratum, non equum inspicit." *The man who inspects the saddle blanket in-*
stead of the horse is stupid.

"M-Maglorius," Valeria stuttered, "I did not mean . . ."

". . . stultissimus qui hominem aut veste aut condicione aestimat," he
finished. The corners of his mouth twisted upward slightly, to let
Valeria know he was truly not angry as he completed his answer to the
question she posed to Quintus about master or slave.

"Yes," Alypia said, repeating the proverb that Maglorius had spoken, as if Valeria were too dense to understand it without help. "The man who inspects the saddle blanket instead of the horse is stupid; most stupid is the man who judges another man by his clothes or circumstances."

But Valeria did not need her stepmother's help. She'd understood full well what Maglorius had meant. Master or slave or freedman serving the wealthy—each was simply a condition of fate.

Valeria felt her cheeks burn, and she wanted to squirm at Maglorius' gentle reproving of her rash question to Quintus. There was something about Maglorius and the way he gave her his attention, something that she could never quite define, something that made her secretly wish he was a Roman of dignified descent and she was a woman of another household. Maglorius always treated her with dignity and respect. She adored the way he showed love to Quintus, too, as if Quintus were his own son. Maglorius who had fashioned Quintus toys by carving them out of wood. Maglorius who had mesmerized her with tales of faraway lands and of noble warriors. Maglorius who was so gentle with the baby Sabinus he now held.

"Of course," Alypia continued archly, "if Maglorius were a better man, he would resist using Latin in a way that makes his barbarian heritage obvious. Disgraced soldier, slave, gladiator, freedman, and now bodyguard. His airs are pretentious and fool nobody."

Valeria did not know what had come over her stepmother in the last weeks. She'd changed too. Alypia was irritable and almost vicious in most of her remarks about Maglorius. She had begun treating Sabinus meanly, leaving the little boy in the charge of servants and slaves. Maglorius, in turn, had simply shrugged off her barbs and given extra attention to the little boy.

Just as now. Maglorius turned and began walking away from Alypia.

"Come back," Alypia said to Maglorius. "You haven't told me what request the messenger from the royal palace brought to you."

"It is of no concern to you," he said.

"So," Alypia said bitterly, "the rumors I've heard about you and Queen Bernice are true?"

Valeria was startled. Maglorius and Queen Bernice? That filled her with dismay. Bernice was the most beautiful woman in Jerusalem. If the rumors were true, how could Maglorius resist her?

"My affairs with Bernice are of no concern to you," Maglorius repeated.

Alypia waved him away, apparently weary of argument. Valeria knew better. Whenever her stepmother lost an argument, she pretended she didn't care in the first place.

Maglorius moved to Quintus and, still holding Sabinus, murmured a few instructions on using the wooden swords. Quintus appeared happy to try the new moves.

Alypia pointed the slave, who had been standing discreetly at the edge of the courtyard, toward Valeria.

The slave set the tray of food down on the couch beside Valeria and bowed slightly before escaping the courtyard and the argument that was sure to follow.

"Eat," Alypia commanded her stepdaughter.

Alypia was now thirty. Her hair was naturally dark, matching Valeria's, but like many other Roman women, she wore a blonde wig made from the hair of slaves from northern Gaul. Her fingers were full of ornate gold bands, her earrings made of bunches of emerald beads. On each wrist was a gold bracelet formed into the shape of a snake. There was no mistaking her wealth or her position as the wife of a high-ranking Roman administrator.

"Eat," she commanded again.

"Oh, Mother," Valeria said, rising and throwing her arms around Alypia's neck, "thank you so very, very much for releasing me from the bondage of an arranged marriage."

"I have done no such thing." Alypia pushed herself loose from her stepdaughter's embrace and forced Valeria back onto the couch.

Valeria pretended surprise. "I don't understand. You asked me to eat."

"It was not a request. It was a demand."

"But, Alypia—" Valeria kept the same pretended surprise in the tone of her voice—"you know my vow. I'll starve myself to death before I allow myself to be sent to Rome to marry an old man. Why would you ask me to eat if I am still expected to do this?"

"Don't play games with me," Alypia said.

Valeria dropped her act. "This is not a game. I would rather die than marry against my will."

Even as she spoke, Valeria felt her mouth water at the sight of the bread and the honey and the fruit.

"Child, child, child," Alypia said.

"Obviously I am not a child if I am expected to become a wife."

"You are a child if you refuse to acknowledge the ways of the world. A woman must marry well. From within the marriage, there are ways of persuading a husband to do what the wife wants, without the husband knowing he is receiving such guidance. And ways for a wife to find pleasure outside the marriage."

Valeria closed her eyes. She knew what her stepmother would recite next. That no Roman father would let a child, let alone a daughter, dictate his decisions. That Roman women were helpless unless married. That a Roman marriage was simply a contract of convenience, often broken if something more convenient arose. That Romans feared and ridiculed the concept of consuming love.

Yet . . .

What was it she felt for Maglorius? Something so deep and profound, something that she must keep hidden at all costs. Something—

A slap across her face jolted Valeria from her reverie.

"Listen to me, child!"

Valeria was stunned. Not once had her stepmother ever struck her. Valeria brought her hand to her face in disbelief, lightly touching the skin of her cheek that was hot with pain.

"I will not apologize," Alypia said. "You are foolish to refuse to eat." She smiled unpleasantly. "After all, most stupid is the man who judges another man by his clothes or circumstances. Accept what life has given you, just like your hero Maglorius has." Alypia let the word *hero* drip with sarcasm.

"Like Maglorius," Valeria said, "I refuse to live a life of falsehood, manipulating the people around me to suit my selfish will."

Alypia's eyes narrowed with an emotion close to hatred. "Is this what you think of me? False and manipulative?"

Valeria let her silence be the answer.

"As for false and manipulative," Alypia said, "there are things about Maglorius that would surprise you greatly. He . . ." She stopped herself.

"He what?"

Alypia glanced to the corner of the courtyard, where Maglorius squatted beside Quintus.

"He what?" Valeria persisted. "If you are going to make accusations . . ."

"Silence, child," Alypia hissed. "You have everything. Wealth, position, and whatever your heart desires."

"To have an old man touch me like a lizard crawling across my skin?" Valeria asked. "How repulsive. You want me to accept my fate because that is exactly what you chose. If you can't be happy you don't want anyone else to be—"

This time, Valeria's eyes were open. She saw her stepmother raise her hand. Valeria accepted the blow with defiance and did not touch her stinging cheek. She stared resolutely at her stepmother for several moments, then leaned forward, lifted the tray of food, and turned it over, letting the dishes crash into pieces on the courtyard floor.

✠ ✠ ✠

Ben-Aryeh caught up with Vitas just before he reached Sebaste's city gates. He discovered that Vitas didn't even have a servant to help him with the two donkeys. "You travel alone," Ben-Aryeh said.

Vitas was in the process of mounting one donkey. A rope tied the second to the first. "Except for these two." Vitas indicated the donkeys. Smiled. "Good listeners, both of them."

"What of the servant I saw with you in the market?"

"Someone I found in the city to watch the donkeys while I looked for you."

"I see," Ben-Aryeh said. He glanced down the road, where it disappeared around the curve of a hill barren of trees. There was no way around it. Florus was in Jerusalem! Getting to Jerusalem as soon as possible outweighed his pride.

"I'd like to travel with you," Ben-Aryeh said. He waited for the Roman to remind him that barely an hour earlier he'd given a couple of insulting reasons why he had no intention of sharing the journey.

Vitas surprised him with graciousness. "I'm glad you changed your mind. You take this donkey then. The other one has a habit of setting its feet down hard, as if it knows how to hurt a man's back."

"Are you suggesting that I am too old to deal with——?"

"You're my guest," Vitas said. "It's that simple."

Again, graciousness when Ben-Aryeh was determined to be rude. Ben-Aryeh hoped that the Roman would soon give him reason to dislike him again.

They departed Sebaste.

Together.

THE SEVENTH HOUR

To meet Maglorius, Queen Bernice had smudged her face with dirt and grease and bound her hair tightly. She'd thrown on the loose clothing of a man and covered her head and face with as much of her headcovering as possible. She'd worn clothing that the Greeks preferred, and since Greeks were clean-shaven, her lack of a beard aided in her disguise.

She felt vaguely ridiculous, disguising herself in this manner, as if she were playing a child's game or rather what she imagined children might have played, for the memories of her own childhood consisted of continuous doting by various servants and no time alone or with other children.

Yet she saw no other way to accomplish what she felt necessary, and she was gambling that among the thousands who moved through the Court of the Gentiles, there would be no particular reason for anyone to examine her too closely.

Still, because of her disguise and because she had no servants or bodyguards in attendance, she felt vulnerable and exposed as she walked down Solomon's Porch. It was a tremendously long covered porch— roughly a quarter of a mile—with hundreds of columns and arches, running north and south at the eastern perimeter of the Temple Mount.

Shaded from the sun, the man she sought stood as arranged, beneath the fifth arch of Solomon's Porch, counted from the southeast corner. As she'd also arranged, he carried two empty turtledove cages and leaned against one of the marble columns that supported that arch.

Because she was simply one among hundreds upon hundreds in the busy Court of the Gentiles, Bernice did not expect that Maglorius would notice her on her approach.

Now that she knew he was there at the appointed time and had not left because of impatience, she slowed to give herself time to examine him, something she enjoyed doing at every opportunity.

There was something about the calmness of his square face that immediately intrigued her. As she walked closer, she was again drawn by the fascinating history written across his face, by the cheeks and forehead that bore long-healed scars, forming slashes of paler skin against his tanned face. The power suggested in the stillness of his alertness stirred desire within her, a siren of desire that she immediately put aside.

As she drew close, he spoke to her. "You make a very poor man," he said. "Walk with less elegance."

It shouldn't have surprised her that Maglorius would see through the disguise. "Thank you for agreeing to this meeting."

"You said you have some information that is of great urgency."

Normally, she preferred banter with him, but she had not lied about the urgency, so she became direct. "It is Florus," she told him. "He approaches Jerusalem with an army." Maglorius was one of the few aware that Bernice had spies who reported any activities of the procurator, so she didn't explain how she knew of what Florus intended."

"The entire city knows this." He smiled softly so that his next words did not seem like a rebuke. "I see no urgency in that information."

"I need you to protect me as we join those who go out to greet Florus and his army."

"You have never struck me as one overly concerned about the Jews," Maglorius said.

Queen Bernice drew a deep breath. Fought the sympathy and regret and outrage that threatened to overwhelm her as she remembered how and why Matthias died in her chamber.

"I can promise you," she told Maglorius, "that has changed."

✛ ✛ ✛

When Sebaste was well behind Vitas and Ben-Aryeh, the Roman broke the silence of their travel with a question. "Could Jerusalem fall?"

"Certainly not!" Ben-Aryeh said, instantly insulted. "Have you seen its glory? The eighth wonder of the world, some call it. The temple is atop a mountain that is like a fortress unto itself. How dare you ask such a question. If you think that Florus and a couple of cohorts could . . . could . . . could . . ."

It was rare for Ben-Aryeh to be speechless, but for the upstart Roman to imply that Jerusalem was like any other outpost of the empire was an outrage.

"It isn't Florus I'm thinking of," Vitas replied, as if deep in thought and oblivious to Ben-Aryeh's reaction. "But whoever will have to clean up the mess that he might start."

"Send five legions," Ben-Aryeh shot back stoutly, believing this was a discussion that concerned national pride. "Or even five more. Ten legions could lay siege, and Jerusalem would be standing twenty years later. The city's walls are unbreachable. It has a water source that can't be quenched. And the storehouses of food inside the city would last for years."

"What I meant was—"

Ben-Aryeh was glad to be angry with this Roman again and would not be stopped. "Every Jewish man in the city would give his life in protection of the temple. You Romans think you can conquer all, but there is no city in the empire that would fight so hard and so long to resist."

"I see," Vitas said mildly when Ben-Aryeh stopped to catch his breath. "You're aware that the empire may lose battles but has yet to lose a war."

"Judea could be laid waste entirely," Ben-Aryeh answered, "but Jerusalem will still be standing. Remember, you are talking about the dwelling place of the one true God. I suggest we end this discussion before—"

"I now understand why your history is filled with so many rebellions," Vitas said. He was grinning, which made Ben-Aryeh even angrier. "Here we have two grown men unable to pass a pleasant afternoon's journey without political speculation."

"Enough! What you call politics is a matter of deep faith to us. God will preserve His holy house until He has sent the promised Messiah." Ben-Aryeh reined in his donkey until it stopped. He allowed Vitas to gain at least twenty yards ahead before he prodded his own donkey forward again.

There, Ben-Aryeh thought, *I will follow at this distance the entire journey.*

It gave him satisfaction when Vitas half turned and noticed the separation.

"Nor," Ben-Aryeh called out, "do I intend to get any closer."

"Suit yourself," Vitas said in good humor.

More reason to hate the Roman. Nothing seemed to upset him. Then Ben-Aryeh half heard something from the Roman. "What was that?" Ben-Aryeh had to shout.

"I asked a question about your prophets. And the temple."

"I know that," Ben-Aryeh said. He kicked the donkey in the ribs. "I just want to be sure I heard correctly."

He reached Vitas again, aware that he'd just broken his promise to remain at a distance and aware once more that he had been forced to overcome his pride. But if this Roman had actually asked what Ben-Aryeh thought . . .

"So," Vitas said, "my question was this. What does it mean 'the abomination that causes desolation,' spoken of by the prophet Jesus?"

"False prophet!" The words shot like venom from between Ben-Aryeh's clenched teeth. "To respectable Jews, He was a false prophet!"

The force of Ben-Aryeh's fury was not lost on Vitas. Yet Vitas persisted. "By referring to the abomination, this Jesus refers to Daniel. Another of your prophets, correct?"

Who is this Roman? Ben-Aryeh could only stare.

Vitas shrugged. "I thought you, of anyone, would be an expert on such things."

Ben-Aryeh focused on the horizon. His mind, however, flashed to a horrible image, an image all too familiar to his people. Suffering. Bloodshed. Three and a half years of grotesque and horrifying torment inflicted on the Jews by a Syrian despot, Antiochus Epiphanes. Worse yet, the abomination that desolated the Holy of Holies in their precious temple—a pagan statue erected to Zeus on the sacred altar.

"Is something wrong?" The genuine concern from Vitas broke through Ben-Aryeh's thoughts.

"You have no ability to understand. I have no urge to waste my breath explaining."

"I see. Pearls before swine."

Ben-Aryeh gritted his teeth, knowing by the smirk on Vitas' face that

Vitas was referring directly to a famous story about Jesus. "How do you know so much about the false prophet?"

"This desolation that Jesus spoke about . . ."

Suddenly Ben-Aryeh's anger was overwhelmed by foreboding in the pit of his stomach—like knowledge of the impending death of a loved one. Could history be repeating itself? In referring to the abomination, had Jesus actually had the audacity to suggest that it would happen to the Jews all over again? Could such an apocalypse really happen again? Would someone more vile than Antiochus emerge on the Jewish horizon? Were the Jews on the precipice of another three and a half years of an enemy's concerted efforts to desecrate the temple?

"You seem angry that I asked," Vitas said, interrupting his thoughts again.

"Everything about you makes me angry."

"Then it doesn't matter if I drown in ten feet of water or ten fathoms, does it?"

"What?"

"If there's no way of asking you questions without making you angry, I might as well ask any I please without worrying about the consequences."

"Why ask any at all?" Ben-Aryeh said. "Why not leave this entire subject alone?"

"I'm on a commission, remember? You may even recall the name of the man who sent me. A certain Nero. I would be remiss if I didn't learn as much as I could about the Jews. And Bernice told me that you were one of the greatest living scholars."

"Humph. Ask then."

"I've read scrolls about the life of Jesus written by a Jew named Matthew. Is there any truth to Jesus' prophecies?"

Ben-Aryeh pulled at his hair and gnashed his teeth.

"Perhaps I'll ride ahead of you," Vitas said. "That question seems beyond your capabilities."

✛ ✛ ✛

In the windless heat of midday, the mushroom of a slowly rising dust plume was visible long before the marching Roman soldiers and the horses and chariots crossed over the final hilltop that divided Jerusalem from the Kidron Valley.

A crowd of about five hundred waited in the shade of olive trees outside Jerusalem, with the city gates and imposing temple structure behind them.

Some were drunk; they were there strictly for the entertainment that a confrontation with Florus promised. Others were familiar faces at any such crowd gatherings. They were the ones who had first brought out baskets the day before to beg coppers for Florus. They served the religious establishment, paid to incite the crowd's mood in whatever direction suited the priests and city leaders. Many, however, were truly angry about the events of the day before.

Bernice sat at the base of an olive tree, well shaded by the tangle of ancient gray branches above her. Nearby, yet far enough so that it didn't appear they were companions, Maglorius sat cross-legged on a quilt of grass. They'd chosen a spot away from the rest of the crowd to have relative privacy.

Bernice asked Maglorius to explain yesterday's events more fully.

"But I'm not a Jew," he said.

"But you know the affairs of the city as well as anyone."

"I find it remarkable," Maglorius said, "that you didn't care enough yesterday to gather reports about the soldiers in the temple. Yet now . . ."

"Tell me," she said. "Why I'm concerned is a private matter."

Maglorius did not seem perturbed at the sharpness in her voice. He explained what he knew. The day before, two dozen soldiers, by order of Florus, had marched in formation from Antonio Fortress, their garrison, around the temple walls, through the main gates, and across the Court of the Gentiles. At the prescribed distance that all heathens must stand from the Holy of Holies, they had supervised the loading of mules and horses with the seventeen talents of gold taken from the temple treasury.

It was a spectacle that had drawn the total focus of all men and women in the open courtyard; money changing, purchase of animals for sacrifice, and any form of worship had all ended immediately. The brief silence in the huge open temple court—′ interrupted only by the snorting of horses and mules and the grunting of men loading those beasts—had been uncanny.

Then, as instructed by the high priest, a dozen men, armed with baskets, had begun rushing among the people, loudly crying for coppers for "poor beggar Florus." At first, their mocking defiance had been greeted with more silence; all in the crowd wanted to be certain that the soldiers in the courtyard would remain restrained.

One person, a former high priest named Annas, had dared to fling a copper. When the soldiers remained stoic, he'd thrown two more, shouting defiance, looking like a hero.

His defiance ignited others. Immediately, the air filled with coppers, and more people began shouting, "Coppers for poor beggar Florus." The open mockery and the avalanche of coins led to great peals of laughter echoing off the temple walls, with Annas bowing at the applause for his initial bravery.

"Our priests," Bernice said bitterly. "Many are as much in collusion with Rome as King Herod and I."

"That's a surprising admission," Maglorius said.

"Truth. Painful truth."

"Truth that makes you want to be here?" Maglorius asked Bernice. "You are an obvious target for the Sicarii."

She didn't reply.

He pressed her. "You risk your life among the crowds when all you would have to do is request a report on the events from the safety of your palace, undoubtedly to be reported to you later."

"You risked your life, too," she said in return. "Certainly if Bellator discovers you serve Vitas, you will be punished."

Maglorius didn't reply.

"Well, then . . ." Bernice caught the teasing tone in her voice, the one she'd used so well for so long when she wanted to flirt with a man. She stopped herself. This was not who she wanted to be any longer. She wanted to be a protector of the children who should not die in the way that Matthias' son and daughter had died.

"Well, then," she began again in a more sober voice, "it looks like we'll each have our own secrets."

"The coin of the realm."

"I don't understand," she said.

"Secrets. The temple is riddled with them. Secret tunnels beneath. Secret passageways with holes to listen in on conversations of others. Secret meetings. Spies throughout the city. Secrets. Secrets. Secrets."

"I doubt it is strictly a Jewish trait as you imply," she said. "The fact that you are here is ample proof of that."

More long silence. Uncomfortable for Bernice.

"I'm here," Bernice finally said, "because I need to be part of my people again. I've spent too many years imprisoned by the luxury of the palaces of Herod. Too many years ignoring the evils of Roman occupation because of the benefits that come with it. Is that enough answer?"

"If it is true."

"It is true," she said, thinking of waking up to a man holding a knife to her throat.

Shouting interrupted whatever she might have said next. Some of the men near the road had seen the first of the soldiers crest the hill. People around them stood. Moved closer to the road.

"Remember," Maglorius told Bernice. "Whatever happens, I will be nearby. Whatever happens, don't run. You are safest when you allow me to stay close."

She bowed her head in acknowledgment of his instructions, then slowly moved to join the others at the road.

She wasn't tall enough to see over the shoulders of the men who lined the road, so she grabbed the branches of an olive tree, and with a discreet glance back at Maglorius for his approval, which he gave with a slight nod, she hoisted herself higher to get a better view.

The soldiers marched in a formation of two abreast at a steady mile-eating pace. Within minutes they were close enough for Bernice to see their breastplates of armor, the gleam of their short swords.

She looked for the centurions, the men with the feather-crested helmets, and counted five.

Five hundred soldiers.

And horses.

And chariots.

With Florus bringing up the rear in a brightly colored chariot and the reins in his hands.

The movement of the army was a low ominous rumble.

At first, the applause was inaudible above the marching of the soldiers. But as the people in the crowd became bolder, the applause grew
louder, until it was unmistakable in its clarity.

And intent.

Once more, the Jews were mocking Florus.

The Roman commander waited until the bulk of the army had passed
the crowd. Then he barked orders to his centurions, who in turn gave
sharp commands to their men.

As if one body, the entire procession stopped.

"People of Jerusalem!" Florus shouted. "Hear this!"

He was a large man, with only his upper body showing above the
chariot. His helmet flanked both sides of his face, effectively hiding any
expression. His body armor shielded the rest of him. It was an almost
disembodied voice that cried across the sudden silence of the valley.

"Do not mock with pretended courtesy one whom you revile!" The
voice had a deep rasp and held all the authority of Rome behind it.
"Today I order you home! Tomorrow those of you who have mocked
Rome and therefore Caesar himself will be punished. Do you understand?"

No answer greeted him. No further applause.

"Centurion!" He pointed to the one nearest him. "Send fifty horsemen to drive these people into the city ahead of the army. Any who protest, take captive for immediate crucifixion at the roadside. This army
will not be preceded by mockery as it enters the city."

Low murmurs spread among the people. Some began to move toward the city even before the horsemen began wheeling into another
tight, well-trained formation.

Still perched in the tree, Bernice felt a hand on her ankle.

Maglorius. Who had moved to stand directly below her. "Get down.
Now. I will be immediately behind you," he said. "Remain in the middle
of the crowd."

Bernice climbed down. She joined dozens of men who moved together down the road, past the motionless soldiers. A few men spit, but
none dared openly speak any insults.

For a moment, it looked like some of the younger men might break loose, but the sight of all the soldiers and the imposing height of the horsemen on their great warhorses proved too intimidating.

The moment passed, and people at the edges of the crowd hurried away. Like water pouring from a bowl, others followed, and it became an exodus from the soldiers, with people fighting to get through the city gates and into the safety of Jerusalem before the soldiers could harm them.

✠ ✠ ✠

As Vitas rode forward and away from Ben-Aryeh on the road to Jerusalem, Ben-Aryeh shouted with rage.

"Stop! Right now!" Ben-Aryeh dismounted from his donkey. He grabbed the reins of Vitas' donkey, held them, and glared at Vitas, his face only inches away. "You ask about the prophecies of Jesus?"

"I do," Vitas said.

"If you are one of the followers of Jesus, tell me immediately. Because I would rather crawl back to Sebaste than journey any farther with you."

"I am not a follower," Vitas said. "Merely curious. Most people are forgotten, even by their closest friends, within a couple of years of their death. This man Jesus, however, of no obvious wealth and political power, seems to become more important with the passage of time."

"Where do you get this information?"

"I am a curious man, Ben-Aryeh." Vitas stared him directly in the eyes, and for the first time, Ben-Aryeh got a sense of the strength of this quiet Roman. "I'm not afraid of asking questions. Or of the answers I might hear, as long as it is truth."

"But you are obviously afraid of questions asked of you. Where did you get this information? The scroll?"

"All right then. From a woman. A Jew. Who told me about this Jesus." For a moment Vitas looked away from Ben-Aryeh.

There, Ben-Aryeh thought. *I've found it. The man's weakness. He speaks of a woman and looks away because he does not want me to see into his soul and his need for her.* Perhaps there was some sense to this man's determination to remain unknown in Judea, when any other man of his rank would have come heralded and demanding banquets.

Yes, Ben-Aryeh thought as silence hung between them. *A woman.*

Yes. A man who only wants to learn how Florus mistreats the people of an occupied land does not read a scroll and decide he needs to get to Jerusalem on another matter so quickly that he will actually travel through the night alone.

A woman. One whom Vitas had left Rome to find. The letter had held the seal of Bellator. Was she employed in the Bellator household? Was that how they met? In Rome when the Bellator family lived there?

Against his will, Ben-Aryeh felt sympathy for the Roman. He wasn't asking questions from the arrogance of a conqueror but because he truly wanted to know. And, if Ben-Aryeh had guessed correctly, a man who wanted to know for one of the purest and deepest motives. Love.

"If you want to know about the Jews, I will tell you this," Ben-Aryeh said more softly. He loved his own wife so deeply that if another man found that gift, he would never begrudge it, not even to a Roman. "Much as this Jesus of Nazareth was a blasphemer, learning about Him and His preposterous claims and the equally preposterous claims of His followers will tell you much of what you need to know about our people."

"Let me listen," Vitas said.

Ben-Aryeh gave the reins back to Vitas.

Mounted his own donkey again.

Rode beside the Roman.

"You see," Ben-Aryeh said, "although I will insist he was not the Messiah God promised us, we are waiting for one. But you need to know our history from the beginning to truly understand it. Are you sure you want to hear all of this?"

Vitas nodded.

"It's a good thing we have a long journey ahead of us," Ben-Aryeh said.

"I will confess this is the very reason I invited you to join me," Vitas said. "A man can only learn so much from books."

"Very well," Ben-Aryeh answered. "First and foremost, you have to learn the nature of the relationship between God and man. We have sinned, beginning with Adam, and because of it, God barred us from the Tree of Life. He wants to create for us a new Jerusalem where we will be able to eat from that tree again. All of our Scripture points to the end of all times and that New Jerusalem."

"Adam?" Vitas said. "The Tree of Life?"

Ben-Aryeh closed his eyes and swayed on the donkey's back. "You know so little."

"Teach me," Vitas said humbly. "We have time."

"In the beginning," Ben-Aryeh said, as if he were addressing a boy in the synagogue, "God created the heavens and the earth. . . ."

✝ ✝ ✝

As Bernice and Maglorius entered the city, the surrounding crowd began to fan out. Bernice turned.

Maglorius, as promised, was immediately behind her. Still protecting her.

They separated themselves from the crowd, and he escorted her through a narrow side street, upward toward the palace.

"Don't you find it strange," she said. "Florus and his army are already here. Yet only yesterday he was publicly insulted at the temple."

"I wondered if that would occur to you," Maglorius said. "He had already assembled his army and begun to travel. Before the incident occurred."

"It was planned," Queen Bernice said. "My spies have informed me of that."

She was angry with herself. Before this morning, she'd been content to remain a spectator to the battles between Florus and the Jews. Because her power and wealth came from Rome, it didn't matter to her what information the spies brought about him. But now . . .

"You of all people know that Lucius Bellator is definitely not a supporter of Florus," Bernice told Maglorius. "My spies also tell me that Florus is looking for any excuse to set his soldiers loose. And if they are loose, who knows what might be deliberate yet appear as damage done in a riot out of control?"

"You are suggesting that Florus might send soldiers into the upper city with orders to murder Bellator."

"I'm saying," she said, "if you are in their employ as a bodyguard, then tomorrow do what you can to protect the Bellator family."

14 AV

THE SEVENTH HOUR

Tell me, Roman, why do you hate the Jews?" Despite the wording of his question, Ben-Aryeh spoke to Vitas with a degree of friendliness and banter.

After traveling through most of the night, stopping every hour to rest, and traveling through the morning at a constant pace, they had just passed through Givat Shaul, a town that overlooked the place where the road from Caesarea joined the road from Sebaste to continue the last three miles into Jerusalem.

It was a relatively cool day, the afternoon was still pleasant, the green of the date trees an equally pleasant sight against the hills and sky. There had been no incidents with bandits, and with Jerusalem so near, Ben-Aryeh was far more relaxed than he had been at the beginning of the journey.

"You accuse me of hating Jews?" Vitas asked mildly. "I find that interesting."

The manner of this Roman had also contributed to Ben-Aryeh's relaxed state. Ben-Aryeh had observed over his life that the rigors of travel with another person added to whatever friction might have existed previously, observing too that since he usually found fault with another man's traveling habits, the friction was inescapable.

Vitas, on the other hand, was so relaxed and quiet and polite, such an intelligent man of debate, that Ben-Aryeh had been forced to admit to himself that the journey had actually been enjoyable.

Except for the fact that the man was a Roman.

Even that was less of a problem now. Ben-Aryeh knew the same intimacy of spending hour after hour of travel with a man that caused friction was also an intimacy that could bond men quickly if they were of the same mind and heart.

"I don't accuse you of hatred," Ben-Aryeh said, "although I do reserve judgment on your motives for coming here to Judea. It is the Roman attitude in general that makes me curious."

Their conversations over the previous thirty-five miles had ranged wide and far with each hour, and it had become easier for Ben-Aryeh to talk to the man without getting angry or taking insult. So he was fully prepared for an honest answer, which Vitas provided.

"It's not hatred." Vitas grinned. "More like contempt and anger."

"I feel much better. Remind me to abandon my life in Jerusalem for the welcome I would receive in Rome."

"Certainly," Vitas said. "I sensed immediately upon meeting you that you were well suited for mixing among strangers and would enjoy immense popularity wherever you traveled."

"Humph."

"Your race has been conquered," Vitas said in a more serious tone. "To the educated Roman—"

"We have not been conquered."

"There," Vitas still spoke mildly, "that explains it. Soldiers of the empire occupy your land. You pay taxes to Caesar, yet you act as if we don't exist. To a Roman, when a country is subjugated, the people in it lose their right to their religion unless Rome grants it."

"Faith is between God and the people. It is outside of government laws or control."

"Not to Romans. Political life and religion are intertwined. We serve our gods for what they can give us."

"You try to bribe your gods," Ben-Aryeh snorted. "I've heard of your prayers. 'If you give me this,' you say to a god, 'I'll give you that.'"

"What are your temple sacrifices if not bribery?"

Hours earlier, Ben-Aryeh would have bristled at such a question. Now he understood that Vitas was inquiring strictly for the sake of new knowledge.

"Our sacrifices," Ben-Aryeh said, "are payment for our sins. They allow us to approach God, through an intermediary, the priest. You'll remember I explained the relationship between God and man, beginning with creation."

"You did. And that's something else that Romans can't understand. Worship of something unseen without a visible symbol to represent it. It's an utter rejection of every other religion in the world. Which leads me to another point. The stubborn, uncompromising attitude of Jews, with religious rites so exclusive to all others."

"Our God—"

"And circumcision," Vitas said. "We certainly don't understand that."

"I told you about the covenant," Ben-Aryeh began impatiently, then saw that Vitas was trying to hide a smile. "Humph," Ben-Aryeh said again.

"You Jews keep together and help each other at any cost. You remain a closed community to outsiders, even when you occupy the cities outside your land. I think it is part of human nature to be suspicious of a group like that."

"Have you any idea how often the Jews have been persecuted?" Ben-Aryeh asked. "From our point of view, it is a necessity to help each other and be wary of outsiders."

"Point conceded," Vitas said. "I'll keep that in mind as I move through Judea."

The road in front of them was not empty of travelers but sparse enough that a single figure approaching them was readily recognizable to Ben-Aryeh.

It was Olithar. His assistant. Waiting ahead, just before a dip in the road. Holding the halter to an unsaddled donkey and a foal.

The sight of the young man brought back to Ben-Aryeh the dread he had been trying to avoid the whole journey. Florus had brought his army here to the city. What horrors had happened? What message was so important that Olithar had come out to find him?

Time with Vitas was now almost finished. Ben-Aryeh had been waiting as long as possible to ask his final question, wanting to establish as much rapport as he could. "Tell me, Roman," Ben-Aryeh said softly, "truly. Why are you here?"

Ben-Aryeh expected either an evasive answer or to find out more about the woman who he speculated had brought Vitas to Jerusalem. What he heard surprised him.

"I'm tired of death," Vitas said, equally softly.

"Death comes to us all."

"I'm tired of killing. Especially of the killing caused by Rome."

Ben-Aryeh sensed this was not something he should interrupt, as if Vitas had wanted all along to speak of this.

"I fought a campaign in Britannia," Vitas said. His eyes were focused on a distant hill. "The Iceni revolted because of a bad governor and were slaughtered in that revolt. At the end of my campaign, I was involved in something that . . ."

Vitas took a deep breath, paused so long that Ben-Aryeh wondered if he'd finished speaking. "On my return to Rome," Vitas said, "I expected that I'd never have to see such killing ever again. In fact, I made sure of it by molding my political career toward the confines of the imperial palace."

Ben-Aryeh wondered what Vitas had nearly said about the end of the Iceni campaign and why he had changed the subject to Rome.

Vitas gave Ben-Aryeh a wan smile. "Even in Rome, I could not escape more killing. As you might know, however, Nero has found a new group to persecute. The Christians. And so the killing continues. You ask me why I'm here. I can't live in Rome any longer and continue to see it happen."

"And there happens to be a certain woman here in Judea?"

Vitas smiled. Enough of an answer.

Olithar saw that it was Ben-Aryeh and began to wave. He was a tall, skinny man with a sparse beard.

"My assistant," Ben-Aryeh explained, noticing that Olithar's waving had drawn the attention of Vitas. "I'm not sure it will do you or me any good if we are seen together. Nor would Bernice want anyone to guess at the arrangements she had made between you and me."

"Stop then, on your donkey, as if it is giving you trouble," Vitas said. "I'll hurry forward and when I pass him, I'll lower my head so he doesn't see my face. You can join him and follow behind on your way to the city."

Ben-Aryeh nodded. To Olithar, it would seem as if he and Vitas had had only a few words on the road, not something unusual on a busy highway like this.

"Before I go, let me tell you the truth, my friend," Vitas said. "If I can return to Rome at a safer time and show Nero how a bad procurator is cutting into his tax revenue, Florus will be gone. And with him gone, perhaps you Jews won't have a reason to die the way the Iceni did. That is why I am here."

Ben-Aryeh glimpsed something elusive in the Roman's eyes. A sadness that had surfaced before the man could hide it completely. "There's more, isn't there?" Ben-Aryeh said, truly feeling compassion for the Roman.

"Of course," Vitas said, spurring his donkey forward and speaking over his shoulder as he left Ben-Aryeh behind. "Isn't there always?"

☩ ☩ ☩

Queen Bernice ignored all the attention given to her and her five attendants as she walked through the Court of the Gentiles, past the livestock enclosures and money tables. She ignored the stares, the pointing, the whispering, the occasional catcall. She preferred traveling in the privacy of a litter and rarely walked in public so conspicuously, because she knew this was the treatment to expect.

This morning, however, she needed to see the high priest, and the two messages she had sent to him had been ignored. Since he would not come to the palace, she had been forced to visit the Temple Mount, where her litter and the servants carrying it were not permitted entry.

Inside the Court of Women she did not hesitate. She moved directly to the priests who were sorting through firewood for the altar. "Ananias," she commanded. "I need to see him immediately."

There were four men at the stacks of wood. All four straightened, fully aware of who spoke to them.

"You—" Bernice pointed at the shortest, a man with a mole on his left cheek, this the tiny blemish that defiled him and condemned him to menial labor in the priesthood—"tell him that Queen Bernice waits. And remind him that my brother has the power to remove and appoint high priests as frequently as he wants."

She hoped her unmistakable confidence that the priest would obey was enough to get him moving before he wondered why any priest should follow the commands of a person from outside the temple.

Fortunately, her bluff worked.

The priest shuffled forward, across the courtyard, up the steps, and into the Court of Israel, with the altar that guarded the Holy of Holies inside.

Bernice retreated to the shade of the gallery along the outer wall of the Court of Women. Early in the morning, it was already hot.

She expected that the indirect threat of removal from his office would force Ananias to meet with her. Although five years had passed—with a succession of high priests during that time—since Annas the Younger had made a political miscalculation and angered her brother Agrippa II, thereby losing his priestly office, all high priests were extremely conscious that the latest in the line of Herods would not hesitate to use the power granted to the royalty by Rome.

This was proven when she saw Ananias—long flowing robe, long gray beard—hurrying to meet her.

"This, Your Highness, is not the most convenient time," Ananias said upon reaching her.

They were out of earshot of anyone in the Court of Women, but the other priests watched them with intense curiosity.

"Obviously," she answered. "I'm certain it was so busy that you didn't even have a chance to read either of the messages I had delivered to you already this morning."

She said it with haughtiness and scorn. This was not a moment for weakness or vulnerability. Ananias was not an ally, nor would he ever become one, for Ananias was simply a pawn of the wealthy Sadducees.

After Annas the Younger had been banished from the high priest-hood, effectively ending the long reign of power of his family, a consortium of the upper class had influenced Agrippa II to appoint whoever would serve them best. In the end, for all the courageous actions that a certain priest named Ben-Aryeh had taken to rid the temple of the Annas family, it had actually made the situation worse. As for Ben-Aryeh, he would never be a candidate, for he was too strong willed to serve that consortium of wealthy men.

"I have no time for messages," Ananias said. He was a tall, thin man with a full head of thick gray hair to match his beard, and the robes of the high priesthood gave him an intimidating appearance. "As you've surely heard, Florus and five hundred extra soldiers occupy Palace Antonia. Dealing with Florus is an extremely urgent matter."

"I've also heard that you and the chief priests did nothing to discourage the crowds from insulting him yesterday as his army approached the city."

Ananias snorted. "Seventeen talents taken from the temple treasury the day before that! How could anybody stop the crowds from reacting as they did?"

"You say you have little time," she said, "so I will speak with directness. It is no secret that you and the high priests before you have had a tradition of paying people to blend in with the crowds and incite them with your agenda. In short, the crowds behave as you direct. Or are you suggesting that the great priesthood truly has no power over the people?"

Ananias smoothed his robes. "As you say, I have little time. Florus has summoned a delegation of leaders. I must go."

It was a bluff and she knew it. At this point, he would be very curious to find out what had been important enough for her to send two messages and then appear in person. So would the Sadducees whom he reported to.

"That is why I am here," Bernice said. "I am begging you to do exactly as he requests. Give him no reason to unleash the dogs of war."

"You are giving me political advice?"

"It is not advice. It is a request. More than a request."

Now that she had reached the main purpose of her meeting with him, she would show weakness. If that was what it took to let him know how much it mattered, she would swallow her pride. "If you wish," she said, "I will get down on my knees and literally beg this of you."

"This is not the imperious, arrogant Queen Bernice who has antagonized the priesthood for the last decade. The Queen Bernice whose immoral appetites have made her a laughingstock among good Jews."

His words stabbed her. She deserved them.

"No," she said, swallowing any attempt at defending herself. "It is not. Against Florus, we must set aside our differences."

"Are you suggesting we actually battle Rome?"

"No. Any fight we will lose. And our people will be slaughtered."

"*Our* people? Since when do the descendants of Herod care about the Jews, except as vassals to support the excesses of royalty?"

Bernice forgot to keep her pride in control and snapped without thinking, "The same argument can be made of the priesthood."

"We serve God."

"And the priests live very well doing it."

"I believe our conversation is over," Ananias said. As well he should. Now that he knew why she'd requested the meeting, he was certainly satisfied.

"Please. I am sorry. I was wrong to suggest what I did. And you were right. Until now, the excesses of royalty have done nothing except leech from our people. But the future does not have to be the past."

Ananias appeared genuinely puzzled at her humility. "This new policy has official approval from Agrippa?"

Bernice said nothing.

"He is in Alexandra, congratulating the ruler there on having obtained the government from Nero. Am I correct?"

"He is in Alexandra."

"A shrewd political move, of course. I am to believe then, that the man currying favor from our powerful neighbors is the same man who suddenly tells me through you to place the welfare of peasants above the welfare of royalty?"

"The peasants are without power. They depend on us for—"

"So, you don't speak for your brother. And you come to me, the high priest, daring to tell me how to conduct my business with Florus."

"Florus is looking for any excuse to set his soldiers loose."

"That is obvious. But he must also be accountable to Rome for his actions. That will check any excesses beyond what he has already done."

"You don't understand. It is just as easy for him to blame the Jews for any riots as it is for the Jews to blame him. And who would Caesar believe? His actions then—whatever the excesses—are easily explained to Rome."

"What I don't understand is why you have this sudden concern. The Herods are powerless lapdogs of Caesar. Regardless of what happens with the rest of the nation's difficulties with Florus, nothing will change about your life. You'll still flit from palace to palace according to the season." He paused and sneered. "Pampered and hedonistic."

"Please," Bernice said. "Whatever Florus requests, give it to him. If it is money, I will replace it for you."

"He already has our money. Remember? Seventeen talents."

"Please . . . ," she repeated.

Ananias sighed. "Strangely enough, I feel compassion for your sudden interest in keeping peace. But there is nothing to fear. Florus is going to demand that we hand over the troublemakers who insulted him yesterday."

"Will you do it then?"

His sigh became one of exasperation. "I will explain this to you the way I would explain it to a child. As simply as possible."

"I will listen as a child."

"The troublemakers Florus wants are the same people who, as you so indelicately put it, have been bribed by us to incite the crowds. If we hand them over, who would ever work for us again?"

"And you lose some of your power over the people . . ."

"Not power—" he smiled—"influence."

"Let our people be more important than that. Just this once. Please."

"Your concern is impressive. Truly. Unfathomable after all your years without but impressive." Another smile, genuine. "Your fear is misplaced. This is the way it will happen. We will gather our leaders and chief priests and meet with Florus as he's requested. He will demand an apology. We will give it to him in private. This way, our people know that publicly we have stood up to him. We keep our power. He keeps his. It's part of a game that every procurator plays. It is a delicate dance that has been playing to the same music for the last hundred years. Nothing will change."

Bernice thought of what her spies had delivered. "I believe you are wrong. I believe he is like no other procurator Rome has sent before. He wants war."

Ananias frowned. "War would be convenient for him if he could start it somewhere in the provinces. But here, too many people of influence would be able to present to the governor of Syria any of the wrongs done by Florus. He dares not risk beginning a war here."

"What if he believes that war will distract the governor and distract Rome from looking into his affairs in Jerusalem? Look how easily he was able to get all these extra soldiers into the heart of the city."

"Perhaps, Your Highness, you should return to the way of life that you have been content to lead for so long until now. Your grasp of politics is too poor for you to try to meddle. Trust me, by late afternoon, Florus will be on his return to Caesarea with his army and the money that he stole from us. That's all he wanted in the first place. As for us, we won't really miss what he's taken, because the temple treasury is far vaster than he can comprehend. And the people will again believe we fought him to a standstill. Everyone will be happy." Ananias paused. "Anything else?"

Bernice bowed her head. She knew it was useless to spend more time trying to convince him.

"Good," he said. "Trust my words. Nothing will go wrong."

✝ ✝ ✝

A growing population had forced development outside the city of Jerusalem, on a site yet to be enclosed by protective walls. Here, farthest away from the mansions of the upper city yet still within Jerusalem proper were the extensive leather operations, a thriving industry because of the thousands of sheep and cattle slaughtered for temple sacrifice. The leather industry had been placed there, not only because of the distance from the mansions but because prevailing winds blew the stench away from the city.

Yet within this quarter, not even the winds could totally disperse the heavy rotten-egg odors that came from all stages of leather production—from scraping the raw hides, to curing the leather in vats of tannin, to hanging them to dry. For those who lived in the quarter, the stench seeped into their hair and skin. Given its lack of walled protection and the continuous nauseating smell that hung over it, it had soon become the quarter to house the poorest of poor.

Here, Sophia was employed by an absentee owner of one of the largest leather warehouses. As an unmarried woman with no family, she had few other choices in employment.

She was draped in a sheep hide when Maglorius came into sight from behind the vats of tannin; she was glad for the excuse to set it down.

Although he'd never come to this quarter to visit, she smiled at his unexpected arrival.

Maglorius had become a good friend over the previous months.

Daily, she thanked God for that friendship and how He had arranged for them to meet. Most surely it had not been coincidence. Maglorius was an ex-gladiator, and she was a freed slave, each born in different parts of the world. Yet, after the ship's journey from Smyrna to Rome where they had first met, here he was in Jerusalem. And to think that they had literally bumped into each other in the crowded market. God worked in wonderful ways.

"Come with me," Maglorius said without his usual welcoming smile. "Immediately."

There were dozens of other workers around her, most of them older or maimed in some way; those who had the ability to work anywhere else did not lower themselves to employment here.

"I cannot," she said, gesturing around her. "I—"

Maglorius surprised her. He stepped forward quickly and took her elbow.

She winced. "What are you—"

"Listen to me," he said in a low, confidential voice. "I have very little time. Come with me now."

His actions had drawn the attention of others, who began whispering. Sophia was embarrassed. Maglorius was an attractive man and she was a single woman. The conclusions they would draw were quite natural.

"I'll follow you to the street where we can talk," she said in an equally low voice. "But you are hurting my arm."

He eased the grip but did not entirely let go, and he guided her away from the vats and the other workers. When they reached the narrow street, he did not stop as she expected but continued to lead her toward the city.

"No," she said and shook her arm loose. "What has come over you?"

"I will explain, but I have to get to the market. With you."

"Not a single step until I hear more," Sophia said. "You know how stubborn I am."

"I do," he said.

He picked her up and threw her over his right shoulder, her legs draped over his chest, her hair hanging straight down over her face, giving her a view of his sandaled heels and the packed dirt of the street.

She screamed.

Several nearby people glanced at them.

"Disobedient wife," Maglorius yelled. "Sometimes one has no choice."

The men nodded with understanding, and Maglorius marched ahead.

"Maglorius!" Sophia shouted. "Have you lost your mind?"

He ignored her.

She flailed her arms, and her hand hit the hilt of his sword. She grabbed it, pulled it loose in a swift move. "Stop," she said, "or I'll cut you open."

That was effective.

He stopped, set her down, and with blinding swiftness, grabbed the wrist of her sword hand. She pulled but didn't even move his arm.

"Florus is about to send soldiers through the city," Maglorius said, his face set with determination. "They will have orders to kill any citizens in sight."

"How do you know this?" By his unblinking stare, she knew he believed he was telling the truth. "Florus would never——"

"Yes, he would. Come with me. Now. Valeria is in the market and I must get her next."

"But if that is true, these people here . . ."

Maglorius spun away from her. He stepped close to an old man who had been watching them through rheumy eyes. "Citizen," he said, "go through this quarter and warn others to find a place to hide. Soldiers are on their way."

The man's eyes widened. He smacked his gums several times, then tottered off toward the men down the road who were loading a cart with finished hides.

Moments later, Maglorius was back with Sophia. "He may tell them; he may not," he said. "I've been giving the same warning as often as possible on my way here, and most people laugh at me."

"Soldiers . . . ," Sophia said. "Not in Jerusalem."

"That's exactly what I've been told. But it is going to happen. Soon."

When he took her arm, she did not protest. If something had happened that affected Maglorius in this way, she would be foolish not to listen.

"I need to make a confession to you," Maglorius said as they walked up the slight incline toward the city walls. "If I don't survive the next days, and if Vitas doesn't make it into the city or find you, then—"

"Vitas!"

If daily she thanked God for her friendship with Maglorius, twice daily she asked her Father to watch over Vitas, even convinced as she was that when she'd refused to stay in Rome with him, she'd lost him forever.

"Walk faster," Maglorius urged.

"Vitas?!"

He sighed. "It was not an accident that I met you in the market. I'd been searching for you. Myself. And through others."

"Searching for me?"

"We have so little time. Interruptions make this more difficult."

They reached the Ephraim Gate, with the temple towering above them. Three young men loitered at the gate, eyeing Sophia.

Maglorius moved toward them, and they watched him with insolence in their stances.

"Here's your chance to be heroes," Maglorius said. "When you hear the disturbance in the city, make sure the gate cannot be shut so people can flee into this quarter."

All three laughed.

"At least wait nearby," he said over his shoulder as he headed back to Sophia. "You'll see."

They laughed scornfully again. But, as Sophia noticed, they remained where they were. This was the effect Maglorius could have on people.

"Vitas?" Sophia asked. "You must tell me."

"I've been in correspondence with Vitas. Under strict orders not to let you know of it. He asked me to find you and arrange for your continued safety."

They were hurrying up the narrow street that would take them to the heart of the city. To the crowded marketplace.

"You are not my friend, then," Sophia said slowly, trying to grasp this. She'd been in Jerusalem half a year. "Not a friend but a bodyguard."

"Others have been your bodyguards. I have been your friend almost from the beginning."

In anger, Sophia stopped walking. "Others? Spying on me?"

He turned to her. "Two weeks ago, that man who attacked you near dusk as you were on your way to a meeting of the followers. And the two others who stopped him."

"They were spying on me?"

"For your protection," Maglorius said. "As part of my pledge to Vitas. Please, we need to get to the market."

"No."

"Valeria is there. I can't choose between the two of you. I can't leave you behind and help her, or abandon her to be with you."

At the anguish easy to read on his face, Sophia relented. But she was furious. "You are telling me that Vitas hired you to—"

"I owe Vitas a debt of gratitude. I would never work for a Roman. Ever."

"You are employed in the Bellator household," Sophia blurted out. Immediately she felt irritated with herself. Why was she arguing with Maglorius about something that trivial?

"No," he said gently. "I'm there because of my son."

That was as perplexing to Sophia as anything else he'd said. "You're not married," she began slowly. "You . . ." She stopped herself, suddenly comprehending.

"It's changed," Maglorius said quickly. "You should know that. I ended what was wrong and deceitful. Since you helped me become a believer."

"So that's not a pretense? The time you spend in worship with us? Your belief in the Resurrection?"

"I found you at the request of Vitas. Once I had arranged for your protection, I was under no obligation to spend time with you. I did it freely. In fact, I'm sure Vitas would have preferred that you not know of my presence in Jerusalem."

Making it all the more difficult for Sophia to grasp was the urgency of pace that Maglorius forced upon them. She wanted time to sit down—alone—and absorb it all and reflect on what it meant.

Vitas? Coming to Jerusalem? Arranging for her protection?

Maglorius? With a son in the Bellator household? How did he know about Florus and the soldiers? What did he owe to Vitas?

She settled on one question first. "Vitas, when will he arrive in Jerusalem?"

"If a messenger found him in Caesarea before Florus did, and if Vitas went to Sebaste as Bernice requested . . ."

"Bernice? Queen Bernice? Why would—?"

"Judea is far from Rome," Maglorius said impatiently. "Vitas offers her political favors there for her help here. It's the way of the world."

"And Vitas then will be here . . ."

"I expect his arrival in the next couple of days. He wanted to find you himself. But Florus and the army changed everything. Vitas may get here soon. Or later. I can't say. As for you, once I get you to the royal palace, you'll be safe. Vitas can find you there when he finally arrives."

She was slowing down to try to comprehend this new information. In the royal palace?

He took her by the arm again. "Please," he said, "don't make me ask again. Hurry!"

✛ ✛ ✛

When the brigands attacked from the gully in the dip of the road, it took Ben-Aryeh several seconds to comprehend the source of the screaming and motion. Part of the screaming came from Olithar, his assistant, who was already running from the road into the hills above it.

Ben-Aryeh saw four men, all brandishing curved swords, running forward from huge boulders that clung to the hillside above the highway.

Brigands!

Here, almost within the shadows of the walls of Jerusalem, it verged on preposterous that brigands had so boldly attacked.

Yet there was no denying it was actually happening.

Ben-Aryeh leaned forward on the donkey, clutching the beast's neck. It brayed as he kicked it forward. He hoped to burst through the wall of brigands.

But failed. The donkey spun sideways, and Ben-Aryeh hit the

ground hard and groaned from the pain of smashing his ribs into a round stone.

The brigands moved forward and gathered around him.

Ben-Aryeh stared upward as one of the men swung a club at his head.

THE EIGHTH HOUR

Uitas found himself outside the city again.

On the final stretch of the road to Jerusalem, from the top of the Mount of Olives, he had been awed at the magnificence of the temple, its golden burnished dome so bright with reflected sunlight that he'd been forced to look away.

From the temple, he had turned his gaze to the magnificent mansions beyond it, glimpsing the deep green foliage of the private gardens. And the walls of the city! Massive, perched on the edge of the sharply dropping cliffs. It truly seemed like a city that might house the God of Israel. Yes, he had thought, even with his anxiousness to get inside and begin searching for Sophia, Jerusalem truly was the eighth wonder of the world. He'd read about it, heard about it, but had not been able to remotely comprehend its glory until finally seeing it.

He'd walked through the gates, been forced to take a wide detour around the temple, and, asking directions again and again, had finally found his way through the labyrinth of streets to Ephraim Gate.

And stepped back outside the walls.

Just like that, all the wealth and luxury were gone; ahead were huts and hovels on freshly packed dirt streets. And the smell.

Vitas grimaced.

Not from distaste but from remembered horror.

There was too much in the air that reminded him of his time in Britannia, of torched wagons, of corpses of horses and humans, of headless bodies hung from posts as an unsuccessful deterrent to other tribesmen.

He closed his eyes and endured the stab of remorse that came with any reminder of those days in Britannia.

Even this close to Sophia, he could not escape it.

The moment passed, and Vitas stepped forward, sidestepping dung from oxen that pulled carts loaded with hides. Here in the leather district, no taxes were paid for someone to tend to the cleanliness of the streets.

Vitas left Ephraim Gate behind and moved farther into the near slums of this quarter.

This was where Sophia had chosen to live and work? This was what she'd found after refusing to stay in Rome? What was it that drove her to it? Yes, she'd explained her faith in the man crucified by Pilate, but as much as Vitas had tried to understand, he found it was impossible.

The squalor here made it even more difficult to understand.

As he strode forward, an ironic grin crossed his face. Sophia had explained that following her faith meant reaching out to the sick and the poor. Here, most certainly, was the place to find them.

With each step, Vitas became both more certain and more uncertain. More certain that he'd made the right decision to leave Rome and look for her. More uncertain as to what her response might be. After all, she'd rejected him once already.

He could only hope that she would see him with new eyes once she realized he had been willing to travel halfway across the world to see her again.

And there was something else. Something that Ben-Aryeh or Bernice never would have believed.

Vitas truly did want to expose Florus and his abuses.

Vitas had seen how the injustices of Roman rule had driven the Iceni to revolt. Had seen the horrors inflicted upon them. Seen the families torn apart. Seen mothers and sons . . .

There it was. The stab of remorse again.

Ben-Aryeh and Bernice never would have believed that Vitas wanted to use his power and influence to prevent revolt from forcing Rome to destroy yet another of its provinces. But it was truth.

Maybe, in the end, that would be an added reason for Sophia to look at him with new eyes.

With this uncertain hope in his heart, Vitas found the leather warehouse as Maglorius had described it in the most recent correspondence.

He breathed relief.

Whatever her reaction to his unexpected arrival, at least he could take her to the palace and keep her safe from the army that had entered the city.

Vitas moved past the vats of tannin and stepped directly into an area where women lifted and dropped scraped sheep hides into short vats full of dark, vile liquids.

They all stopped movement immediately.

Vitas was glad not to be in expensive dress. He would have been embarrassed at the contrast to the poverty etched in the faces and hands and clothing of these women.

"I'm looking for Sophia," he said.

"You and every other man in this district," one of the women cackled.

"Hush," another one said. To Vitas, the second woman said, "She was here, but left with . . ."

"With a large man," the first screeched. "One I would have gladly entertained myself."

"How long ago?" Vitas asked the second woman.

"Not long."

"Right before some fools came running in here and warned us that the soldiers might attack the city," the first woman said.

"What?"

The first woman nodded, her dark eyes gleaming. "That man, the one that took Sophia, he tried telling men on the street that the soldiers would attack."

"What did he look like?"

When the first woman finished her description, Vitas knew without a doubt that it had been Maglorius.

And if Maglorius had warned about an attack . . .

"Hey!" the first woman yelled at Vitas. "Where are you going?"

He broke into a run.

"Come back," she shouted. "You're better looking than the other one." Her laughter followed him.

And then he was back on the street, uncaring of the startled glances of those who saw him running toward the city walls.

And then the distant screams reached him.

✠ ✠ ✠

Valeria was standing at the entrance of an alley into the main street of the market when an urchin slipped behind her and stood so close that the knife he pulled was invisible to any observers.

Valeria had been using the vantage point to pretend a casual surveillance of the crowds, as if she were simply a pilgrim overwhelmed by the diversity and noise of the marketplace. Truth was, she'd been bored among the luxuries of home. Here was life in all its confusion.

From the alley behind her came the smell of raw lamb, for in the less desirable side streets, butchers set up shop, hanging meat from hooks and waving away the flies that tried to settle on the gleaming carcasses of lamb and chicken. Fishmongers, too, set up stalls here, with the unblinking black eyes of their wares staring upward at the awnings that sheltered them from the sun.

The large, shady halls along the main street to her left and right held the more desirable goods provided by goldsmiths, jewelers, and importers. Had she wanted, Valeria could have purchased from a dazzling selection of luxuries from India, Persia, Egypt, Greece, Media, Arabia, and Italy—jeweled cups, silks, purple wall hangings, ointments, perfumes.

This activity she craved. She did not want to become the wife of a wealthy old man, an accessory like jewelry for him to show off in public places. She wanted to be part of all this.

She'd listened as a nearby writer, reed behind his ear, haggled with a pilgrim over the cost of a letter that the pilgrim wanted to dictate to send back to his family in Parthia. She'd found the pilgrim's nasal whining amusing and thought of how she might retell it to a friend, if she ever had one outside the sheltered existence of her family's mansion.

Then came a tug on her purse.

By the time she turned and realized the straps had been severed by the urchin, the dirt-smeared boy had already begun to run, dodging among the people of the crowded market who were oblivious to the theft.

Valeria thought of calling out but hesitated. She'd escaped the upper-city villa and was here without permission. Calling attention to herself might lead to repercussions greater than a stolen purse.

As she hesitated and watched the urchin escape, there was a flash of movement ahead. A man stepping out of another alley lifted his arm and held it horizontal to the ground. The thief, who'd been looking backward to see if there was pursuit, slammed his neck into the arm and fell backward as if a giant beam had dropped onto him from the sky.

The man grabbed the boy by his collar and lifted him effortlessly.

Maglorius! In simple peasant clothing, almost indistinguishable from most of the other men on the street. Unless one looked closely and saw the solid bulk of muscle beneath the rough cloth.

Maglorius smiled grimly as he hauled the urchin back toward Valeria.

A few people moved as if to question Maglorius, but on closer examination of the determination and anger on his face, parted for him.

Maglorius still held the boy completely off the ground as he reached Valeria. The boy was blinking from a greasy face, obviously not recovered from the stunning impact and suddenness of his fall.

"You have this young woman's purse," Maglorius told him. "I advise you to return it to her."

He was too dazed to comprehend the command.

Maglorius shook him several times. "The purse."

The boy handed it to Valeria.

Maglorius kept his grip on the urchin's collar. "There is a reason you have strict orders not to leave the villa without me or one of your family's slaves," Maglorius told Valeria. "And this rascal is one of them."

Valeria responded by opening the purse and shaking it upside down to show Maglorius it was empty. Nothing fell from it.

"And there is a reason," she countered, "that I keep my gold in a purse hidden inside my clothing and use the outside purse to fool thieves. Your protection was welcome but hardly necessary."

"This is a dangerous city," Maglorius growled, as if he'd forgotten he was still holding the thief at arm's length. "If you are going to steal away from the villa, at least dress in a way that doesn't scream to the world that you are a Roman from the upper city." He shook his head. "And at the very least, don't dress in such a way that even a corpse would sit up and take notice of your beauty. That only adds to the danger."

"Danger?" Valeria certainly did not want to acknowledge that at his compliment, her heart had begun to beat faster. "Greeks, Romans, Egyptians, and Parthians. All live in Jerusalem in peace. You yourself have told me it is one of the most cosmopolitan cities in the world."

"Every city has its underworld," Maglorius said. "This one too."

The urchin coughed to get their attention.

"One moment," Maglorius told Valeria. He swung the boy around to look him directly in the face. "You attempted to rob a Roman citizen," Maglorius said. "Is crucifixion how you want to end your short life?"

The urchin shuddered. Crucifixion was a torture that lasted for days. Maglorius was making no idle threat; this was often the fate of thieves.

"Or would you prefer being sold to the arenas? Wild beasts would enjoy a morsel like you. And the crowds would be delighted to watch your limbs torn from your body."

The boy began to squirm.

"Frightened?" Maglorius asked. He didn't need an answer. "Good. Don't be stupid. Look for work. Not plunder."

Maglorius held the boy as he dug into his own pocket for some coins. Then he dropped him, who remained motionless in disbelief.

Maglorius extended his other hand and showed the boy the silver. "Take this."

The boy's eyes widened at the sight of a month's wages. He reached for it.

Maglorius clamped his wrist. "Spend it wisely and find work instead of thievery. Now go, before I change my mind."

The boy tried to yank free.

"One last thing," Maglorius said. "If Roman soldiers start attacking the citizens, run hard and far and give as much warning as possible to as many people as possible. Do you understand?"

The boy nodded.

Maglorius released him.

Like a mouse darting into refuge among grain bags, the urchin disappeared.

"A month or two ago," Valeria said, "I believe you would have dismembered him yourself. And now you grant him freedom? and money? What has come over you?"

"We need to leave the market area," Maglorius said.

"Avoiding my question, Maglorius?"

"Walk with me." He took her arm so she had no choice.

"May I presume it was coincidence that you were nearby?" Valeria asked.

"Hardly," Maglorius answered. "Walk faster. It is unseemly to drag you along."

The terseness of his voice was alarming to Valeria, but she pretended not to have heard it. "If not coincidence, then I can conclude you followed me from the upper city."

"That is my duty. I am, after all, the bodyguard and watchman."

Valeria wondered what destination Maglorius had in mind. They were not climbing upward on the cobblestone street to the wealthy part of the city. But down. Toward the temple, where smoke rose from the altar sacrifices.

When Maglorius spoke, it sounded like he was straining to be casual. "Walking the markets is hardly anything one would suspect a young woman who has not eaten in three weeks capable of."

"I am resilient and hardy."

"And you also have a servant bribed who hides the greatest portion of each meal and takes it to you in the dark of night."

"How do you know this?"

"Because that servant came to me for permission for it. But if your deception is discovered, there will be little that we can do to help you further."

Without warning, Maglorius turned her onto another side street. Here, flax spinners were intent on their work. It was quieter than the main street.

Ahead, a dark-haired young woman in poor clothing stood in the shade opposite the flax spinners. The woman watched their approach as Valeria answered Maglorius.

"I'm not worried." Valeria spoke in a low voice. "Alypia spends hours each day with slaves attending to her baths and perfumes and hair. Father, he is in love with numbers. Neither really knows what happens in the household. Only you."

"That, too, is my duty."

There was something touching and vulnerable about his protective-ness, and Valeria stopped him.

She was almost hesitant. But there were only days before she would be sent to Rome to be married; it was obvious by now that her hunger strike was not working as a bluff. Unless she truly did end her life—something she'd never had any intent of doing—she would be on a ship, perhaps never to see Maglorius again. She wanted him to know how she felt.

"I cannot see how I will avoid being sent to Rome," she said. "So please let me tell you this now, since I may not have a chance before I am sent away. Many times, I have wished I were a slave in another house-hold. Not the daughter of a dusty old man who barely knows I exist."

She was about to tell Maglorius that as a slave, she might then be free to dream about him in the way a woman dreams about a man.

But his sharp reaction interrupted and surprised her. "Do not be so harsh on Lucius," Maglorius said. "You are judging him by his saddle, the past that has taken him to where he is now."

She'd never thought of her father as anything except an old man. She'd never wondered about him as a young man, always assuming he'd spent his life among the accounts of taxes. "Are you suggesting he is any-thing but what he appears?"

Both were standing where Valeria had stopped Maglorius. She no-ticed again the dark-haired woman staring at them and was vaguely jeal-ous. Even in peasant's clothing, the woman was beautiful. And she seemed to be interested in Maglorius. Too interested.

Distant shouts and screams reached them. Maglorius took her arm and moved her so forcefully that she stumbled.

The screams continued. The flax spinners around them stopped work and cocked their heads to listen.

"Maglorius!" Valeria said.

Maglorius ignored her and called ahead to the dark-haired woman. "Sophia!"

She stepped forward.

"It is as I feared," Maglorius said.

"Who is this?" Valeria asked.

Again, Maglorius ignored her. "Sophia," he said to the woman, "I will not lead both of you into danger. We'll go to the lower city, and I'll leave you there where you'll be safe."

✣ ✣ ✣

Ben-Aryeh came to consciousness in the gully off the road. Flies crawled across his face. He spat blood and sat up, wiping slowly at his face.

His donkey was gone.

Ben-Aryeh rolled to his feet and staggered out of the gully and up to a high point to look for help. The nearest caravan was at least a mile away, just beginning to ascend to Jerusalem. Ahead, another half mile away, were the gates of the walls of Jerusalem. But no one between here and there.

No one near.

He took deep breaths to regain his composure. No bones felt broken. His head throbbed, but if that was the worst of it, God had truly smiled upon him. Whatever had been stolen could easily be replaced.

But where was Olithar?

Ben-Aryeh took a step forward, then cocked his head. Had he heard correctly? Muffled sobs?

"Please . . ." It was a woman's voice.

From behind one of the massive boulders on the opposite side of the highway, where the hills rose.

"Please . . ."

Ben-Aryeh adjusted his sandals. Then his cloak. He began to climb toward the sound. The sobbing had a heart-rending quality to it, and when he rounded the boulder, he discovered why.

The young woman was bleeding across her face. Her dark hair, loosened from a shawl, was spread over the ground where she lay. Her dress was torn.

She had curled into a ball, knees tucked into her arms. "Please . . ." Her sobs made her incoherent.

Ben-Aryeh rushed forward and threw his cloak over her. He knelt. It did not matter to him that contact with her blood defiled him and that he would now have to go through the weeklong cleansing ritual.

The woman had been beaten. Probably by the same brigands who had attacked him.

She opened her eyes as his shadow fell across her. She flinched and sobbed louder.

"My child," he said, "I am a Sadducee. A priest of the temple. I am here to help not to harm you."

How he wished he had water. But the leather bags were attached to his donkey. And it was gone.

She reached for him with bare arms.

"My child," he repeated. "My child."

She squeezed him and clutched him as he helped her to her feet, careful to make sure that his cloak covered her and let her retain her modesty.

Together, Ben-Aryeh and the injured woman tottered down the hillside and back onto the road. Their progress was so slow that the caravan behind them was much nearer now.

"We'll wait here," he said, pointing back at the wagons. "There should be someone with water. And you can rest as one of the wagons takes you the remaining distance into the city."

"No! Please no!"

"My child . . ."

"Is it bad enough that you, a total stranger, must see my shame? How many men will there be in that caravan? Merchants to enjoy my loss of innocence."

"But—"

"I can walk. Help me. In the city I have friends. Just take me to the city gates."

She clung to him, begging until he consented then, holding his cloak, took her first limping steps toward the gate.

"I will get stronger," she said. "I promise."

THE NINTH HOUR

This is absolutely unacceptable." Ben-Aryeh's assistant, Olithar, spoke to Queen Bernice. "Ben-Aryeh's arrangement with you was total discretion. By sending a messenger to the temple for me, you risk that secrecy, and you also put me in a bad light."

Vitas sat on a nearby cushion, squirming with impatience. While he had reached the public courtyard of the royal palace a half hour earlier, he'd only just been escorted to this inner chamber. Vitas badly wanted to press Bernice for an escort of men to help him search for Sophia.

They'd barely had time to appraise each other—this after months of correspondence—when Olithar had arrived.

Upon entering the room, Olithar had given Vitas only a quick glance. Again, the fact that Vitas was dressed simply had served him well. There'd been no flicker of recognition, which meant that earlier when Vitas had passed Olithar on the road to Jerusalem, he had not appeared important or unusual enough for the assistant to give him a second glance.

Here, too, Olithar must have decided that Vitas was a servant of some kind, because he ignored Vitas completely.

"Ben-Aryeh's arrangement with me," Bernice snapped, "as you well know, means that Ben-Aryeh provides help when I need it. I do not need to justify my request to him, let alone to you."

Arrangement? Vitas wondered, not for the first time, what it was that had obligated a proud man like Ben-Aryeh to wait in Sebaste for his arrival.

"Furthermore," Bernice snapped, "I did not send for you. I sent for Ben-Aryeh. Where is he, if not at the temple?"

Olithar shrugged. "How am I supposed to know? He went to Sebaste days ago."

Vitas was glad that Olithar's back was to him. That meant Olithar did not see his reaction to what was obviously a lie. It had been two hours since Vitas had left Ben-Aryeh with Olithar just outside the city, as Vitas had recently informed Bernice. Time enough for Ben-Aryeh to make it to the temple. Especially if Olithar had done so. And here, Olithar was pretending he hadn't seen Ben-Aryeh at all.

Vitas, however, said nothing to contradict the assistant.

"Listen to the screams that reach us even here," Bernice continued in a commanding tone. "What led to this? What happened when the chief priests and leaders met with Florus? What caused Florus to send out his soldiers? I can't send him a message until I know."

Vitas remained motionless. Invisible to the two of them.

"I wasn't there," Olithar said.

"Are the priests gathered in the safety of the temple?"

"Yes."

"Then I'm sure you've heard. Tell me now."

Olithar shrugged. "Florus was in no mood for discussion. When the chief priests and leaders arrived, he gave orders that those who insulted him be handed over. Immediately."

"Ananias? What did he say?"

"From what I understand, he began a long flowery speech describing the hotheads as youths at an age when all men make impetuous choices. It sounded rehearsed. He went on to say that even he and Florus had probably done things they regretted later. It was obvious to all of us that the speech had no effect on Florus except to make him angrier, but Ananias spoke as if he were in love with his own voice. When he suggested to Florus—not requested—that it would be fair to pardon the hotheads, Florus exploded. He sent for his centurions and, in front of all the chief priests and leaders, ordered them to take their soldiers and plunder the market and kill anybody in sight and not to stop until they heard further orders from him."

"My worst fears . . ." Bernice closed her eyes and shook her head.

Then made her decision. "You will deliver the message to Florus for me. Wait for his reply and bring it back to me immediately."

"No," Olithar said.

"No? Our people are dying!"

"I want to help," he answered. "But this is not the way. Florus is already incensed at the temple priests. He may not even give me an audience, and if he did, his anger would only increase if he thought I was trying to stop his orders."

"It must be done!" Bernice was frantic. "Take the risk!"

"A lowly assistant going behind the high priest's back to the procurator of Judea? My days in the temple would be over. I would be useless to you and Ben-Aryeh."

Bernice paced back and forth. Finally, she knelt. She untied her sandals. She rose and tossed them to the side. "Get me a sackcloth and ashes," Bernice said grimly to a nearby servant. "I will go to him myself in bare feet, and certainly he will listen to my supplication."

"You cannot go!" Olithar said.

"Who else can?" Bernice asked. She spoke to the servant again. "Send for a horse for me."

✢ ✢ ✢

Maglorius and Valeria reached the next intersection, an even smaller alley, cloaked completely in shadow. Here were the residences of the lower city. Grimy walls, crooked doorways.

Sophia led them.

"Where are you taking us?" Valeria asked.

Sophia spoke quietly, almost shyly. "I have a friend who will help us. She is a . . ."

Sophia glanced at Maglorius. He nodded.

"She is a follower of Jesus," Sophia said. She turned forward again, leading them farther into the narrow alley.

Valeria had heard vague rumors about this new religion. She didn't get a chance to ask Maglorius about it.

"This I must tell you about Lucius . . . ," Maglorius said, speaking carefully as he guided her behind Sophia.

Valeria found it odd that Maglorius referred to her father with the intimacy of her father's praenomen, but she didn't interrupt.

"Although he is wealthy, he is filled with sorrow. He has been denied what he truly wants in life."

The shouting and screaming behind them grew louder.

"My father has no strong desires," Valeria said. "Except for more money."

"You know nothing about your father," Maglorius said.

The sound of confusion behind them was a distraction to Valeria. "How can you say that? I've grown up in his household."

"Lucius has been betrayed repeatedly during his life," Maglorius said. "It is enough to make anyone a tired, dusty old man. I can only imagine his disappointments, living with the results of that betrayal yet taking responsibility for those who depended on him, despite his legal right to spurn that responsibility."

Again, the reference to her father by his praenomen. How strange. "Maglorius, you speak in circles. What responsibilities could you mean?"

"I am as much to blame as anyone," Maglorius said. "In my defense I can only say it happened before I met the Christos. Since then, I have taken steps to change what I can about the life of deception. . . ."

"The Christos? You, too, are a follower?"

A peaceful smile crossed the ex-gladiator's face as he nodded.

Valeria once again became aware of the screams. She glanced around. "The soldiers?"

"This morning the Jews sent a delegation to Gessius Florus, imploring forgiveness for the actions of a few rash young men. He did not give it to them. Florus is determined to stir up a revolt."

"You seem to know a lot about the politics of Judea. Both Jewish and Roman."

"It is my duty."

"I thought your duty was to protect us."

"Which is why I must be aware of the politics. Florus is an enemy of your family, for your father, Lucius, knows too much about the abuses Florus heaps on the Jews. And Florus is desperate to keep reports of this from Caesar. Lucius is respected in Rome and would be a credible witness against Florus."

They had not stopped moving. Valeria was completely lost in the twisted streets of the lower city. "You are telling me much more than I have ever heard from you," she said.

"Events force me. Just as I feel I must tell you the truth about Lucius and my part in his betrayal. Instead of these events, I wish that you were on a ship going to Rome."

Maglorius let the distance between them and Sophia lengthen. He spoke softly, to keep their conversation private. Valeria did the same.

"You wish for me to be married against my will?" Valeria had a wild impulse to take his hand, confess her emotions, and hope Maglorius would take her away from the arranged marriage.

"I wish for you to be safe," he answered.

Sophia stopped without warning and rapped on the door in front of her. She knocked in an odd sequence, and moments later the door opened. Sophia spoke to the person who answered in low, urgent tones. The door opened wider. Sophia beckoned, and Valeria and Maglorius followed her inside.

Even after the dim light of the alley, it took Valeria a few moments to adjust to the even dimmer light inside the house. The few pieces of furniture in it were made of rough wood.

A woman, perhaps only a few years older than Valeria, shut the door behind them. This woman's belly was swollen with pregnancy.

To Valeria and Maglorius, Sophia said, "This is Sarai. She is a follower of the Christos. You can trust her and her husband, for he, too, is a follower."

Maglorius let out a long breath of relief. "I'm going back to get Quintus and Sabinus now. Please wait here."

Confused, Valeria wanted to deny the fear around her. "This is ridiculous. We do not need protection. Take me home." She turned to Sarai and half bowed. "Thank you for your offer, but it won't be necessary."

Maglorius squeezed Valeria's shoulder. "Your family is in danger. Don't you understand? Because of the events of the last weeks, Florus has sent his soldiers into the upper market to slaughter innocent Jews."

"My family is Roman. They are safe."

"I don't believe it is a coincidence that Florus sent soldiers to the upper market as well as to the rest of the city. Your family's mansion is nearby. I believe the soldiers will attack it."

"Why?" The conversation seemed surreal to her.

"No family will be safe. Especially if some, like yours, have been marked by Florus for the silence that will come with their deaths."

"How do you know this?"

"I know."

"Are you suggesting that Roman soldiers will be instructed to kill my parents? instructed by a Roman procurator?"

"I am suggesting that this is an evil world and in the confusion of soldiers sent out to destroy, anything can look like an unfortunate accident. Something a man like Florus would be highly aware of."

"Not my family. Impossible. My father—"

"Lucius does not have the power to stop these events." Maglorius released her shoulder. "Listen to me. You will remain here until I return with Quintus and Sabinus. You will—"

Three Roman soldiers burst through the door, swords drawn. Their faces were flecked with gore, and they screamed with bloodlust.

✠ ✠ ✠

Against the advice of Vitas, Bernice had chosen to gamble.

After dismissing Olithar, she'd argued to Vitas that because it was not a formal battle but a melee of soldiers set loose to pillage and kill, the individual Romans would rather choose targets who were helpless than stand ground and risk their lives unnecessarily by fighting a group of armed royal guards.

Vitas had argued in return that if Florus was determined to have this riot, no amount of supplication would deter him.

She'd said she was going, and he could choose to join her or stay behind. It was a remarkable first meeting.

He'd chosen to go with her. Sophia was in the city somewhere. He would need help to find her, especially under these circumstances.

Cries of horror and screams of pain were constant. Among the confusion of men and women running from soldiers in the crooked narrow streets, it was difficult for Vitas to determine the source of any specific cry of horror. What he could see allowed him to understand that no one was safe, even for those who had chosen to hide in a house or a shop.

Hundreds upon hundreds of soldiers were behaving no differently than a mob rioting and looting out of control. Their military gear gave them a double advantage over mere rioters, however. Soldiers clearly recognized other soldiers, of course, and did not waste time fighting each other. And they were protected by breastplates and leg and body armor, armed with razor-sharp swords, and were at the height of physical fitness. Few among the Jews had a chance in an individual battle; those who seemed to put up good resistance were immediately swarmed by other soldiers.

Because those who fled into the shops and houses were often forced out within minutes by soldiers who broke down the doors, the streets were constantly refilled with people fleeing soldiers, and soldiers pouring back into the streets to pursue them.

The slaughter had been happening for nearly an hour. The streets in places were red with blood, visible even to Bernice on the balcony of the palace. Frequently, those fleeing the soldiers slipped on the blood and were killed where they fell. Not frequently enough, a soldier would fall, and the pursued would gain a short reprieve until another soldier spotted the quarry.

The only advantage the unarmed populace had against the soldiers was the soldiers' greed. They'd been given permission by Florus to plunder at will, and whenever a soldier stooped to search a body for jewelry or coins, it gave any civilians nearby a better chance to escape.

Vitas saw all this from his own horse, as he and a contingent of guards surrounded Bernice.

She sat astride a white horse, wearing a sackcloth. Her hair was loose and gray with ashes, her feet bare. The horse was surrounded by a dozen palace guards, all carrying spears and shields.

She guided the horse at the pace of a walking man, and her mount remained within the protective cluster of the guards on foot and other guards on horseback.

Vitas marveled at her composure. Bodies were everywhere. Stabbed. Headless.

The wounded filled the doorways where they had crawled—if they could—for safety. Other wounded, too butchered to do anything but groan from where they fell, littered the streets.

The blood in places actually flowed, as if there had been a heavy rain, and Bernice's horse snorted nervously, sometimes prancing sideways. It took all her skill as a rider to keep it under control.

These were images Vitas had hoped never to see again, not after his time in Britannia. Yet here he was. And just as helpless to stop the carnage as he'd been there against the Iceni.

As their short journey continued, Roman soldiers occasionally rounded a corner and stopped in surprise at the sight of the phalanx of guards.

Bernice's argument proved correct. Each time, the soldiers ignored them. Some soldiers turned in pursuit of a man or a woman still trapped in the markets. Others were too heavily burdened with luxury goods from the looted shops to do much except continue in the direction they'd been walking.

Finally, they arrived at the gate of the Antonia Fortress.

Bernice called to the guard at the tower.

The gates did not open.

"I am the queen of the Jews!" she called. "I demand an audience with Florus."

The Roman above her disappeared.

Screams from the city streets continued to echo. The smell of burning wood drifted in from some of the shops that were now blazing.

Florus appeared. Above her. At the tower rampart.

"What is it?" He was forced to shout above the horrible noises of the markets.

Queen Bernice dismounted. She knelt on the stones of the street, craning her head upward to send her voice to Florus. "I am here in supplication," she cried. "Barefoot. Bareheaded. I beg of you to call your soldiers away from the killing."

Florus laughed. "I killed your messenger. Why should I not kill you too?"

"I am begging you. Please, please listen."

Two Roman soldiers marched down the street toward them.

She did not notice, but Florus did. "Find a child!" he shouted at them. "Bring the child here and decapitate it in front of the queen of the Jews!"

"No!" Bernice screamed. "No!" She stood, throwing her hands skyward. "I beg of you!"

"Two children!" Florus yelled at the soldiers. "Now!"

"You cannot do this!" Bernice cried. "How can I convince you to stop this?"

"Three children!" Florus shouted at the soldiers, who had begun to trot away at his earlier order. "The younger the better!" He leered down at Bernice. "When will you Jews learn not to infuriate Rome?"

"I beg you!"

Florus laughed. "Perhaps you should offer me more than supplication! It will make up for all the times at banquets you have ignored me as if I were rotting meat. Or perhaps I'll just take you without any offer on your part!"

He motioned to the royal guard beside him, pointing downward. Seconds later, the gate to the fortress opened, and soldiers swarmed toward Bernice and her guards.

"Leave!" the captain of the royal guard shouted at her. "Now."

Bernice hesitated.

The Roman soldiers slowed to a walk and threw up their shields. Standing side by side, the shields made an impenetrable barrier.

As they advanced, two royal guards grabbed Bernice and threw her on her horse.

"No!" Bernice cried. "Florus, stop this!"

"Come up and visit!" Florus taunted from his view. "Show me how badly you want your people spared."

Another palace guard grabbed the reins of her horse and turned it back toward the palace.

Bernice twisted, trying to call out to Florus again.

Yet another guard jabbed his spear into the hindquarters of her horse, and it bolted forward toward Vitas. Her own guards parted to let her through, then fell in rank to face the Roman soldiers.

Vitas looked up at Florus from his horse.

They made eye contact, but Florus did not seem to recognize Vitas dressed in his simple garb. Florus opened his mouth as if to shout something. Then shut it. A royal guard yelled for retreat, and the moment was broken.

Vitas spun his horse around and followed the others as they all fled the advancing Roman soldiers.

✢ ✢ ✢

Maglorius backed Valeria and Sophia and Sarai into a corner and walked forward to face the soldiers. "Please," he said. "Go. Leave this household in peace."

"We leave it in death!" one answered and slashed downward at Maglorius, who leaped backward but grabbed the soldier's arm as the blow continued to the floor. Maglorius kicked the soldier's feet, and as the soldier fell, he slammed his right foot into the soldier's head.

Maglorius had not lost his grip on the soldier's arm. He twisted it, using the soldier's sword to block a blow from the second soldier. It was a small room, and that prevented both remaining soldiers from surrounding him.

With a grunt, Maglorius yanked the sword loose from the fallen soldier and spun hard, blocking yet another blow. He parried once more, then jabbed.

The second soldier fell, gurgling from a hole in his neck.

Maglorius roared at the third, and with swiftness nearly impossible for Valeria to follow in the dim light, thrust and parried and overwhelmed the final soldier in a matter of seconds.

The silence—after the ringing of steel against steel—struck Valeria with the same impact as the suddenness of the attack.

"This . . . this . . ." Valeria could not find words to complete her sentence. She faltered as she noticed Maglorius' head bowed in prayer.

"Forgive me, Father," he said, "for the deaths of these men."

Moaning drew her attention.

Maglorius raised his head and stepped past Valeria.

Sarai was on her knees, staring down with disbelief at the blood that gushed from her hands where she held her belly. In the violence and confusion, one of the soldiers had succeeded in breaching Maglorius' defense.

"My baby," she said so quietly that Valeria wasn't sure the woman had spoken. "My baby."

Maglorius knelt beside Sarai.

"I am not afraid of death, Maglorius. But the baby. I want it to live." Sarai began to weep. The blood flowed freely down the front of the woman's dress.

Maglorius closed his eyes briefly. "This is what they are doing across the city. May the Christos have mercy on the women and children."

Sarai sighed and slumped forward. Her eyes were open and she continued to breathe.

"Hold her hand," Maglorius said to Valeria.

Blood. The intimacy of another person's blood. And a stranger at that. Yet it flashed across Valeria's mind: *None are strangers in the presence of death*.

She knelt beside Maglorius, unheeding of the blood that stained her silk dress.

The woman tried to smile at Valeria. "Good-bye, my baby," she whispered. "May Christos welcome you home with me."

Maglorius placed an arm around Sarai's shoulder and cradled her. She fell limply against it.

"'Don't be troubled,'" Maglorius whispered. "'You trust God, now trust in me. There are many rooms in my Father's home, and I am going to prepare a place for you.'" He paused and stroked Sarai's face. "Remember, these were His words. Take comfort in them."

Sarai's eyes began to close slowly.

Then opened.

"I see light," she said. She smiled. "My child. A boy! We are walking. He holds my hand with his tiny fingers. . . ."

Sarai's eyes widened, but she was looking past Valeria. She cried out in joyful greeting, "Christos!"

The woman died with that smile on her face.

Maglorius set her down gently.

Valeria was transfixed by the woman's smile and did not notice immediately that Maglorius had pulled a dagger from his cloak.

He grabbed Valeria by the hair and pulled her head back so her throat was exposed.

She was too startled to scream.

The dagger came down and slashed through her hair.

"Maglorius!"

He ignored her struggle and hacked until her hair was as short as a boy's. "No one must guess you are the daughter of Lucius Bellator. All Jews hate the Roman tax collectors, and to them he is the worst of all. After I leave, search for clothes here. Sarai's husband's clothes. He works at the sheep dip, and they will serve to completely hide who you are."

Maglorius reached under his tunic. With rapid movements, he untied a belt hidden beneath. "Here," he said, holding it out.

She took the heavy pouch.

"Gold," he said.

"This is a fortune," she said. "Where did you get it? Why? And why give it to me now?"

"When you get to the tunnels—"

"Tunnels!"

He continued as if she had not interrupted. "Those who live beneath the city will kill for a few shekels. Find a place to hide this pouch. You can return to it as you need to, taking a little each time."

"You talk as if I don't have a villa to return to."

"I pray you will," he said, "but Florus is a determined man. And what I've been told makes me fear for the future of any who bear the Bellator name. If my precautions are unnecessary, it will be a simple matter for us to return for the gold later."

"And now?" Valeria asked. "Where do we go?"

"We go separate ways. You must hide. Let no strangers know you are a woman either, for when lawlessness and bloodlust run in the city . . ."

He didn't complete his sentence. Valeria understood. And shuddered.

"Sarai . . . ," Sophia said, kneeling beside her friend and stroking her cheek. Valeria became aware of the other woman's presence.

Maglorius took a deep breath, finding strength to speak. "Each of us will sorrow for her later. And rejoice for her soul. But now is the time to attend to the living."

He moved to the doorway and stopped, a dark outline against the light from outside. "You cannot remain here. Down the street you will find a house with an entrance to the tunnel to the Siloam Pool. The house will be open and empty. I promise."

"How do you know this?" Valeria asked.

"No questions. Listen!" He gave both of them instructions on how to find the entrance and made them repeat it so he was confident they understood.

"Good." He nodded. "I leave here first. Wait until I am safely gone, then hide inside that entrance. That is where I will return to you with Quintus and Sabinus. Wait until morning if you have to."

Maglorius stepped out, then immediately returned and filled the doorway again. "There is a temple priest. His name is Ben-Aryeh. You will find him among the high priests. If I never see you again, he has the answers."

"Never see you again?" Valerius asked. "Where are you going?"

"To get Quintus and Sabinus. Even if it costs me my life."

✠ ✠ ✠

The braveness of the beautiful young woman beside him touched Ben-Aryeh's heart. True to her promise, she had fought to walk without needing much help. Anger burned inside him that she had been so brutally treated.

He walked with her, and occasionally she would stumble and grab his elbow for support.

"The brigands . . . ," he said as they neared the city. "Did they . . . ?"

"Yes. I told you they took my purity." She began to weep, then bit her lip and forced the tears to end. Her voice quivered. "I am engaged to a man in Jerusalem. He and I had a fight. In a moment of foolishness I decided I wanted to be alone. Away from all people. And the men, they found me. Dragged me to a place where—"

She began to weep again.

"They will be found," Ben-Aryeh said. "Justice will be done."

"I don't want justice!" she wailed. "Not even their deaths will give me back what I lost."

"My child, my child . . . ," he soothed, "you still have your honor."

He did not have to explain. If this had happened to an unmarried woman within the town gates, she would be as guilty of adultery as the man, for it was her duty to cry for help during an assault. But in the countryside, where there was nobody to hear her cries, only the man—

or men—would be found guilty. She would not be considered a woman of immoral quality. And the attacker would face death by stoning. This was prescribed by law.

They continued to walk. Ben-Aryeh could think of no other words of comfort, and she lapsed into silence broken by the occasional tears.

Nearer the gates, he could hear screams from the upper city.

Florus and the soldiers!

What had happened?

And his wife, Amaris! Was she safe?

He hurried the young woman forward until they reached the shadows of the city walls. The open gate beckoned. He could see the walls of the temple inside. Whatever was happening in the city had yet to spread to this quarter.

"Here," the young woman said, her voice clearer, "I cannot keep your cloak."

"Certainly."

"It is far too expensive. My dress will cover me."

They stepped through the gates and into the safety of the city. The street was not filled with crowds but at least a dozen men and women walked down the stones between the first houses.

"I insist," she said. "You have already helped me."

Reluctantly, Ben-Aryeh accepted his cloak.

She then startled him. "Help!" she screamed. "Help! Help!"

All the nearby people turned to them.

Ben-Aryeh stepped back, dumbfounded.

"Help!" the woman screamed again. She pointed directly at Ben-Aryeh. "This man has violated me!"

Some of the men moved closer.

"Help me!" she shouted. "Outside the city, he violated me!"

A jumble of thoughts moved through Ben-Aryeh's mind. It would be her word against his. Even if he wasn't found guilty, the suspicion against him would remain for the rest of his life. And what of Amaris? How would this affect her?

Ben-Aryeh knew the city as well as any man.

He made his decision.

If he escaped now, this woman would never be able to find him. The temple had thousands of priests, and if he remained in his mansion over the next days or even weeks, he would be safe from her.

As a few men started to jog in their direction, Ben-Aryeh spun around and darted into the nearest alley.

"Help!" she shouted. "That's the man!"

Twenty steps into the alley, there was a smaller one. Ben-Aryeh turned into it. He kept running, taking another turn and then another, losing himself in the maze of narrow, twisting alleys in this part of the city.

Within minutes, he was safe from any pursuers.

He began to sneak his way back up to the upper city.

Where his wife waited.

15 AV

THE FOURTH HOUR

In one of the upper rooms of the mansion Alypia held the baby Sabinus on a cushion with one hand. With the other, she lifted a second cushion.

Time now for the baby to die. Sabinus had served his purpose. First, he had brought Maglorius to her—the fool had been so delighted to discover he was going to be a father that he'd gladly signed on as a bodyguard for the household. But in recent weeks he'd said he could not continue the affair, that it was wrong in the sight of God. So the baby had become a burden to her in one way but useful in another, because he was her only leverage against Maglorius.

During the previous night, she was glad for Sabinus. She'd slept with the little boy, prepared to put a knife against his throat and threaten to kill him if Maglorius appeared to harm her.

But day had come; Maglorius had not. The baby had no more value to her.

She would sell the property quickly, indeed had long before lined up a purchaser should Bellator die. And now he had. She had hidden in her room while the soliders had slaughtered the household. Now all it would take was a short journey up the street to a wealthy Greek trader.

So, time to kill Sabinus. Especially with the convenient story that the soldiers had done so. She would leave the little boy's body with some of the dead servants in the courtyard. That would speak plainly enough.

She brought the second cushion down and pressed it against the baby's face. No sense cutting the boy's throat while he was alive. That would be too messy. No, when he was safely dead, she would place his body among the others and then run a sword through him as if soldiers had killed him.

She pressed the pillow harder, surprised at her son's strength as he squirmed for air.

✛ ✛ ✛

Because Sophia had been raised in a Jewish household, she was familiar with the laws of the prophets and the histories told by Moses and other great patriarchs. She certainly knew the chronicles of the kings of Judah, and among them had been taught about the acts of Hezekiah.

She had learned how Hezekiah and the prophet Isaiah, son of Amoz, cried out in prayer to God when King Sennacherib of Assyria threatened Jerusalem and mocked the Lord God. She had learned that the Lord sent an angel to destroy the Assyrian army with all its commanders and officers. How Sennacherib returned to his homeland in disgrace and was slain by swords wielded by his own sons in the temple of his own gods, proving yet again that the Jews were God's chosen people and would have a Messiah delivered to them.

Sophia had learned the acts of Hezekiah well enough to be able to quote a certain description of the king, provided and recorded by the ancients in the Chronicles: "He blocked up the upper spring of Gihon and brought the water down through a tunnel to the west side of the City of David."

The existence of Hezekiah's Siloam aqueduct beneath the city then was not the surprise to her that it had been to her companion, Valeria.

The Gihon was a natural spring that rose in a rocky cleft in the Kidron Valley. From it, water ran beneath the city; a primitive tunnel had been carved through the soft strata by the ancients, running nearly a third of a mile to the Siloam Pool. The tunnel was connected to other series of tunnels. It had many false passageways and more than a few secret entrances, known to the priests who fiercely guarded their knowledge. This Sophia had explained to Valeria once they were in the tunnels.

The afternoon before, they had trusted Maglorius enough to follow his instructions. Because of it, they safely made it through the house that had been empty as promised, into a courtyard, and down through a trapdoor almost invisible because of the cunning inlaid pattern of mosaics.

Sophia had expected darkness when the door closed above her, and was surprised by tiny shafts of light that pierced through the floor above her, another part of the design of the hidden trapdoor.

She'd seen steps carved into rock, descending into blackness beyond the reach of the shafts of light. The air was cool and vaguely damp. The echo of her breathing sounded harsh. Sophia and Valeria had rested on the top of the steps. Neither wanted to go farther into the tunnel.

Their hopes for the quick return of Maglorius had faded as the light above them had darkened to night. They'd remained there the night, sleeping awkwardly against the wall, waking to the slightest noises.

At dawn, Maglorius still had not appeared.

So, after morning had passed, Sophia told Valeria to wait while she went out into the city.

✛ ✛ ✛

A man with a water jar. "When you reach the Siloam Pool, look for a man with a water jar." Those were the instructions Queen Bernice had given her servant Hephzibah.

Hephzibah had walked down from the palace, shaded from the early morning sun by the rise of buildings on each side of the narrow streets. Perhaps only fifteen minutes had passed for her to reach the lower part of the city, but, lost in thoughts, she'd been unaware of time.

It seemed that everyone she passed on the streets shared that same daze of disbelief. Gone were the cries of shopkeepers hawking their wares, gone was the buzz of gossip and storytelling as the crowds moved from shop to shop with good-natured jostling. Instead, the streets were nearly empty, and as people passed by others, it was in silence. A silence of mourning. A silence of dread. A silence broken only by wailing each time someone found the body of a mother, father, sister, brother, son, or daughter.

Thousands had been slaughtered. Her queen nearly killed. Why had God abandoned them?

Hephzibah averted her eyes from those kneeling beside the bodies of loved ones. Because yesterday's slaughter had continued until nightfall, it was only now that the survivors were in the streets.

As she neared the lower city, however, the streets became more alive. Crowds were beginning to move upward to the upper markets to gather in protest of the atrocities of Florus. More than once, someone had urged her to change direction and join them. Each time, she'd shaken her head.

And now, with the pool in sight and the royal gardens just beyond as a backdrop, she looked for a man carrying a water jug. Among all the women near the pool, she saw him immediately, as it was unusual for any man to fulfill the domestic task of collecting the day's water for a household. He stood at the pool's edge, the large clay jar at his feet.

Hephzibah hurried toward him. As she drew closer, she indulged her curiosity. Who was it that had the queen's ear?

When she looked into his face, she thought she understood. He was a large man with an air of confidence—not the challenging aura of someone who wanted the world to know he was bigger and stronger and smarter than any other man, but a quiet confidence that spoke well to her soul. The scars on his face and the sadness in his eyes seemed to tell her that he had earned the right to this confidence. It was no wonder that her queen was drawn to this man.

"You are Maglorius?" she asked quietly.

"I am," he said. They stood in direct sunlight, and he squinted as he studied her face.

"I am Hephzibah. The queen has sent me."

"Forgive my lack of trust," he said. "Word for word, what was my message to her?"

"'Send someone you trust with a royal seal to the Siloam Pool to look for a man with a water jar.'"

Maglorius nodded. "You have the seal?"

"I do." Hephzibah had watched Bernice warm the wax and press the royal symbol upon it. Hephzibah passed it to Maglorius.

"So you are one she trusts?" he said.

"I am." Hephzibah pushed aside a tinge of guilt. The queen had been betrayed by many in her life—men, other servants, even her brother. It was to Hephzibah that the queen often confided those broken trusts, yet if the queen knew how Hephzibah had once been disloyal, no longer would that trust exist.

An image flashed in her head. Of the queen weeping in the days after an intruder had nearly killed her. Hephzibah felt her stomach tighten and hoped the man in front of her did not notice her pang of guilt.

"This intrigue," he murmured, absently shifting the seal from one hand to another, "I am tired of it. I wish we lived in a world without spies. Or the need for spies. Even the Master Himself in this city faced intrigue in His last days. . . ." He stopped.

"Go on," Hephzibah said. The Master? Dare she hope that Maglorius shared her faith?

Maglorius stared across the pool in silence, so Hephzibah, who much preferred to listen than speak, took a chance. "It was Passover," she said to encourage Maglorius. "To ensure that no one, especially Judas, knew ahead of time where He had arranged for the disciples to have supper, the Master sent them to look for a man carrying water, a servant of the owner of the house who was providing a room for the Master that night."

Maglorius turned his head sharply, a grimace obvious in the tightening of his lips.

"I'm sorry," she said. "Did I offend you?"

He rubbed the back of his head. "No. It hurts to move quickly." A smile from him. "You've read the letters passed among the believers?"

"I have," Hephzibah said. "So often that much of it I have memorized."

"Does Queen Bernice know of your faith?"

"She does not. Someday, when it is right, I hope to share my belief with her."

And then, Hephzibah thought, she would also confess that Matthias was her brother. Confess how she had helped him into the palace.

"I believe she hungers for it," Maglorius said. "Her soul has a deep need for love."

Hephzibah nodded. She grieved her brother's death. Had not known he intended it. The last day had been horrible. Dealing with his death. Dealing with the aftermath of the riots. It was only through prayer and faith that she'd been able to find hope in this tribulation.

Noises from the upper city reached them. The crowd must have gathered already.

"Time is short," Maglorius said. "Let me tell you what I request of the queen. But first remind her of her promise to me. She will understand."

The wailing of great lamentations echoed through the city. The force of it startled nearby pigeons, and in a blur they rose from the cobblestones where they had been pecking for food.

"She regrets she cannot meet you herself." The queen had emphasized this to Hephzibah, that she must tell this to the man. "In any other situation, she would arrange to see you herself."

"I would not want to put her in danger."

"She barely survived yesterday," Hephzibah said.

"What!"

"You haven't heard?"

"I was . . ." He stopped and rubbed the back of his head again. When he brought his hand down, Hephzibah saw that his fingers were flecked with dried blood. "No, I had not heard. Please tell me."

"Are you in pain?" she asked.

"Tell me about the queen and Florus."

He listened intently as Hephzibah did. The backdrop to her stories was the shouting that reached them, and the name *Florus* was audible here in the lower city.

"He is a treacherous man," he said when she finished. "He sends trouble into every life in Jerusalem. And that is why I need any help that the queen can give. There is a lost boy. From the Bellator household. If the queen can arrange to send as many people as possible into the city to look for him, I would be in her debt. The boy's name is Quintus."

"The boy's parents?"

Maglorius closed his eyes. "Dead."

"I am sorry."

"It was the soldiers sent by Florus. The boy escaped. At least, I pray he escaped. I've left one servant at the mansion, waiting should he return."

"Among all the people in the city," Hephzibah said gently, "and in the time of these riots, it may not be simple to find him."

"He will be wearing a signet ring. He is a Roman citizen. And as the rightful heir, a wealthy citizen. He must be found."

His intensity alarmed her. "Yes," she said quickly. "I will tell all of this to the queen. But come with me. A woman named Sophia arrived at the palace, looking for you."

✠ ✠ ✠

As she fought to suffocate her tiny son, a voice reached Alypia from the courtyard below.

"Hello? Hello?"

Alypia cursed the gods and lifted the cushion. Sabinus began to wail with fright. Alypia ignored him and looked down into the courtyard. A man was calling, a man she recognized from her time in Rome.

Gallus Sergius Vitas.

She whispered a prayer of gratitude to her household gods. Who better to help her claim the fortune that she was owed as a widow than Gallus Sergius Vitas, a man she knew from different functions in Rome, where she had attended as the subservient and nearly invisible wife of Bellator?

Stepping away from the window, she yanked down the left shoulder of her dress to expose enough skin to verge on the point of indecency. It wasn't difficult; hours earlier, at the first light of dawn, she'd already cut and ripped the dress in several places and trampled it to add smudges of dirt. She took a breath and pretended she was trying to compose herself in the way a woman would after surviving the assault of soldiers and an ex-gladiator.

Then she was ready.

She left Sabinus behind to wail alone and walked down to the courtyard. "Hello?" she said with the correct tone of fearful hesitation. "Hello?"

The man in the courtyard reacted immediately to the sound of her voice. He turned away from his inspection of the bodies of slaves and servants sprawled haphazardly where Roman soldiers had slaughtered them the afternoon before.

The peace of midmorning sunshine and the songs of the birds from the rooftop garden were a horrible juxtaposition against the obscenity of the aftermath of that violence. Yet all was not the illusion of peace.

Alypia knew she had the man's attention. She swayed slightly, as if she were on the verge of fainting, ignoring Sabinus' wailing from the mansion.

He moved quickly toward her. She pretended slight alarm and moved backward.

"I'm a Roman citizen," he called to her softly. "I mean no harm."

"Thank the gods." Alypia found a bench and collapsed on it. "After yesterday, I've been so afraid. I'm alone with no one to help! My husband was killed!"

Cautiously, the man moved even closer. She watched his eyes carefully, waiting for them to be drawn to the exposure of her upper body. A seduction now would be very convenient, especially given this man's family background and his power in Rome. Although she was disappointed that his eyes remained steadily on her face, she knew it was only a temporary setback. It was just the two of them here in the upper-city mansion, and she was a vulnerable woman appealing to a man's protection. And she'd already let him know she was without a husband.

He looked briefly past her as the baby wailed again, as if seeking the source of the cries. "You are Alypia," he said.

"Yes."

"I am Vitas." He sat on the bench but kept his distance from her. "Gallus Sergius Vitas."

"Not the same who serves as one of Nero's trusted advisers in Rome?" she asked, knowing the answer.

He nodded.

"Here in Jerusalem? Why?" This she did not know. Still, it was a gift from the gods. The only bad thing about his arrival was that he had heard the cries of the baby. Now she could no longer claim that soldiers had killed Sabinus.

"Yes, I am from Rome. To meet with your husband. On behalf of Nero."

"You are—" Alypia's voice caught in her throat—"one day too late."

Vitas allowed her the silence of grief.

She milked it, annoyed that Sabinus' renewed crying was a distraction from the portrait she wanted to present. She hoped Vitas would put an arm of comfort around her shoulder.

"The soldiers," he said. He put his cloak around her, but to her irritation, discreetly kept his distance. "Did they attack you when they killed your husband?"

"No!" Alypia gave an outburst of anger.

This seemed to startle him.

"He was murdered by one of this very household."

She had his full attention and enjoyed it. She turned to face him directly and bit on her knuckles. "An ex-gladiator named Maglorius. I'm afraid if he comes back . . ." She reached across, putting a hand on his forearm. It was important to touch him. "You do have a sword, don't you?"

"Maglorius?"

"If you've heard his name in Rome, it is the same man." She left her hand on his arm. "Once famed in the arenas."

"Maglorius."

"He was half dead after a sword gutted him in Asia, and when he arrived in Rome, too weak to return to the arenas, he was set free. Surely you heard that gossip."

Vitas was watching her closely.

"He joined our family as a bodyguard." Alypia wondered if Vitas had heard any rumors and decided to proceed as if he had not. No sense admitting to her affair with Maglorius until forced to. Especially now that it was so completely finished. What an impetuous period that had been in her life. But no longer would she allow love to affect her. It was only money and power that she wanted from men. "He traveled with us here to Jerusalem as part of his employment. And yesterday, after the soldiers were gone, he . . . he—" she sobbed—"it was terrible!"

"You are saying that he killed Bellator?"

"Yesterday afternoon. Just after the soldiers left. I'm sure he thought they would be blamed for it. But I saw it and—"

Alypia threw herself onto Vitas. "He murdered my husband! Help me. I'm the one who witnessed it. He'll want me dead, too. I think he believes he can plunder this mansion and our wealth if we are both gone."

"Was he by himself?" Vitas asked.

Alypia was not so lost in her acting that she was oblivious to the muscle of the man's arms or the solidness of his chest. Vitas was a rich man. A powerful man. And extremely attractive. What a pleasure he could be after years with Bellator, who'd been a rich and powerful man but old and extremely unattractive.

"What kind of question is that?" Alypia said, beginning to stroke one of his biceps. "Who else would be with him?"

Vitas extracted himself. Stood in front of the bench. Then knelt to look directly in her face. "I will make sure you are protected."

There it was again. The irritating cry of Sabinus.

She caught the look of concern in the glance that Vitas gave toward the sound again.

She knew the baby boy was frightened. The baby, however, was much more of a problem than a distraction to Vitas as she desired to seduce him.

Now that Quintus had disappeared or been murdered, Sabinus alone stood in the way of Alypia inheriting the bulk of Bellator's wealth. It wasn't the fact that the boy was her son and only child that had prevented her from suffocating him during the night. She'd never been maternal anyway, and with her hatred for Maglorius added to the idea of the wealth she would gain with the murder of Sabinus, she would have had no hesitation blaming the boy's death on the soldiers who had ransacked the mansion.

Now, too, she didn't want the baby to be an impediment to any romance she would entice Vitas to consider. Most men did not want a woman who brought with her the baggage of a previous marriage.

Then, as the baby's cries grew louder, a thought popped into her head that could be nothing short of inspiration. "The baby of one of the dead servants," she said.

Yes, that was it! Not her baby but one that belonged to a servant. She'd been so focused on creating the story about Maglorius and the murder of her husband, anticipating questions and ensuring it would stand up against any doubts, she'd not given the baby's situation the thought it needed. But this story worked too! For after yesterday afternoon's attack of the mansion by Florus' soldiers, she had ample choice of dead servant girls unable to deny motherhood.

"I don't know what to do," she continued. "I hold it but it just keeps crying. What will happen to the child now?"

"And your children," Vitas said. "What of them? Valeria and Quintus."

"Not my children," she said quickly. "Stepchildren. They belong to Bellator and his previous wife."

She wasn't going to explain that those children, like the baby boy, carried only Bellator's name not his blood. They had been fathered by someone else, for as she well knew, Bellator had been incapable of siring children.

And she certainly wasn't going to explain her plans to ensure that Quintus did not survive the next week in Jerusalem. It was a blessing, in a way, that the boy had fled believing his hero Maglorius to be a murderer. If Quintus returned, she would find a way to take care of him. And the same for Valeria, the little witch, if she'd actually survived the attack in the marketplace.

"Where is Maglorius now?" Vitas asked.

Couldn't this man see what was in front of him? A beautiful, impassioned woman.

"Maglorius," she almost snapped. "Hopefully the soldiers killed him after he fled here. If not, maybe he died somewhere in the city during the night."

Vitas stared past Alypia. Again, that look of concern for the crying baby.

"What can I do?" she said, wanting the man's full attention. "I'm now a widow. This city is full of danger. You can't leave me alone here."

"Florus will be—"

"Florus? He undoubtedly sent his soldiers here. He's hated Bellator since our arrival."

"As I was about to say," Vitas said calmly, "Florus will be no protection. I've been a guest at the royal palace. I was safe there last night. I have no doubt you will be welcome there too."

That explained it, Alypia thought with a flash of jealousy. Queen Bernice was notorious for being a man-eater. And the attentions of a Roman of the status that Vitas held would be of great value to her. That explained the lack of attention that Vitas was giving Alypia at this moment. He undoubtedly was more than a guest at the royal palace.

"I don't even trust that," she said. Alypia had no intention of going into the palace and competing with Bernice there. "Who knows if Florus might send spies into the palace to get to me?" She drew herself up. "All I need is a way to leave the city," she said, wanting Vitas to insist on staying with her.

His reply was not what she'd expected.

"I don't think the danger is as grave as you might believe. Bernice is urging the high priest to take the necessary steps to keep Florus happy. And Maglorius—"

"You must protect me from him. Have him arrested. Immediately crucified."

Vitas hesitated for a moment, then finally nodded. "Yes, I will take care of him."

THE FIFTH HOUR

Be prepared for the worst," Maglorius told Sophia when they reached the upper city. One of the queen's servants had found him for her, and she was very grateful for it. "Florus sent his soldiers this far too. And the Bellator household did not escape."

Be prepared for the worst.

It did not take much for Sophia to imagine the sights and sounds of soldiers here in the upper city. The bricked streets were wider than the ones leading from the market area to the poor parts of the lower city; the walls that hid the households from the streets much higher and thicker. Still, the clanging of swords, the screams of the victims, and the shouts of pursuit would have rung along these streets no differently than the horrors of what she'd heard the day before.

"You were here then before . . ." Sophia didn't have to finish her sentence. In the short time they had walked together from the royal palace to this point, Maglorius had explained that he'd spent the night looking for Quintus. But this was only after Sophia had reassured him that Valeria was still waiting for him beneath the city where he had directed them to safety during the height of the slaughter.

"I was there." Maglorius had a heaviness in his voice, as if holding an untold story. "Too late to do much except comfort the dying."

Directly ahead of them was an archway that led to the outer courtyard of the Bellator household. The iron bars were broken and twisted, evidence of the recent violent attack of soldiers.

"And the mistress of the household," Sophia said. "Alypia. She was not hurt."

For a moment, Maglorius looked away. As if hiding something. "I would expect you to find her there," he finally answered. "And, of course, Vitas, as we were told at the palace."

"Surely she will want to hear about Quintus. Yet you will not enter with me. Vitas will want to see you too."

"No." Maglorius spoke without hesitation. "I need to keep searching for Quintus. You deliver the news."

"Where will we find you later?" Sophia asked.

"I will find you," he answered.

"Maglorius, you are troubled."

"Alypia will have with her a baby boy," he said. "His name is Sabinus. Please ensure that the baby is doing well. I'm afraid that Alypia's maternal instincts aren't strong. Without servants to help her with him . . ." Maglorius let out a deep breath. "At any rate, that is the one favor I would ask of you. Look after Sabinus. Even volunteer to stay with Alypia until she can find another servant to help with the boy."

"Come in with me," Sophia invited gently.

"Make me that promise. Please."

"I do. Come in with me."

"I cannot," he said. "Soon enough you'll find out why. And when you do, remember you have made the promise."

"If I will find out soon enough, why not tell me yourself?" Sophia asked.

"Because then truthfully you cannot be found guilty of helping a fugitive. My crime would be your crime."

"Crime?"

"Go," Maglorius said gently. "Find Vitas. Watch over the baby."

Sophia had one last question. But she could guess the answer. "Sabinus is your son?"

Maglorius nodded. "My son. Until you helped me find my faith, he was my only reason to live." With that, he turned and hurried down the street toward the lower city.

Sophia entered the courtyard. She'd been promised that Vitas was here, waiting for her.

She called his name.

The only reply was the wailing of a baby.

✛ ✛ ✛

"Last night," Queen Bernice said to Vitas, "when I asked, you explained that you wanted to be here without official recognition but were reluctant to tell me why."

A messenger had found Vitas at the Bellator household and delivered an urgent request for him to return to the palace. Upon his arrival he'd immediately been delivered to Bernice at one of the upper-palace courtyards.

Vitas did not want to be here. He wanted to be back in the city looking for Sophia. He'd expected to find her at the Bellator household with Maglorius. Instead, Alypia had made her accusations with no mention of Sophia. Vitas could not believe Maglorius had murdered Bellator. But if he had returned to the Bellator household in the afternoon, Sophia had not been with him. Where was she?

"And last night," Vitas answered, impatient for Bernice to get to the point, "when I asked, you agreed that Ben-Aryeh was obligated to you but were equally reluctant to go into details."

"You know his son," she said without hesitation. "Or you certainly know of him. A Jew named Chayim."

It took Vitas several moments to place the name. "Chayim. The Jew residing in the imperial palace in Rome?"

Bernice nodded.

Curiosity was enough to temporarily distract Vitas from his thoughts about Sophia and Maglorius. "I thought he was a member of the Herod family."

"Now you understand my reluctance to tell you about him. Especially because of your closeness to Nero. Telling you this exposes my deceit. I misrepresented his lineage when I sent him to Rome."

"But that raises other questions."

"Like, for example, why Chayim was offered as a hostage when he isn't of Herodian descent?"

"That would be my first question," Vitas said. It was common enough. Kings of different countries sent Nero their sons, ensuring that they would not revolt: "And my second would be why did Ben-Aryeh agree to it?"

"You spend enough time in the imperial palace. Surely you know or at least have heard a thing or two about Chayim."

Vitas snorted. "If Chayim is the son of Ben-Aryeh, that is like saying the sun gave birth to the night."

"So Chayim hasn't changed."

"Was he a womanizer and devout disciple of wine and parties here in Jerusalem?" Vitas responded.

Bernice nodded, smiling faintly. "You can imagine how much difficulty that presented to Ben-Aryeh."

"That, then, is the answer to my second question. Ben-Aryeh must have found it very convenient to see Chayim go."

"Yes," Bernice said. "Which is also the answer to your first question. Because it was convenient for Chayim to go, it put Ben-Aryeh in debt to me. Where I wanted him." She hesitated. "There's more."

"Ben-Aryeh is one of the most powerful men of the temple," Vitas said, "and it would never hurt you to have a way to control that power."

"You understand quickly."

"I deal in the politics of the imperial palace."

"Of course, which is why you want your presence here unknown to Florus?"

Vitas merely smiled. This question was not why she'd sent a messenger for him.

"Florus is a dangerous man," she continued. "You know that too."

"Yesterday's events are enough proof of that." Thousands killed. It was doubly important now that Florus not discover the presence of Vitas in Jerusalem. Vitas grimly looked forward to delivering a report of his atrocities to Nero, knowing that whatever version Florus gave Rome would immediately be exposed as a lie.

"Would you go to Florus directly if you knew it might save countless lives today?" Queen Bernice asked.

"What do you know?" Vitas asked sharply.

"Despite assurances he might give to the temple authorities, he intends to instigate another riot."

Vitas rubbed his face. Would Florus listen to warnings about Nero's wrath, or would Florus take the opportunity to kill Vitas for the silence it would ensure?

"What I say or don't say will not make a difference to Florus," Vitas finally said. "If I make it back to Rome, however, I can ensure that he loses his procuracy."

"I feared you might say that."

"Is my assessment wrong?"

"Probably not. But I don't know where else to turn."

"What about Ben-Aryeh? You reached me by messenger. Surely you can find him and use your leverage to make him speak to Florus."

"It's too late," Bernice said. "He's already with the delegation in front of Florus."

✠ ✠ ✠

"I understand you were successful in persuading your people to return to their homes this morning." Florus spoke from a large chair, looking down on the delegation of priests, Ben-Aryeh among them.

The room reeked of pomp. Florus wore his robes of power and was surrounded by soldiers. The priests wore their temple robes, and stood in a group of about two dozen, all of them men of greatest wealth and influence in the city.

"We were," Ananias replied. As high priest, he was the designated spokesman.

Ben-Aryeh, like Ananias and all the other Jews, was well aware that a single political misstep among these Jews of influence would result in a delegation approaching Agrippa to relieve Ananias of the high priest's position.

"Are you satisfied that there will be no talk of further riots in protest of how Rome governs the Jews?" Florus asked. It appeared that he was deliberately allowing a smile to play across his face, as if he were taunting Ananias into arguing that the riots would not have occurred except for the actions taken by Florus.

Ananias merely bowed his head.

Ben-Aryeh could only guess how much self-discipline it cost Ananias to remain silent. Earlier in the morning, for nearly a full hour, the priests of greatest authority, including Ben-Aryeh, had pleaded with the great crowd gathered in the upper market, where the soldiers had begun their slaughter the day before. The leaders of the city had beseeched the people not to provoke Florus further; many of the priests had torn their clothing and fallen down before the crowd. These people had all suffered deaths in their immediate families because of the soldiers, had seen their shops or homes looted. Some of them—even Jews with Roman citizenship—had been whipped by soldiers. The gross unfairness of such punishment forced upon them by Florus had some ready to charge the fortress unarmed.

Yet, finally, the priests and leaders had persuaded even the most seditious that discretion would serve the city far better than continued protest. And Florus had sent for this delegation to visit him here in the Antonia Fortress as a result.

"Speak clearly," Florus ordered Ananias. "You are satisfied that there will be no talk of further riots in protest of how Rome governs?"

"There will be no talk," Ananias said. "There will be nothing done to provoke you or your soldiers."

Tense as it was in the room, Ben-Aryeh felt a hateful stare, as if it were a physical presence pushing on his soul. He glanced sideways and saw Annas the Younger. Smiling.

Annas the Younger, while no longer the high priest, still counted as one of the leaders of the city. Ben-Aryeh, who'd been triumphant in getting the last of the Annas family removed, had made efforts not to lord his triumph over Annas, and indeed, on the advice of his wife, Amaris, had made great efforts to shun gatherings where Annas or his brothers might be.

This, however, was unavoidable.

Their eyes met, and Annas continued to stare. Continued to smile. Ben-Aryeh believed he was a stronger man in all aspects than Annas the Younger. But he was unable to outlast Annas in this naked contest and returned his attention to Florus.

At least part of his attention. Part of Ben-Aryeh's thoughts remained on Annas. Had someone recognized Ben-Aryeh the day before when the woman shouted for help and accused him of violating her? Had someone recognized him as he fled, an action that surely would have been seen as guilt of the crime? Had someone told all of this to Annas the Younger? Was that the reason for his wolflike smile?

"Nothing done to provoke me or my soldiers," Florus was saying. "You may believe that among yourselves, but you Jews are a contentious, stubborn people. I certainly find no reason to believe it myself."

"The city will remain quiet," Ananias said. "Unless—" He cut himself short.

"Unless?" Florus seemed amused, seemed hopeful that Ananias might attempt to cast blame on Florus.

"The city will remain quiet," Ananias repeated.

"Your word means little to me. Actions, however, speak loudly. This is what I want from you and your people. I have two cohorts of soldiers arriving today from Caesarea. I want a peaceful demonstration. I want your people to greet my soldiers with silent salutes of respect. If they can do that, then I will be satisfied that your troublemakers are truly under your control. And I promise no further punishment will come to the city."

On the surface, it seemed like a simple enough request. But Ben-Aryeh knew better. A minority of the Jews were angry enough to start a war. The abuses of Florus had been going on too long, and Jerusalem was a covered pot ready to boil over.

"Procurator," Ananias began.

"Are you going to inflict another long speech on me?" Florus asked, his face beginning to darken with rage. "Such as you did yesterday when you refused to deliver the troublemakers to me? Have you already forgotten the consequences of your defiance in that speech? Or should I invite you to go outside and listen to the wailings of those who mourn?"

"It will be done," Ananias said quickly. "We will assemble our people and send them to greet your soldiers with respect."

"Good," Florus grunted. "Now leave before I change my mind."

THE EIGHTH HOUR

The temple authorities were able to accurately guess how many people the Court of the Gentiles could hold, not by counting the people themselves, but because of their accurate calculations of the number of lambs slaughtered at the altar every Passover. At twelve people per lamb, they knew the court was capable of holding a hundred thousand people.

On this day, Ben-Aryeh was able to cast an expert eye over the crowd and decide that only a fifth of the court held people. It was a crowd then, he knew, of roughly twenty thousand. All were assembled to listen to the chief priests.

It was the second occasion that day—and also only the second occasion in the last eighteen months—that circumstances had forced Ben-Aryeh near the physical presence of Annas the Younger. In front of Florus, Ben-Aryeh had managed to stay on the opposite side of the room, as far as possible from Annas.

Here, on a hastily built stage of rough lumbers, Ben-Aryeh was almost close enough to touch Annas, and he was very conscious of his enemy's presence.

This, however, was a mild concern for Ben-Aryeh in comparison to his greater worry. In the public eye here on the stage, every one of those twenty thousand gathered would be able to see him clearly if he moved to the front of the small group of priests.

And the woman who'd accused him of violating her could well be among this crowd. His safety to this point had been in the likelihood that she would never see him again in the crowded city. He had not expected to be required to be part of an assembly in front of a crowd of this magnitude.

It was his goal, then, to remain hidden among the other chief priests.

As Ananias the high priest raised his arms and brought the crowd to silence, Ben-Aryeh allowed himself a wry smile. This was the first time in his life he was grateful for his relatively short stature. As long as he stood behind all the others, he would be nearly invisible.

"People of Jerusalem," Ananias began. "You well know that destruction is almost upon this city and our families!"

Dust was sprinkled heavily in Ananias' hair, as it was with all the other chief priests, including Ben-Aryeh. They were dressed in their magnificent temple robes, and the contrast of the dust of humility and the glory of the temple was a powerful and rarely seen sight for the people.

"Yet by our actions we can save ourselves!"

Ananias had no need to shout. The acoustics of the temple were superb; had there been a hundred thousand in attendance, with all of them silent, even a slight cough from the stage would have carried to all of them. Ananias shouted because he wanted the drama that all of the chief priests had agreed upon earlier as a necessity for swaying the crowd.

"Two cohorts of soldiers arrive today from Caesarea. Florus already has enough forces in the city to defeat us, yet more arrive. We must show Rome that we want no battle, and the city will be saved!"

Ananias raised his arms. "People of Jerusalem, we must leave this temple as one person, travel outside the city gates as one person, and quietly salute those soldiers as one person. Only this act will prove to Florus that there are none among us who wish more trouble from Rome!"

"What benefit is a salute to soldiers who serve Rome?" one man cried. "I say death to Caesar! Over three thousand died yesterday! Women, children! Even infants! We leave this temple and fight them now before the cohorts arrive! We are God's people. We shall prevail, for God has promised us a Messiah!"

Shouts of agreement rose.

Ananias pointed at the man, and temple police converged upon him, dragging him away.

Despite the anxiety that came with the fear that the woman would suddenly shout and point an accusing finger at him, Ben-Aryeh allowed himself another wry smile.

Had Ananias truly wanted the man silenced, he would not have waited so long to summon the temple police. No, the man's protests and his arrest had been orchestrated earlier. Outside the temple, he would be released and sent home, two coins of gold richer.

"No!" Ananias called. "No!"

The chief priests had wanted an open argument started to give them reason for what happened next.

"Bring out the holy vessels!" Ananias cried. "Show all of the sacred treasures we must protect for the sake of our God!"

All of the temple's harpists and singers—hundreds upon hundreds—poured out of the Court of Women, overwhelming the crowd with a glorious hymn. Following them came every priest in the employ of the temple—from lowest in status to highest—some carrying a holy vessel of gold or silver, some carrying ornamental garments trimmed with gold threads.

Never before had the people of Jerusalem seen such a display of the wealth hidden within the Holy of Holies. Some actually fell back in the presence of such sacred objects. Some fell to their knees.

Ananias signaled the harpists and singers, and instantly a silence fell upon the temple, the reverence of the crowd a palpable sensation.

Now Ananias spoke quietly. "We are a great people, serving the great and only God. It is to Him and for Him that we must show control and discipline to honor Him and His treasures that we have successfully preserved for untold generations. Shall we yield to the few troublemakers and have the entire city and this temple laid waste because of them? Or should we remove all reason for any war that Florus might inflict?"

"Death to the troublemakers!" came another shout. This, too, had been orchestrated. As were most of the other shouts of agreement.

Before there could be any unanticipated shouts of defiance, the harpists and singers filled the court with another glorious hymn. Even though Ben-Aryeh knew all of it had been planned as tightly as any temple service, the music still touched his soul and brought tears to his eyes.

He looked past the shoulders of the chief priests in front of him and saw many people openly weeping. This was exactly the effect that Ananias had predicted.

The crowd was theirs.

When the last strains of the music died away, Ananias raised his arms again. "Do any of you wish to cause trouble? Do any of you wish by the harmful actions of an individual to deny this city freedom and peace?"

He let the words hang.

Now if anyone answered, they were to be instantly swarmed by temple police and bludgeoned to death.

But the music and the sight of the thousands of holy vessels gleaming in the sunlight and the thousands of ornamental garments were enough to control any remaining troublemakers.

"Then follow us!" Ananias commanded. "We will lead you outside the city to the soldiers!"

Ben-Aryeh knew then that he was safe. He could remain hidden among the chief priests until they were down from the temporary stage, where he would be out of the public eye.

"You think I don't know who arranged for Agrippa to remove me from the high priesthood?" The hissing voice of Annas the Younger broke Ben-Aryeh from his thoughts.

Ben-Aryeh turned, almost startled. In the five years, neither had addressed the other directly during the few, brief occasions they were close enough to speak, let alone alluded to Annas the Younger's fall from power and how Ben-Aryeh had orchestrated it. But each knew the other was aware of the events. And each knew the other was aware of the hatred between them that remained like a sword. So Ben-Aryeh knew exactly what Annas meant as he continued to speak in the temple courtyard.

"You shall pay for it, Ben-Aryeh," Annas said. "Finally. I lost my position. But you shall lose your life. And I will be the first one to cast a stone."

Before Ben-Aryeh could reply, Annas the Younger flashed another wolflike smile that seemed to stay in Ben-Aryeh's vision as Annas shuffled forward among the other chief priests.

✠ ✠ ✠

These had been the instructions from Maglorius: "Wait with Vitas until my return."

Except Vitas had not been anywhere. The opulent Bellator mansion had been abandoned. Sophia had stepped past the bodies in the court-yard already buzzing with flies around the eyes and noses. She'd consid-ered dragging the bodies into the shade and looking for blankets to cover them, but the crying of the baby had drawn her inside.

She'd found Sabinus alone near the body of a servant woman, tug-ging on the hem of her dress. Sophia's first impulse had been anger that the baby had been abandoned to crawl among the bodies. She'd pushed aside the anger and fled from the body with Sabinus, then searched through the household for food to quiet his cries.

The wealth around her was staggering—more than she could imag-ine belonging to a single person. It also filled her with sadness; whoever lived here had been able to satisfy every earthly desire yet had lost it all. So how much was it truly worth?

These thoughts were soon replaced with wonder for the miracle of life as she held Sabinus and fed him. She marveled at his tiny fingers and toes. Marveled at his charming little smile. Crooned to him as he crooned to her. Fought away any hopes at all that someday she might be able to hold a child of her own.

Time did not seem to pass at all; then she heard voices in the court-yard.

Holding Sabinus, she rushed out and discovered two large men lift-ing the body of a fallen slave. Greeks, she knew by their clothing. Bearded, wide-shouldered, obviously laborers. She saw that they had al-ready moved a couple bodies onto a cart, arms and legs hanging haphaz-ardly over the side.

The taller of the two noticed Sophia in the archway. He dropped the legs of the body he was holding. His partner cursed him for his clumsi-ness, then turned to see where the first man was pointing.

Directly at Sophia and Sabinus.

The second man dropped the upper half of the body with a thump.

"Who are you?" the tall one asked.

"I was about to ask you the same," Sophia replied. Something felt wrong, but she wasn't going to show fear.

"We've been sent here by the new owner," the second one an-swered. Both edged toward her. "To clean things up."

"New owner?"

"Sold by the wife," the first one said. "No less than an hour ago. From what I hear, it was a steal. Her husband's dead, and she's in quite the hurry to get to Caesarea to find a ship back to Rome. Not that I blame her with Florus and his army camped in the city."

"Don't blame her at all," the shorter one said. "A lot of lootings and killings have taken place. Not all by soldiers either."

They were closer now. Almost leering.

Sophia pressed backward.

"See," the first one said, talking more to his companion than to Sophia, "if her body is piled with the others, who's to say how she died?"

They were only a few paces away now. Close enough that she could see their eyes, red from drinking early in the day. Close enough to smell clothes that had obviously been slept in, probably night after night for weeks.

"Just another dead slave," the second agreed. "But we could have some fun with her first."

"We were told the place was empty," the first one said. "Why not?"

Sophia realized if she tried to run with Sabinus it would be easy for them to tackle her from behind. There was too much risk that the baby would be hurt badly as she fell.

How could she save the little boy's life?

✛ ✛ ✛

Events had transformed her world so quickly that Valeria could hardly believe this was reality. The afternoon before, she'd been part of the buzz of the marketplace. Then had come the screams and terror as the soldiers attacked innocent people at random.

Could she even trust her memory?

Again and again in her mind she saw the sudden violence of Maglorius defending her against Roman soldiers. Again and again she heard the heartbroken sadness of Sarai as she bid good-bye to her un-born baby, heard the startled joy as she cried out to Christos moments later.

Had all this really happened? Had the soldiers reached her villa as Maglorius feared? What of Maglorius? What of Quintus?

In the light that came from beneath the door that guarded the tunnel, Valeria raised her hands, saw the blood that had dried on her fingers. The pouch jangled as she shifted her legs, a reminder of what Maglorius had given her after killing the soldiers. Each breath she took carried the sour decaying smell that clung to the clothes of Sarai's husband that she'd put on. Each movement brought the roughness of its fabric against skin that had felt only silks and cottons.

Yes, she told herself, *this has happened.*

And Maglorius had not come for her. Nor had Sophia returned as promised.

Did she dare go look for Maglorius?

Valeria forced herself to move, to block the fear from her mind. First, she must hide the gold. Deeper into the tunnel she went, grateful that all she needed to do was look up to see the hope that the light from above gave.

Where to hide the gold?

By feeling around above her head, she found a crevice large enough to hold the pouch. Before placing the pouch in it, however, she counted the paces from the bottom of the steps.

Twelve.

Satisfied she could find it again when necessary, she reached upward and hid the pouch.

Another thought struck her.

She took it down and removed several coins.

Replaced it again.

Then she returned to the bottom of the steps to wait for Maglorius. She would wait a few more hours, she told herself. She tried to distract herself from her worries, but she could not escape the questions that arose in the dim, cold hiding place.

Her questions brought guilt.

Valeria had sneaked out of the villa, forcing Maglorius to follow her. Because of it, they'd arrived at Sarai's house without Quintus, and probably much earlier than they would have if she had not sneaked out. What if they had arrived later? Would Sarai have been elsewhere in the house with a chance to escape from the Roman soldiers? Had she then caused Sarai's death?

And had she risked Quintus' life now too? After all, if she'd remained at the villa, Maglorius would have been able to remain with both
of them instead of leaving Quintus behind.

More questions troubled her. How did Maglorius know all he did
about these events? And if he knew the family was in danger from
Gessius Florus, why hadn't Maglorius warned her mother and father?

Uncomfortable as it was to be sitting on the cold steps in smelly near-
rags of men's clothing, Valeria began to drift into sleep as she leaned
against the wall of the tunnel. Her last waking thought was about the
final moments of Sarai's life, and how Maglorius had tried to comfort
the dying woman.

Who, Valeria wondered, *is the Christos?*

When she woke, her mouth dry and her muscles aching, she blinked,
trying to remember where she was. A noise grew louder, the noise that
had tickled her subconscious and awakened her.

Maglorius?

The door above her opened.

Slowly.

But the figure was not of the ex-gladiator who had protected her for
the last year.

✝ ✝ ✝

Ben-Aryeh let the threats of Annas the Younger echo in his head. Cast a
stone? That was the punishment for adultery. What did Annas the
Younger know?

Ben-Aryeh was not guilty of violating the woman. He'd done nothing except try to help. Yet the sensation of guilt washed over him, and
he fought the urge to flee.

As he stepped down from the stage, he saw a familiar face.
Maglorius. Big, broad shouldered. Calm.

What was the man doing here? In such a public place? They'd
agreed it would be wise not to be seen together, yet now Maglorius
was stepping away from the crowd with purpose. In Ben-Aryeh's direction.

Perhaps Ben-Aryeh could make it look like a chance encounter, as
if Maglorius were simply one stranger among many in the crowd.

With pretended nonchalance, Ben-Aryeh kept walking along the path that would take him to Maglorius. "My good man," he said loudly for the benefit of anyone who might be too near, "if you'll excuse me . . ."

"Listen." Maglorius stepped close and grabbed Ben-Aryeh's shoulders. "This is so important I had no choice. Bernice received a message from her spy in the camp of Florus."

Ben-Aryeh glanced around to see if any of the chief priests had noticed. All seemed preoccupied with getting into position where they could lead the massive crowd out of the temple and the city.

Ben-Aryeh began to relax. Then froze.

It was her! The young woman he'd saved from the brigands! Walking directly toward him, searching faces in the crowd.

Had she seen him yet?

"Not now! Not now!" Ben-Aryeh was normally a calm man. Yet he'd fled the day before from the woman when perhaps he should have stayed and vigorously denied the charges. Now the chance to declare his innocence was lost, for the Sanhedrin would surely be able to find witnesses at the city who had seen him run, and that action would prove him guilty in all their eyes.

"Listen!" Maglorius said again, clutching Ben-Aryeh's shoulders. "There will be more slaughter if—"

The woman had not seen him yet. But she was looking. Her eyes were about to sweep in his direction!

Ben-Aryeh felt panic. He threw a fist into the stomach of Maglorius. It wasn't enough to knock the man over but enough to shock him. Ben-Aryeh took advantage of that and twisted loose from the strong grip of the Roman.

He stepped into the flow of the crowd, once again grateful that his height made him invisible among those towering above him. He pushed through people, ignoring their protests.

Ahead was the Court of Women, and ahead of that the Court of Israel. Once he reached it, he could run past the altar and to the Court of Priests.

He was certain the woman had not seen him.

Once he reached the Court of Priests, he would be safe. He knew the secret tunnels beneath the temple as well as any man alive. He could

hide there for the remainder of the day. At dark, he would escape the
Temple Mount unseen and return to his mansion in the upper city.

Where he would finally be safe with his beloved Amaris.

Vitas roared.

He'd entered the courtyard, seen the two men pressing in on Sophia,
one of the men lifting a knife in threat.

She'd cried out his name.

They turned as he sprinted toward them, still roaring, drawing his
short sword from his tunic.

They separated, showing the wiliness of street fighters. The other
one drew a knife too, a short curved blade.

Vitas slowed, now that they weren't a direct threat to Sophia.
He glanced around, taking in his surroundings, a natural unthinking response of a fighting man hoping to take advantage of the ter-
rain.

Vitas stopped and evaluated his opponents. They were big, mid-
twenties. One's arms were badly scarred. The other was missing a front
tooth. Both were grinning—obviously they'd been in situations like this
before and were far from afraid.

"Run," Vitas told Sophia. He kept his voice calm, though it felt like
the pounding of his heart would distort his words. "Now."

Whatever happened, he'd make sure it lasted long enough for her to
escape. Then he could give her no more thought.

The man on his right circled behind him. Vitas was forced to dance
delicately, keeping the other in his peripheral vision.

Without giving his body conscious directions, he made the first
move. A faked lunge. Surprise was his only chance. That man jumped
back, giving Vitas an opening toward the wall.

Because Vitas hadn't committed fully to his lunge, he was able to use
his momentum and a sudden direction shift to get to the wall of the
courtyard, beneath the shade of an orange tree. He grabbed one of the
fruits with his free hand, hurled it clumsily at the second man, who
ducked and laughed.

They pressed in on him. The wall at his back gave him some advantage of defense, for it didn't allow one or the other to move behind him. But it trapped him as well.

"No reason to rush," one man told the other. "Get as close as you can without bringing that sword into range. Soon enough, one of us will have a chance at his unprotected side."

As the man spoke, he reached into the dirt beneath the tree and scooped up a handful. His intent was obvious. To throw it at Vitas and distract or blind him.

The men edged closer.

Vitas heard his own breathing. Heavy. The adrenaline of battle filled him. Yet he'd learned it could be an enemy as well, causing men to act without caution.

He squatted, trying to keep both men in his vision. He, too, scooped dirt into his free hand. The tactic could work both ways. He stood.

One moved close. Vitas whirled on him, whipping his sword blade through the air. The man danced back. Vitas was spinning the other way, anticipating an attack from the second.

Instead, the man was several steps away. Laughing at Vitas.

The other moved in again. Vitas was forced to defend as viciously as possible, then again, swing his sword to the other side in anticipation of the second attack. Again, only empty air. The other man still had not moved.

So that was the plan: One would wear him down; the other would wait.

Then came a slight whistling sound. And a thud and a crash. And the second man was down as if thunder had struck him from the sky.

Vitas blinked as he tried to understand the shards of pottery around the man's head and shoulders.

Then came another crash. This time to his left. At the feet of his other opponent.

Vitas risked a glance upward. Caught a glimpse of long, dark hair from a figure on the second story.

Sophia?

A flash of movement from his left. Vitas managed a half step backward and grunted as pain seared his side. The knife had bounced off his ribs.

The half step had been enough to throw the other man off balance, and his attack carried him forward. Vitas smashed the butt of his sword down on the man's head, then brought his knee upward to pound the man's chin.

It was enough.

His opponent collapsed. His body trembled, then stilled.

Vitas looked up again, just in time to see another clay pot in midair. He jumped sideways and it broke on the ground at his feet. "Hey!" he shouted.

Now he could see Sophia's face. She was wincing, obviously alarmed at how close she'd come to hitting him.

He grinned at her. "Don't think this changes things," he called to her. "I'm still mad at you."

✠ ✠ ✠

Valeria's knees buckled·in relief as she recognized the figure. It was Quintus! Her brother! Alive!

Surely Maglorius was near. Everything would be fine now. Maglorius would take care of them.

She stepped upward from the darkness.

Quintus reacted instantly. "What have you done with my sister!" He brought his short sword high and slashed at her. The weight of it was too much for his arm, however, and he wobbled for balance. The sword fell harmless at her side.

"No!" she cried.

He bowled forward, butting his head into her stomach.

She fell backward on the steps, gasping.

He began to pummel her face with his fists.

She rolled, taking him with her. Finally, when she was on top of him, sitting on his stomach, she grabbed his wrists and pushed them to the steps behind his back.

He began to knock his knees into her back, twisting and flailing, screaming.

"Quintus!"

He stopped.

"Quintus," she said more quietly, "it's me. Valeria."

His eyes were wide. "Valeria?"

Then she remembered. Her hair. Maglorius had cut it short. And her clothes. It was not surprising that he hadn't recognized her.

"Valeria?" he asked again.

"Yes," she said, smiling gently. She rose with a graceful movement and helped Quintus to his feet.

He touched her hair. "You don't look like Valeria . . ." He sounded genuinely puzzled.

"Maglorius cut my hair. He said it would be safer. He told me to wait here while—"

"Maglorius," Quintus said, spitting. He pushed her aside and picked up the short sword. "I hate him. I swear it here and now. I will pierce his heart with this sword."

"Quintus?" She saw that his tiny face was screwed up in pain. Tears began to leak from his eyes. "Quintus?"

He tried to speak, but emotion overcame him and he began to sob.

She pulled him close, held him, and waited until he finished.

"Maglorius . . ." Quintus gulped back a sob. "Yesterday afternoon. He came into the courtyard and found me practicing with the wooden sword. He gave me this."

Quintus touched his sword. "He told me if the soldiers came that I should hide in the cistern. He said Roman soldiers might attack and if anything happened, I should wait until it was quiet and I was sure they were gone before I came out of the cistern. He told me how to find the house in the lower city and how to get to the tunnel. He told me where I would find you."

Quintus hugged her. "Last night I was too afraid to move through the city. I waited until this morning. I'm so glad you're here."

"Maglorius," she prompted him gently. "And Mother and Father . . ." She was still trying to comprehend. Roman soldiers in their house? What had happened to her father and mother?

She pushed aside her fears. "Tell me about Maglorius," she said more firmly. "Tell me what happened after the soldiers—"

"Mother said it was because of the riots. That he thought he could safely blame it on the soldiers."

"Blame what? And Mother! Where is she?"

Quintus began to sob again. Valeria could see he was trying to remain brave, but he was, after all, a little boy.

"I don't know," he said. "After all the fighting and screaming and noise, she was gone."

"Gone?"

"I came out of hiding. The servants were . . ."

More sobs.

"Dead," Quintus wailed when he found his breath. "Dead! I close my eyes and I see them. On the floor. I see their blood. I hear them scream. All dead."

Death was not part of their world. Their world was safety, servants, luxury, petty squabbles between brother and sister. Had Valeria not seen the unexpected violence of the Roman soldiers the day before, she would not have believed Quintus.

She squeezed his shoulders and kept trying to comfort him. She needed to calm him, to find out what had happened. "You came out of hiding and the servants were dead. And Mother?"

Guilt overwhelmed her. Mother could not be dead. All they'd done over the last few months was quarrel. She needed to be able to tell Mother that she didn't mean any of the horrible things she'd said.

"Mother wasn't there. Or Maglorius. But all the servants—"

"I know, I know," Valeria soothed. "You're here. You're safe. Tell me about Maglorius."

"Maglorius." Quintus was suddenly savage. He set his jaw. It would have been a comical sight, with the tears so fresh on his face, except his eyes blazed. "I saw it myself. Mother, she called for me. She called for the servants. From Father's study. He murdered our father. That's why I'm going to kill him."

"Murder." Valeria sat down. This was too much to comprehend. "Murder," she repeated, barely able to breathe out the word.

Quintus sat beside her. He placed the sword in his lap. His anger seemed to give him strength, and the tears dried on his face as he spoke with detached resolve. "Father was on the floor," he said. "His head was toward the door. Maglorius was lying knocked out and crossways to him, across Father's body. He was holding a knife."

"Father?"

"Maglorius. He'd stabbed Father. Maglorius still had his hand on the knife. And the knife was in Father's chest. There were pieces of clay everywhere."

"Clay?"

"From a wine jug. Mother had walked into the study just as Maglorius stabbed Father. She grabbed the first thing she could and hit Maglorius across the head. When I got to the study she was on her knees. Screaming at Maglorius. Begging Father to live."

Quintus shuddered. "Father was dead. Mother saw the short sword in my hand, the one that Maglorius had given me in the courtyard. She told me to kill Maglorius."

Quintus lost his strength as suddenly as he'd found it. "I couldn't do it. Not then. I would do it now. But then I couldn't believe it. Maglorius woke up and saw me standing there. I looked into his eyes, and I couldn't kill him. Mother tried to take the sword. She said she would kill him herself for taking away our father. That's when the shouting reached us. The soldiers had broken into the courtyard. Mother screamed at me to run."

He fell silent. Drained.

Valeria ached with love for her little brother. There would be time to grieve. Later.

Now she had to do everything possible to protect him.

THE ELEVENTH HOUR

I feel guilty about this," Sophia told Vitas.

"You had no choice. I would have forced you here by the point of a sword."

Sophia liked it, that Vitas had understood what she meant without asking for an explanation. On the journey from Smyrna to Rome, they'd spent countless hours in conversation, leaning on the railing of the ship, staring at the horizon. Then, as now, it seemed each could read the other's mind.

Now, however, they were not looking at the place where sea met sky. They were on a balcony of the royal palace. The moon had just risen and sat low on the horizon. It seemed within reach if she stretched a hand toward it. A breeze caressed her face, and she wished instead it was the gentle touch of the man with her.

Vitas had taken her to the royal palace this afternoon, insisting it was the only refuge in Jerusalem. His words had been prophetic; when the slaughter began again, the streets had been blocked with soldiers and citizens in panic.

It was this that brought her the tremendous guilt. She had survived. Too many others had not.

"Listen," he said, "if you could have done anything at all to stop the soldiers but didn't, you would have the right to condemn yourself. But these events were set in motion by circumstances far beyond any one person's control. What do you suggest? That you take up a sword and stand in the streets and die?"

Vitas placed a hand on her shoulder. "Despite the logic of my argument, I feel the same way you do." He smiled. Spoke softly. "Emotions don't listen to facts."

They were both staring at the dark outline of the hills against the sky. The glittering of the stars. Because to look in another direction would show the glow of the fires of the temple portico. The Jews had destroyed it to keep the soldiers from entering the temple.

"I should know," he said a few moments later. "I'm here because I ignored the facts."

She turned to him. His face was lost in the darkness.

"These are the facts," Vitas said. "I met a woman, a slave in Smyrna. Stubborn. Intelligent. I guessed that she might even be beautiful, if a person could look past her distinctly un-Roman taste in clothing."

"Is that how you judge beauty?" Sophia shot back. "If so—"

He laughed. "Quick tempered and quick to take insult too. Those are the facts." He grew serious. "I decided that first night that I wanted to know you more. You were a slave. It was in my power to arrange your freedom. So I did."

He shrugged. "If my impulse was wrong and my heart would not be drawn to you, then you had the gift of that freedom. If, however, my heart was right, then when I pursued you, your response to me would be that of a free woman. I would never have to wonder if your interest in me was that of a slave with no choice."

Sophia was listening carefully.

"Here is another fact. After days and days on the ship back to Rome, I realized that my heart truly had been drawn to you. But you know that. Because I asked if you would stay in Rome with Paulina so I could continue to court you."

Sophia knew that. It had been an agonizing choice. To say no to this man.

"You left me," he said. "You returned to Jerusalem. Your family was more important to you than the attention of a Roman citizen. Those are the facts."

"Vitas, I—"

"If humans operated purely on logic, I would have forgotten about you. I tried to. But could not. You know that Maglorius sent me reports. When I discovered you could not find your family . . ." He sighed. "I could not ignore my heart. Even though it meant that I would once again give you the chance to say no to me."

"Vitas—"

"Let me finish. Please. It was worth the risk. I've finally allowed myself to understand that a man cannot live life unless he is prepared to love. I've spent years in a cocoon, trying to pretend all I needed were the trappings of my life as a Roman from a good family with enough wealth to live comfortably. You changed that. So, whatever answer you give, I want to thank you."

He moved to the edge of the balcony and stared at the moon.

Long moments passed.

"No answer, then," he said. "I suppose that in itself is an answer."

"Vitas," she answered gently, "you didn't ask a question."

"Oh. I assumed . . ."

She laughed. "Assumptions can be dangerous. Especially when it comes to matters of the heart."

He drew a breath, as if seeking courage. He turned, kept his distance from her. "Will you return to Rome with me?"

She still didn't answer. She knew that Roman men were accustomed to procuring mistresses.

"As my wife?" he asked.

Her heart soared. She had abandoned him when the ship arrived in Rome, torn between her love for him and her duties to family. Now she had a second chance.

At the same time, she could not speak her heart. She could not accept.

✠ ✠ ✠

"I am so glad you're alive!" As she spoke, Amaris rose from a couch in the outer courtyard of the family's upper-city mansion and rushed to Ben-Aryeh.

Night had draped the city with merciful darkness. Oil torches flickered and burned. The light breeze across the mountaintop of Jerusalem did not reach this courtyard.

Ben-Aryeh had passed by five temple police standing at the arched opening to the courtyard. Under normal circumstances, he would have been slightly embarrassed to have any witnesses to the long, tearful hug that Amaris gave him.

These were not normal circumstances. Although he knew all five men were watching, he returned her hug with fervent love, stroking her hair, whispering endearments, kissing her forehead.

The sun had set on the slaughter of hundreds more in the city, dead at the hands of Roman soldiers. Ben-Aryeh had been among those fighting near the temple. He was thankful and relieved—with the guilt of a survivor—to have returned home. And to have a home waiting.

When Amaris relinquished her hold on him, Ben-Aryeh turned to the men at the archway. "We would like our privacy now."

These were temple police he'd sent to protect Amaris during the height of the fighting, an indication of his high political status that they would obey at that point. He saw no need for any other way to speak but as a curt command.

They slipped out through the archway toward the dark street.

Ben-Aryeh led Amaris to the couch and sat beside her.

"My love," she said, "the noise that reached me here in the afternoon! What has been happening?"

He held her hands as he explained. How Florus had told them to send a crowd out of the city to greet and salute the soldiers to prove that they could remain at peace. How the soldiers had refused to acknowledge the salutes. How they'd struck with no warning as a single troublemaker shouted an insult.

From there, the riot had grown so quickly it was difficult to comprehend. From horseback, armed with clubs and swords, the soldiers had begun to kill without discrimination. Many died by the soldiers' swords, many from the horses that tramped them, and many more as those in the crowds panicked and fought each other to escape into the city.

At the city gates, it worsened. The great crowd jammed at the narrow opening. Dozens suffocated under the weight of those pressing from behind. Dozens more were crushed so badly that their bodies were beyond recognition.

The soldiers pursued them into the city, and when Florus brought his other garrisons out of Antonia Fortress, it became obvious that the attack had been well planned, and that the soldiers meant to seize the temple.

The citizens rallied. In the narrow streets, the soldiers lost any advantage that horses and organized fighting gave them in the open. With the streets blocked and many citizens throwing a hail of darts, pottery, and stone blocks from the rooftops, the soldiers were forced to retreat.

At this point Ben-Aryeh left the tunnels beneath the temple. He first dispatched bodyguards to his mansion, then joined those who had begun tearing down the cloisters that connected the temple to Antonia Fortress.

Darkness had fallen as the fighting finally ended. But the wailing had just begun, as once more, relatives went into the streets with lit torches to search for those who had not returned home.

When he finished relaying all of this to Amaris, Ben-Aryeh kissed her forehead again. "I fear," he said, "for the city. By deceiving us into greeting the new cohorts today instead of protesting their arrival, Florus now has enough soldiers within the city gates to begin a measured and deliberate war, quarter by quarter. In short, we have let the enemy inside, and the temple will eventually be taken."

"Something can be done. Surely."

"Our own resistance was in the heat of panic. Emotions can only sustain our fight so long. Florus is no fool. He will most surely begin to go from one household to the next to eliminate resistance. When that is finished, the temple and its treasury are his."

"What about us?" she whispered.

"I will do everything in my power to see that nothing harms us. The city will always be here. So shall we."

"And if something is out of your power?"

"Wealth and connections," Ben-Aryeh said. "Unless there is more rioting, we will not suffer. Again, I reassure you. Now that Florus has enough military power in the city, he will proceed in a way that will keep him in control."

"But what if you lose your wealth and connections? If—"

"Nothing will harm us!" In his determination to quell her fears, he missed the pleading edge in her voice.

"Please tell me," she said, "that you have done nothing to betray me."

"What?"

"You love me and have always been faithful to me. That is what I need to hear. Not about your money and your politics. All I really want is you and your love."

Ben-Aryeh stood. "I have never betrayed you. Nor ever contemplated it!"

"Never?"

For a moment, he again considered telling her about the brigand attack, about the woman he had rescued, about fleeing her at the city gates. The evening before, here on the same couch in the same courtyard, he'd come very close. Yet Amaris had been so happy that he'd returned from Sebaste and survived the first day's riots that he had not wanted to dampen her relief, especially since it seemed unlikely that his false accuser would ever be able to identify him after his successful escape.

If he told her now, she would wonder why he'd kept it secret a day earlier, and whatever he said would be tinged by her suspicions, unjustified as they might be.

And circumstances had changed since the woman had almost seen him at the temple earlier in the day. The city was once again in great confusion. Chances were she'd been killed in the riot. If not, the next few days promised a systematic war that would reduce further the likelihood that he would be seen by her, let alone accused again.

Why then, Ben-Aryeh told himself, should he worry his beloved Amaris with the story? Despite the fact that keeping silent was a form of falsehood, he was an innocent man and had not been unfaithful to her. That was what was important.

Ben-Aryeh knelt beside her. "You are my one true love. Nothing will change that. I have never been unfaithful to you. I would never consider it. I would rather rip my eyes from my head than look at another woman with lust in my heart."

She stared at him for several moments. In the torchlight, her face was serious as she searched his eyes. Finally, she sighed. "I believe you."

"Very touching." The voice came from behind them. A voice from the entrance that led to an inner courtyard and the mansion beyond. "Very touching indeed."

Ben-Aryeh recognized that voice.

He stood and whirled. "Leave this home!" Ben-Aryeh commanded. "You have no right to be here."

"No?" Annas the Younger's voice was silky. As if filled with pleasure. "Guards!" he barked.

Immediately, the temple police that Ben-Aryeh had dismissed from the outer archway stepped into sight. They'd been waiting.

"Ben-Aryeh," Annas said, "these men are here to place you under arrest."

"I have committed no crimes."

"The Sanhedrin will judge otherwise, I am sure," Annas said. "Perhaps you are missing this necklace?" He dangled it from his fingers.

Even in the dim light given by the torches, Ben-Aryeh knew. Without thinking, he reached for his neck where it had hung for years.

"Yes," Annas said, "I see that you are. It was given to me by a woman. She took it from you as she was clawing to escape your grasp."

"No!"

"No? I'm sure she'd like to tell her story to the Sanhedrin. Unless, of course, you are not the one. But why don't we ask her?"

From the inner courtyard and into the torchlight stepped the woman whom Ben-Aryeh had rescued from the brigands the day before.

"Yes," she said without hesitation, pointing directly at Ben-Aryeh, "this is the man who robbed me of my purity outside the city gates."

✛ ✛ ✛

As soldiers escorted Queen Bernice and her attendants onto a south-side balcony of Antonia Fortress, she was highly aware of the fist-sized rock pressing hard into her belly.

She wished it were a tent peg. She remembered one of the stories of her people's history. In the time of the Judges. The Israelites had been oppressed for twenty years by Jabin of Hazor, a Canaanite king. The commander of his army, Sisera, had thousands of soldiers and nine hundred iron chariots. On the day that the Lord gave the Israelites victory over Sisera, he fled and came to the tent of Jael, wife of Heber the Kenite. She offered him shelter, gave him milk to drink, and covered him with a blanket. As the milk began to digest and sent him into sleep from exhaustion, she crept up with a hammer and a tent peg and drove the peg through his temple into the ground. From that time on, Bernice remembered from the story, Israel became stronger and eventually overthrew the power of King Jabin.

For this meeting with Florus, she'd allowed slaves to help her bathe, perfume, and wind her hair into fashionable braids. She'd uncharacteristically dismissed them, however, before dressing in her undergarments. She wanted no witnesses to the girdle that held the rock in place, no one to suspect after Florus was dead that she had found a way to murder him.

"Queen Bernice." Florus greeted her in a flat, almost unwelcoming voice as he turned from the balcony. He leaned against it, the top edge reaching his waist. Below was a drop of forty feet, into a courtyard paved with rounded stones. This, too, was something Bernice was aware of with the same intensity that she was conscious of the rock she intended to smash into his skull as soon as he was too drunk to realize her intent.

"Frankly," he said, "I'm surprised that you requested this visit. Especially after how you fled from me yesterday." Again, his tone was flat.

She knew that stance and posture. It was of a man trying to appear uninterested in her. But it was a lie; she'd attended too many banquets where she'd caught him staring at her from across the room.

She also knew how to play such men. "I much prefer choosing my man instead of having a man choose me."

The last of the evening's sun was full on his face, and she caught the slight widening of his eyes. He shifted slightly toward her, and that told her enough.

"Where shall I send my attendants?" she asked Florus. "And be kind to them. They may be waiting awhile for me."

"Send them back to your palace," he said. There was a quickness to his words. "I'll have my soldiers escort you home." He paused and grinned, showing large stained teeth. "When you are ready."

The arrogance of men, she thought. Provided a slight opening, they were all too eager to throw the door wide open. Subtlety—and understanding how much a woman appreciated subtlety—was lost on them.

Already Florus was puffing his chest slightly in his delight that she'd shown interest in him. As if he were the most desirable man in Judea.

"And your soldiers?" Bernice asked. "You'll have them stay?"

"Dismissed, of course." He raised his voice. "Immediately." He did not have to repeat the command.

During the time it took for the attendants and soldiers to file back out the entrance to the balcony, Florus studied Bernice.

Unattractive as he was, she knew he was not a totally stupid man. He would notice the care that she'd taken to present herself. He would be aware of her reputation as a woman of few virtues.

Bernice pretended not to notice his vulgar examination. She knew what she wanted to accomplish.

✛ ✛ ✛

In the dark Valeria could not guess at how much time had passed.

Then came a voice they had loved.

"Valeria!" It was Maglorius. "Quintus!"

They heard his footsteps above.

For a moment she wanted to rise and run to him.

"He'll kill me," Quintus whispered. "He knows I saw him murder Father. He'll kill me. Then he'll kill you too to keep it secret."

Still, Valeria hesitated.

"He knows we are here because he asked both of us to wait for him here. He planned it all. Sent us to a place where he could find us and kill us," Quintus said.

"No." Valeria would not believe it. Yet had not Maglorius recently admitted to her that he had betrayed Lucius? And had not his ambiguous conversation suggested much more of a secret, one that Lucius knew? Was it enough of a terrible secret that Maglorius had taken the opportunity to kill Lucius when it appeared he would never be blamed for the murder?

"I will be like the retiarius," Quintus hissed. "I will run now, but when I am bigger and stronger or if I can catch him when he least expects it, I will kill him."

Maglorius? The man who had slept on the floor in front of her doorway every night for the last year to make sure she was safe?

Valeria wanted to call for him, but Quintus made the decision for her.

He hopped to his feet and moved downward.

Into the black of the tunnels.

The voice of Maglorius echoed behind them.

But they were gone from him.

Beneath the city.

Alone.

✝ ✝ ✝

"I am a follower of the Christos," Sophia said. "You are not. Can you live with that?"

Images of the tribulation that Nero had inflicted upon the followers in Rome flashed through Vitas' mind. The tar jackets on men and women hanging from lampposts. The lions in the arena. He realized the risk that marrying a Christian involved.

Still, he knew his answer. "Sophia, I can live with it. But can you live with the fact that I do not believe?"

"I'm not sure," she said slowly. "To be yoked with an unbeliever . . ."

"What if I promise to listen to what you have to say about it? What if I encourage you to worship as you choose?"

This was an easy promise for Vitas. It was the Roman way, tolerance of different religions.

"And what will happen in Rome?" she asked. "My beliefs will be a threat to my life. To yours."

"Let me ask," he said. "Are these beliefs something you intend to put on public display, regardless of whether or not you are my wife?"

Sophia appeared to consider it. Then answered as he had hoped. "I would not deny my Lord if asked. In these times, followers of the Christos do not proclaim their beliefs publicly. Until the Tribulation ends, we are to persevere."

Vitas vowed to himself that he would renew his efforts to use his power with Nero to stop the tribulation in Rome. He would argue again the practicality of ending the persecution. That it was growing unpopular with the masses. That perhaps there could be a special tax placed upon the Christians. Somehow he would find a solution. But this was not the moment to tell Sophia.

"So then," he continued, "if you had the freedom to worship in our household, that would be enough. If you and Paulina could—"

"Paulina!"

"She's remarried. To a good man. They don't live far from where you would live in Rome. And the baby girl is fine." Vitas grinned. "In Rome you would have a friend and freedom to worship in private. That should be enough of a promise."

She did not answer as he hoped. "It is not enough," she said. "I must share my faith with those I trust. And always, I would pray for you to believe too."

"It is that important?"

"You tell me. How important is eternal life?"

"I understand," he said.

"No," she said simply, "you don't. Because when you do, then you will believe that the Christos died for our sins in order to save us from the wrath of God, He was resurrected, and all who trust in Him have that hope of a resurrection after death." Sophia clutched his arm. "That is my hope, my purpose, my peace. If you are the man that I will share my life with, I must also share that."

"I want you to be my wife. If I tell you I believe so you will be my wife, it is a belief forced upon me."

"I'm not saying believe and I will become your wife. I'm saying . . ." She hesitated, as if struggling with her decision. "I'm saying that I want you to promise to be open to that decision. You are right. A man cannot live alone. But there is more. A man cannot live without God."

He stroked her face, feeling the tears. "The answer is yes, then?"

"I want it to be yes," she said.

Vitas knew he could not deny his conscience any longer.

In all their hours of conversation on the ship from Smyrna to Rome, Vitas had never hinted at the degree of power that he held in Roman politics. He'd been frank about his family background, less than frank about the extent of his family's wealth and his own inheritance. He had wanted her to be interested in him, not in his power or money. Indeed, many times after she'd left Rome he had wondered if telling her about those assets might have kept her there.

And now?

If she knew that he was part of the closest circle of advisers to Nero, she might walk away because of what Nero had done to other believers. At the very least, she was right. Her beliefs would be a danger to her life—and to his.

But she had to know the truth. Vitas took a deep breath. "There are two things I must tell you. Two things I have kept from you during all the times we spent in conversation on the ship." He forced himself to continue before he changed his mind. "The first is this. In Britannia, there was a woman. Of the Iceni tribe. We were married. We had a child."

Because of the shock on her face, he knew this was the way it had to be done. If she found out later from someone else, she would never trust him again. "I have not spoken of this to you because I never speak of it. She is dead. As is my son."

It took Sophia a moment to speak. She was hesitant. "Did you love her?"

"Yes." The truth was the only way.

"I'm glad," she said.

Her reply startled him. "Glad?"

"Who you were before we met is nothing you or I can change. I would hate to think of you as a man capable of having a son with a woman you did not love." She paused. "Why do you never speak of it?"

Vitas closed his eyes and shook his head. "Let me tell you when I am ready."

Several moments passed before she finally nodded. "I trust you."

"You should also know that I serve Nero directly as an adviser."

She recoiled. Almost in revulsion.

"I've lost you," he said softly. "Haven't I?"

"You've seen what he does to the Christians. You know of his evil. Yet you accept it."

"I don't," Vitas answered. "I do everything in my power to turn him away from it." How could he explain the complicated dance between Nero and the Senate and his role as the stabilizer? "Listen. In Britannia, I saw . . ."

Memories of the final battle there overwhelmed him, and he had to collect himself. "In Britannia," he began again, "I vowed that I would do everything possible to ensure the empire treats all people with justice."

"You serve Nero," she said simply. "I cannot live with that."

Yes, he thought, *I have lost her.*

Then her eyes widened. "It was you!" She grabbed his arm. "It could only have been you!"

"I . . . I . . . don't understand."

"Tell me." Her voice was low and urgent. "I was not in Rome long but long enough to hear a story among the Christians there. About a night when Nero dressed as a beast and God sent an earthquake to free the men and women held captive. Some say it is a falsehood. Some swear it is true."

Vitas remained silent.

"Some tell about one man who defied Nero that night. A man who set the Christians free." Her grip on his arm grew tighter. "I want to hear from you something that will let me believe it was you."

"You will not trust me unless I offer proof?"

"You want me to commit my life to you."

"There were two men and two women," Vitas said. "If I'm going to help the Christians, I need you."

She hugged him. Stroked his hair. Her face was close against his, and he felt her silent tears. "That is enough."

"I want you to be my wife. Come to Rome with me."

Her silent tears became sobs. "I love you. But how can I abandon my people now when it looks like Jerusalem will be destroyed?"

"I love you."

He knew what he had to do now. If this was going to be the last night of his life, he wanted to take the memory of those words to his death. Holding Sophia. In the moonlight. As she clung to him.

If there is a God, Vitas thought, *the God that Ben-Aryeh proclaims, a God who sent His Son as Sophia proclaims, I want to thank this God for love.*

And wanted from this God any help he could get.

"Sophia," Vitas said quietly, "I must leave you right now. Please pray for me."

✠ ✠ ✠

"You knew he was there?" Ben-Aryeh ignored Annas and the temple police and the woman. He spoke to Amaris. "You gave me no warning?"

"He showed me the necklace. The woman told me where and when and how she got it." Amaris' voice broke. "I asked him for a few minutes alone with you. I wanted to give you the chance—"

"To confess?" His shock turned to anger, and his voice rose. "*You* believed *them. You* betrayed *me* by hiding his presence in my household."

"I . . ." Amaris swallowed hard and kept her composure. But did not speak.

"A man who forces himself on a woman robbed by brigands has no moral high ground," Annas the Younger said. He was obviously enjoying the scene. "I see the true Ben-Aryeh now. Blaming those around him."

The temple police surrounded Ben-Aryeh and looked to Annas for a signal. Annas shook them off, smiling in his triumph.

Ben-Aryeh turned on Annas. "You set this up. That's how she found me."

Annas laughed. "So you are admitting you know this woman."

"I admit nothing."

"I think otherwise. I am witness to your words. As are these temple police. *'That's how she found me.'* It certainly sounds like a guilty man who not only recognizes this woman but knows she is looking for him because he fled her earlier. Yes, the Sanhedrin will have no difficulty judging you worthy of death for adultery."

"You . . . set . . . . this . . . up." Ben-Aryeh strained to keep control. "How else would she know to come here?"

"She saw you on the platform at the temple," Annas said. "She came to me and described you. Told me her story. I am here to see that justice is done."

What had Annas hissed earlier in the day? *"You shall pay for it, Ben-Aryeh. I lost my position. But you shall lose your life. And I will be the first one to cast a stone."*

His neck bulging with rage, Ben-Aryeh spat out his words. "You are here to seek revenge for . . ." He choked back the rest of his thoughts.

"For how you manipulated our leading citizens into sending letters to Agrippa to relieve me of my position after the execution of James the Just?" Annas smiled broadly. "Would this be a reason for revenge? Or have you plotted against me in other ways?"

Ben-Aryeh gritted his teeth and breathed hard through his nostrils. *That's how she found me. You are here to seek revenge.* Blurting out both statements would hurt him. Badly. And he considered himself one of the most controlled and politically astute men in the city.

No, he was a fool. He had delivered himself into the hands of the man who hated him most. Worse, he'd lost any chance to convince Amaris of his innocence. If only he'd told her yesterday about the false accusation and the stolen necklace. If only he'd told her minutes earlier when they were alone in the outer courtyard.

The city was doomed, but what did that matter against what he'd lost with Amaris? She would forever believe he was guilty, and he would die with the searing knowledge that she in turn had betrayed him.

In front of Annas, Ben-Aryeh let out a slow breath, careful to hide the sigh from his enemy. "What will you do now?" he asked calmly.

"Remain with you as the temple police escort you to a prison cell. Call for a meeting of the Sanhedrin as soon as it is convenient. Then fulfill my duty by throwing the first stone as your death sentence is carried out." Annas chuckled. "All of it is simply following the letter of the law. As I'm sure you would do, were you truly a righteous man."

"I am a righteous man," Ben-Aryeh said. "I welcome the chance to prove my innocence in front of the Sanhedrin." He gestured at himself. "I'm sure you are not such a petty man that you will prevent me from removing this filthy clothing. I was fighting the Romans down at the temple while you were here waiting for me."

"Ah, the self-righteous Ben-Aryeh. A rapist, but one determined to show that he was serving God at the temple. Does it not occur to you that I served God better by ensuring justice for the woman you violated?"

"The war is upon us. I may be in prison a long time before you convene the Sanhedrin," Ben-Aryeh said. "I wish to wipe away today's sweat with a towel and washbasin and change my clothing before I leave my household."

"As you wish."

"Amaris?" Ben-Aryeh asked. "No matter what you think of me now, I ask you to visit me in prison."

She did not answer.

Ben-Aryeh squared his shoulders. Marched past Annas the Younger, who grinned openly in delight at Ben-Aryeh's trouble.

Ben-Aryeh crossed the tiles of the inner courtyard, walked the familiar walk through the mansion, guessing he would never be able to walk through it again.

He reached his laundered clothing.

Changed quickly.

He stopped in the bedchamber, where he kept hidden a small clay jug filled with gold coins. He filled a leather purse with the coins and hung it around his neck beneath his clothing. Then, without hesitation, he climbed out the window and slid down a vine on the outer wall.

When he reached the street, he landed softly.

And fled into the night. There was only one man who could help him now.

✛ ✛ ✛

When Bernice and Florus were alone, Florus pointed at a table that held a jug of wine and various delicacies. "You are my guest," he said. "What would you like?"

Someone with decent social graces, she thought, but of course kept that to herself.

Bernice moved to the table and poured wine. It would give him a sense of power that the queen of the Jews had served him. More importantly, it gave her a chance to make sure his goblet held far more wine than hers.

"Your brother is in Egypt, I hear," Florus said.

Did she imagine that his eyes glittered as the light began to fail? "Yes," she replied. "Egypt."

Was this man incapable of interesting conversation? He was essentially a king himself in this part of the world. No, more than king, because she and Agrippa held no power against what he might decide, except in the form of sending a formal complaint to the governor of Syria or to Nero himself. Florus held the power of life and death, had traveled the world, had dined with the famous and infamous. How could he be so unbearably dull and uncharistmatic?

In a flash, she understood.

Because he was so focused on his own desires. She wasn't a person to him. But a commodity. And since his position essentially allowed him to take what he wanted at will, he didn't understand the give-and-take of pursuit.

"Agrippa gone then. And you in Jerusalem. Word reached me it is part of a holy vow. . . ."

"Yes," she replied. "Holy vow."

"You Jews confuse me. What is it you hope to gain by placing faith in what cannot be seen?"

A real conversational gambit, Bernice thought. Was there a part of him that could prove interesting?

Before she could answer, however, he lifted his goblet. "Not a good wine," he said. "I hope you'll endure it."

She smiled over her own goblet. "I shall."

"So," he said, "let's not waste time. What payment to you expect?"

"I . . . don't understand."

"I find in these situations that it saves time to negotiate in a direct manner."

"These situations—?"

He snorted. "You're not the first prostitute I've enjoyed."

Bernice could not help herself. She threw her wine in his face. She expected him to hit her.

He laughed instead. "You think I'm stupid? How many social occasions have brought us to the same banquets? Yet you completely ignored me. And now suddenly, when I bring my army to Jerusalem, you show up perfumed and oiled and want time with me in private. You want something from me, and it is obvious how you intend to secure it. So let me ask again, what payment do you expect?"

He held up a hand to stop her from speaking. "Don't misunderstand me. I don't expect you to be cheap. Nor do I intend to be cheap. I'm a man of wealth, and a night with you would be worth a great deal to me."

Bernice blinked a few times.

"Remarkable," he said. "You've lost composure. I believe it's the first time, isn't it?"

She should not have underestimated him. She turned to the wine jug and refilled her goblet.

He gulped back some wine and held out his goblet for more, then gulped more and wiped his mouth with the back of his hand. "What shall it be?"

Your drunkenness, she thought. *Then a stone against the skull, the same stone that a poor peasant struggled to hold aloft as he watched your bandits kill his family. And once you are unconscious, your death when I push you over this balcony. A death that I could claim was an accident.*

"What shall it be?" he repeated.

She poured him more wine. "Florus, my dear man, perhaps you might actually find it enjoyable to be very slow and deliberate in your negotiations. After all, a man offered me a kingdom to be his bride when I was only thirteen. Do we really have to be so shortsighted as to think I might be here only for a night?"

He leered. Drank more wine. "What exactly are you saying?"

She pretended to drink her own wine. "Let me ask you this. Do you think Rome would really believe the reports of how badly you have stolen from the Jews if the queen herself became your wife?"

"Reports of how badly I have stolen from the Jews?" Florus stood quickly, a move so abrupt that it surprised her.

Bernice reminded herself that the Romans were, above all, warriors. No matter what this man seemed to be now, at one time he had been a physical specimen to be feared. She needed to be very, very careful around him. The drop from the balcony that she hoped would kill him was also a drop that could kill her.

"You are suggesting I'm afraid of Rome?" He half roared, and a spray of wine from his mouth touched her face.

"Of course not," Bernice said.

He grinned and sat again, motioning for more wine. "I like a horse that can't be intimidated. Something about controlling a beautiful beast that—"

"I'm not suggesting it," she said. "I'm saying it directly. You are afraid of the governor of Syria, Cestius Gallus, because he doesn't want problems in his jurisdiction. And you are afraid that if Rome looks too closely into your affairs here that you will face severe legal actions."

He stood and roared again. "Insolence!"

"Shut your mouth," she said with appropriate weariness, although her heart hammered with fear. All he had to do was reach out with one of those meaty fists. "There's no audience for you to impress." She pushed his chest and made him fall backward.

For a few heartbeats, it seemed he was going to rush forward and beat her. Then he grinned. "Prostitutes cower from me. You're proving to be a lot more interesting."

Bernice relaxed but hid her relief. "You want war. That's obvious.

You make an outrageous theft from the temple, and when a few hot-headed youths unsurprisingly insult you as you ride to Jerusalem, you set your soldiers loose upon helpless citizens. When the people show too much control and refuse to riot, you spark it again with more slaughter. Even now, your soldiers are at the ready to attack at dawn."

Florus belched. "A war might be convenient. What of it?"

"You forget that reports of the war and how it started will put you in a bad light. After all, as much as you might like to, you can't kill every single resident of Jerusalem. Someone will survive to present to Caesar the injustices that caused this war."

Bernice sipped her wine. She noted with satisfaction that most of his was gone. She refilled her goblet and casually reached across to do the same for his. "War is not the answer," Bernice continued.

"No?"

"Today, great as your force was, you still had to retreat. Jews may not be motivated enough to muster a good offense, but our defense of what is dear to us is so fierce as to be unbeatable. Even by Rome."

"The temple."

"Of course. Not the gold inside, but what it represents. Surely you know enough of recent history to understand how fanatical our people are about serving the one true God."

She walked around behind him. She began to massage his shoulders, glad that he could not read her contempt of him in her face. It also gave her an excuse to set down her goblet while he continued to drink.

"Tomorrow," she said, "you either attack or not. If you do, it will be the same as today. Every Jewish male in this city will fight to his death to protect the temple. You know you can't defeat that. Your retreat then will cause you a tremendous loss of face."

He grunted with pleasure as her fingers worked muscles that had gone soft with easy living.

"Leave the city in peace," she said. "Go back to Caesarea."

"And then . . . ?"

"What will be of more importance to Caesar? Reports from Jews and temple priests who complain on a regular basis? Or a letter from the queen of the Jews supporting all the actions you have taken so far?"

"With the queen at my side as a wife." The wine seemed to finally be

having an effect. He snorted laughter. "Yes, what a prize that would be."
He sucked in air. "Tell me, my little seductress. It's obvious all that you
bring to a marriage. Wealth. Beauty. A title. Even respectability. But
how do you benefit?"

"You tell me," Bernice said. She stopped massaging him.

He reached up and pulled her hands onto his chest, forcing her chin
to rest on his head.

She found it extremely repulsive but did not pull back.

"Roman citizenship," he said. "Safety from military reprisals. And, of
course, a luxurious lifestyle."

"With a powerful, fascinating man," she finished for him.

"Why now? We've been together at the same banquets before.
You've never shown the faintest interest in me."

"You've never shown so boldly that you were willing to use all your
power."

He lurched sideways. "You find that attractive?"

"Most women do. At least women like me."

He pulled her down farther, twisting his head to try to kiss her
mouth.

She pulled away. "What is your hurry?" she asked in a teasing voice.
She found another jug of wine and offered it to him.

He nodded, blinking slowly. "Hurry? No hurry. But only a fool buys
a horse without checking its teeth first. I'm not so sure I should agree to
marriage without an adequate appraisal."

He reached for her waist.

The rock! He must not discover it!

She spun away, laughing. "Ah yes, but why would one buy a cow if
one could get the milk for free?"

He puzzled over that for a moment, addled by the wine. When he finally understood, he laughed until he began to cough. "Suddenly you're
a woman of virtue?"

"Maybe I always was," she said. "Rumors can be vicious, you know."

"Perhaps," he said. "But I am a man unaccustomed to being refused.
And if you find my power so attractive . . ."

Bernice smiled, forcing herself to feel seductive. She lifted her hands
to loosen her hair. Was he drunk enough?

As she loosened her hair with one hand, she half turned and made it appear that she was about to disrobe. She took the stone that she would use to crush his skull.

Then she turned and approached him with the murder weapon hidden behind her back, a seductive smile across her face.

Florus leered. "Better," he crooned. "Much better."

"You'll call off your soldiers?" she asked. "You'll leave the city in peace?"

"Certainly. And you'll give me a taste of what it will be like to have you as a wife?"

"Of course."

"Come here then."

She backed away, keeping her smile in place. "Call for your head centurion. Tell him that the soldiers are not to attack the temple tomorrow."

"Call him now?"

"I like to know a man is serious about his desire for me."

"I could always call him again at dawn and tell him I've changed my mind."

"Not the great Florus. He wouldn't want to seem indecisive."

He grunted. "Soldier!" he yelled.

Almost instantly, two guards entered the doorway and stepped onto the balcony.

"Take this message to the commanders," Florus said. "Tomorrow all of our cohorts but one will return to Caesarea."

Each saluted him. He dismissed them immediately.

"Satisfied?" Florus asked.

Bernice gave him a leer of her own. "Not yet!" She walked to the door and barred it in place. "In a few minutes, however, that may change." She thought of his broken and dead body on the ground far below. "Yes," she said. "Give me a chance and I'll be well satisfied."

He grinned. A very drunken grin. He stripped off his shirt, showing a wide chest of graying hairs. "Come here then, my queen."

Bernice glided to a nearby torch. She capped it and extinguished it. And the next. And the next.

It was nearly dark on the balcony now.

What she didn't expect was how quietly the large man could move, even as drunk as he was.

As she reached for the final torch, his hands suddenly wrapped around her waist. "I'm tired of waiting," he said. "I——" He stopped. Turned her to face him. Held her shoulder with one large hand. Groped her hidden hand with the other.

"What is this!" He pushed and pulled at the stone until his muddled mind made sense of it. "Is this a weapon? You came here to kill me?" He pushed her away. "Guards! Bring me my sword!"

She knew she was about to die. And was at peace with it. At least Jerusalem was safe. She had saved the city.

"Guards!" he shouted. "Sword!"

✝ ✝ ✝

"I'm hungry," Quintus said in the pitch-black darkness.

Valeria had forced him to wait long hours in the depths of the tunnels beneath the city. If indeed Maglorius did want them dead, she needed to be sure he was gone.

"Soon," she said, "we will have plenty of gold to buy whatever we need. Then we will pay for a journey to Caesarea and from there, a ship to Rome. We are citizens, after all. Lawyers will help us recover our father's estate. And we will rebuild our lives from there."

Quintus fought back another sob. He clutched her hand as they slowly navigated the uneven sewer floor. The stone was wet, slippery. Her only way of sensing direction was by keeping her free hand against the wall and making sure they moved upward.

"Soon," she repeated to Quintus, as much for her own comfort as his.

The gold that she'd hidden . . . it was their lifeline. Money would ensure they had food and shelter and a way to get to Rome. Money would ensure they received the inheritance due to them. And until Quintus was old enough, she would look after him as if he were a son not a stepbrother.

It was the gold that gave her hope.

Yet when they finally reached the steps that had brought them down into the sewer, the pouch of gold coins that she'd hidden was gone. Disbelieving as she was, she searched frantically but could not find it.

"Valeria?" Quintus asked. "What is it?"

"Let me hold you," she said, concealing her fear and panic. "We'll make it through this night. That's what's important. We'll face tomorrow when it comes."

And somehow, she vowed, she'd find a way to get them to Rome.

☩ ☩ ☩

Aware he was half drunk, Florus struggled to open the door. He kept roaring for the guards to bring him his sword. When it finally opened, he was savagely delighted to see three guards waiting for him.

But no sword.

Florus blinked, wondering if the alcohol had addled his mind so thoroughly that he was seeing a vision in the light of the oil torches of the hallway.

"I understand you've given orders to send the soldiers out of the city tomorrow morning," the man behind his guards said.

"Gallus Sergius Vitas!"

"Sent by Nero," Vitas replied calmly, arms crossed. "Caesar will be glad to hear of your restraint. It is difficult to tax a region when a representative of Rome is obviously guilty of forcing its people into war."

Florus blinked again. *Gallus Sergius Vitas.* Despite the betrayal by Bernice, perhaps some good would come of this night. Like an insect in a spiderweb, Vitas had actually come to him.

"Guards!" Florus spluttered. "Seize him."

Vitas would be dead by morning. No more threat to Florus.

The guards parted, and Vitas moved forward.

"Guards!" Florus, apoplectic with rage, was aware of his saliva splattering as he yelled.

"Imagine my relief," Vitas said, "when I discovered that two of your centurions served in Britannia alongside me and Titus."

"Guards!"

"Imagine their joy," Vitas continued, "when they learned that I need merely speak the word, as I did, for them to be transferred to the city police of Rome. Easy living, higher wages."

"Guards!"

"You're wasting your breath," Vitas said. "They've seen the orders from Nero, orders giving me safe passage through the empire."

Florus fell backward and leaned against the door.

The worst had happened. Once Vitas returned to Rome, Nero would recall Florus as procurator. At the very least, there would be disgrace. More likely, execution.

Vitas pushed Florus aside, and Florus staggered to keep his balance.

"Queen Bernice," Florus heard Vitas say, "I trust you are ready to return to the palace and to your people?"

TWENTY-TWO MONTHS
AFTER THE BEGINNING
OF THE TRIBULATION

{AD 66}

ROME

CAPITAL OF THE EMPIRE

This calls for wisdom.
If anyone has insight,
let him calculate the
number of the beast,
for it is man's number.
His number is 666.

—Revelation 13:18

VENUS

HORA SEXTA

Let's talk about Vitas," Helius said. "After all, he's just arrived here in Rome from an extended vacation with his new wife."

"The incorruptible Vitas?" Tigellinus sneered, cleared his throat noisily, then spat on the clean marble floor of the palace hall.

Helius averted his eyes from the result. "There are times," he said archly, "that incorruptible is easier to bear than disgusting."

"Just as there are times that incorruptible is easier to bear than unearned snobbery. Why do you want to talk about Vitas? He's back to make our lives miserable as the conscience we never asked for, and the less I'm reminded of him, the better. You've read his reports about Florus and the Jews? When Nero hears of it, you and I will lose a substantial part of our income."

Helius touched Tigellinus on the elbow and pointed him at an archway that led to a garden. "Let's talk in a safe place."

Tigellinus shrugged. Followed.

Outside, an unseasonably warm December morning made the garden pleasant.

"What I find ironic," Helius began, "is that we are plagued by an incorruptible man, when Nero would actually tolerate nearly every vice known to man."

"You should know," Tigellinus said, grinning.

"*We* should know."

Tigellinus shrugged again modestly. "I'm sure Nero gives Vitas the power he does because it keeps us off balance."

"Did," Helius said.

It took several moments for Tigellinus to comprehend. "Did? *Did* give Vitas power?"

"Yes, my brutish friend." Despite his fastidiousness, Helius did have real affection for Tigellinus and knew it was returned. "What's the one thing that Nero won't tolerate?"

"Betrayal."

"You said that without even a second thought."

"Because you know it's true. But Vitas would never betray Nero." Helius smiled.

Tigellinus frowned. "You are not suggesting . . . ?"

"That the incorruptible Vitas has finally made an error?"

Tigellinus grinned. "You *are* suggesting that. I can see it on your face. If you were a cat, you would be licking your whiskers. What is it?"

"A woman."

"For a moment," Tigellinus said, showing disappointment, "I thought you actually had something. Nero doesn't care if Vitas is unfaithful to that new wife of his. Nero would applaud."

"That new wife of his," Helius said, "is a Christian."

Tigellinus had been turning away from Helius, but this brought him spinning back on his heel. His eyes narrowed as he stared at Helius.

"Meow," Helius said, pretending to lick his hands as if they were a cat's paws.

"The Jew he married is a Christian?" Tigellinus repeated.

Helius nodded. "One of the slaves who serves their family brought Nero the news today."

"Is it too much to hope that Vitas himself has joined in her faith?"

"Too much. But the fact that Vitas is hiding a Christian in his household is enough to make him a traitor in Nero's eyes. Imagine what the mobs would say if it gets out that after all Nero has done to eradicate the Christians, one of his inner circle does the opposite."

"Imagine." Tigellinus' teeth gleamed as he gave a wolflike grin. "And imagine what that would do to the credibility of the reports about Florus that Vitas has brought us."

"Tigellinus," Helius said, "those reports won't even see the light of day. Once Vitas is dead, will there be any need to pass them on to Nero? And Florus will continue to fatten our purses for as long as we choose to support his cause with the emperor."

"Wonderful," Tigellinus said. "Shall we throw dice to decide who has the pleasure of telling Vitas that he has an invitation to the amphitheater prisons?"

"Not so fast."

"Nero's actually going to let him live?"

"Nero has a different fate intended for him. After all, wouldn't it be nice to strip Vitas of his land and money and reputation before he's executed?"

"And his wife?"

"That's the genius of Nero's plan," Helius said. "It will nicely take care of her too." He explained Nero's plan.

"Yes, indeed." Tigellinus pounded Helius on the back with delight when he finished. "Lucunda macul est ex inimici sanguine."

What a pleasant stain comes from an enemy's blood.

✠ ✠ ✠

"Welcome back, brother." Vitas hurried through the garden to hug Damian.

"Shouldn't I be saying that to you?" Damian returned the hug. "Isn't this your first week back in Rome? And all I brought from my travels was a wretched slave for the arenas. You've returned with a wife."

"Sophia," Vitas said. That one word never failed to fill him with a heady mixture of emotions. Sophia. Romans were supposed to marry for convenience or politics. Vitas felt blessed that her presence in his life was so much more. And he found it ironic that he now thought of it as a blessing; much as he wanted to resist, her quiet demonstrations of faith in the one true God had moved him closer and closer to that faith himself.

Vitas blinked and realized that Damian was regarding him with a quizzical, humorous look.

"She does have your heart, doesn't she?" Damian said. "And are the rumors true? She's the Jew you rescued in Smyrna, right? Then followed to Jerusalem?"

"And the rumors about you are true? A slave hunter beyond compare?"

"Are you changing the subject?"

"Are you?"

They both laughed. Vitas pointed them to a bench under the shade of a tree.

When they were seated, Damian's face lost some of its humor. "What of Maglorius? Is it true he murdered the elderly Bellator and is now a fugitive?"

Vitas sobered too. "It's true he's been accused of it. And it's true that he disappeared in Jerusalem."

"You know more than that, don't you?"

"Alypia, I'm told, is in Rome now in charge of Bellator's estate."

Damian grinned. "I remember her well. She's without a husband now, you say."

Vitas shivered. "Stay away from her, Damian. That one would steal your soul."

"Maglorius survived her."

"As a fugitive from the law. He—" Vitas paused—"you haven't been hired to find him, have you?"

"No, but you'll find it interesting who did hire me, almost as soon as I stepped back into the city." Damian waved away the question before Vitas could ask it. "First, Maglorius."

"Bellator left behind two children. A daughter almost grown and a young son. They, too, disappeared during the riots in Jerusalem. I'm convinced Maglorius is still there, looking for them."

"And his own son? With Alypia?"

Vitas looked around before he answered, even though he knew they were in total privacy in the garden. "The boy's name is Sabinus. He's with us, but this is a matter of extreme discretion."

"Of course. I'll say nothing."

"Sophia promised to care for the boy until Maglorius can return."

Damian shook his head. "There you are, collecting more strays of the world."

Vitas thought of the old Jew in their household too. "You don't know the half of it. But we've got enough money. Why not?"

Damian shrugged.

Vitas said, "Tell me, brother, who has hired you now?"

"First," Damian said, "let me thank you for starting me in this career. I find myself suited to hunting for slaves."

"Probably because it's still a shocking endeavor to the truly respectable families in Rome."

Damian laughed. "Naturally."

"And the person who hired you?"

"I'm sure you'd find out as soon as you return to the imperial palace," Damian said. "Helius."

"Helius!"

"Yes. And he's offered a large reward to find the man. You might find this interesting, too, since the fugitive is a Jew. And I've been sworn to secrecy. But since you'll soon know from Helius anyway . . ."

"Who could Helius possibly want that badly?"

"His name is John. Son of Zebedee. Apparently claims to be one of the disciples of Jesus."

"I know of him," Vitas said quietly. He was careful not to let a new set of emotions cross his face. He knew how important Sophia's faith was to her. How could he tell her that his own brother was about to join the persecution? And worse, would be in pursuit of the last living disciple who had followed Jesus?

"How could you possibly know of him?" Damian asked.

Here was a secret Vitas needed to keep from his brother. To protect Sophia. Vitas did not want to contemplate the horror that would occur if Helius or Tigellinus found out about her faith.

"He is the author of a letter that's been circulating among the Christians," Vitas answered. "This letter has caused Nero a lot of trouble."

This was one of the few secrets he'd kept from Sophia. That Helius and Tigellinus had spoken of the letter with Vitas, wondering how to deal with the threat. There were moments—many of them—when Vitas hated Sophia's faith for the trouble it might bring to the happiness of their marriage.

"I haven't heard of the letter." Damian leaned forward. Less a brother and more a professional hunter of men.

"That's the way Helius wants it," Vitas answered.

"Tell me more."

Vitas hesitated. Helius obviously had an agenda for sending Damian in pursuit of John. If Helius had not given Damian information about the letter, it was for a reason. Vitas could only guess at that reason; if Damian knew of it, it might be leverage someday against Helius.

Yet Damian was his brother. Who knew if the information might someday protect Damian? Vitas made his decision. "Here is what I know," Vitas said. He began to explain.

Fifteen minutes later, Sophia entered the garden, interrupting the two of them.

Vitas rose, smiling.

Sophia! She was dressed as a Roman wife, and servants had tended to her hair.

What beauty! His heart ached to think that she loved him as he loved her.

"Damian," Vitas said, "please meet—"

"We've met," Damian said, standing. He gave her a hug. "Remember? Smyrna? Long ship journey where my brother spent every one of his waking moments with you and probably every moment of every dream as he slept?"

"I wanted to introduce her to you as my wife," Vitas said.

"I'm not big on formalities," Damian answered. He turned to Sophia. "Welcome to the family, small as it is."

Sophia leaned toward Vitas and whispered something in his ear.

"Really?" Vitas said. "You are not joking?"

"Really," she answered, her smile glowing on her face.

"And I can tell Damian?" Vitas asked her.

She nodded.

"Brother," Vitas said, "our family won't be so small anymore. Soon you'll be an uncle."

"Congratulations!"

Vitas could see that Damian meant it sincerely.

It seemed like the perfect day.

As long as Vitas could force from his mind that his brother was about to begin pursuit of John, the last disciple.

As Vitas stood there in the garden, arm around Sophia, he wondered if there was some way—perhaps by trading political favors with Tigellinus and Helius for the first time ever—he could convince them to drop that pursuit.

Without, of course, revealing that his own wife was a follower of Jesus. Because that would be death for both of them.

✠ ✠ ✠

"Do you remember me?"

Leah had carefully chosen the place for this confrontation. A crowded marketplace. With competing vendors of wine, live chickens, pottery, fresh vegetables, all shouting to be heard. In a public place like this, her conversation would be as private as if she were alone in a court-yard with the slave she'd finally found after six months of searching. And here, with hundreds of people milling from one vendor to another, she was as safe as if a dozen soldiers protected her.

She'd just touched the elbow of the slave and when he turned, she glanced at his forehead for confirmation, stared directly into his eyes, and asked the question.

"Do you remember me?" she repeated. She knew this was the man. Although there wasn't anything distinctive about his size or features, the brand on his forehead was unforgettable: a triangle with a circle in the center.

The slave's brand was as unforgettable as the circumstances that had brought him briefly into her life. "My brother was Nathan, son of Hezron. A week after he died . . ."

Leah took a deep breath. The memories were painful. It still seemed like only a day had passed since Nathan had been martyred. Not months. A year. "A week after Nathan died," she said, "you were the one who ap-peared for the letters he had hidden in our household. You drew the Greek symbol, spoke the password that Nathan had instructed me to lis-ten for, took the letters, and left without speaking."

The man blinked. "No. You are mistaken."

But his cheek muscles had tightened slightly, and since she'd been hoping to surprise him, she knew he was lying. "Secundus Nigilius Barbatus," Leah said.

He flinched again.

"He's the ex-governor of Greece," she continued. She pointed at the brand on the man's forehead. "As it is plain for the world to see, you serve in his household as a slave. You're an administrator for him, in charge of household affairs. That, I presume, is why you freely roam this market."

He shook his head in denial.

"Your name is Cornelius," she said. "It took me months to learn what Roman used the triangle brand to mark his slaves and then weeks to find you."

"I have no time for idle chat with a strange woman," he said. "So if you'll excuse me . . ." He tried to push her aside. He was about her height and hardly any larger in width, and he was unsuccessful.

"I know who you are," Leah said. "I want my questions answered. So don't try to run from me. I'll scream that you've robbed me."

He looked from side to side, as if estimating his chances.

But she'd calculated correctly. Too many people. If he ran, it would look far too suspicious.

"I want those answers," Leah said. "You are one of them. If you don't talk, I'll turn you in to the authorities. And you know exactly what charges I'll accuse you of. Sedition. You'll die in the same way my brother Nathan did. In the arena."

"This is plainly ridiculous," he answered. Without conviction.

She stared directly into his face. "I may scream for help right at this moment. I'm sure the cohort of soldiers at the far end of the market will be very interested in what I have to tell them about you."

A moment later, his shoulders slumped. "All right then. What are your questions?"

HORA SEPTINA

αre you a follower of the Truth?"

This dangerous question was not what Chayim, the son of Ben-Aryeh, had expected upon his invitation to a small garden that over-looked the lake on the palace grounds of the Golden House of Nero.

Chayim sat on a shaded bench, facing the two on an opposing bench who had invited him. Helius. Tigellinus.

"I am most assuredly not," Chayim said, trying to hide the fact that he could not find moisture in his suddenly dry mouth.

Helius and Tigellinus said nothing to Chayim's vehement denial of faith in Christ. They simply stared at him, unsmiling.

Helius was refined, smooth, silky.

"Ask my slaves," Chayim said quickly. "Ask anybody in the palace. I do not leave at night. All my associates are known to be faithful to the emperor. I am not a follower of the Truth."

"All right then," Helius said in an ambiguous way. Without pream-ble, he turned to Tigellinus. "Shall we discuss the problem that Antonia's marriage refusal presents?"

"It's not a problem," Tigellinus growled, as if Chayim were not sit-ting on a bench opposite theirs. "Nero has already instructed me to have her killed. He is furious she rejected him."

"That goes without saying," Helius replied. "Our problem is a matter of how her execution should be presented to the mobs. Otherwise most will believe Nero is simply getting rid of the last of the offspring of Claudius."

Months earlier, Nero had kicked Poppaea, his previous wife, to death in a fit of anger after she chided him for coming home late from chariot races. Along with his wife died the baby in her womb. This, of course, was the reason Nero was now looking for a new wife.

Yet against all that, there was a compelling reason for Antonia to accept his offer. What Nero wanted, Nero took.

"Antonia?" Helius said. "She was a fool to reject him. We denounce her. There have been rumors floating that she was prepared to stand at the side of Piso if his plot to kill Nero had succeeded."

Tigellinus shrugged. "Whatever. I'll get the letter drafted that invites her to open her veins."

Helius laughed. "She'd better be more efficient at it than her half sister."

Octavia, Antonia's half sister and Nero's first wife, had died too slowly to suit the soldier sent to kill her. Her veins were open, but terror slowed the blood flow, so she was suffocated and beaten so badly that when Poppaea finally received her head, it was beyond recognition.

"I'm delighted you mentioned Piso," Helius said, "for that brings up another matter. Gallus Vitas."

Tigellinus sighed. "Let's get these tedious matters out of the way quickly. I have a chariot race to attend."

Chayim wondered why they spoke so openly about this after they'd invited him here. After that mysterious question about whether he was a follower of the Truth. Was it to let him see the corrupt power they exercised so openly and freely?

"Nero's already decided Vitas' fate," Tigellinus said. "Why bother me with details?"

"You need to give me the soldiers to send to his estate," Helius said. "I know his slaves are fiercely loyal to him. We need to make sure that everything is taken."

Chayim knew this was true. When Nero appointed a magistrate these days, invariably his instructions were simple: "You know my needs. Let us see that nobody is left with anything."

"Also," Helius continued, "Nero's asked us to come up with a reason to present to Senate. Word will get out quickly after tonight, and I'd prefer the mobs did not know about the support Vitas has for Christians—"

"Had," Tigellinus said mildly. "Get into the custom of speaking about Vitas in past tense."

Helius grinned. "Of course. As for the reason behind it, I'd like to suggest that Vitas had involvement with Piso. That plot against Nero was an endless spiderweb. Does it matter if Vitas was actually part of it?"

Tigellinus obviously saw no reason to protest.

Helius turned to Chayim. "Nero's invited Vitas and his wife to tonight's dinner party. It suits Nero to copy something that Caligula had done on occasion at similar banquets. I think you'll find it amusing."

Helius explained the rest of the details as Chayim was forced to listen, still wondering why they discussed it in front of him.

"We'd better have excellent guards in attendance," Tigellinus said. "Vitas has a remarkable reputation as a soldier."

"Of course," Helius said. "This goes without saying."

"Then don't say it," Tigellinus snapped. He stood abruptly. "You handle the rest of this." He strode away without bidding either farewell.

"Such a beast, wouldn't you say?" commented Helius to Chayim. "I find his unpredictability so attractive."

Chayim hoped Helius had not decided he was attractive. They were very secluded out here in the vast garden.

"You're not a follower of the Truth?"

"No." Chayim kept his voice steady.

"That, of course, is a good thing. Tigellinus and I, well, you might have guessed we are efficient at dealing with matters that disturb Nero. It would disturb Nero if a member of his court were seditious in any manner at all."

Yes, that was the reason they'd spoken so freely. To show him their deadliness and power.

"Have you a coin?" Helius asked.

The sudden changes in subjects bewildered Chayim, keeping him off balance. He guessed that, too, was deliberate.

Chayim fumbled to find one, noting the shakiness of his fingers. Yes, he was afraid.

"Look at Caesar's portrait," Helius directed Chayim. "What is he holding?"

Chayim examined the coin. Nero was engraved on the back of the coin. Holding seven stars.

Helius nodded when Chayim pointed this out. "And although you are a Jew, you understand the significance of those seven stars. Yes?"

Now Chayim nodded.

"Explain it to me," Helius said.

"Rome has seven hills. Stars are bodies of the heavens. Nero . . ." Chayim faltered. All of the religious training of Chayim's youth urged him to say that Nero *claimed* to be divine. Yet to dispute Nero's claim to be a god meant death. Especially in the presence of Helius.

Chayim chose life. "Nero is divine. He holds those seven stars."

Helius smiled. As if his question had been a test of sorts.

Chayim pushed aside his conscience for denying the one true God of his father and his people.

"You would agree then," Helius said, "that for any other man in the world to claim those seven stars in his right hand, it would be an act of treason? That man would essentially be claiming what is Nero's?"

"Certainly," Chayim said, feeling on safer ground. He knew of no man who had done so.

"That leads to our little problem," Helius said. "I've heard rumors of a new letter circulating among followers of the Truth. A revelation, they call it, with a leader described in the letter as holding seven stars in his right hand. Certainly a treasonous letter, wouldn't you agree?"

Helius gave a catlike smile, as if he had actually licked his whiskers. "Had you been a follower, Tigellinus and I would have ordered your torture to learn more about those claims. It would have saved us some time. And, of course, offered amusement. Nero himself would have watched. Not everyone, you know, is privileged to provide Nero with entertainment."

"I am not a follower," Chayim said vehemently.

"So you've informed me." Helius seemed to be enjoying himself. "And you can rest assured that neither am I. Nor Tigellinus. But that leads to another difficulty. We are Nero's protectors. At his orders we must find out all we can about this matter. I have obtained a copy of the letter, and although I understand the language, as it is written in Greek, believe me, the letter is not always clear."

Chayim felt his brow furrow in puzzlement, something Helius caught immediately.

"There are many parts of it," Helius said, "that need interpretation. I believe, however, that a full understanding of the letter will provide Nero another legitimate reason for his persecutions of the Christians."

"I see."

"Afraid of our ruthlessness?" Helius asked.

"Yes."

"Terrified?"

"Yes."

"Good." Helius stood and began to pace slowly. "This is your opportunity, Chayim. I want —"

"My Greek is not strong," Chayim said. "I'll do my best to interpret but—"

"You should not speak until I am finished. Apologize. Kneel and apologize."

Burning with humiliation, Chayim lowered himself. "I am sorry for offending you."

"Think nothing of it. Remain on your knees and listen." Helius continued as if the brief incident had not occurred. "Now is the opportunity to repay Nero for your life of ease in the palace."

"How—" Chayim snapped his mouth shut, very conscious of his recent apology and the fact that he was still kneeling.

"You learn fast," Helius said. "I will finish. You see, if I have followers of the Truth tortured and questioned about this letter instead of being merely tortured and killed, it will appear to Rome that we actually fear their treason. No, I want it done discreetly. And that is how you can serve Nero." He paused. "Unless you aren't interested."

Chayim's tongue felt like a chunk of wood. "I would be delighted to help."

"Good, good. You are wise to what happens to those who reject Nero." Helius extended his hand to Chayim to help him to his feet. "Now that you are Nero's friend," Helius said, "join us tonight at an intimate dinner party. I'm sure you will find it amusing to see the fate that awaits Vitas."

Chayim bowed his acceptance of the invitation.

"Oh yes," Helius said, "about this matter of the seven stars."

Chayim lifted his head. Found the catlike eyes staring into his.

"We need a spy, an infiltrator, a Jew to move among other Jews to get us a full interpretation of the letter," Helius said. "You, my friend, are going to pose as a follower of the Truth."

✞ ✞ ✞

"If the reward is great enough, I can tell you where to find the one you now hunt."

At those words, Damian glanced up from the uninteresting view of sweat dripping onto his knees from his forehead. He sat on a bench in the public bath, dressed only in a towel wrapped around his waist. Standing behind him, Jerome, a large slave with a shaved head, kneaded Damian's shoulders. And now, directly in front of him, the stranger who had approached moments earlier.

"The one I hunt," Damian repeated to this stranger, affecting disinterest. It was midmorning, and the baths were quiet at this time. This was why Damian came, because he could be found easier in the steam now than later in the day when the bath was crowded.

"Yesterday," the man began to answer, "you visited the master of my household and asked him about—"

"Move toward me," Damian ordered. Through the wisps of steam, he had seen what might be a scar across the man's forehead.

Without question, the man complied, the second indication that he might be a slave, accustomed to taking orders from a Roman.

Damian stood from the bench for a closer view of the man to confirm his guess about the stranger's identity. "Are you here with the permission of Barbatus?" Damian said.

"I didn't tell you that my master was—"

"Don't take me for a fool," Damian growled at the slave. "His mark is plain across your forehead."

The slave was much shorter than Damian. He had a lean face, and if Damian had to guess further, he would have presumed the man was an administrator or physician, because he was not muscular. Aside from the scar of the hot-iron brand—a triangle with a circle in the center— that had once been pressed against his forehead to mark him, there were no apparent healed wounds that would indicate a life of hard physical labor.

If Damian was an expert on anything, it was on slaves. Offhand, he could probably identify hundreds of brands of different patrician Roman families. The pattern of a triangle with a circle in the center belonged to Secundus Nigilius Barbatus, who had once held the prestigious post of governor of Greece.

As the man hesitated, Damian spoke again. "Don't lie to me. If Barbatus wanted to deliver a message, he would have sent a litter for me and given it to me himself."

Jerome stopped massaging Damian's back and placed another towel across his shoulders. Damian didn't acknowledge this; slaves did not expect courtesy.

"Already you are at a disadvantage," Damian said to the slave in front of him. "If I report to Barbatus that you left the household as you did, he will consider you an escaped slave."

Unspoken, because it didn't need to be said, was that Barbatus could have the fugitive slave immediately killed or, worse, sent to the arena.

"I'm a trusted administrator," the slave answered, showing a flash of pride. "I come and go as I please."

"So he knows you are approaching me for the reward I offered yesterday?"

"Of course not," the slave said.

"I doubt Barbatus would appreciate this act of secrecy. And he is known for harshly punishing those who disobey him. Tell me what I need to know or face his wrath."

"If you have me punished," the slave answered, "would any other slave ever seek you out here again?"

Damian grinned. At the man's unexpected show of resolve. And at the new deduction this allowed Damian. The slave obviously knew enough about Damian's methods and reputation to have approached with such confidence.

"Well, then," Damian said, "at least tell me your name."

"Cornelius," the slave answered.

"Obviously, you know about the reward. Do you know where I can find the fugitive from the island?"

Strictly speaking, the man whom Damian now hunted, a Jew named John, was not a fugitive from the barren island off the coast of Greece, where he had been exiled. The man had not escaped but had been released. He was only a fugitive now because Helius, Nero's secretary, had hired Damian to find him. And rumors had placed the Jew here in Rome.

As for his captivity on Patmos, John had been released because a group of wealthy and influential men had approached Barbatus during his governorship of Asia. Within his jurisdiction were Greece and the islands off the coast. Damian had had no problem securing the names of those men from Barbatus, who knew Damian now owed him a political favor. After getting the names, Damian had made a point to delay his departure and stop in the gardens of the estate to talk at length with one of the slaves tending a hillside of olives. This, for Damian, was a customary tactic. Slaves formed the majority of the population and provided an incredible network of hidden information.

"That reward is not enough," Cornelius said.

"The reward I offered yesterday is ample," Damian said. In truth, he would have paid ten times the amount, but to offer that would have shown how important the fugitive was. And that had the potential to lead others to ask too many questions about the Jew. Helius had stressed that Damian must keep his quest secret; if word ever leaked out that Helius had hired Damian, not even Damian's family status could protect him from imperial punishment.

"Without my help, it might take you months to find the Jew," Cornelius said. "I know where he is and enough about him that I can help you place an ambush."

"When?" Damian demanded abruptly.

"I can make the arrangements tomorrow and report back to you. John will be yours by sundown of the day after. That should be worth enough for you to buy my freedom from Barbatus."

"Your freedom for another man's death," Damian said.

Cornelius shrugged. "Whatever he did to cause a man of your reputation to begin the hunt probably means he deserves whatever fate befalls him."

"So you know of my reputation."

"What slave doesn't? And what slave doesn't fear the day you might begin pursuit of him?"

"I will buy your freedom," Damian said. "After I have this man captured."

"Before his capture," Cornelius said firmly. "John is a popular man among many slaves. I want to be away from the estate of Barbatus before word spreads that I betrayed him."

"Today, then, you will be a free man. You know my reputation, but I warn you anyway. If you don't return tomorrow with the promised information, I will hunt you as relentlessly as I have hunted all the others."

Damian glanced back at the large bald man who had resumed massaging his shoulders. There was another reason that Damian let it be known that informers could find him here at the baths every morning at this time. In the baths, men could not conceal knives or short swords. And in unarmed combat, there wasn't a man alive who could compete against Damian's slave.

"Jerome," Damian said, "show this man a sample of the consequences if he disappoints me."

With phenomenal agility and speed, the large man sidestepped Damian and clamped Cornelius by the throat. With a single massive arm, he lifted the slave completely off the ground.

"If you are lying," Damian said to Cornelius, "if you don't make the arrangements for me to capture the fugitive, or if you try to run from Rome after I've purchased your freedom, Jerome will rip your head off your shoulders. That mark on your forehead would make it impossible for you to live openly ever again if you become a fugitive. Do you understand?"

Cornelius made a high-pitched squeal that sounded like agreement.

"Good," Damian said. He motioned for Jerome to set Cornelius down, who instantly heaved and gagged for air.

"Leave now," Damian told the slave. "Tomorrow, at the same time and place, I fully expect you to tell me how and where to find this John."

✠ ✠ ✠

"I know what you've told me before," Vitas said to Ben-Aryeh. "But now that we are in Rome, surely you'll reconsider."

Ben-Aryeh sat on a bench in the outer courtyard of Vitas' home. His eyes were closed. His face was tilted to catch the sun.

Vitas found himself admiring the lines on the older man's face. Lines of character.

"You are speaking about Chayim," Ben-Aryeh said.

"I can provide you a litter to go to the imperial palace," Vitas said. "You'll be safe, of course. Reports of the accusation against you in Jerusalem will not have reached Rome."

"You've told me that repeatedly. And each time it emphasizes the fact that I am of so little importance that no one in Rome would care that I have escaped Jerusalem."

"Except Chayim. Your son."

"Congratulations," Ben-Aryeh said. "I understand Sophia is with child."

"Don't try to change the subject."

"When you are a father, perhaps you will understand how much it hurts to be estranged from your firstborn."

"Don't be stubborn," Vitas urged. He and Ben-Aryeh had argued so much over the months that it was second nature for both of them to freely speak their minds. "Now is your chance to reconcile."

"I will not go to the palace."

"I can send for him to join you here," Vitas said.

Ben-Aryeh finally opened his eyes. "So that I can tell him myself that I am a fugitive? That if I return to Jerusalem, I will be put to death by stoning? That I have abandoned my wife and his mother because I am too afraid of that fate?"

"I doubt it's fear," Vitas said. "I know you rage against the injustice of it. You are an innocent man. Your enemies are trying to destroy you."

This was clear to Vitas. He remembered that morning with Queen Bernice, when the assistant named Olithar had lied about Ben-Aryeh. That had been enough proof of Ben-Aryeh's innocence for Vitas to help when Ben-Aryeh had shown up at the royal palace, asking for safe-conduct out of the city. Vitas had had no regrets since—he was beginning to love the older man like a brother.

"*Trying* to destroy me?" Ben-Aryeh said. "I'm stuck here with a Roman family. In Rome. Don't get me wrong. I'm extremely grateful, and someday I shall find a way to repay you. But my enemies have succeeded extremely well."

"But they weren't able to kill you."

"You find that ironic, don't you?" Ben-Aryeh said. "All your questions about this Jesus and how He accepted crucifixion despite His innocence. And here I am, a man of the law, breaking the law."

"Shall I send for Chayim?"

"No," Ben-Aryeh said. "If he has changed and is a Jew dutiful to God, I will only shame him. If he has not changed, he will shame me."

HORA DUODECIMA

Late-afternoon sunshine warmed Damian as he walked through a small market area.

He did not look back to confirm that Jerome was shadowing him as he moved through the crowded market. That was a given. Always. They were a team. He assumed that Jerome remained because he was content with the monthly wage that Damian paid, but Damian never asked, assuming that every man and woman always did what each felt was in his or her best interest.

It was with this assumption that Damian hunted slaves, as he was doing this morning on his way to a pottery maker.

In his quiet moments—and for Damian there were many—he wasn't afraid to contemplate the satisfaction it gave him to make a business of pursuing slaves. It allowed him a form of defiance against the status quo that had been thrust upon him, born as he was into a patrician family. And most of all, it satisfied his instinct to hunt.

For who else to match wits with than another human being? Especially a desperate human being, trying to avoid the torture and death that would come with capture.

It was not the prospect of their punishment that drove Damian. That was simply a fact of the Roman world, and slaves knew the consequences of disobedience or theft or murder, so he felt no pity for them once captured. No, it was the pursuit, often so challenging that after capturing an especially clever slave, Damian was tempted to release that slave again with a month's worth of living expenses and a week's head start.

The hunt!

Damian began with that assumption—that men always did what they felt was in their self-interest. But what added to the challenge was that he'd learned how widely varied one man's self-interest could be from another's. Many slaves were entirely predictable in their flight, and those he found quickly and with a sense of boredom. The others—the minority—presented him with a fascinating array of needs and desires, from the depraved to the sublime. These slaves—the unpredictable and intelligent—gave him the most satisfaction.

To hunt them, he'd learned to add another basic rule: Think like the prey.

Thus, again and again he would slip into the role, indeed the very psyche of those he pursued, spending hours—even days—in the household interviewing other slaves about the habits and friends and desires of the one escaped. Whatever distance the pursued gained while Damian patiently remained to ask those questions was quickly lost once Damian understood whom he pursued.

In a way, then, he was disappointed that today he expected to hear from the slave from the ex-governor's household of a time and place that John would be captured. From all that Damian had learned about John, the man was intelligent. And John's motives were difficult to discern, which made him all the more unpredictable as quarry. Damian had hoped for a battle of intellect against intellect in seeking John. It would be a shame that a betrayal might end any chance John had of remaining free.

Still, Damian was not going to assume the capture would end as expected. So this morning, he moved through the marketplace as if the pursuit would be protracted. On the chance that John did escape immediate capture, Damian wanted to peer into the man's mind. And what better reflected the way a man thought than his writings?

There was more.

In hiring Damian, Helius had made a passing comment about the uselessness of rumors of a letter that this John had written to a growing circulation in Rome and Asia.

Damian believed this was one of the few mistakes Helius had made over the last few years. Helius, as the second most powerful man in the empire, had great political acumen. Helius should have known his comment would not deter Damian but spur him to investigate the letter further.

If, for some reason, Helius did not want Damian learning more about the letter, Damian wanted to know the reason. Even if John was soon captured and delivered to Helius as promised.

For in Rome, political knowledge was power. As were secrets.

☩ ☩ ☩

The dimly lit shop was cramped and had the comforting smell of damp clay. An unfinished pot sat on a nearby wheel, draped with a wet cloth. On a bench were other large squares of clay, equally protected from the heat by damp cloths.

The owner of the shop was Darda, a tiny old bearded Jew who sat in the doorway on a stool. He ignored the passersby and squinted at a scroll with intense concentration.

"What is it you want to know?" the old Jew asked when he finished.

"Some of it makes perfect sense," Damian said. "And some of it is obviously symbolism."

Darda nodded, keeping his watery blue eyes directly on Damian's face. "And?"

"I am paying you to interpret it," Damian replied. "Am I not? So begin."

"Have I seen your money? Is it in my hand?"

Damian sighed theatrically, hoping to amuse the old Jew. "I simply don't understand how the Romans rule the Jews instead of the opposite."

That earned the slightest of smiles. Or perhaps the twitch around the old Jew's mouth was Damian's imagination.

"Besides," Darda said, "there is one who could make much better sense of this for you. But I'm not sure you would have enough gold for him. He hates the empire and he hates the Christians because he lost his sons to both."

Darda scratched his beard. "And you would have to find him first. He is one of our greatest rabbis, but he has hidden himself and his daughters because he fears Nero."

"Tell me his name," Damian said. There was no such thing as information that could not be used in some manner. And the letter intrigued him.

"Hezron, son of Onam. The sons who died were Caleb and Nathan. He has one daughter named Leah. The other, her name slips my memory."

"Do I owe you for this precious knowledge?" Damian wasn't afraid of sarcasm.

Darda shook his head.

"But for you to interpret what you can of this . . ."

Darda named an amount.

"That's outrageous," Damian said. Without heat. For what Helius was prepared to pay for the capture of John, the sesterces involved here were meaningless. Besides, Damian liked to cultivate the reputation of one who wouldn't hesitate to pay handsomely for deserving information—knowledge and secrets, after all, were power.

"Would you rather waste time trying to find another rabbi willing to help a hated Roman?"

Damian cocked his head and regarded Darda. "You don't strike me as a man who is willing to compromise for money."

Darda finally smiled. "This letter, it is dangerous. I enjoy the chance to cause a little confusion and grief for Nero by spreading its message among your people."

Dangerous. For Nero. Damian hid his reaction. But perhaps his instincts were right. Perhaps Helius truly was afraid.

"And, of course," Damian said, "it is all the more satisfying to be paid by a Roman for this."

"Of course."

"You shall be paid," Damian grunted. "Now tell me what you can."

"The money first."

Damian made a show of disgust, but it was merely a show. He had not expected anything else from the old man.

Darda took the money and disappeared inside his shop to hide it in a safe place.

"Don't trust me?" Damian said upon his return.

"Not the slightest. In fact, I'm afraid that Nero himself sent you. I will tell you what I can, answer what I can, except for one question."

"That was not part of our deal."

"I'll return your money," the old man said, rising.

Damian motioned for him to sit. "Tell me what you can."

✛ ✛ ✛

Chayim was conscious of the perfume that clung to the silk sheets rumpled around him on the bed.

He inhaled. And tried to find enjoyment in a moment. Normally, he would freely admit that he found no shame in his circumstances, that pleasure, luxury, and wealth intoxicated him.

Just as he would freely admit that his father's God was not his God. His expensive education in Rome had convinced him that the Jewish religion was superstition, and he'd readily rejected it. But he'd truly rejected it years earlier, while living in Jerusalem.

So when his grim-faced father, Ben-Aryeh, had informed him that he was to be sent to the emperor's court as an envoy, Chayim had immediately seen it as a gift of freedom—even after Ben-Aryeh explained that Chayim's life in the court depended on a continued harmonious relationship between the Jewish royalty, the temple priesthood, and the powers of Rome.

Until the meeting with Helius and Tigellinus, nothing had altered Chayim's optimistic view of his new life. He'd dropped his Jewish mannerisms and immediately entered the life of riotous rich living, pretending to be just another prince among the half dozen held as de facto hostages to ensure that their fathers in various kingdoms did not begin revolts against Rome.

At the meeting with Helius and Tigellinus, however, the skeletal fingers of palace intrigue had first clutched him and had brought him a new realization.

It seemed that his pleasures did have a price.

"Wine?" a woman's voice called. She appeared in a robe at the doorway, holding an ornate clay jug and a goblet.

This was Litas. A slave from Parthia. Tall, dark-haired. She had a wide smile and sensuous eyes. Chayim was intrigued by her appearance and had not yet tired of her. As a gift from the emperor, she had no choice in what Chayim chose to do with her, but she was never unwilling.

"No."

She frowned at the sharpness in his voice.

He realized his mistake. And in that moment, he knew he was more his father's son than he'd have guessed until this first danger. Chayim's political instincts, untested until the order given him by Helius, surfaced. Litas was a gift from the emperor; who was to say that she was not also a spy.

Chayim needed to pretend nothing was amiss. "My head hurts from wine at lunch," Chayim said, as if this explained his curtness.

"I hope it improves soon," she said. "A dinner with Nero tonight! I so look forward to it. And to the entertainment. Who was it that will be publicly humiliated?"

"Vitas. A war hero. And his wife. Some Jewish woman." Chayim now regretted telling Litas what Helius and Tigellinus had planned. She'd seemed to enjoy the prospect of it too much. And now, wondering if she was a spy for Helius, it made him uncomfortable to have such a heartless woman so close to him.

"Go ahead and return to the baths and wait for me," Chayim said. He needed to be alone to think.

Litas gave him her wide smile. Before, he would have enjoyed the lasciviousness in it. Now he found it vaguely repulsive. He forced himself to smile at her, and she nodded and disappeared.

There was no one Chayim could speak to about what troubled him. This, too, was a new realization. Until now, he'd had no troubles. All of his friends were simply acquaintances who shared the lifestyle of parties until dawn, with long sleep to follow during the day.

As for his troubles, they were obvious.

Helius had commanded him to infiltrate the cult of the followers. He had even told him the time and place that such a group would gather next. Helius was not to be disobeyed, for Helius and Tigellinus were easily able to bend the will of Nero.

Yet Chayim had been commanded to engage in treason against Nero. At any time, Helius could deny that he'd given the order to Chayim and, quite simply, have Chayim publicly tried and condemned for that treason.

Chayim was well aware of how those who followed the Christos were killed. Whether he died because he joined the cult or because he refused to join the cult, dead was still dead. In short, this might be an unstoppable strategy on Helius' part to eliminate Chayim.

Chayim had tried to remember if he'd somehow insulted Helius over the last months and came up with nothing. Had Helius made a suggestive overture to Chayim that he'd innocently rejected? It took less than that for the capricious Helius to choose enemies.

The alternative, one that Chayim hoped for, was that Helius and Tigellinus truly did want what they'd requested. The subversive letter that was rumored to be circulating among the followers. If so, it made sense that Helius knew a time and location for the next meeting of the cult.

But to get that letter Chayim needed to trust that Helius had no other motive and then act upon that trust, fully joining the cult at the risk to his life.

What if, for example, Chayim was publicly exposed by another source, a source unaware of the order given by Helius? Would Helius then protect Chayim against the rage of Nero?

It seemed to Chayim that he was doomed either way. He couldn't refuse Helius, but indulging Helius presented great danger, even if Helius had no evil intentions for Chayim.

Unless there was a way to keep Helius happy and still ensure there was no possibility of being accused of being a follower . . .

"Chayim!" Litas' voice came from a hot bath in the next room.

Helius wanted the letter that was circulating among the Christians. If Chayim could get that without placing himself in danger . . .

"Chayim!"

Chayim gave it more thought. If Helius was setting Chayim up to be caught among the Christians, Helius' plan would only work if Helius knew when and where to find Chayim in the compromising situation. Therefore, if Chayim could find another group of Christians, he would at least be eliminating some of the risk as he tried to acquire the letter.

"Chayim! The water gets cold!"

But how to earn the trust of a Christian well enough to learn where and when they met? Their fear of persecution—well justified—made them secretive and wary of outsiders. Torture and bribery probably wouldn't work, even if Chayim could find a Christian to approach. So how could Chayim convince a Christian to invite him to a meeting?

"Chayim!"

Litas' insistent voice finally broke through his thoughts. Chayim frowned. She was a mere slave, not some centurion ordering him around as if he were a soldier.

With that silent aggravated thought still echoing in his mind, Chayim saw his solution in an inspired flash. One that would involve very little risk to himself. All of it unfolded quickly in his mind, proving again that he was much more his father's son than either of them would have expected.

First, though, he would need to find a Christian and infiltrate the cult at a time and place of his own choosing, not one set up by Helius.

Perhaps among other slaves . . .

And, despite her arrogance, Litas was a slave. Who must certainly know the activities of other slaves . . .

"Litas," he called as he sprang from his bed, "let's talk. I want some information that only you might know."

✠ ✠ ✠

"This is the first thing you need to know about the written history of the Jews," Darda said, as if he'd been prepared for the question. "It is the redemption plan of God, from the beginning of creation to the arrival of the Messiah He has promised us."

"Redemption plan? What do we need to be redeemed from?"

"Whatever drives you away from God," Darda countered.

"That's an obscure answer. My sesterces are not meant to pay for obscure answers."

"Someday, if you are blessed, the answer won't be obscure."

Damian scowled. "Speak less obscurely about this letter."

Darda pointed a clay-encrusted fingertip at the scroll in Damian's hands. "If one were to believe that the man named Jesus was the Messiah sent by God, then this letter is the culmination of all the writings of our prophets. But remember, that is only if you believe in the other letters about Jesus that are circulating."

"Since I am unaware of those letters and will probably find little of interest in them, tell me about the man who wrote this letter." Damian unrolled it to the beginning. He read again the introduction. "Yes, tell me about this John who calls himself God's servant and wants us to believe an angel brought him to a great revelation and then writes of such horrifying events."

"John? While he has chosen to place his faith in Jesus as the long-expected Messiah, he is obviously an educated Jew. And, for what it is worth, he is one of the original twelve disciples who followed Jesus."

"You sound hesitant about calling him intelligent." This was how Damian worked. Filtering the perceptions that other people had about his prey.

Darda shrugged. "It's a contradiction to me. An intelligent man. Yet one who places his faith in the prophecies of Jesus."

Darda scratched his ear, inspected whatever he'd found on his fingertip, and continued. "Educated? Nearly two-thirds of his writings in this letter allude to the writings of our ancient prophets. Ezekiel. Daniel. Isaiah. That shows his education. And because of all his allusions to previous writings, the symbolism will make sense only to one familiar with the Jewish prophecies."

"So I have no chance of understanding it without those reference points."

"Definitely not. You would end up speculating and coming up with ridiculous conjectures."

"What about the other third of this letter? That doesn't borrow from previous writings."

"Where John doesn't use symbolism that we should understand from our ancient prophets, he explains clearly."

"Give me an example."

Darda closed his eyes and recited from memory. "'For the time has come for the wedding feast of the Lamb, and his bride has prepared herself. She is permitted to wear the finest white linen. (Fine linen represents the good deeds done by the people of God.)' See? He tells us exactly what he means by *fine linen*."

"Lamb?" Damian made a face, because that was the one image that had caught his attention. "Lamb? Sheep are stupid beasts. Smelly and need constant attention."

"You are thinking like a Roman. Not a Jew. You want to interpret the symbols in a literal sense. But symbols are so much richer than mere words. They show us things that are invisible."

"I can see a lamb. And you are saying it is more than a lamb?"

"Every Jew understands on an intellectual level the significance of the

Lamb, but more importantly, the symbol speaks on a profound level to our souls. We've all seen a lamb sacrificed for our sins, seen the terror in its eyes, watched the knife cut its throat, seen the blood spill across the whiteness of its struggling body, heard the bleating fade as it died."

Damian felt frustrated. There was so little he knew about this. Perhaps it would just be easier to give John over to Helius and move on to the pursuit of another slave. But there was the fact that Helius was willing to pay so much for John. And a more macabre yet fascinating mystery existed. Damian knew that two previous slave hunters had tried and failed to find John, and had died unexpected violent deaths in the slums afterward. What was hidden here?

"You mentioned Isaiah," Damian said, "Ezekiel. Daniel."

"These prophets of our people, all of whom encouraged us that God would send a Messiah."

"Prophets," Damian echoed. "Making predictions about the future?"

"Yes," Darda answered, as if speaking to a simpleton. "A true prophet makes no prophecy that is false or unfulfilled."

"Then this John must be a false prophet," Damian said. "He speaks of things that haven't happened."

Darda sighed. "That is the danger of a non-Jew imposing his own view upon our writings. Prophecies can refer to the fore future, the far future, and the final future. All the Hebrew prophets moved in and out of those time categories, and John does the same. But to understand them, you need to read them in context, and to do that, you need a thorough knowledge of all our Scriptures."

"Tell me this, then. You said some believe the Messiah did come as promised."

"Yes, there are radicals among our people who argue that since Jesus was the promised Messiah, God's covenant with us is fulfilled."

"Radicals?"

"I don't dispute the witnesses and their stories about Jesus. In a Jewish court of law, much of what they testify would be considered acceptable. He was a miracle worker, and I might not dispute that. But . . ."

"But what?"

"Let me back up. In a time-honored tradition of all our prophets, Jesus, like John, used language that all Jews would understand came from previous prophets. He doesn't steal from them, but alludes to them and makes them even more significant. But Jesus' words must be interpreted in light of the previous prophets, and unless you are familiar with all their writings, His prophecies make little sense."

"You are saying that to a Roman like me, unfamiliar with Jewish writings, John's letter is an elaborate code?"

"Sea," Darda said abruptly. "Waters of the sea. What does that mean to you?"

"A place for ships to sail."

Darda snorted. "There's my proof. The sea to a Jew, understood in a symbolic sense, means chaos and confusion. In this letter of Revelation, when the Beast rises from the sea, it says much more to a Jewish reader than to you."

"Jesus, then, uses this rich symbolism?"

Darda nodded.

"And His prophecies? Do they show Him to be a false prophet or a true prophet?"

"In His final days He made one prophecy that completely destroys His credibility. He promised that the temple in Jerusalem would be destroyed in this generation. As that is plainly impossible, Jesus was obviously not divine. He—"

"Enough," Damian said. Darda was getting too passionate in his hate for Jesus. Damian wanted to focus on John, the author of the letter, the man feared by Helius. "You said John was obviously educated. Can you make any other guesses about him?"

"John verges on genius. I've read and reread this. The writing is powerful and layered, so complete that I would almost believe that it came to him in a divinely inspired vision. Except then I would have to agree with him that Jesus was the Messiah."

Another shrug from the old man. "And the temple still stands and cannot fall. One false prophecy shows the prophet is not a prophet from God, for God is not fallible."

"Why is the temple in Jerusalem so important?" Damian asked.

Darda nearly sputtered. "Without the temple, we cannot approach God with sacrifices. And without God, we as Jews are totally desolate. If the temple ever fell, how else could we seek redemption?"

Redemption. That bothersome word again. Yet Damian doubted Helius feared this John and his vision because of religious matters and the notoriously famous and invisible God of the Jews.

Damian unscrolled the letter to a portion that had interested him during his first quick reading. He studied it more slowly. The sounds of the market faded away.

Darda was patient.

"It seems that this is a grand story," Damian finally said. "There is a hero in here and an antihero."

"The Lamb against the Beast," Darda said. "I'm impressed. That is the heart of the vision, is it not?"

"You are asking me?" Damian said. He was enjoying this. The pursuit of knowledge.

"I am. You've read the vision. Who is the Lamb?"

"This Messiah."

Darda nodded. Again with a faint twitch of a smile. "It is the Lamb against the Beast. Do you understand the significance of this?"

Damian recited a portion from the letter. " 'Wisdom is needed to understand this. Let the one who has understanding calculate the number of the Beast, for it is the number of man. His number is 666.' "

Then Damian sketched out the Greek symbols in the dirt at their feet. "I've seen it represented as this graffiti."

$$\chi \xi \varsigma$$

"But I don't have the understanding," Damian said. "That is why I have enlisted your help. Who is the Beast?"

Darda stood abruptly. "Our conversation ends here. I warned you about one question that I would not address. And that was it."

"Surely you are joking," Damian said. "What harm can there be in—"

"I will speak nothing more on the subject."

"What about your desire to spread confusion against Nero?"

"Not at the cost of my life," Darda said. He turned and stepped inside the shop and quickly shut the door.

A clunk of wood told Damian that the old Jew had barred it in place.

Interesting, Damian thought. *Very, very interesting.*

PRIMA FAX

Here was Nero, stepping forward from his dinner companions, with a strange hunger in his eyes that immediately deepened the foreboding that had steeped Vitas' soul since the invitation to Nero's palace.

To arrive at this inner chamber, its entrance guarded by six soldiers of the Emperor's Guard, a slave had led Vitas and Sophia through the halls. During the long walk, their sandals slapping on polished marble, they'd exchanged frequent glances that mirrored their unspoken opinion of the grossly ostentatious luxury that reflected the crass taste and sheer megalomania of an emperor well past the edge of madness.

Nero reached to clasp the forearms of Vitas in greeting. "Back from Jerusalem!"

Nero's breath smelled of wine and garlic. His hands on Vitas' forearms were hot. Nero's blond curly hair was thinning, and it clung to his scalp because of a sheen of sweat. His once handsome face was swollen from years of wine and food and decadent living. The table behind him was piled high with delicacies.

Vitas accepted Nero's greeting without recoiling and managed to keep his eyes directly on Nero's face as the emperor continued his effusive greeting. "I understand you were able to step in and quell the disturbances in Jerusalem."

"I had little to do with that," Vitas said. "I merely happened to be there during the few days of riots."

312 HANEGRAAFF • BROUWER

Nero stepped away and inspected Vitas up and down. It gave Vitas a sense of violation, but he smiled and nodded as if they were brothers.

"Modest as always." Nero began to applaud slowly but emphatically. "All of Rome salutes you. Indeed, Caesar salutes you."

Immediately, the dozen dinner guests standing in clusters nearby did the same.

Vitas took no satisfaction from this accolade from the man who held the most power in the entire world.

Still, there was the sense of foreboding that Vitas could not escape. "When Nero pretends to be a friend," the wags in the forum were fond of saying, "beware what he takes with one hand while his other arm holds you in an embrace."

There was another reason Vitas wished there had been no applause. He now led a secret life, married to a Christian.

"And here we have a wife whom the hero obviously deserves." Nero cast his eyes on Sophia. This inspection, unlike the one bestowed on Vitas, was more than cursory. Nero allowed his eyes to caress the woman's curves and did not hide a smile of predatory satisfaction. "Welcome too. May your evening with the Caesar be a memorable one."

One of the dinner guests chuckled.

Vitas recognized the almost womanly tones and did not glance over to confirm. Helius.

Sophia returned Nero's inspection with a fixed smile. Vitas could only guess how she felt. True thoughts about Nero were best kept hidden, even after the evening ended and they were absolutely certain they were alone; who knew when a slave might betray carelessly spoken words?

"Please," Nero said, "let me make introductions. Some you know, of course, but others you don't."

He waved his arm dramatically and began with a short man whose dark eyes glittered with intensity. "This, my friend, is Chayim," Nero said unnecessarily. Vitas wondered why Nero was making a point of telling Vitas what he already knew. "A Jew. You know what they say. You don't have to be a Jew to be stupid, but it helps."

Chayim lifted a wine goblet in the direction of Vitas and forced out a laugh that fooled no one but Caesar.

Nero pretended to suddenly remember something. "I'm sorry! I'd forgotten, Gallus Vitas. Your wife, too, is a Jew, is she not?"

Now Vitas understood. It gave Nero the chance to insult Vitas and Sophia. Vitas's skin prickled with renewed foreboding. Before, Nero had always treated Vitas with respect. What could this mean?

"She is a Roman citizen," Vitas said.

Nero applauded again. "Well spoken!" He continued the introductions. "To the left of Chayim is Aulus Petillius. He was once handsome, I'm told, but as you can see, he hasn't aged well."

Aulus lifted a glass and forced a smile. Nero's words were truth; Aulus had heavy jowls beneath a round face and a heavy thatch of dark hair. Although his hair was his own, he dyed it, and most believed it was a wig.

Nero moved on, guest by guest, passing by Helius and Tigellinus, who seemed to be eyeing Vitas with anticipation.

Vitas shivered and hoped with desperation that he and Sophia would survive an evening with the madman.

As Nero finished the introductions, Vitas concentrated on remembering each face and name. He hoped Sophia was doing the same. He had warned her to drink only watered wine and to keep her senses about her. Tonight was not a night for social blunders.

✝ ✝ ✝

Caius Sennius Ruso paused on the path of his hillside garden and surveyed the last living man of the twelve disciples who had once walked in Galilee with Jesus. John, son of Zebedee.

John, ahead up the hill on a bench beneath an olive tree with a nearby lantern giving him light, seemed unaware of Ruso's approach.

Ruso did not think that John was in prayer. No, John was gazing at a slightly upward angle, as if looking into the sky beyond the twisting dark branches of the tree, smiling as if memories were speaking directly to him.

Not for the first time did Ruso wonder about these memories that John must have of the three years spent with Jesus. Whenever John spoke of Jesus, it was as if only days had passed since their time together, not more than three decades.

These were memories that glowed behind John's eyes when he spoke of his faith. John was now in his midfifties, and although sun and wind had creased his face with wrinkles, he had none of the fears and worries or greed and selfishness usually etched into a man's face by that age. His dark hair had begun to pepper, but lean living had kept his face thin, and from a distance, especially when he was walking, his energy and carriage made him appear much younger.

Ruso realized he'd been staring, and with a self-conscious cough, he moved forward again. John did not like to be the center of attention, whether it was from one man or a group.

Ruso was careful to greet John well before arriving, as if to compensate for the moments he'd paused and watched his older friend. "Things are well?" Ruso asked as John rose and smiled.

"Always," John said. "You are too kind."

Ruso snorted. No sense beginning the usual argument with John, the one where Ruso tried to extend every available luxury that came with his wealth and where John politely and insistently refused.

Ruso had inherited a substantial fortune. As a senator, for years he had lived a life of luxury here in his estate on Capitoline Hill in Rome. Yet with all he had, for most of his adulthood, he'd also been unable to escape a nagging sense of emptiness. On a business trip to Ephesus, he'd heard of a remarkable teacher, and curiosity had led him to the teacher—John. Ruso's conversion to faith in Jesus had been gradual, yet certain.

He'd grieved for John when political circumstances forced him into exile on Patmos and rejoiced at the chance to be among those who had helped John leave the island a few years later. When John had insisted on coming to Rome to comfort believers in the midst of the Tribulation, Ruso had had to fight long and hard to convince him to stay here on the estate instead of in the slums of the city. Even so, John declined any special treatment and insisted on his daily visits into the depths of the city.

"You are rather well dressed to visit the prisons with me today," John said. "And you are home much later than usual."

"Today, unfortunately, I'm forced to meet with some lawyers."

It was a lie. Ruso intended to meet with a couple of military men to make travel arrangements. Their connections would ensure the secrecy his plans required. Ruso deeply regretted the need to lie to his friend. But he had no choice.

"Lawyers need comfort too," John said dryly. His eyes met Ruso's. "But I doubt you came here just to tell me that."

Had John heard the lie in his voice? As a senator, Ruso was an expert at public oratory, and proud of the inflections he could put into his voice as needed. But John was uncannily perceptive.

"I'm here to beg you to leave Rome," Ruso said, hoping his calm voice masked his unease. With John, there was no sense in trying to ease into a subject; he always seemed to see past any conversational screens. "Your life is in danger."

"So are the lives of all believers here," John answered with a smile of irony. "This is the solution then? All of us leave the city? Including you?"

"There is a slave hunter of great repute. Named Damian. You are the only one he is pursuing."

John sat on the bench again. "My friend, you are asking me to flee the same tribulation that I have encouraged all believers to endure with the same faith in God shown by our Master."

"You don't understand. If Damian is on your trail . . ." Ruso paced beneath the branches of the olive tree as he spoke. "I did not fear the other two slave hunters seeking you for bounty in the last months. They weren't as bright, men who lived in the lower-class world and had no access to this world."

Ruso put up a hand to stop the protest he knew would come from John. "Yes, in our Father's eyes, there are no divisions between classes. But in this world, where we both live until we can be with the Father, economics dictate certain things and for convenience in conversation, I speak of lower class and upper class. Most slave hunters can never breach the upper-class world, but Damian comes from a patrician family of great influence. He knows how to move among the upper classes, indeed, is welcomed by them. For he may be a contemptible slave hunter, but he is also the brother of a war hero, and a member of one of Rome's oldest and most distinguished families."

Ruso continued pacing. "And he is good, John. Very good. For the last six months, he has searched the entire world for the slave of a senator who escaped with a chest of valuable jewels. The entire world! And found the slave too, bringing him back to justice in Rome. I've used all my connections to inquire as to who has recently hired him to find you, but so far, I've learned nothing. But it must be a man of great power and influence. That has me worried."

"I will find another place to live," John said quietly. "It is unfair to put you and your family at risk."

"I am not worried for me!" Ruso realized he had raised his voice and apologized. "I worry for you, my friend. Yesterday Damian was at a neighboring estate and interviewed Barbatus."

John cocked his head in recognition of the name.

"Yes, Secundus Nigilius Barbatus. Who released you from Patmos. Damian was inquiring as to who secured your release and why."

"You are in danger then," John said softly, obviously understanding the implication.

When Ruso and some of his friends had approached Barbatus, Nero had not yet begun his persecution of the believers. Barbatus had had no reason not to release John, who'd been placed on the island by local officials tired of the trouble that John's preaching caused in the Jewish community.

"Barbatus is no fool," Ruso said. "He would be glad to do a favor for Damian. Moreover, he'd be reluctant to protect you by refusing to help Damian, not with Nero determined to use believers as a scapegoat for the Great Fire."

"Damian will have your name," John said. "You were among those who petitioned for my release from Patmos."

"Yes, but I am not afraid. Officially, I had broken no law by helping you before Nero's edict against Christians."

"But if you continue to help now . . ."

"Let me repeat," Ruso said. "I am not afraid for me and my family. We can easily travel out of reach of Nero until he tires of the persecution. But Damian will eventually find you. Don't you see? The other two hunters never even discovered that sort of information, never made it past the sewers of Rome in their inquiries. Damian will find you. And then . . ."

Ruso bit back a description of the consequences. John well understood them. Every day John was in the prisons, comforting those captured by Nero for their faith. Every day John literally walked into the lion's den. Every day Ruso prayed with gratitude when John returned by God's grace.

"Listen to me," Ruso said. "Damian will have most certainly offered a reward to the slaves of Barbatus. And he will offer the same reward to my slaves when he comes to interview me, as he most surely will. You know that on my conversion, I offered freedom to my slaves, and that those who stayed did so because their lives here are much better than the lives of most freedmen. Yet if Damian offers a substantial reward, it might be enough to tempt any of them. You are not safe here."

"I am not afraid of death."

"John! I've memorized the letters of Matthew and Mark and Luke. I've listened to your stories. Wasn't there a time when our Lord and Master Himself avoided the tetrarchy of Herod because it was unsafe for Him to travel in that territory?"

"He understood politics, if that is what you are suggesting," John said.

"And the politics of Rome dictate that you leave," Ruso said.

"Your argument is a two-edged sword," John said with a smile. "For our Lord and Master still returned to Jerusalem for Passover when He also knew that the politics of the situation had forced all the ruling powers to join in an effort to kill Him there."

"Surely," Ruso pleaded, "you can leave Rome until the Tribulation passes. Even the mobs are starting to express sympathy for the Christians, and Nero will eventually have to bow to their will. In the end, all emperors must. Couldn't you leave now? Aren't you needed to minister to the seven churches in Asia?"

"They have my letters and the vision of the revelation," John said. "I was among them before the Tribulation began, and if God wills that I survive, I will return."

"How can you not say that God wills for you to leave now that you've received ample warning? How can you not say that God has sent me to you this morning?"

"How can you not say that God has chosen this as my time to die?"

Ruso shook his head.

"I want to remind you of words of hope," John said. "Remember

Paul in his letter to the church at Thessalonica?" John drew a breath and quoted, as if Paul were speaking directly to Ruso. "'Brothers, we do not want you to be ignorant about those who fall asleep, or to grieve like the rest of men, who have no hope. We believe that Jesus died and rose again and so we believe that God will bring with Jesus those who have fallen asleep in him.'"

Ruso could not help himself, frustrated as he was with his friend, and he finished Paul's words for John. "'I can tell you this directly from the Lord: We who are still living when the Lord returns will not rise to meet Him ahead of those who are in their graves. For the Lord Himself will come down from heaven with a commanding shout, with the call of the archangel, and with the trumpet call of God. First, all the believers who have died will rise from their graves. Then, together with them, we who are still alive and remain on the earth will be caught up in the clouds to meet the Lord in the air and remain with Him forever. So comfort and encourage each other with these words.'"

"We have discussed this many times," John said. "Our hope as believers is the final resurrection. Because Jesus came back to life, so will all believers."

"Will this happen before the Tribulation ends?"

"That I cannot say." John smiled, and serenity lit his face. "It would be foolish to make that prediction. Yet I want you to know this. Should you or I die before He comes again, when we are with God, time will mean nothing. The Second Coming will be as immediate to us as it might be to someone living in another millennium. And the time of His coming is not nearly as important as the hope of our resurrection through Him. That is why I do not fear Damian."

John continued to smile. "I'm sure that all believers would wish to be whisked away, taken up into thin air, to avoid the Tribulation. Yet that would be a false hope, especially if it replaces the true hope of the Resurrection, for the resurrection of Jesus and the resurrection promised to us because of it are what give us the hope to endure troubles. In this age. In any age, even should it take thousands of years for the Second Coming."

"You will not go, no matter what I say?" But Ruso knew the answer.

He and John had discussed John's vision on Patmos countless times. John had been given a vision of the fore future, and of the far future, and of the final future. John had seen heaven and the end of time. Because of it, he feared nothing.

John answered as Ruso expected. "I will not leave Rome, even if Damian was walking up the path at this very moment with soldiers to capture me."

Ruso gave an involuntary look down the hill and shuddered, as if seeing Damian and the soldiers at that very moment. "I pray to God it won't happen," he said. "I pray it is His will that your light shine in this world for many years longer."

✠ ✠ ✠

"Your wife," Nero said, placing a hand on Vitas' shoulder with half-drunk familiarity, "she brings to mind a shy doe at the stream. The hesitation, the awareness. As if danger might lurk in the shadows of the trees, ready to pounce. It is—" Nero stopped himself and belched— "yes, it is quite alluring, I find."

Other conversation quieted. It was a couple hours into the dinner. Already, many of the guests had risen from the couches to vomit in a nearby room before returning to gorge, some of them several times already.

Vitas struggled for words to fill that silence. His foreboding deepened even further.

"That one is like a fox in heat." Nero pointed at a woman who was lifting a plate of hummingbird tongues, her fingers greasy and flecked with food. "She radiates a sense of hunger for a man. It is a different kind of attraction, I must admit."

The woman—Gloria, if Vitas remembered her name correctly— smiled as if the emperor had bestowed upon her a wonderful compliment.

"This one—" Nero pointed at another woman—"is rather too fat for my taste. Her expensive dress hides defects that only a husband should be aware of." He giggled. "One might ask how I know."

The husband, quite drunk, simply shrugged.

"Does your wife please you?" Nero asked Vitas, his eyes returned to

Sophia. "Does she please you the way a woman should please a man? Or is her shyness pretended?"

Before Vitas could think of a suitable answer, Nero stood. He tilted forward slightly and recovered his balance. "Actually," Nero said to Vitas, "I have suddenly decided I am not interested in your opinion. Not when the Caesar can decide for himself in the tradition of Caligula."

Vitas grew cold with shock. Surely Nero would not . . .

"Come, my dear." Nero extended a hand to Sophia. "I have a bed in a nearby room. We shall not be long. And when I return, I will give all of our guests a frank appraisal."

As Vitas shifted to find his feet, Nero placed a hand on his shoulder and forced him to remain on the couch. "Surely," Nero said, his eyes half closed, "you would not deny the deity?"

When Vitas pushed upward, Nero tightened his grip, digging his nails into Vitas' shoulder. "Caesar takes what he wants." Nero spoke sweetly, a tone that belied the viciousness of his clawlike grip. "Because a god will not be denied anything from mortals."

Again, silence. Some, like Tigellinus and Helius, had amusement on their faces. Others, like Chayim the Jew, carefully studied the contents in the bowls of food in front of them.

"I . . . ," Vitas began.

Sophia's pleading eyes transfixed Vitas. Nero's other hand was still extended to her.

"Might I remind you that Tigellinus," Nero said, "is cocaptain of the cohorts. He is very familiar with the punishment handed to those who defy a god."

In response, Tigellinus belched.

Nero released his grip on Vitas and took Sophia by the hand, forcibly lifting her to her feet beside him. "I take it then," Nero said to Vitas, "that I have your permission?"

Sophia shuddered.

Six guards outside the room. Tigellinus nearby on his couch. And Nero, a man who had people killed for falling asleep at the singing performances he forced upon them.

Vitas could utter the words he wanted to speak. It would result in his death. Merciful and quick if Nero was inclined. Or slowly if Nero was not. Either way, Nero would still take his wife. And perhaps have her killed as well.

"I do have your permission." Nero smiled. "After all, I would not sample her without it."

Inside Vitas, helpless rage fought against the impossible choice he faced. To ensure that his wife was not killed and to keep his own life, he would have to allow the unthinkable.

"Please," Nero said. His bloodshot eyes seemed maniacal. "I must hear it from you. Yes?"

Vitas' mind told him to agree, but his heart and soul would not let him.

Nero shrugged. "I'll be happy to take your silence as permission."

Nero pulled Sophia forward. "Well, then, I shouldn't be long. I'm sure all our guests are anxious to know how well or badly this young woman is capable of pleasing a god."

He led Sophia through a curtained doorway at the back of the room.

She did not meet Vitas' eyes as she followed.

Then rage and love overpowered all of Vitas' rational thoughts. With a roar, he rose from his couch and charged forward, instinctively reaching beneath his toga for his short sword.

But it was gone, taken from him during the earlier search by the guards.

Still he roared. And still he charged, with a killing hatred filling his every sense.

Nero had begun to turn, a look of sudden fear on his face.

Then Vitas was on Nero, reaching for his neck. His fingers closed on the soft cartilage of Nero's throat and he began to throttle him.

Then Tigellinus was upon Vitas, battering his head with the hilt of his sword.

Vitas clung to Nero, clung to consciousness. Blood streamed in his eyes, but Vitas fought on, blind.

As the hilt came down again and again with savage force, Vitas was dimly aware of another sound.

Applause. From the dinner guests who were well amused by the scene.

And moments later, the applause dimmed to silence as blackness took away any conscious thoughts Vitas held.

SATURN

HORA QUARTA

Loud cries of pain came from the hillside olive grove below the mansion. Chayim lifted the hem of his toga and hurried toward the sound. He'd walked from the palace through the streets of Rome to get to the countryside manor of Aulus Petillius, an acquaintance who owned the mansion, and was sweating heavily in the morning sun.

The cries of pain continued, and as Chayim moved into the shade of the first olive trees, he also heard a pattern of thuds punctuating the screams.

The ancient trees with their twisted trunks and labyrinths of low-hanging branches blocked his vision, but the screams grew louder. It wasn't until he reached an oil press in the center of the grove that he realized fully what was happening.

Chayim immediately recognized the person swinging a small wooden pole down on the huddled body of a young woman. Aulus Petillius: the older, fat man with the heavy thatch of dark hair on his scalp who had sat near him at the banquet the night before.

The woman was in slave's clothing. She was not screaming in protest, for it was an owner's right to administer punishment at whim. Her cries of pain were involuntary exclamations that each new blow from Aulus forced from her body.

"Petillius!" Chayim shouted. "Petillius!"

Chayim's voice stopped Petillius at the top of his swing.

Petillius turned, startled. His face seemed vacant from thought, and it took him several seconds of blinking before he replied, almost as if

Chayim had awakened him from a dream. "Is it that time already?" He sputtered out his words, breathing heavily from exertion. "I'd forgotten you promised to visit this morning."

The slave on the ground shifted slightly and whimpered. Chayim saw that the young woman had short hair and her face was splotched from tears.

"Normally I would not mind returning at a more convenient time for you," Chayim said, "but it was a distance to travel."

"I would hear nothing of it," Petillius said. "It will be a simple matter to call a slave to prepare us food and drink." He scowled. "But not this one. She is worthless. Claims that illness has made her weak. But I know it is nothing except sheer laziness." Petillius poked her with his pole. "Am I right?"

"It is a fever. I sleep poorly and I'm always thirsty." The young woman spoke from beneath a protective arm over her head.

"You disagree with me?" Petillius thumped her again. He looked over at Chayim. "You'll excuse me while I finish this task?"

"Please," Chayim said. "Don't."

"Come, come," Petillius said. "You've come this far. What can it matter how long I delay lunch?"

"I have plenty of time. But—" Chayim stepped forward and knelt beside the slave—"she appears seriously injured. As a friend, I would hate to see you face any legal difficulties."

"Bah. The laws that protect slaves are theoretical. No one I know has faced a judge for punishing one." Petillius prodded the slave with the end of his pole. "No blood. See?"

Chayim stood. "She is not an animal."

Petillius was astounded. "Of course not. She's a slave. Do you have any idea how cheap slaves are these days? Animals, on the other hand—"

"She's human," Chayim said quietly.

"I beg your pardon?"

"She's human. I believe if you treat her with kindness you'll see in time that—"

Petillius laughed so hard his jowls swayed. "It's early in the day for drunkenness, my friend!"

"Let me buy her," Chayim said. "You said slaves are cheap."

Petillius stopped laughing as abruptly as he'd begun. "My slaves

aren't cheap, however. And this one has a child." He named an outrageous sum.

"You just finished telling me that she's lazy," Chayim observed mildly.
Petillius cut the sum in half.

"Look at her," Chayim said. "It will take days, perhaps weeks, for her
to recover from the beating."
Petillius cut the sum in half again.

"It seems," Chayim said, "that we have come to an agreement. Now,
if you don't mind, would you be able to provide me with water and food
for her?" Chayim paused as he touched the woman's neck lightly with
the backs of his fingers. "And a blanket. The poor woman is shivering."

☩ ☩ ☩

"Today?" Ruso said, trying to hide his anger but fairly certain it was obvious. "It's enough of a danger to all of us that you brought someone up
here at all. But you do it today?"

"I had no choice," Cornelius said. "She threatened to turn me in to
the authorities. I met with Damian today and made arrangements.
Without me, what of our plans for tomorrow?"

The sun was beginning to set. They were on the hillside, just beneath the
grove of olive trees that John used as a private retreat. Ruso had never asked
John but guessed it reminded John of the Garden of Gethsemane outside
Jerusalem, the garden that Jesus had often used as a similar retreat.

A young woman stood on the hillside, watching them.

"This is not good at all." Ruso's lips tightened as he looked past
Cornelius at the woman, who was just out of earshot. "If she found you,
obviously, someone from the meetings has been indiscreet."

Cornelius offered the faintest of smiles. "That, at least, is not one of
our worries." He rubbed his forehead. "Her name is Leah. She is the sister to Nathan, son of Hezron. Nathan had instructed her to hold the
copies of the letters of Matthew and Luke and of the one of John's vision. I was the one you sent to retrieve them, remember?"

"That was months ago," Ruso said, slowly and sadly. He continued to
stare at Leah while speaking to Cornelius. She did not look away from
his steady gaze. "But how did she ever find you in a city this large if
someone did not tell her about you?"

Cornelius rubbed his forehead again. Closed his eyes. "I'll never escape this mark. On the days she went to market, without her father knowing, she began to make inquiries about it until she learned which household branded slaves this distinctly. After that, it was only a matter of time . . ."

"But if she hasn't turned you in to the authorities, what does she want? Money to keep her silence? If so, I have plenty. We'll send her on her way. You know John will be gone before she can return and make further trouble."

"No, not money," Cornelius said. "In the days after Nathan died and before I arrived, she'd read those letters. She wants to know more about them."

"She searches for our faith?" Ruso asked in astonishment. "Even after what happened to Nathan?"

"Especially because of what happened to him. She says she's not able to stop wondering why he allowed himself to be killed in that manner."

"But here," Ruso said. "Why bring her here?"

"To meet John." Before Ruso could protest, Cornelius rushed on. "After all, tonight will be his last night on this estate."

"Only if you are successful with Damian," Ruso answered.

"Either way, John will know we've betrayed him," Cornelius said. "Do you think he'll stay here on the estate after that?"

Ruso didn't need to answer that question. "As you wish," Ruso said to Cornelius after a short grim silence. "Take her up to meet with him. But first let me know exactly what arrangements you made with the slave hunter for tomorrow. It is extremely important that John does not suspect anything."

✝ ✝ ✝

Chayim followed Petillius toward the mansion. They did not move quickly. Although it was less than a hundred yards to the gate, Petillius stopped to rest often.

"Were you impressed?" Petillius said, leaning against a tree. "Because I can tell you that I was. I've never been onstage, of course, but looking back, I think I have a natural talent. Don't you agree?"

"The beating was severe enough," Chayim said.

a code of multiple variations. I could spend hours expounding on this, and believe me, I have given the number much thought since studying the letter for you."

Azariah had an empty scroll beside him. He picked it up and made some quick markings.

"This, as you know, is a triangular," Azariah said. "A simple example. It's the triangular 21, which forms two triangles with an inner triangle of 6 and an outer of 15, in a total of 6 lines. As the triangular 21, the total number of 21 is the sum of all the numbers from 1 to 6. If you extend this pattern all the way out to 36 lines, adding up all the numbers from 1 to 36, you form the triangular 666. I won't bore you with the calculations; trust me when I say that the triangular 666 is the 'fulfillment' of 105, a 12-fold triangle with a periphery of 30 x $3\frac{1}{2}$, a reckoning that also adds up to the fatally limited reign of 1,260 days that the letter prophesies for the Beast. Incredible code. Astounding, actually."

Azariah shook his head in awe. "It's even eerie, especially when you understand the name of the Beast."

Damian was impressed at the rabbi's reaction of wonder and admiration, yet was too impatient to want more discussion of the matter. "I have far less interest in your calculations than in the name of the Beast," Damian said.

"But these numerical relationships are very significant," Azariah protested. "You came to me because—"

"The name of the Beast," Damian interrupted. "That's what's important to me. It seems to me that John is plainly saying that I should be able to identify the Beast by its number. Except I can't."

"You are not Hebrew." Azariah gave Damian a broad grin. "Which, of course, is why you came to me."

"You are saying you have the answer?"

"It is as plain to me as it would be to any other Jew reading it."

✢ ✢ ✢

Scraping of iron against iron.

Vitas must have dozed, because it wasn't until the prison cell door was completely shut again and he heard rustling in the straw that he realized he wasn't alone.

"Hello?" he croaked. The cell was so dark he couldn't even make out the figure of the person who had stepped inside.

"Helius will arrive in the next couple of hours," the voice answered. "We have little time."

"Who are you?"

"Drink this." A hand touched his shoulder, then followed his arm down to his hand. When something cold touched it, Vitas realized it was the smooth side of a clay jar.

Vitas lifted it. With greed, he gulped a few swallows, then recoiled at the liquid's bitterness. "What is this?" Vitas gasped.

"You will thank me for it later."

"Who are you?"

"Drink again."

Vitas was so thirsty, he gulped a few more swallows. "Surely you can tell me who you are."

"I cannot." A pause. "If it ever reaches Nero's ear that I was here, I will die in the same way he intends for you to die. Now drink until it is empty."

Vitas tried a few more gulps. The bitterness seemed less intense. "Tell me, please," he said. A warm glow seemed to rise from the center of his belly. "Do you know anything about my wife, Sophia?"

"I do not. Nor do I want to know anything. About her. About you. The less I know, the better. Now drink. Hurry."

"You are here but don't know who I am?"

"I have been given instructions. Listen carefully. I was told the future of your wife and unborn child depend on it."

Vitas straightened.

"First," the man said, "I am going to leave you with a letter. You must decipher it to find the answers you need."

"Answers?"

"You cannot listen carefully if you are speaking." The stranger was curt. "Shall I continue?"

"Yes."

"Second, there is an obscure matter that Tiberius once brought to Senate vote. You will find it somewhere in the archives. It will be marked with a number."

"I'm still listening."

"Then remember this, for the life of your family may depend on it someday.

"I'm listening. What is the number?"

"It is the number of the Beast. Six hundred and sixty-six."

✛ ✛ ✛

"Let me remind you I'm paying good money for that answer," Damian said, a trifle impatient. "Give me the name of the Beast."

"Not so fast." Azariah was obviously enjoying this. "Let's talk more about the Beast. I must repeat how ingeniously the author accomplishes so much in so little writing. He says one thing and it can mean three things. The Beast, for example. To our people, in one sense the Beast refers to the Roman Empire, but in another sense, as given by the number 666, it is also about an individual emperor. Here . . ."

Azariah took the letter from Damian, unscrolled it, and scanned it. He paused, searched for a specific portion, found it, and took a breath before reading it as if he were preaching in the synagogue. " 'Now understand this: The seven heads of the beast represent the seven hills of the city where this woman rules. They also represent seven kings. Five kings have already fallen, the sixth now reigns, and the seventh is yet to come, but his reign will be brief. The scarlet beast that was alive and then died is the eighth king. He is like the other seven, and he, too, will go to his doom.' "

Azariah looked up. "Tell me without giving it much thought. What numbers are significant and why?"

Damian did as instructed. " 'Seven hills,' Rome. That is very obvious. I understood it the first time I read the letter, as would anybody in the world. 'Five kings have already fallen; the sixth now reigns'? Any child who knows Roman history will answer that." He ticked off on his fingers as he named the emperors in succession. "Julius Caesar, Augustus, Tiberius, Caligula, Claudius, and now Nero."

Azariah nodded. "Strictly speaking, Julius Caesar did not allow himself to be called emperor, but he was a de facto emperor and everyone since has referred to him as one. So, yes, it is an obvious reference to the first six emperors after the fall of the Republic."

"So . . ." Damian spoke more slowly as he tried to think it through. "'The seventh is yet to come.' The next emperor? A brief reign? Then the eighth who will go to his doom?"

"One could easily read into that the prediction of a rapid succession of emperors. 'Doom' suggests unnatural deaths."

Damian felt another surge of excitement. "This is suggesting assassination?"

"Several in succession. Perhaps civil war."

Damian's mind whirled. Nero would be very agitated to hear of this. He was highly suspicious of plots against his life, especially after a failed one a few years earlier.

Damian's excitement, however, was tempered by another thought that he spoke to Azariah. "The thought of civil war is ridiculous. The empire is stable and prosperous. A tradition of passing imperial powers from one emperor to the next is well established."

"I agree," Azariah said. "And keep in mind, John's letter is merely a prophecy. But, as you know, one that would strike fear into Nero if he knew of it. His reputation as a superstitious man, after all, is known far and wide."

"Why fear?" Now Damian knew he was getting to the heart of it.

Azariah rubbed his face, leaving behind grease from the chicken drumstick he had earlier set aside. "I would say that John is writing this letter to give comfort to all the followers of Jesus during this time of persecution and tribulation. He is saying it will not continue indefinitely, and he is promising great rewards to those who persevere."

"Tribulation?"

"The one that is very obvious to all Romans and Christians. It began shortly after the Great Fire, when Nero laid the blame for it on the Christians, and continues with their horrible public executions."

"There is an ending to the Tribulation." Damian recalled what he'd read in the letter. "An ending that happens because the Beast dies. And then the unthinkable. Civil war."

Azariah shrugged. "If the prophecy were true."

Yes, Damian thought, *this is why Helius fears the letter! Prophecy of Caesar's death. Nero's instablility would be worsened to hear of this.*

Except for one thing. The Beast in the letter could not be Nero. So Nero would have nothing in this letter to fear.

"I have tried gematria with all the names of rulers I know," Damian said. "The number 666 does not give me a beast I would recognize. And certainly not Nero."

"It doesn't?" Azariah smiled, then wrote a vertical column of letters on the scroll. "Look, here is the Hebrew alphabet. And here—" he sketched a second column beside the first—"the Greek alphabet. Simple, yes?"

"All right."

"The first ten letters of both alphabets correspond to the first ten numbers, 1 through 10. But the second ten correspond to the next ten *tens.*"

"So *kappa,* the tenth Greek letter, is 10, but the eleventh, *lambda,* is 20."

"Good. And the third ten letters—"

"Are hundreds, of course," Damian said, impatient. "I understand that Hebrew gematria uses the same principles as Greek. But John's letter was written in Greek so why discuss—?"

"Because the writer expects much of his audience to be Hebrew," Azriah said, obviously anticipating Damian's objection. "And he knows they will apply gematria accordingly."

Azariah took the scroll and etched out a few more letters. "As a Roman, you cannot be blamed for not knowing that Hebrew does not use vowels. This is how we spell *Nero Caesar.*"

נרון קסר

"Six hundred and sixty-six," Damian said after a brief calculation. "Nero is the Beast!"

✙ ✙ ✙

In the prison cell, the stranger grabbed Vitas by the hand. "Are you drowsy yet? warm?"

"Who sent you?" Vitas asked. His tongue felt thick. "What was it I drank?"

"Do you feel this?" the stranger asked.

Vitas was vaguely aware of a pinching sensation on the back of his hand. "Yes," he mumbled. "I'm not dead yet."

"Drink more."

Vitas had no willpower to refuse when the stranger put the jug up to his lips again.

"Empty?" the stranger in his cell asked.

"Who sent you?" Vitas asked again. Or thought he asked again. It was difficult to tell if he'd spoken or simply thought the question.

"Do you feel this?" came the question once more.

"Feel what?"

The stranger dropped Vitas' hand.

Vitas was dimly conscious of it landing on his own thigh. "Felt it," Vitas announced with great seriousness. "That was my hand. It's at the end of my arm."

"Excellent, excellent."

More rustling. Had the stranger just draped something around Vitas' neck?

Then came a hard blow directly across Vitas' face.

"Wait!" Vitas protested. He tried to lift his hands to protect himself, but his arms were rubber.

Another blow landed.

And another.

✛ ✛ ✛

"Was the letter coded this way to get past the censors?" Damian asked the rabbi.

"The author of this letter probably knew his treason would be obvious to any careful reader," Azariah said. "There is enough in it already to suggest that the Beast is Nero. But there is an element of safety, because a Roman censor scanning it would definitely not see Nero as 666, while most of John's audience would. More important is how uncanny the coincidence between the gematria of Nero's name and all the layers of symbolism that a Jew sees in 666."

Azariah's voice dropped to a whisper. "Almost as if an angel truly had given John the vision."

Damian had no interest in alleged supernatural inspiration of the letter. Only in finding out what he could about John. And more importantly, finding out what Helius feared about John and John's vision.

"Could Helius or Nero know of this naming of the Beast?" Damian said.

"All they would have to do is ask questions as you did. Darda and I aren't the only rabbis in Rome."

"So, in essence, the author of this letter says that Nero is the Beast who opposes the Lamb. . . ."

"The Beast identified, but the empire itself is also the Beast, and will continue to reign even after an apparently mortal wound."

"Civil war." *There it is,* Damian thought. *That far-fetched implication again.*

"If you can believe that would ever happen," Azariah said.

"And it predicts when Nero will die," Damian said calmly, hiding his reaction. A prediction of when Nero would die! What an incredibly important document! Nero placed great faith—and fear—in any omens or prophecies that alluded to him. And to have one that spoke of his death!

"Yes. But remember the other improbable prophecies. That the temple in Jerusalem will fall, for example. If you've ever seen the temple high on the mount, you'd know how . . . well . . . how stupid that prediction is."

"Just for a moment, consider what if the impossible happened, that the temple *did* fall, as the self-proclaimed Messiah Jesus also claimed," Damian said. "What would that say about Jesus?"

John was Damian's prey, but by nature Damian was curious. And here, Azariah had made the same statement about the fall of the temple as had Darda. Yet to have a prediction about Nero's death! If there was any way Damian could find validity in the prophecies of the Revelation, it would be that much more valuable to him.

"Vindication, I suppose," Azariah said slowly. "On several occasions Jesus called judgment on those who were about to kill Him. Used a Jewish prophecy phrase that means exactly that and was used repeatedly in our ancient writings: *coming on clouds.* He combined that phrase with another from a psalm of coronation and exaltation. Jesus declared to them, 'Hereafter you will see the Son of Man sitting at the right hand of power and coming on the clouds of heaven.' I remember the wording I read because of the absolute audacity of Jesus' claim. In effect, He was claiming deity in pronouncing judgment over Jerusalem, and if Jerusalem and the temple were to fall within the near future—may it not be so—it would mean that Jesus, not Caesar or another Jewish messiah, is Lord and King."

Azariah paused before continuing. "And there would be an incredible irony. He claimed to be the Lamb that was slain to redeem us. With the temple gone, there would be no other way to reach God but through Jesus. If He truly was divine."

"What do you think of the accuracy of the other predictions John made?" Damian asked. Knowledge was power, a secret like this that much more so.

"As I said, the way it is written is so incredible I could believe it was divinely inspired. Yet the obvious impossibility of the events happening as predicted—the falling of the temple, civil war in the empire—lead me to one conclusion. . . ."

Azariah let out a deep breath. "John is vainly trying to comfort those fools who already believe in the equally impossible notion that Jesus was resurrected and was and is the promised Messiah."

Damian nodded, very glad that his brother, Vitas, had told him about Helius and the letter.

But he knew Helius would not see it in such a harmless manner. Helius would immediately understand what Damian understood. The danger of the prophecy to Nero's peace of mind. And that Nero's perception of such a threat would make life very difficult in the palace. And throughout Rome.

This would make John a valuable captive indeed.

But the fact that two other slave hunters had died under mysterious circumstances gave Damian good reason to worry about his own life.

If John, son of Zebedee, held the key to this, there was a double reason for Damian to capture him.

✠ ✠ ✠

The stranger held Vitas up in a sitting position as he struck Vitas again and again.

Vitas was acutely aware of the sound of the beating. Of the thud of wood against his flesh. How long it continued, he didn't know.

And barely cared.

Without warning, the blows stopped.

The stranger dropped him in the straw. Vitas barely felt the man's touch as he slipped what felt like a scroll inside his clothing and against his chest. A moment later the man patted Vitas' chest, as if satisfying himself that the scroll was in place. Then Vitas listened as the stranger crunched across the straw toward the cell door. Torchlight silhouetted the stranger briefly as he opened it.

Then Vitas was alone again.

HORA UNDECIMA

Sophia sat in the garden near the stable, singing a lullaby to Sabinus. Aside from prayer, pouring her love out to this baby was the only way she was able to quell the fear and speculation about the fate of Vitas. And her own fate, too.

Ben-Aryeh approached, leading five Roman soldiers. This was the moment she had been dreading all day.

The night before, guards had dragged Vitas' unconscious body from the feast. Nero, almost too drunk to stand, had continued to move her into a private chamber. Moments later, he'd passed out. She had stared at him for some time, shuddering at the evil written across his face, even as he lay unconscious. She'd wondered if she could do anything to help Vitas and had realized the only thing to do was flee the palace and do what she could the next day.

Repeatedly Ben-Aryeh had urged her to flee the mansion on the hillside, telling her that Nero would regret allowing her to escape so lightly. But she could not leave the estate until she knew what had happened to Vitas. She had sent servants back to inquire about him, but no news had reached her; some servants had yet to return. And if they had any information that might allow her to help Vitas, how then could she do so?

She'd lost her family in Jerusalem. Would she lose the man she loved now?

As hour after agonizing hour passed, prayers had been her spiritual comfort; Sabinus and his good-natured play at her feet had been her earthly comfort.

As she rose, holding Sabinus, to meet Ben-Aryeh, a young servant girl hurried from where she had been waiting nearby.

"Take the child and go," Sophia told the servant. She wrapped Sabinus in a blanket. "You have been instructed."

The servant girl nodded.

Although Ben-Aryeh had not been able to convince Sophia to leave, the wily priest had insisted they plan for the worst. A letter had already been sent to Sophia's friend Paulina, asking her to care for Sabinus should it be necessary.

As the servant girl walked toward the stable, Sophia watched the soldiers intently. If they tried stopping the girl, all was lost. They ignored her, and she was able to leave the garden before the soldiers reached Sophia.

Sophia closed her eyes briefly, offering a prayer of thanks. Nero had not decided to destroy all of the family. Only her. For if death was not involved, a messenger would have arrived. Not soldiers in full military gear.

The lead soldier stood three feet away and appraised Sophia. Ben-Aryeh stood to the side, his face inscrutable. His shoulders were bowed, as if he were making himself as small as possible. She had never seen him this abject.

"Her servant does not lie to us," the leader said to the others, his eyes full on Sophia's face. "This is his wife. I saw her with Vitas last night." Then he spoke to Sophia, offering a scroll. "Nero has orders for you."

"I do not read Latin," Sophia answered. She felt faint. The situation was unfolding as Ben-Aryeh had predicted. Early in the morning, he'd gone to the head servants of the household to ask them about the ways of the Romans and grimly reported back to her.

First would come the soldiers. With the scroll.

"Very well," the soldier said. "Nero invites you to open your veins."

Suicide.

She had been prepared for this, but the calmness of the soldier's words still unnerved her. Sophia drew several deep breaths, forcing herself to behave with dignity. "You will allow me as is customary to free the household's slaves?"

The soldier grunted and nodded.

"Let me ask you," she continued. "Does he want my head?"

It was a relevant question. She'd heard about Octavia, Nero's first wife, and the soldier who had severed her head to take back to the emperor as proof of her death.

"What does that matter to you?" the soldier asked. "Dead is dead."

"If Nero wants my head, I should like to have my makeup and hair prepared," she said coolly.

"He does not want your head," the soldier growled. "Nor do I have the time to wait."

"Allow her a hot bath," Ben-Aryeh interceded. "At least make it painless for her." He pulled a pouch from his tunic and shook it, making the sound of the coins inside very obvious.

The lead soldier nodded. "Very well."

Ben-Aryeh tossed him the gold. "I will order the slaves to prepare a bath," he said to Sophia.

"As hot as a person can stand," Sophia said. "And have them leave wine."

"As you command."

Ben-Aryeh hurried ahead, leaving the soldiers to escort her from the garden back to the mansion.

✠ ✠ ✠

Tri via.

Damian stood at an intersection of three roads. The major of the three was the Via Sacra, just south and east of the center of Rome.

As was customary for any intersection of three roads—known to the Romans, of course, as tri via—a sign had been placed in a conspicuous spot. On the sign were the postings of any minor matters that passersby felt were important enough to write down for the public to know.

As he waited along the Via Sacra for the slave named Cornelius, Damian scanned the trivial postings. A wedding announced. Rewards for lost valuables. A plea to help find a donkey that had disappeared.

It was an ingrained habit for Damian to read anything in the path of his eyes. In this moment, however, during a calm and cloudless mid-afternoon, his mind barely registered the postings.

His thoughts should have been on the imminent capture of John, son of Zebedee. The arrangement that Damian had made with Cornelius was simple. Cornelius would take him into a nearby alley that John traveled through every day around this time. Cornelius would wait, hidden with Damian, and when John passed by, make identification of John so that men hired by Damian could make an immediate and discreet capture.

His thoughts should have been on this. But because Damian had become an expert at surprising his prey with similar and sudden captures and because he trusted the men who were already in place and waiting to make the capture, Damian allowed his mind to drift to that meeting with Rabbi Azariah earlier in the day.

It was a given, unless something unexpected happened, that John would be captured well before sundown. Yet now Damian wasn't quite sure if he should deliver John immediately to Helius.

Because Damian now believed he understood exactly how much John was worth to Helius.

☩ ☩ ☩

Helius arrived with three guards, each carrying a torch. He, however, refused to enter the squalid cell that held Vitas. He sent the guards in to pull Vitas into the hallway.

When the guards dropped Vitas, he fell to his knees.

Helius grabbed Vitas by the hair and lifted his head. Then gasped and stepped away. "By the gods!" Helius said. "Your face!"

In the time that had passed since the stranger had entered Vitas' cell and administered the quiet and efficient beating, Vitas' face had swollen monstrously. He saw through the slits of his puffed eyelids. His forehead was knotted with purple bruises. His lips were like sausages.

Vitas could keep his balance only by remaining on his hands and knees, like a dog. He felt the weight of the scroll sagging against his tunic. Even had he found the emotional and physical energy, reading the scroll would have been impossible in the darkness of the cell. But it was obviously important, and he knew he must keep it from Helius.

"The guards had fun with you," Helius said, laughing. "It's just as well that Sophia can't see you now."

"Sophia!" Vitas found energy. "Sophia!"

His teeth were not broken, nor were there any cuts on his face. The wooden dowel used to beat him had been strangely padded.

"Your precious wife," Helius sneered. "I suppose you want to know her fate?"

"Sophia!"

"I'd prefer to let you speculate. Much more fun for me, letting you twist in the wind, so to speak."

"Sophia!"

"You attacked the emperor," Helius said. "Definitely one of the gravest crimes possible." He pushed Vitas with his foot.

Vitas toppled. He made sure to fall on the scroll hidden in his clothing. "Sophia . . ." His burst of energy gone, her name came out as a groan.

"Pathetic," Helius said. "But by tomorrow evening, she won't be of concern to you. I'm happy—no correct that—I'm delighted to tell you that you are scheduled to appear in the arena."

He paused, examining Vitas. "I'd thought perhaps it would be amusing to let you fight some gladiators. After all, a military hero should provide good entertainment. But now that I see your pitiful condition, it may have to be the lions."

Another pause. "No," Helius said, "perhaps an elephant. We'll have you tied to a tusk. Your face is already beaten beyond recognition. The same fate may as well await your body." He shrugged. "No matter. What's important are the provisions of your will regarding your entire estate."

Vitas stared straight ahead. All he saw were the boots of the guards. The dark walls of the subterranean hallway with the torchlight gleaming off the stone.

"Normally," Helius said, "it would be expected that you bequeath your entire estate to the emperor. That, along with a confession of your guilt. But I have a proposal for you."

The feet of the guards in Vitas' vision shifted. Then walked away.

Helius had dismissed them. He knelt beside Vitas, whispering in his ear. "You have certain properties on the coast. I think it would be appropriate if you gave them directly to me. Nero won't miss them."

Vitas tried to spit. But his lips were so big that they had almost cracked under the pressure of the blood throbbing through them. He couldn't work up the moisture.

"Ah," Helius said, "I sense anger. I am correct, aren't I? It's very difficult to read your emotions when your face looks like a melon." He flicked Vitas in the face several times with his forefinger. "Fascinating, absolutely fascinating. I'll have to have more criminals beaten like this."

Vitas tried to swing a punch, but from the ground it was impossible.

"Behave," Helius said. "You are going to die, so do it with dignity. And do it in such a way that you spare Sophia from the same fate as yours."

Vitas became very still.

"Ah, I do have your attention." Helius knelt closer. "If you draw up the will as I request, she will live. I promise."

"Guarantee . . . ?" That simple word took several seconds for Vitas to speak.

"What guarantee do you have that I will deliver on that promise? Perhaps none. But you do know she won't be spared if you cross me." Helius seemed to ponder it further. "Actually, request for your lawyer to send her to a safe place before the will is executed." Helius laughed. "*Executed.* Such a fitting word, don't you think?"

He prodded Vitas. "Really, you should keep a sense of humor about this. It's all you have left."

"Send . . . my . . . lawyer. Will . . . do . . . it."

"Excellent." Helius rose. "Don't you feel much better now?"

"Send . . . Sophia . . ."

"I think not. Nero wouldn't approve. Most definitely not approve. He's quite upset, you know. At both of you. He looks forward to watching you die in the most horrible way."

The feet of the guards returned into Vitas' narrow range of vision. Rough hands lifted him to his feet. They began to drag him back into the cell.

"The lawyer will be here first thing in the morning," Helius said. "Do get a good night's sleep."

☩ ☩ ☩

Chayim found himself alone against five men holding knives in outstretched arms. He backed away from them until the outer wall of a warehouse stopped his retreat.

"What's the only thing better than a fool alone near the wharves?" the largest of the five asked his companions.

Since the question was not directed at Chayim, he didn't answer.

"A rich fool!" the same voice laughed.

Chayim was in a district of Rome unfamiliar to him. Down by the Tiber, where the ships were unloaded during the day.

"Let's strip him and fillet him like a fish!" one voice said from the darkness.

Chayim edged along the wall, feeling behind him with his hands.

"Ho, ho!" the leader said. "There'll be no escape for you. The rings on your fingers are worth a year's wages, no doubt. You'll have no need for them anyway, as we'll be chopping your fingers off to get them."

"My advice to you is to leave," Chayim said. "I'm not here looking for trouble."

"We have a jester!" The leader had a scarred face and wore an eyepatch. "A jester come down to the slums for entertainment. What is it you seek? A girl? A boy?" The man waved his knife closer to Chayim's face. His voice turned nasty. "Whatever it is, rich fool, it has cost you your life."

"Enough," Chayim said. "I offer you one last chance to leave."

"Otherwise, what?"

Chayim kept silent.

"Boys, let's gut him."

The small thud was barely audible. But the groan of surprise was louder.

The leader fell to his knees, and his knife dropped to the cobblestone. He twisted in agony, revealing the thrown military sword that had pierced the center of his belly. He held the sword with both hands, looking down with his mouth gaping in disbelief.

Before any of the others could react, six guards of the prefect rushed forward. All were in full armor, including head plates. The others formed a line behind their shields and brandished their short swords.

Shouts of dismay greeted that action, then the thumping of feet against cobblestone as the street gang fled.

Chayim stepped around the man on the ground. The soldier who owned the sword pulled it out. Blood streamed from the blade.

"I'll see that your pay for services is doubled for each of you," Chayim said to the soldiers. He pointed at the first soldier's sword. "Please wipe that clean. We don't need to terrify our prey with all that fresh blood."

HORA DUODECIMA

Lengthways," the soldier said. He'd been sent up by the centurion to supervise Sophia's death.

"I'm not sure I understand." Sophia wore a robe and stood just inside the chamber where a hot bath had been prepared for her.

The soldier stood at the entrance. She followed his eyes as he scanned the room, making sure there was no possible way for her to escape. A knife and a jug of wine had been set beside the bath. There was a pile of towels too. Otherwise, the room was empty, except for the vapors rising from the hot water.

"If you cut your wrists lengthways," he said, not unkindly, "the bleeding is much more efficient." He motioned on his own wrist, tracing a path along the tendons. "Trust me," he said. "I've been sent on more than one of these assignments. From all I can tell, it is a painless way to die. You'll faint and then—"

"Thank you," Sophia said curtly.

He moved his eyes to her face. "You can't take this personally, you know. These days, Nero looks for any excuse to confiscate an estate."

Sophia bit back another curt remark, telling herself that this young soldier truly was trying to help. "You're a good man," she said slowly. "And one I trust will allow me the modesty I require."

"Of course." His young face colored with embarrassment. "I'll wait outside." He took a step.

"How long?" Sophia asked, stopping him.

He understood immediately. "If you have the courage to make the cut deep, five minutes, perhaps. The hot water helps you bleed faster."

"Good-bye then," she said.

"I'm sorry for you," he answered. "And I'm impressed that you are behaving like a Roman."

Instead of a Jew, she thought silently.

He nodded once and left her alone.

Sophia winced at the scalding heat of the water but forced herself in as quickly as she could. Once totally submerged, she took the jug of wine and poured half of it into the water. Then she took the knife and placed the blade against the softness of the underside of her wrist, testing its sharpness.

A small cut opened immediately. She was amazed at how easily the cut deepened and widened. She placed her wrist in the water and watched the blood swirl and fade, a tiny tendril that disappeared like a fleeing snake.

She wasn't ready, however, to finish slitting her wrist.

Not for the first time since Vitas had been taken away did she silently ask herself a question she wished she could ignore. Was this the consequence of her marriage to an unbeliever? When he'd proposed, she'd convinced herself she could help all Christians by marrying someone with influence with Nero, but now she wondered if it had only been a rationalization brought on by her selfishness and passion for Vitas.

And this was the result. The reputation and estate and household of Vitas in ruin. Vitas captive somewhere. And these orders for her own suicide.

Yet she knew God loved her. She clamped her other hand over the small wound, closed her eyes, and prayed. She prayed for Vitas. She prayed for her unborn child. And she prayed for courage.

Finally, she was at peace.

Ready for what was ahead of her.

✝ ✝ ✝

"Everything is set?" Cornelius asked as he stepped forward toward Damian. Cornelius had hidden himself for as long as possible by walking just behind a group of peasants who were driving goats toward the center of the city.

Damian swallowed his distaste. A distaste for the slave, who was willing to sell another human being into captivity. And a distaste for himself, because as Damian could not deny to himself, he was willing to broker the sale.

"How I conduct my business is of no concern to you," Damian said. "You should worry more whether John, son of Zebedee, will take his customary route as you promised."

The bleats of the goats faded, but the approaching sound of soldiers' sandals slapping the cobblestone replaced it.

"I don't want John to see me," Cornelius repeated. The approaching soldiers—a dozen of them—obviously bothered him. His eyes shifted from one direction to another, alert for any threat.

"What difference does it make?" Damian asked. "He won't live long enough to return and punish you."

The soldiers passed by without any incident.

"I don't want him to see me," Cornelius repeated. He rubbed the triangular brand on his forehead nervously.

"Don't waste my time," Damian warned. He didn't want this slave to have a sudden attack of conscience. Damian pointed at the mouth of the alley, barely wider than two men with their arms spread. "We need to be ready for you to identify him."

Cornelius looked at the ground. As if he had just realized the consequences of his actions. Still keeping his eyes downcast, he spoke. "He cannot know it was I who betrayed him."

"You will do what is necessary to identify him for me as he passes by."

"No," Cornelius said with resolve that surprised Damian. He lifted his head again and stared directly at Damian. "Otherwise I will walk away right now."

"I have already purchased your freedom from Barbatus."

"I will return to him and become his slave again. I do not want John to see me."

Damian sighed. "Then we will do it your way. As long as it gets done."

Cornelius gritted his teeth briefly. A muscle along the side of his jaw twitched. "It will be done," he said. "I will deliver him to you as promised."

✢ ✢ ✢

Chayim rapped on a door hidden in the recess of an alley. He wondered if he'd heard movement inside.

He rapped again.

And a third time.

"'I am the way, the truth, and the life,'" Chayim said. This, the slave Rikka had told him in the morning, was the code. Three times a knock at the door. Then the phrases that all inside would recognize. "'No one can come to the Father except through Me.'"

The door opened, and Chayim saw the light of dozens of candles.

"Hurry." A man's arm reached out and pulled him inside.

Chayim stumbled through the entrance. As he blinked and tried to make sense of the room, another person shut the door behind him. "Welcome, brother," said the man who had pulled him in. "Welcome in the name of Christ."

It was a small room and smelled of fish. The small windows had been covered completely with dark blankets for privacy. The candles were perched on tables and ledges, revealing about a dozen men and women. A meal had been prepared and filled the top of the biggest table, centered among them.

"Thank you," Chayim said.

He saw with satisfaction that on another table several scrolls had been set aside. If the letter he needed was among them, his troubles were over tonight!

Movement from the corner of his eye.

A woman had stepped forward. She took both his hands in greeting. "Rikka cannot be here tonight, as she is too badly injured. But she told me of you and how you saved her. I, in turn, have told the others. We all rejoice to have you among us."

The gentleness in her voice hit him with the impact of a falling mountain, and because of it, the woman's words of greeting barely registered in Chayim's conscious thoughts. For the first time he could remember, he was at a loss for a reply of any kind.

It wasn't that the woman was exceptionally beautiful, although there was no doubt that any man would have given her a second and third look as she moved through a marketplace. No, Chayim had never feared a woman's beauty and knew how to use it against her, for he believed that all women had insecurities that could be leveraged by a man with the insight to find them.

But in this moment, as her eyes met his, Chayim felt a savage hunger to possess this woman.

Lust.

Later he would reflect again and again on this moment, enjoying and marveling at it as if it were a precious stone throwing exquisite light in different ways from different angles every time he looked at it anew. His hunger for her overwhelmed any other hungers he'd had in his life, and he vowed he would do what it took to satisfy it.

"Come, come! Introductions all around!" This came from Corbulo, the rough-handed fisherman who'd first opened the door for Chayim.

Still, silence.

Had the others understood his immediate reaction of lust? Was his intent to take her and possess her in any and all manners so obvious to all that they shared a silent horror?

Chayim wrenched his own stare away from her and forced composure upon himself. The rest were now looking at him expectantly.

Before arranging to seem like a hero to Rikka by intervening in her beating, he'd decided a false identity was the only way to ensure safety in a group of Christians who might be arrested for treason at any moment. The story he would give them now must be the same story he'd given to Rikka. He almost stammered as he gave all of them what he had so carefully prepared earlier.

"There is not much to say about myself," Chayim said. "My name is Chayim. I am a Greek from the city of Agrigentum in Sicily. My father has sent me here to pursue contracts for his shipping fleet."

Chayim pretended a modest shrug. "It is my father's work and wisdom that built the family fortune. I cannot claim then a true ownership of whatever wealth allows me to stay in Rome, nor should I get undue credit for helping Rikka today."

"A Greek?" one man asked. "Chayim sounds Jewish."

Chayim had also prepared himself for this. The alternative, he'd decided, was a false Greek name, but the danger in that was his unfamiliarity with it. If someone addressed him by the Greek name and he didn't respond, it would raise greater suspicion than the innocent question that had just been asked.

"It is Jewish," Chayim said with a practiced chuckle. "But please don't ask for the complicated story behind it. For my family was touched with scandal, and I prefer to let that sleeping dog lie. Especially here in Rome, where those who meet me are not prejudiced by the local gossip on the island."

By the nods of the people, Chayim believed this falsehood had served its purpose. Cloaked him in mystery and deflected further questions. And it would make him look like a hero to the woman he wanted so badly to possess.

He dared another glance at her. Her eyes were on his face. He wanted to take her right here, hold her, drag her away, and he didn't care whether or not she shared those feelings.

Chayim set his face into a mask of patience as one by one the others told him their names and their backgrounds. He wasn't listening. He was counting them down until the woman who had greeted him had a chance to speak.

"Leah," she said. She was the final person in the group. "My brother was among those who died in the Tribulation that began after the Great Fire in Rome. I am not a believer, but I seek the faith, so I am here tonight."

Leah.

As she spoke, Chayim memorized her every feature. The long dark hair parted in a way that framed her high cheekbones. Her slender fingers, motionless as her hands rested gracefully on her lap. The unadorned dress. And her lips with a slight pout.

The fire within him grew. In his mind he could already taste her kiss. He tingled, thinking that she might protest, and that added to his sense of hunger.

"Leah," he repeated aloud. He'd repeated all the other names, giving the illusion that he was attempting to remember each of them. But it was only Leah that mattered.

Chayim was about to move toward her, hoping to sit nearby as the group began the meeting. But Corbulo took him by the elbow and sat him opposite Leah. Chayim tried to hide his stare in her direction as the group sang a hymn unfamiliar to him.

They shared a meal, breaking bread and drinking wine in honor of the flesh and blood of Christ, a ritual that made little sense to Chayim. He pretended to match their reverence and joy, but his mind—and eyes—turned to Leah again and again.

Where did she live? How could he meet her again after what he knew would happen tonight?

As he speculated, the group continued with the meal. More hymns.

Chayim tried to plot a way he could have her. He felt as if he were in a pan of water slowly coming to boil. He knew what he had wanted before entering this room. Yet it had all changed from the moment Leah took his hands.

And soon everything would change again, because of events he'd started in motion earlier. Perhaps now was the time to warn them all to flee.

But if he did, they'd know he was responsible. And that knowledge would most certainly drive Leah from him, before he'd taken his chance with her.

Chayim's heart rate increased with dread and anticipation. How could he protect Leah without her discovering the betrayal he planned? How could—?

The door suddenly burst open.

And six armed Roman soldiers marched into the room.

✝ ✝ ✝

"You look exhausted, my friend," John said to Ruso. "Did you have visitors late into the night?"

"I did," Ruso answered. "Military men consulting with me on Senate matters." He was lying to his friend. The two visitors were highly ranked in the military, but nothing about the Senate had been discussed. If John knew how little sleep Ruso had had the night before or the reason for the long hours with those men, John would begin to suspect too much.

Ruso wanted them to move to a safer subject. "As you know," he said, "I, like all the other believers, have taken great comfort in the eyewitness accounts about Jesus written for us by you and Matthew and John Mark and Luke."

John stopped walking and faced Ruso. He smiled an invitation for Ruso to continue, as if he sensed Ruso was leading to a question.

They were returning from the hours spent together visiting families of men in prison for refusing to renounce their faith in Jesus. Ruso's role was one of silence as John spoke quietly to each family. Ruso was simply glad that he had the resources to help them with money and food. But it was John whom the men and women leaned on for much more than material gifts. He answered their questions, absorbed their fears, and spoke of Jesus with such certainty that in each household hope replaced despair.

Ruso knew that such effort exhausted John, and usually their trips through the streets back to the peace of the hillside were completed in companionable silence.

It was unusual, then, for Ruso to interrupt John's thoughts during the walk. "I've never asked you," Ruso continued quickly, "but . . ." He hesitated, conscious of his reluctance to press on their friendship. John, although he shrugged it off, was often elevated by their fellow believers because of the special relationship he'd had with Jesus. Ruso avoided taking advantage of his friendship with John to ask about Jesus in a way that seemed he was only interested in the celebrity aspect of John's reputation. In general, John seemed relaxed with Ruso, often glad for the reprieve from the demands placed on him by other believers.

Yet . . .

Of any time that Ruso wanted John distracted, it was now. And Ruso had genuine questions that he doubted he'd ever get a chance to ask John again.

"But . . . ?" John echoed to encourage him.

They had stopped. Passersby flowed around them. They were in the shadows of apartments that lined a crowded street. A marketplace square was behind them and ahead was the Via Sacra, the main thoroughfare they usually took out of the center of Rome toward the household of Ruso.

"Let me put it this way," Ruso said. "In Matthew's account of the time Jesus spent on the Mount of Olives, he tells his readers that Jesus prophesied the abomination that causes desecration in the temple. Yet Luke's account makes no mention of it. We know that's because Matthew was writing to a Jewish audience who would immediately understand the importance of Jesus speaking those words. And Luke wrote to the Gentiles, who would find much less meaning in that. So the accounts differ."

"Of course," John said.

"And will you agree with me that the truth behind any event can be presented in as many ways as there are witnesses to it? For example, a great battle. The generals will report it differently than the soldiers, and the soldiers differently than the cooks at the supply wagons, and the defeated enemies yet again from another perspective."

John smiled. "Such is human nature."

"Yet none of the accounts would be false. And blended together, they would give a far greater view of the truth of the event than any one account. Just as the different accounts of Jesus give us a more complete perspective. Differences. Not contradictions."

John nodded. "I cannot disagree with you. Why do you ask?"

"Judas," Ruso said. Inwardly, he winced to say the name. "The betrayer. I've always wondered about your account of that night."

John's face clouded briefly. "Yes," he said slowly. "What about Judas?"

"On your Passover evening with Jesus," Ruso said, "Judas was allowed to depart from your last supper with Him. Yet Jesus had told all of you that one would betray Him. Didn't any of you wonder when Judas slipped out?"

John sighed. "He was the keeper of the purse. Jesus spoke in a low voice to him. It appeared to us that he was sent out to purchase bread or something else that our Master needed. He was the most zealous of us all. We never dreamed he was the betrayer. Although . . ."

John had begun to walk again.

Ruso took his elbow and gently slowed him. Ahead and too soon, the slave Cornelius would be waiting with Damian, the famed slave hunter. Too soon, Ruso would never see John again.

John was deep in memory and didn't seem to notice that Ruso had slowed their pace. "I remember," John said, "that before Judas left, Simon Peter leaned toward Jesus from his cushion beside the Passover table and asked, 'Lord, who is it?' And Jesus answered, 'It is the one to whom I give the bread dipped in the sauce.' Jesus then dipped the bread and gave it to Judas."

"It wasn't plain then that Judas was the betrayer?"

"Not plain at all. Peter and I exchanged glances but didn't see the significance of it. Judas was fiercely proud and had taken the seat of honor. It was expected that Jesus would hand him the bread first."

Ruso understood. A trusting man is easily deceived. He did not have to look any further than John's trust for him to know that.

"That proves my point about the truth behind an event," Ruso said. "Matthew was there in the room yet does not record the conversation between Peter and Jesus."

"He didn't hear it. Only Peter and I were close enough to Jesus." John shook his head. "And Judas of course. That poor, poor man."

"You speak of him with such compassion." Inwardly, Ruso winced again, thinking about betrayal. He hoped in the days ahead that John would speak of him, too, in such a gentle manner.

"I cannot be sure," John continued, "but I believe Judas turned Jesus over to the authorities to force Jesus to act against them. Think about it. We had spent three years with Jesus, witnessed His miracles, seen Him calm a storm, watched Him walk on water. Judas, as a Zealot, burned for Jesus to overthrow the temple authorities, for they worked closely with the Romans. And most of all, as a Zealot, Judas wanted the Romans gone. All of us disciples believed that if Jesus so desired, an army of angels would have appeared to do His bidding. Judas, I am almost certain, thought that if Jesus was captured, He would have no choice but to fight."

John stared off into the distance. "None of us understood until later our Master's true purpose. The despair we faced during His trial and crucifixion. We were all cowards." John straightened. "Then the Resurrection! We all became fearless confessors of that which we had seen with our eyes and that our hands had touched. Our Master! Resurrected! We were no longer afraid to walk in the Truth."

"I wish I could have been there in those exciting days," Ruso said.

John turned and clasped Ruso. "I know you share my faith, my friend. You know you've met Him through that faith. And you and I are nearing our final heartbeat when we will see Him as He is." John's certainty and peace glowed across his face.

Ruso wanted that to be his last memory of John, not what was still ahead.

✝ ✝ ✝

When a key rattled in the cell door's lock, Vitas thought the time had arrived for him to enter the arena. He had a vision of himself, stepping into the sunlight, squinting after all his hours in darkness, feeling the crunch of sand beneath his feet, hearing the great crowds eagerly awaiting his slaughter.

But more than fear for his death, he was filled with sorrow. He wanted to live to be old with Sophia, to be a good father. Death would take that away from him. Why couldn't he have the faith that she possessed?

The door opened and shut quickly, and a person carrying a small torch slipped into the cell.

"Don't be long," the guard's voice said from outside.

Even this dim light was far more than Vitas had seen since the departure of Helius. He blinked, trying to focus on his visitor.

The man was about the size of Vitas, with light-colored hair. He wore a hooded tunic. "Gallus Sergius Vitas," he said. He was carrying a small bag, closed at the top by the leather strings used as a strap.

He squatted beside Vitas and set a wineskin in his hands. "Here. This should help. I've also got food." The stranger opened the bag and pulled out bread and cheese, and handed them to Vitas.

Vitas was suspicious, remembering how he'd been drugged earlier, then beaten. He set the food in his lap and sipped the wine carefully. Nothing tasted unusual. "If this is poisoned or drugged," Vitas said dourly, thinking of his strange visitor the day before, "you probably wouldn't tell me, would you?"

The wine moistened his taste buds, and Vitas decided he was too hungry to care about the answer one way or another. He ripped into the bread and swallowed almost without chewing.

The man gestured at another wineskin that he'd just pulled out of the bag. "The potions are in this. For me." Beside the second wineskin, the man set down a wooden dowel wrapped in leather. He didn't try to stop Vitas from picking it up.

Vitas slapped it against his hand, considering it as a weapon.

"Not yet," the man said. "There are things I want to tell you first."

Not yet?

"My name is Jonathan," the man said before Vitas could ask that question aloud. His voice trembled. "What I have to say I have rehearsed many times in the last hours, as I know we have little time."

Vitas recognized that tremble. He was well familiar with it himself. It sounded like fear.

"I am a slave," Jonathan said. "My master owns a large farm north of Rome with many slaves. I have a wife and three children. If I had all day and all night for ten years, I would not be able to fully tell you how much I love them. I understand this love now. It is the love of our one true God, given to us and given through us."

Vitas grew very still. Was this man a believer like Sophia?

"Remember: I have rehearsed this. Of all that I can say in the time we have, I thought it important to tell you about God. And His Son. For I believe that God walked this earth and allowed Himself to be crucified as an atonement for all I have done wrong in this life. Through the Christos, God welcomes me while I am alive in this body, and He also has a home waiting for me when I leave this failing body in anticipation of resurrection."

"Don't bother me with religious nonsense," Vitas growled. Not because he didn't believe. But because the man could well be an informer attempting to get Vitas to admit the very same faith, and in so doing, condemn Sophia. This was a trick that Helius was capable of. "Nero's killed hundreds upon hundreds for that belief."

"Which is why my family and I have been sent here. To the arena. It is a belief we refuse to deny. All of us have been sentenced to death."

If this was true, Vitas could only feel horror. If the man was lying, it was an evil thing.

"I don't understand," Vitas said, washing some cheese down with wine. If he was going to die, at least he would die with a full belly. "You walk the underground prisons as if free."

"I will explain. I just wanted you to first know the belief that changed my life. No matter how great the tribulation that any of us might ever face, it is faith in the resurrection of Jesus that gives us hope enough to withstand it. Perhaps you, too, will consider that great truth."

"You are here to preach to me on my deathbed?" Vitas was beginning to believe the man might actually have the faith. "The guard let you into my cell for that?"

"The guard was bribed. I tell you about my faith to spare you regrets. Even if you never think of the Christos again, please believe me when I say I am glad for this opportunity."

"Opportunity?"

"I do what I do willingly."

"Whatever it is, your voice still trembles."

"I am not a brave man," Jonathan said in a whisper. "But if the Christos could do what He did for me . . ."

"Who bribed the guard? Why?" Vitas wanted to ask more, but the man beside him abruptly put his head down in prayer. Vitas gave him silence.

Then Jonathan lifted his head again. He took the second wineskin and drank from it deeply. He sputtered and forced himself to drink more.

"I am ready." Fear was still in the man's voice. He took his final gulps from the wineskin and set it down. "Help me with what I need to do next," Jonathan said. "My hands may not be steady for much longer."

✛ ✛ ✛

"I am glad there is no need to mutilate her body." Ben-Aryeh had joined the soldier outside the bath chamber and spoke with his head bowed. "She was well loved. Although she granted all her slaves their freedom, they will stay here and ensure she has a proper and decent funeral."

"The same cannot be said for her husband," the soldier said.

"No?" Ben-Aryeh pretended a degree of disinterest.

"Tigellinus told us he will die to the lions."

"Did you pass that on to her?"

The soldier shook his head. "Bad enough the emperor invited her to die. Was there any reason to add to her grief?"

"Thank you," Ben-Aryeh said. He was glad the soldier showed compassion; it would probably save the soldier's life. Still, everything depended on what would happen once they both entered the bath chamber.

Ben-Aryeh reached inside his tunic for another pouch of coins. His

368 HANEGRAAFF • BROUWER

hand brushed against the handle of a knife. He hoped he wouldn't have to use it. "Please take this. You have been decent to her."

The soldier hesitated.

"Nero gets what you don't take," Ben-Aryeh said.

The soldier shrugged, then accepted it.

Good, Ben-Aryeh thought. *He is one step closer to keeping his own life.* "Let me see if the mistress is dead," Ben-Aryeh said.

"Not without my supervision."

"Certainly."

The soldier followed Ben-Aryeh inside.

Sophia's body had slid down so that only her head rested on the edge of the bath, tilted back, her eyes closed. One arm was folded across her chest as if she'd vainly tried to clamp her other wrist to stem the flow of blood. That she'd been unsuccessful was obvious to Ben-Aryeh and the soldier. The bathwater had a red hue so dark that her naked body was completely hidden.

A strangled cry left Ben-Aryeh's throat. He rushed forward, leaving the soldier at the entrance. He reached into the bathwater and pulled out Sophia's limp arm. He held it so that the cuts were visible to the soldier behind him. Blood still seeped from the wound.

He placed her arm gently in the water again.

Ben-Aryeh hunched over and began to sob.

✠ ✠ ✠

Chayim stared at the soldiers. They blocked the door, each poised with a sword drawn.

"By the authority of Caesar," the tallest soldier said, "we place you under arrest for treasonous activities."

He was the only soldier among them that Chayim knew. Arminius Gavrus. Gavrus was an imposing figure even without his military equipment, a large man with a square face and dark eyes that showed no expression. With his sword and full armor, he inspired terror.

When they'd made their arrangement earlier in the day, Gavrus had made it very clear that if Chayim did not pay the amount they'd agreed upon, he would kill Chayim without hesitation. This, Chayim had thought, was simply a good sign of the man's seriousness about the evening's task. Chayim felt the money promised was money well spent, for Gavrus had impressed him as an intelligent man, very capable of accomplishing Chayim's plan.

Gavrus stepped forward, raising his sword. His bulk seemed to fill the small room. "Any who resist will lose an arm."

Corbulo was the first to break the shocked silence. "We are friends gathering for a meal. There is nothing treasonous about this."

The others in the room sat motionless. The dim light given by the candles flickered across their faces. Chayim noticed that Leah had moved closer to the older woman beside her and had placed a protective arm around her shoulders.

In discussing his plan with Gavrus, Chayim had stressed that neither of them could anticipate how the Christians might react. Chayim had simply told Gavrus what he wanted to accomplish, told the soldier to hire the right men to help, and adjust to the situation as it unfolded.

"I repeat," Corbulo said, "we have done nothing treasonous."

"That is not for me to decide," Gavrus said. "I am following orders."

Perfect answer, Chayim thought. Presented like a soldier truly sent by Nero. It would have been strange for Gavrus to enter a debate with the accused on whether the charges were valid.

Corbulo pointed at Chayim. "It was you, wasn't it? You led these soldiers to us."

"Silence!" Gavrus said. "As I call you one by one, step forward and accept the shackles."

Chayim thought of Leah. Of how he could not answer the accusation that Corbulo had just hurled at him. But it was all in motion now. Too late to stop.

A soldier at the rear of the group moved beside Gavrus, holding a sack that he emptied on the floor. The shackles clanked as they fell in a heap.

"Wait," Chayim said.

Gavrus was swift to react. In one step, he reached Chayim and pushed the tip of his sword into Chayim's belly, just below his sternum. "You dare tell a soldier under Nero's orders to wait?"

Chayim gasped. Although he knew Gavrus was acting, he wished the soldier had not been quite so enthusiastic about the pressure of the sword. "Hear me out," he said. "You can obey Caesar and still line your pockets with gold."

"Insolence!" Gavrus knocked Chayim in the face with his other hand, sending Chayim to the ground. "Shackle him first," he ordered one of his men.

As the irons bit into his wrist, Chayim made another plea. "Give those of us who are faithful to Caesar a chance to declare their allegiance now. How can Caesar find injustice in that? And perhaps those who are true to Caesar will show you gratitude for that chance at freedom."

This was the brilliance of Chayim's plan. To force these Christians to choose between Nero and their faith. Those who did not choose Nero would be taken away by half the soldiers. After that, those who did choose Nero would be threatened with further punishment unless they helped Chayim. After all, Chayim had judged, these people would also be likely to further betray their cause and divulge whatever Chayim needed to find out about the treasonous letter circulating among the Christians.

At the same time, by remaining behind with those who chose Nero, Chayim could also renounce any belief in the Christ of Nazareth and clear himself of any danger with Nero, especially if Chayim delivered those who did not renounce the Christ to the authorities for death in the arenas.

With the scrolls so near on the table, Chayim should have been very pleased about his decision to infiltrate the meeting and instruct soldiers to arrive when they did. The plan had been brilliant and was working to perfection.

Except now there was Leah. And the hunger that must be satisfied.

"At least consider what I am asking," Chayim said to Gavrus. "Give those who choose Nero their freedom. And you will have their gratitude."

"Gratitude at the chance for freedom," Gavrus repeated. The big soldier made a show of studying Chayim and of considering how to respond. "How much gratitude?" Gavrus finally asked.

"I suspect you can name your price," Chayim said, "especially since those who choose the Christos are guilty of treason and will face death in the arena."

Gavrus pretended to consider that as he paced back and forth in front of the small group.

Chayim stared at his feet, feeling a flush of hatred for the soldier. Earlier in the day, this arrangement had seemed like a perfect solution to the task that Helius had placed upon him. Now, Gavrus and what they had planned stood between Chayim and Leah.

"Fine," Gavrus said. "Let's find out who wants to escape the arena. As for payment, whatever gold or silver or jewelry we find among the group should be enough. Those who are going to die will have no need of it, and those who live will find it a small price to pay."

Gavrus pointed a sword at an old man whose hands were folded in prayer. "You. Tell me that Nero is god and you will continue to live as a loyal subject of Rome."

The old man's eyes were shiny with tears. He did not hesitate. "I follow the Christ, and I am happy to give my life for Him as He give His for me."

"Shackle him," Gavrus said in a flat voice. He pointed at the next, obviously the son of the older man. "And you. Tell me that Nero is god, that you will no longer believe in the superstitious nonsense about a man risen from the dead. Save yourself from the lions and gladiators."

Silence. The silence of agony.

"My father's faith is my faith," the son said, barely above a whisper. "I go to the arena with him."

"Shackle him too." Gavrus moved to stand in front of a middle-aged woman, who had a peaceful smile on her face. "Do you serve Nero? Or do you choose death?"

By the expression on her face, Chayim had no doubt what she would answer.

"Death for Christ gives me life," she said. Her voice grew in strength. "Nero is the Beast that John warned us about in his revelation. I reject his mark."

"Shackle her."

"Nero is the Beast that John warned us about in his revelation."

Before Chayim could puzzle over that remark, Gavrus faced Corbulo. "Will you serve Nero?" Gavrus asked the fisherman. "Will you bow before his image in the temples?"

"Yes," Corbulo said. He glanced around the room defiantly. "I have a family to feed. Children who depend on me. Should I condemn them too?"

No one made a sound but Gavrus. "Step over to the side of the room."

Corbulo was stony-faced as he took trembling steps to stand alone.

"Peter betrayed the Master too," a woman whispered to Corbulo. "And he was forgiven."

"Silence!" Gavrus struck the woman's head with an open hand.

She fell sideways. With great effort, she shifted to a sitting position. "I choose my Master," she said. "His Spirit fills this room and gives us comfort."

At the woman's words, Chayim became aware of a supernatural presence so strong that even Gavrus hesitated before moving to the next person. And the next. Both refused to call Nero god. Both were shackled.

A young woman and a man who held her hand rose wordlessly before Gavrus could face them and joined Corbulo where he stood.

Leah was the last. Of all before her, only three had renounced their faith. The others had chosen arrest and the certain tortured death in the arena before thousands of spectators.

"You!" Gavrus said to Leah. "Will you throw your life away too?"

✠ ✠ ✠

In conversation with John, Ruso began to walk again, leading John toward a small alley off the Via Sacra.

"So . . . ," Ruso said as casually as he could, doing his best to mask the emotions storming inside him, wanting John to remain distracted by questions, "that is why you added your voice to the accounts of Matthew and John Mark and Luke? To give a more complete account of the time Jesus spent on earth?"

John put a companionable arm across Ruso's shoulder. They separated again as a peddler led a loaded donkey between them, and then resumed the conversation at a comfortable walking pace.

"Jesus is the true God and eternal life; He is my Lord and King," John said emphatically. "It was my calling and sacred trust to record the events and describe them for others."

Ruso nodded. "It is important for the world to know what He did."

"Yet all of us with Him could not have told everything. As you might remember——" John smiled, as if showing Ruso that he was quoting from his own letter now circulating among the believers——" 'if all the other things that Jesus did were written down, the whole world could not contain the books.' "

"I wish I could have been there," Ruso said, "as you were."

Ruso had turned into the alley. Afternoon shadows engulfed them. As did the odor of rotting garbage. They were alone, and even though they were only a few paces from the main street, it was much quieter.

"This is odd," John said. "Usually we choose a different way to——"

"There is someone I want you to meet," Ruso said. "It is important." He began to walk quicker, so that John wouldn't change his mind and retreat to the broader and busier street.

Once he was confident that John would stay with him, Ruso turned to him. "Of anything you might remember about me, it is that I have always considered you my friend. A brother."

"You speak as if these are our last moments together," John said.

Ruso was grim. He noticed that four large men stepped out of a nook in the alley and quickly approached from behind John. "These *are* our last moments together," Ruso said.

John blinked. Before he could speak, the largest of the men threw a dark hood over John's head. The other three were on him instantly, binding him with rope.

John did not struggle in the slightest. "Ruso," he said, his voice muffled by the hood, "are you there? Have they hurt you?"

Ruso was too overwhelmed by guilt and regret and sorrow to answer.

John didn't speak as the men bound his legs and arms. It was, without doubt, dawning on him that Ruso had not been attacked, and that meant Ruso had betrayed him to this capture.

"You are loved," John finally said, voice still muffled. "If these are our last moments together, that is what I want you to remember of me. God will never turn away from you if you reach out to Him. I wish Judas would have understood that."

Ruso still could not find his voice. He motioned for the four men to take John away.

They did, lifting him from the ground and carrying him as if he were nothing more than a log. Farther down the alley, they stopped to get a large piece of woven tapestry they'd kept there in preparation.

They rolled John into the tapestry, completely engulfing him. Nobody watching them walk down the street would have guessed they carried a man inside. They looked like workmen delivering a tapestry from a local shop.

Ruso watched the men until they were out of the alley, his eyes blurred with tears.

It is done, he thought. *There is no turning back.*

✛ ✛ ✛

"What is your answer?" the soldier had demanded.

I choose Nero, Leah thought.

She was not a believer. She wanted to tell the soldier the truth, that she was only at this gathering of believers because she was seeking answers.

Why had her brother Nathan given up everything—including his life—for this Jesus? Why had he turned his back on what he'd been taught since childhood about the Jewish religion, knowing how much it would hurt his father and the rest of the family? How had he managed to believe with his whole heart that Jesus was truly the promised Messiah?

These questions had haunted Leah so much that she, too, had betrayed her own father. He was desolate with grief that he'd lost Nathan to the lions in the arena and Caleb to the soldiers of the emperor because of Nathan's faith. He would be insane with fury if he found out that she had risked her life to meet with people who had the same faith that had destroyed their family.

But she'd had no choice if she wanted to find the answers.

At first, she'd read the letters that she'd promised Nathan she would keep until someone showed up at their household to take them from her safekeeping. Letters from friends of Jesus. The one from Matthew told about the few years of Jesus' teaching. Another from John Mark. And the letter of Revelation from John that described his incredible vision of awe and wonder and horror and hope.

But reading those letters again and again in secret had only raised more questions. So finally, Leah had started joining these believers at their meetings, hoping to learn from them about the mystery of their faith and peace throughout the tribulations they faced. She'd even found a way to speak to John himself.

That's the truth she wanted to tell the soldier.

Indeed, the fear that overwhelmed her screamed at her to deny Jesus and proclaim Nero as divine.

Images filled her mind. Of men and women hanging from lampposts by their wrists, wearing tunics covered in tar through the heat of the day until finally at sunset soldiers lit them on fire with their torches. Of her brother, crowded into a cell with other desperate men and women. Of the children, desperately crying as they were led away from their parents to be sold into slavery. Of the massive lions, snarling and fighting as they tore apart those same men and women in the arena, of the terrible snapping of bones that she hadn't been able to block from her hearing as she wept in the arena on the day of her brother's death.

As all of this flashed through her mind, Leah could not help but turn her eyes on the stranger who had brought the soldiers and this death into their midst.

Chayim.

The presence of the soldiers was almost as great a shock as the fact that he had betrayed them by leading the soldiers here. For Corbulo was most certainly right. Who else but Chayim could have been the informer?

When he'd first walked into the room, she'd felt a sensation that was strange to her, of her heart seeming to leap out of her chest at the astonishment of what had happened when their eyes first met. This man had such an effect on her that she was scarcely able to look at him. Was it love? or a physical hunger that she should deny?

And now that she knew he was the betrayer, she had to look at him to confirm her disbelief of the situation, as if she really didn't expect his face to have the same mystery and charisma that had drawn her so instantly to him.

Yet even now, there was something in the intensity of the way he regarded her, and she felt disloyal to all her friends for not hating him far more than she had first been attracted to him.

"What is it, woman?" Gavrus snapped. "I haven't all night."

I choose Nero, she thought. *Not lions or tunics of pitch that would burn me alive.*

I choose Nero.

But she couldn't say it.

Because there were other images in her mind. The images that had brought her to these meetings to seek answers.

Images of her brother singing hymns in the prison below the arena. Of him standing tall on the sand as the lions were loosed. Of the beauty of the songs that rose as the lions circled. Of the peace on his face as he knelt and prayed and waited for his death from those savage teeth and claws.

In that moment, Leah finally stopped asking questions about Jesus and opened her heart in a silent prayer, beseeching Him for the faith that had made her brother strong enough to face the lions with peace.

And in that moment an incredible peace filled her too. An indescribable tranquility and joy as the holiness of an unseen Spirit filled her, like the sigh of an eternal wind.

She thought for an instant that she, too, had seen the Lamb on the throne as John had described it in his letter and heard the sweetest songs of angels that John had listened to in the heaven of his vision.

This is it. Leah knew with certainty. *This is the faith that brings me to God, faith in the Jesus who is His Son and who died on the cross on my behalf, taking the punishment for all the selfishness and sins that made it impossible for me to ever cross the chasm between my imperfection and the utter holiness of God.*

This is it.

Fear fell away from her.

"I believe," Leah said to the soldier. "I believe that Jesus is the Son of God. I will gladly suffer for my Master." She looked directly at Chayim. "And I will pray for those who do not yet have that strength."

✝ ✝ ✝

Ben-Aryeh sobbed beside the bath.

Sophia's eyes were closed, of course, so she could not see the soldier standing in the doorway. She knew, however, what was happening.

This had been Ben-Aryeh's plan.

Earlier in the day, when he'd discovered it was likely that soldiers would be sent with orders for Sophia to commit suicide, Ben-Aryeh had slit the throat of a goat and collected its blood in a large jug. The jug had been hidden beneath the towels beside the bath, and once in the hot water, Sophia had poured its contents into the bath and covered the jug again with the towels.

Then had come the difficult part. Cutting the wrist of her left arm—the side facing the doorway—deep enough so that a casual inspection would show sufficient damage but not so deeply that it would threaten her life. Beneath the water, she'd been clamping her wrist with a small cloth in her right hand to prevent most of the bleeding.

Ben-Aryeh had done as promised. Entered with the soldier and lifted her left arm to show the cut. Then he had carefully placed it back beneath the water and used his body to hide any movement as she resumed clamping her wrist with her other hand to minimize the blood flow.

Because they had planned this carefully, Sophia knew that Ben-Aryeh was using the contortion of his heaving sobs to keep his right hand tight against his belly, close to the handle of the knife he had hidden beneath his tunic.

If the soldier decided to closely inspect Sophia or to ensure she was dead by plunging a sword into her, Ben-Aryeh would kill him. And their escape would be rushed and uncertain. Horses were prepared in the stable, and they would hope for enough time after the discovery of the dead soldier to get to the stable and flee.

On the other hand, if the soldier was satisfied that Sophia was dead, Ben-Aryeh would spare the man's life.

As she waited, Sophia took only tiny breaths through her nostrils, making sure the water around her did not show movement and betray that she was alive.

Moment stretched after moment.

She could not see that the soldier remained at a respectful distance, allowing Ben-Aryeh to grieve with dignity. That compassion saved the soldier's life. He finally turned away and left Ben-Aryeh alone with Sophia.

✠ ✠ ✠

There it was, Chayim thought. Leah had chosen torture. Humiliation. Death. All that beauty would be torn apart before he could taste it, before he could devour it himself.

Chayim nearly groaned.

Gavrus turned to Chayim. "There. Are you satisfied? The four of you have freedom."

Gavrus waited for Chayim to answer as they had planned earlier. Some soldiers would take away the Christians for arrest. Then Chayim would take the scrolls already in the room. He would force Corbulo and the other two to tell him anything else he needed to know about the letter of the Revelation that Helius sought. Through all of this, Chayim would guarantee that he had given Nero no reason to believe him a traitor to the empire, and Chayim would probably earn some personal reward for his actions.

Yet against all that Chayim had believed he wanted until this evening was one inexorable fact: Speaking the words that Gavrus expected to hear would seal Leah's fate and the fate of the other Christians with her. In that moment, the room seemed to shift for Chayim, as if an earthquake had struck.

"Well?" Gavrus demanded. "What say you?"

Chayim opened his mouth to croak out the words that would kill Leah. He felt as if another man were about to speak for him. He stopped and drew a breath. He made his decision. "Four?" Chayim asked. He pointed at Corbulo and the other two nearby. "I only see three."

Gavrus blinked. This was not what they had discussed earlier. "I would assume," Gavrus said, "that you are the fourth. That you also choose Nero."

"Assume instead that I simply want to spare those who would choose Nero."

"Are you telling me that you do not choose allegiance to our emperor and his claim to divinity?"

Chayim drew another breath. "I do not," he said. "I will stand in the arena with those who are unwilling to give up their faith."

The room full of soldiers and condemned followers was quiet with tension and dread.

Until Chayim deliberately broke it.

"It was you!" Chayim lifted his shackled wrists and pointed across the small room at Corbulo. "You brought the soldiers here!"

"I did no such thing." Corbulo took a step forward in anger.

Chayim shook the shackles and the clinking sound seemed to echo. "You are free," he told Corbulo. "You chose Caesar. We are not."

"Enough," Gavrus growled.

Chayim knew he needed a diversion, anything to get outside with Gavrus, anything to let him speak to the Roman soldier in private.

"Betrayer!" Chayim shouted at Corbulo, ignoring the sword that Gavrus raised. "And you dared accuse me!"

"I did not bring the soldiers," Corbulo said. He made an appealing gesture to the others in the room. "I did not!"

Gavrus repeated himself louder. "Enough!"

"You've betrayed our Master." Chayim continued to ignore Gavrus, knowing that he was safe from the soldier, no matter how much Gavrus might be confused by the situation.

Still holding his hands high and pointing at Corbulo in accusation, Chayim searched his memory for the name he needed. During his time with Rikka, he had asked the slave for as many of the stories about the Christ as he dared, hoping she wouldn't realize he was not a follower. "You're no different than . . . than . . . Judas himself!"

"No," Corbulo wailed.

"Enough!" Gavrus shouted.

"We die anyway." Chayim spit at the feet of Gavrus. "I will not let you intimidate me." He spit again, directly on the chest of Gavrus.

At last, a gleam of understanding seemed to come into Gavrus' eyes. "You dare insult a soldier sent by Caesar!" he said.

"I do not serve Caesar! That much should be clear! What are you going to do? Take me outside right now and kill me?"

There it was, the order directed at Gavrus. Would he understand?

Gavrus laughed. "That will be a pleasure." He turned to the other soldiers. "Guard them. This won't take me long."

Gavrus, a much bigger man than Chayim, grabbed Chayim by the shackles and dragged him through the doorway. "What game are you playing?" he hissed into Chayim's ear as soon as they were in the alley. "I thought you were going to join those on Nero's side and send the others to the arena."

"You are one of them," Chayim said. "A Christian."

"What?"

"You took me in the alley to prevent a real fight. You are trying to protect me. That is what you will tell the others when you step inside. But tell them that only after you have released the three who chose Nero."

"What!"

"Listen to me. You are one of them. You have a spy in Nero's court who tells you when a group of Christians is discovered."

Chayim was thinking it through as he spoke, and he found the rush of adrenaline exhilarating. "You learn of a location and arrive well before the soldiers who are truly sent by Nero to arrest them. You then test the Christians as you did to rid them of the ones who are false to their faith."

"Winnowing the chaff from the wheat," Gavrus said. "I'll even apologize to that woman."

Chayim grinned. "You are a quick study."

"What about the ones who chose Nero?"

"Tell it this way. You always send them away before you inform the others that it was a test. Doing it in such a manner, Corbulo and the other two will never know about the fate of those left behind."

"And those left behind?"

"Apologize for frightening them as you did. Tell them it was necessary to protect them and that they now know they can trust everyone in the room who chose to die for the Christ. And now that will include me."

"Chayim . . ."

"Yes?"

"You are a devious snake."

"I will take that as a compliment."

Chayim was proud of himself. Now his presence among them would not be questioned. He could learn more about the letter that Helius sought. Gavrus could always be called upon as a witness that Chayim wasn't actually a Christian. And best of all, in Leah's eyes, he would undoubtedly be a hero.

"I go then," Gavrus said.

"One more thing."

"Yes?"

"Before you send him away," Chayim said, "tell Corbulo that Caesar thanks him for leading you to the group. I want everyone inside to believe he truly was a traitor."

As Gavrus walked back into the room, Chayim smiled, thinking of Leah. Yes, indeed, Chayim congratulated himself, he truly did know how to impress a woman.

✛ ✛ ✛

"There are two small jars at the bottom of the bag," Jonathan said in the cell with Vitas. "Take them please."

Too curious to protest, Vitas reached into the bag and felt for them. One was larger than the other.

"You'll have to apply the dye," Jonathan said. "It can't be found on my hands."

"Dye? Who sent you? What is going on?"

"The larger jar. That dye goes in your hair."

"It will not."

"It must for you to live."

"Live?"

"What color is my hair?" Jonathan's words had lost their crispness.

"Light. Blond?"

"The dye will bleach your hair to look like mine. When you are finished, rub the darker dye into my hair."

"And then what?" Vitas said. "I walk out and leave you here?"

"Yes," Jonathan said simply.

The utter sincerity of his answer froze Vitas.

Then Vitas snorted. "Yesterday someone beat my face beyond recognition. Yours seems to be untouched. No one would confuse you for me."

"Soon enough they will. Please. Open the jars."

Vitas stared at Jonathan.

"There is a ship on the Tiber," Jonathan said. "Your passage has been paid. You need to arrive there before dark. It will sail tonight."

Vitas continued to stare, beginning to comprehend what was happening. The wooden dowel wrapped with leather . . .

Jonathan described where to find the ship. "There's more," he said. "You'll need to give them the words that will identify you. 'These are the ones coming out of the great tribulation. They washed their robes in the blood of the Lamb and made them white.' Repeat this so I know you understand."

Vitas was hesitant, only because this was so strange.

"Repeat it," Jonathan said.

"'These are the ones coming out of the great tribulation. They washed their robes in the blood of the Lamb and made them white.'" Vitas frowned. "What kind of code language is this?"

"Language to save your life and get you away from Rome."

"You are telling me," Vitas said, "that I am going to walk away from this prison? Today? Alive?"

"I was sent here to make that possible."

"But you will . . ."

"Remain here in your place," Jonathan finished.

"No. I cannot let you die for me."

"Please," the man said, "remember the comfort I find in my faith. And remember something else. I will die knowing that it has allowed me to save my family. For that was my bargain. If I take your place, they will be spared."

"Who arranged this?" Vitas leaned forward and pulled at the clothing on the man's chest. "Who sent you?"

"Can't say."

"Won't?"

"Won't. Can't. I had my instructions. That is all." Jonathan slurred his words. "Don't you think I'd be happy to tell you right now?"

"Sophia!" Vitas said.

"Sophia?"

"My wife. She—"

"No!" Jonathan's voice was sharp. "If she finds out you are alive, she will be killed. I was told to tell you that. If you aren't on the ship, she is assassinated. Those are the terms."

"If I don't accept them?"

"Please. My family has already been taken from the arena. If you don't make it to the ship, they will be returned and sent to the lions."

Vitas felt like his head was spinning. Who had organized this? Why? Why couldn't he go to Sophia? "Where is the ship going?"

"I've told you all I can. I am begging you to go. The hood will cover your face until you are well away from the arena. There is a litter waiting outside the amphitheater to take you to the ship. You'll know it is for you because all the slaves carrying it are bald."

Jonathan took the second wineskin and tilted it. He squeezed it, looking for more. "May I have your wine?" he said to Vitas apologetically. "I'm afraid I'll still feel too much."

Vitas let the man take the other wineskin, understanding why Jonathan felt the need to gird himself.

Vitas picked up the wooden dowel wrapped with leather. Now he understood why the blows yesterday had not cut him open. There were no sharp edges on the wood. Whoever had arranged for this meant to make his face unrecognizable. So that when Jonathan—the same size and same build—stepped into the arena, all who saw from the stands would believe it was Vitas dying.

"I am sorry for my cowardly behavior," Jonathan said. "When the soldiers at the cross offered my Savior wine mixed with myrrh, He had the courage to refuse it. And what He faced was a death much worse than mine."

"I don't think I can do it," Vitas said. The wooden dowel felt heavy in his hand.

"You have no choice. Should both of us die? And my family too?"

Vitas felt anguish and guilt. Yet offered a reprieve from death, he could not escape sudden joy. It would give him a chance to return somehow to Sophia.

"I will do it." Vitas raised the wooden dowel in preparation of the first blow to the man's face.

"Please," Jonathan said, "extinguish the torch. I don't want to see the blows coming."

VESPERA

After his men had captured John and after Damian had sent the slave Cornelius on his way, Damian had been in no hurry to speak to his prisoner. Instead, he'd given his men instructions on where to deliver John. Damian had no intention of delivering his captive to Helius immediately.

First of all, Damian suspected that Helius might find it convenient for Damian to die a sudden and mysterious death once John had been delivered to the imperial grounds, and Damian needed to make some arrangements to prevent that.

Second, Damian wanted to learn as much as he could from John. Knowledge, of course, was power. And third, Damian was truly curious about John's vision and hoped that John would answer questions more fully than either of the two rabbis had been able to do.

So it wasn't until evening that Damian first met with the man he had captured.

The safe house where he'd hidden John was a shed on the estate grounds of Damian's father. Years earlier it had been used to hold cattle, and it still smelled faintly of long-dried manure. For Damian, it was not an unpleasant smell. He had many happy childhood memories of running free on the estate.

He unbolted the door and stepped inside the shed, holding a lamp. He gave a brief nod of satisfaction. He'd held other captives here, and the usual arrangements had been made.

The man inside was tethered to the wall by iron bands around his wrists and legs, with long chains that gave him room to move comfortably. Damian had no interest in inflicting more pain than necessary on his captives, and he took pride in handing them over to their owners in the healthiest shape possible.

A bucket for the man's wastes had been provided, along with fresh straw and clean blankets for bedding. Fresh water was nearby and a basket with bread.

Damian noted with more satisfaction that much of the food had been eaten. This was a good sign. If a captive did not eat, it was an indication of the depths of despair.

"Good evening," Damian said in a pleasant voice. "I'm sorry to keep you this way, but I don't want to complicate things by posting guards outside. I hope you understand."

His face glowing in the lamplight, John looked up at him and smiled but said nothing.

This is strange, Damian thought. He'd had sullen prisoners before who refused to speak, but this man's silence came with a friendly smile.

"I won't hide this fact from you," Damian said. "I'm a slave hunter. A man of great power sent me to find you. But before I deliver you to him, I'd like to ask you some questions about your vision."

More silence. Same gentle smile. But more silence.

Damian thought he understood. "I can't give you back your freedom if you speak to me, but I can promise you I will do everything possible to make your captivity comfortable. Is that a fair exchange? Comfort for answers?"

His captive shifted slightly, and the chains that held him to the wall rattled.

Damian knelt. "Come on," he said. "What is it going to take to get you to talk to me?"

The man in chains said nothing.

✠ ✠ ✠

"You must speak the truth to me." Sophia's words broke a long silence between her and Ben-Aryeh.

Earlier, as night fell, Ben-Aryeh had led them up from the Via Apia into a small ravine well away from the road. He had hobbled the horses and then shared fruit and cheese with Sophia.

No fire. It was too dangerous.

No inn.

They had enough gold; Ben-Aryeh had made sure of that before they'd abandoned Vitas' mansion. But there was still too much risk that someone might recognize them.

To the world—and more importantly, to Nero—Sophia was dead. If word reached Tigellinus or Helius that she had not committed suicide, Sophia and Ben-Aryeh would be fleeing to the corners of the empire, never certain that capture and death might be only a day away.

So they rested near the horses. Each in a blanket.

"I have not lied to you," Ben-Aryeh replied.

"Nor have you been your usual self. No caustic remarks. No sarcasm. Not even any complaints about the Romans."

"Think of our day," Ben-Aryeh said.

"No." Sophia was firm. She did not want to know. But she needed to know. "You have learned something about Vitas. I can sense it."

"It is true," he said. "I have not told you everything. This morning, even before we made our plans, a messenger arrived with a strange letter. In this scroll, I was instructed to flee Rome with you immediately and that the remainder of the letter would direct us where to go once we were safely away from Nero. Yet . . ."

"Yet?"

"The letter uses such symbolic language that it is obviously coded. I haven't been able to give it much thought since. Only to wonder at who delivered it and why."

"You haven't answered my question about Vitas." Ben-Aryeh did not speak, and that confirmed it for her. "Tell me," she said. "Everything."

"My child," he began slowly, "the solider told me that Vitas was to face the lions in the arena today."

Sophia pulled her knees closer into her body. She pretended her heart was stone. Vitas . . . gone.

"Sophia?"

"Let me rest," she told Ben-Aryeh. "Weren't you the one who insisted that the next days must be filled with long travel?"

"Sophia."

"Enough," she said. "Please."

He gave her peace.

But she could not turn her heart to stone.

The child of Vitas was within her. She must live for that.

She closed her eyes against the night. Tears fell as she began to pray. She knew that without her faith, her future would be without hope.

☩ ☩ ☩

The man in chains said nothing as he faced Damian.

For good reason.

Damian did not know it, of course, but the man in chains was not John, but John's friend Ruso.

Ruso knew that the moment he opened his mouth, his accent would betray the fact that Damian had captured the wrong person. Would betray the fact that Ruso had had John captured and sent away to safety, then continued himself down the alley toward Damian, where as planned earlier, Cornelius had identified him to the slave hunter as John.

The longer Ruso remained silent, the farther away John would be from Rome.

And only Ruso knew John's final destination.

☩ ☩ ☩

In the dark of night Vitas boarded a small ship on the Tiber, calling out the password when requested: "'These are the ones coming out of the great tribulation. They washed their robes in the blood of the Lamb and made them white.'"

A man whose face was indistinguishable led him wordlessly to a cabin in the belly of the ship. It launched only minutes after his arrival, slipping downstream on the black, silent currents of the river.

It took Vitas out into the night.

But he was leaving Sophia behind.

The cabin was oppressive. Smelled of fish and vinegar. He moved onto the deck. Wanted to watch the outline of the hills of Rome.

Noise from the city taunted him, calling him back. Only at night were commercial wagons allowed into the city. Reaching him was the grinding squeal of wooden wheels on wooden axles of thousands of carts, the bellowing of oxen, the cursing of the drivers trying to find room on the crowded streets.

Wind tugged at the loose edges of the sails, still furled. He was still wearing the tunic with a hood, but here, where no one could see him, he'd pushed the hood back. The wind plucked at his hair, though he couldn't feel it against the skin of his face. The swollen marks of the beating were too fresh.

His pain, however, was much more than physical.

What would become of Sophia? of their unborn child? of Sabinus, the son of Maglorius whom Vitas had sworn to protect? Would Helius keep his word and spare them?

Every fiber of Vitas' being told him to jump off the ship. To find a way back to Sophia.

Yet it would be suicide. Literally.

He, like most soldiers and sailors, could not swim.

So he stood on the deck, trying to squeeze his emotions into a tight ball that he could hide deep inside. He vowed he would survive whatever was ahead, survive to return to Rome.

Yet the pain and grief refused to be set aside.

Taunting him further, clouds slipped away from the moon, and a silver light bathed the hills. He could almost see the fold of the ridge that overlooked his mansion, the mansion taken from him by Nero.

Nero! Vitas was convinced that no man in history could match Nero for pure evil. He vowed to return some day and find revenge. Would he find the power to do it in the strange promise about a Senate vote lost in the archives, marked by the number 666? And the letter he carried, given him by that stranger. What was written on it? And why was the letter so important?

That was one more frustration adding to all his others. It was so dark he had no chance of reading the letter until morning. And by then, Rome would be far behind.

He stared so hard at the city that his eyes began to fill with tears. The water of the Tiber slapped against the hull. Then the outline of the hills blurred against the darkness as clouds covered the moon again.

Still, Vitas did not move. He gripped the edge of the railing so hard that it felt as if his knuckles would split open.

Was there truly a God who loved His children as Sophia claimed? If so, how could this God allow a man the burden of such an injustice, the memories of love taken away, the fears of what might happen to those left behind?

In his pain, Vitas wondered if he should fall to his knees.

If he should pray as Sophia had tried to teach him to pray.

If he should let go of his determination to control his own life and place his soul in the hands of a greater power.

But did he really have a soul? Was there one true God who would hear his prayers?

Vitas groaned in his anguish. He wanted the peace that he knew Sophia had. He wanted to believe. But could not. He'd never been emptier, never been filled with so much despair.

Clouds slipped away from the moon again. He looked for the hills of Rome, but the ship had traveled too far.

That's when Vitas noticed he was being watched. Instinctively, he slipped his hood over his head. His face was too easily remembered; if anyone connected his bruised face with the man who was going to die in the arena for him, Nero might discover that Vitas was still alive.

From within the shadow of his hood, Vitas looked closer. At the front of the deck, the moonlight clearly showed the silhouette of a man seated on coils of thick rope, the shadow of a motionless figure.

Vitas hardly cared. He was a bruised mixture of hope and hopelessness, of resolve and helplessness, of anger and fear.

"I heard you cry out," the man said.

"Whatever you heard," Vitas said, "it is my business. Not yours." Roman men—especially Roman soldiers—did not share their pain. His lips cracked open as he spoke, and Vitas tasted blood.

"Of course," the man said from the coil of rope.

Vitas stared past the man, hoping for one last glimpse of the hills of the city.

"It seems we are on the same journey," the man said. "Perhaps you can tell me the ship's destination."

"If you knew how and why I was on this ship, you'd know that you are asking the wrong person." Vitas licked away the blood from his lips, trying unsuccessfully to moisten them. He could not escape the stirrings of curiosity. "And unless you were put on this ship as a captive, you're a fool if you didn't bother to find out before it sailed."

"I've been called a fool before," the man said, his face in shadow. "But in this case, at least, it is a false accusation." He raised his hands to show they were bound and that the rope was tied to the railing.

The man *was* a captive.

Because the man didn't ask for help, Vitas decided to move closer. "Who are you?" he asked. "Why are you here?"

"I'm on this ship," the man answered, "apparently because a friend believed I would be safer here than in Rome."

Vitas asked the natural question. "Why would you be in danger?"

"All of us marked by the Lamb are hated by those marked by the Beast."

Marked?

In the moon's light, Vitas looked more closely at the man. He saw no slave brand on the man's right hand or forehead. Yet there was something familiar about him. The man's gray hair . . .

"You're not a slave," Vitas said. Where had he seen this man?

"I would guess that if you want to know what I mean, enough time together lies ahead of us. Because if you are on this ship, perhaps you, too, are fleeing the Beast."

Vitas began to untie the rope from the man's wrists. "Who are you?" he asked again.

The man spoke with such certainty, it was uncanny. "I remember your voice. You've been sent to me again."

"Sent?" Vitas struggled to comprehend.

"With my God," the man said, still laughing as if appreciative of an irony, "there are no coincidences."

It came to Vitas. Where he'd seen the man before. "I know who you are!" Vitas said. "That night. When the earthquake struck. You were among the four who faced the beast . . ."

Clouds covered the moon again. Vitas heard the reply come out of near total darkness.

"Yes," the man answered. "I was one of the captives you set free. I am John, son of Zebedee."

AFTERWORD

The Last Disciple presents an alternative to the Left Behind understanding of end-times events based on a *methodology* called *Exegetical Eschatology* *(E²)*. I coined the phrase *Exegetical Eschatology* to underscore the fact that above all else I am deeply committed to a proper *method* of biblical interpretation rather than to any particular *model* of eschatology. Put another way, the plain and proper reading of a biblical passage must always take precedence over a particular eschatological presupposition or paradigm. (More on this in an upcoming book titled *Exegetical Eschatology* [Tyndale House].)

For example, the pretribulational rapture model featured in the Left Behind series interprets Revelation 13 in a strictly literal fashion. Thus, Antichrist dies and resurrects himself physically in order to vindicate his claim to be god. The following passage from *The Indwelling*, volume 7 of the Left Behind series, communicates the point:

> Carpathia catapulted himself to a standing position in the narrow end of his own coffin. He turned triumphantly to face the crowd, and David noticed makeup, putty, surgical staples, and stitches in the box where Nicolae's head had lain.
>
> Standing there before now deathly silence, Nicolae looked as if he had just stepped out of his closet where a valet had helped him into a crisp suit. Shoes gleaming, laces taut, socks smooth, suit unwrinkled, tie hanging just so, he stood broad-shouldered,

fresh-faced, shaven, hair in place, no pallor. Fortunato and the seven were on their knees, hiding their faces, sobbing aloud.

Nicolae raised his hands to shoulder height and said loudly enough for everyone to hear, without aid of a microphone, "Peace. Be still." With that the clouds ascended and vanished, and the sun reappeared in all its brilliance and heat. People squinted and covered their eyes.

"Peace be unto you," he said. "My peace I give you. Please stand." He paused while everyone rose, eyes still locked on him, bodies rigid with fear. "Let not your hearts be troubled. Believe in me."

Murmuring began. David heard people marveling that he was not using a microphone, but neither was he raising his voice. And yet everyone could hear.

It was as if Carpathia read their minds. "You marvel that I speak directly to your hearts without amplification, yet you saw me raise myself from the dead. Who but the most high god has power over death? Who but god controls the earth and sky?" (*The Indwelling*, 366–67).

In sharp contrast, The Last Disciple series exegetes Revelation 13 in light of the whole of Scripture. Thus, Satan can *parody* the work of Christ through "all kinds of counterfeit miracles, signs and wonders" (2 Thessalonians 2:9), but he cannot literally do what Christ did— namely, raise himself from the dead.

What is at stake here is nothing less than the deity and resurrection of Christ. In a Christian worldview, only God has the power to raise the dead. If Antichrist could "raise [himself] from the dead" and control "the earth and sky," Christianity would lose the basis for believing that Christ's resurrection vindicates His claim to deity. Further, if Satan possesses the creative power of God, this would subvert the post-resurrection appearances of Christ in that Satan could have masqueraded as the resurrected Christ. Moreover, the notion that Satan can perform acts that are indistinguishable from genuine miracles suggests a dualistic worldview in which God and Satan are equal powers competing for dominance.

The point here is not to call into question the orthodoxy of the Left Behind authors. We are committed to the same goals: reading the Bible for all its worth and inspiring hope in the Second Coming of Christ. Collegial debate in the interest of truth, however, is essential to the health of the church, while we adhere to the Christian maxim: "In essentials, unity; in nonessentials, liberty; in all things, charity." We must debate this issue, but we need not divide over it. The point is to demonstrate the dangers inherent in the interpretive method they and other dispensationalists employ.

Such dangers are not solely theological. Placing the Beast in the twenty-first instead of the first century poses historical difficulties as well. For example, the apostle John tells his first-century audience that with "wisdom" and "insight" they can "calculate the number of the Beast, for it is man's number. His number is 666" (Revelation 13:18). No amount of wisdom and insight would have given them the ability to figure out the number of a Nicolae Carpathia character in the twenty-first century.

Furthermore, while Daniel was instructed to seal up prophecy because the time of fulfillment was in the far future (Daniel 8:26; 12:4, 9; cf. 9:24), John was told not to seal up his prophecy because its fulfillment was fore future (Revelation 22:10). John's repeated use of such words and phrases as *soon* and *the time is near* demonstrate conclusively that John could not have had the twenty-first century in mind.

Finally, the horror of the Great Tribulation included not only the destruction of Jerusalem and the temple but the persecution of the apostles and prophets who penned the Scriptures and formed the foundation of the Christian church of which Christ Himself was the chief cornerstone. Thus, the Great Tribulation instigated by Nero is the antitype for every type and tribulation that follows before we experience the reality of our own resurrection at the Second Coming of Christ.

For these and a host of other reasons The Last Disciple series places the Great Tribulation precisely where it belongs, in a first-century milieu in which "the last disciple" comforts believers in the throes of the mother of all persecutions.

Visit decipherthecode.com

✚ Read the exciting prologue to the next book
in this best-selling series.

✚ For more information on future releases in this
exciting new series.

OTHER BOOKS BY HANK HANEGRAAFF

OTHER BOOKS BY SIGMUND BROUWER

CHRISTIAN
RESEARCH
INSTITUTE

The Christian Research Institute (CRI) exists to provide Christians worldwide with carefully researched information and well-reasoned answers that encourage them in their faith and equip them to intelligently represent it to people influenced by ideas and teachings that assault or undermine orthodox, biblical Christianity. In carrying out this mission, CRI's strategy is expressed in the acronym EQUIP.

The *E* in EQUIP represents the word *essentials*. CRI is committed to the maxim "In essentials unity, in nonessentials liberty, and in all things charity."

The *Q* in EQUIP represents the word *questions*. In addition to focusing on essentials, CRI answers people's questions regarding cults, culture, and Christianity.

The *U* in EQUIP represents the word *user-friendly*. As much as possible, CRI is committed to taking complex issues and making them understandable and accessible to the lay Christian.

The *I* in EQUIP represents the word *integrity*. Recall Paul's admonition: "Watch your life and doctrine closely. Persevere in them, because if you do, you will save both yourself and your hearers" (1 Timothy 4:16).

The *P* in EQUIP represents the word *para-church*. CRI is deeply committed to the local church as the God-ordained vehicle for equipping, evangelism, and education.

CONTACT CHRISTIAN RESEARCH INSTITUTE:

By Mail:
CRI United States
P.O. Box 7000
Rancho Santa Margarita, CA 92688-2124

In Canada:
CRI Canada
56051 Airways P.O.
Calgary, Alberta T2E 8K5

By Phone:
24-hour Customer Service (U.S.): 949-858-6100
24-hour Toll-Free Credit Card Line: 888-7000-CRI

Fax:
949-858-6111

For information (Canada):
403-571-6363

24-hour Toll-Free Customer Service (Canada):
800-665-5851 (orders and donations only)

On the Internet:
www.equip.org

On the Broadcast:
To contact the *Bible Answer Man* broadcast with your questions,
call toll free in the U.S. and Canada, 888-ASK HANK (275-4265),
Monday–Friday, 2:30 P.M. to 4:00 P.M Pacific Time.

For a list of stations airing the *Bible Answer Man* or to listen to the
broadcast via the Internet, log on to our Web site at www.equip.org.

SUSPENSE WITH A MISSION

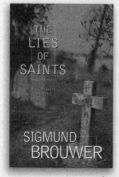

THE WEEPING CHAMBER

by SIGMUND BROUWER

Foreword by HANK HANEGRAAFF

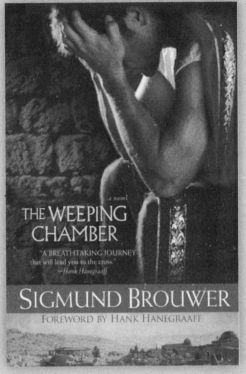

SOFTCOVER ISBN 0-8423-8715-3

The Weeping Chamber transports us into the heart of ancient
Jerusalem during the turbulent last days of Christ.

"A breathtaking journey that will lead you to the cross."
- HANK HANEGRAAFF